Dylan's Nam

Tom Faustman

Blue Sky Ventures
175 Tryon Street
Glastonbury, CT 06073

This book is a work of fiction. Names, characters, places, and incidents either are products of the author's imagination or are used factiously. Any rememblance to actual events or locales or persons, living or dead, is entirely coincidental.

Cover Design by SubjectExperts

Manufactured in the United States of America

Like many other unlikely soldiers, I found my world turned upside down when sent to Vietnam. Why me? Don't they know I'm just a kid? How would I do in combat? Would I have the courage? In desperation, I surrounded myself with fellow soldiers who loved their family and friends; people I could trust when things went sour. Although it's been decades, I still see those strong faces that helped me survive. To my brave brothers, eternal thanks.

Dylan's Nam

The conspirators never met in the same place twice, always arrived separately, at lengthy intervals. Each had served multiple tours in Nam, lifers. Like most soldiers, they were gung-ho and patriotic on the first tour.

Everything changed during the 2nd tour; the brutality, greed and hopelessness became overwhelming. Their initial meeting was pure chance, the jaded views of war rolled after too many Jack Daniels, playing pool at the Quang Tri USO years ago. It didn't take long for the conspiracy to unfold. They decided to cash in on the opportunities of doomed war.

The first step was for all to become MP's, not too hard to connive, not many wanted to be the most hated people on base. Each of them had special skills, the division of labor was easily determined; no one in charge, the money split evenly. At first it was the easy pickings: stolen cigarettes, booze and food. Prostitution soon became a more lucrative venture, and more fun. It didn't take long to figure the big money was weapons and munitions. Treason was the last step, it didn't bother them for long, the war was corrupt; why should the civilian contractors make all the money?

The 3rd Division MP Motor Pool was today's meeting place. Sgt Ben Burton ran the place, made certain no one was there to overhear the discussion. Although Ben didn't have the title, he actually ran the whole MP outfit. Nobody ever saw Ben do any real work, he just somehow ran the Motor Pool, USO club, Post Office and other miscellaneous functions. While appearing disconnected, these operations had one thing in common- money poured through them. He was an expert on currency manipulation, a trade he learned in the real world. Ben called today's meeting, wanted to report on the latest heist.

"Biggest haul yet, cleared $75,000 from the sale of RPG's, mortars, Thompsons and ammo. Shouldn't be no problem gettin' it to our accounts." Ben was very smart, used his poor grammar intentionally to make people underestimate him. The other conspirators nodded nonchalantly, before one asked, "How many casualties?" Ben hesitated, "Only four dead. One dumb ass MP wandered where he shouldn't a been, the rest grunts. Probably woulda died soon anyway, Tet's comin." One of them nodded, not much reaction to the deaths. As they were starting to leave, Ben threw in, "Got new MP's comin'. I like messin' with the new meat."

DYLAN

I ran like hell as the incoming rockets hammered Ben Hoi airfield. Our TWA flight had just landed; we had been warned during the plane debriefing "that Charlie might give you a reception party."

My dour buddy Fleming was seated next to me, leaned over after the speech, "More bullshit, they're just trying to bust our balls." I remember nodding agreement; they were just trying to scare us. It was a beautiful sunny day in South Vietnam as we deplaned.

Then I was tearing into the airport hangar, looking for cover. The noise was what I'll never forget. Slow, high arcing, whistling sounds then thunderous detonations. You felt the explosive pressure but the deafening sound was the worst part, it left you disoriented, scrambled. I tried to find a safe spot inside the hangar but the flimsy building was more like a big tin hut, no real place to hide. I found a spot in the corner but noticed the walls were open at the bottom to let air circulate. How could this be safe?

The sound was different now. More like a dull hum before the compact, thumping explosion. These bombs seemed targeted at the airport hangar where I lurked, but they were falling short, toward the other side of the building. I decided to stay put rather than look for another spot. When we got our plane debriefing, the Sgt told us to always find protection in the corners of buildings. If the bombs knocked the building down, it would be easier to crawl out of the debris. As I looked at the wide-open bottom, I wondered about that advice.

More stunned than frightened, I huddled in the corner, watched the other soldiers. The thunderous concussions left them immobile, almost paralyzed. I was the only one looking around. For some reason, I kept my eyes open, looking for some sign to guide me. If a bomb hit the building, maybe I should run? The phrase "scared shitless" never made any sense until this moment. I felt empty; everything was gone. Before being drafted, I worried about having the courage to survive the terror of war. Now I was in the middle of it, I'd kept my wits. I told myself to keep thinking, look for the safest place, get my ass ready to move. My adrenaline had kicked in; I was fully alert, surviving.

Then it was over, deathly silent. My ears still hummed, I felt like I'd just run a marathon. My heart was racing; my shirt was drenched in sweat. I heard a loud whistle, which I came to learn meant "all clear." I stayed on the ground; watched a few soldiers taking their places behind the counters.

One soldier announced on a loud speaker, "Welcome to Nam, newbies. Don't worry, pretty soon that shit won't mean nothin'. I aint even bull shittin." Was he saying this happened all the time?

I got to my feet, looked for Fleming and Callahan. They weren't in the hangar, so I went outside; still nowhere to be seen. I got nervous, started thinking what I'd do if I lost my only buddies from Basic Training and MP school. Joe Callahan and I had been best pals in Basic Training but had a bad incident in MP school that left us estranged. We were cordial, just not close anymore. I met Fleming at Ft Gordon MP School; we hit it off immediately. Fleming was always cranky, on the verge of rant, believed nothing was ever quite good enough; somehow he amused me greatly.

Then I heard yelling. I spotted them getting out of the TWA jet. They had run back inside the plane when the shit storm started. "I tried to get that asshole pilot to take off but he told me to piss off," Fleming moaned as he approached.

"He did too," confirmed Callahan. "You should have seen Fleming begging the guy. The pilot thought he was nuts." Callahan just shook his head in disbelief. He was not prone to making jokes; he was usually serious. It was easy to picture Fleming berating the pilot.

I was glad to see them; they were my only connection with home. We were the only MP's sent to Nam from our Advanced Individual Training (AIT) class at Ft Gordon.

Actually, there was one other guy, Mike McCarthy, but I never knew him at AIT. McCarthy was on a different flight, would join us later that day. Hoped he got a more peaceful reception.

My hearing was apparently off since Fleming whined, "You're screaming like a mental patient. Take it down a peg, Dylan." That cracked me up; we headed for the truck that would take us to Ben Hoi Army base, just outside of Saigon. Ben Hoi was called "the Distribution Center" for Nam. I remember thinking: I had never been "distributed" before.

As we rolled away from the airport hangar, I got a better look at the airport area. It was a depressing sight. The roads were unpaved, clouds of dust poured over us. Surrounding the airport were tall barbed wire fences with spools of concertina wire looped above. Every 100 feet or so were bunkers of armed soldiers poised to prevent unlawful entry. There was a single entrance with dozens of heavily armed MP's on alert. As we pulled away from the airstrip, it made sense to me that the area was so primitive. Why put up substantial structures if they were getting bombed daily?

Fleming sat next to me, but Callahan stayed near the rear of the truck. I hoped one day we'd work out our problem; I liked the guy a lot. We left the airstrip; headed on a dusty ride toward Ben Hoi. No one talked. I sat there thinking how my world had turned upside down in the last 6 months. One day I'm celebrating my college graduation, then bang, on a plane to Nam. My thoughts flashed back to that lousy day last summer when I got my draft notice.

THE PHILLY SUBURBS

As I drove my Honda motorbike through the streets of Drexel Heights, in suburban Philadelphia, I remember wondering if this was this the best of times, or worst of times? I was more prone to playful mayhem, but the turbulent times forced the philosophical musings. On the best side, it was 1970; I'd just graduated as an English major from Westminster University, after an unspectacular basketball career. I'd just landed the sweetest job imaginable, the summer director of a nearby playground. Each day I was forced to make challenging decisions, should I play horseshoes, basketball or shuffleboard? If that stressed me out, I played arts and crafts with the little kids until my angst subsided.

As I zoomed towards the basketball courts, I thought about the bad stuff. Vietnam dominated everything. The country was hostilely divided between hawks and doves. College campuses became protest circuses; families fought bitterly about what was "right."

While some of my friends supported the government, most screamed with outrage. The ones that screamed the loudest were those with low draft numbers. Because the troop counts were low and interest in joining the armed forces was at historic levels of disinterest, a draft lottery was held. Each of us got a draft position based on our date of birth. The lucky ones got a high number with no likelihood of service. The unlucky got low numbers. These low picks were sure to be drafted, with Vietnam the next stop. Based on random luck, you were screwed royally. I was part of the royalty.

Nearing the courts, I saw a guy called Frog shooting half-court set shots. Nicknames were huge if you played at the basketball courts in Drexel Heights. Frog wasn't named that because he was tall and handsome. An older friend, Jimmer Keilmann, was the self proclaimed "Commissioner of the Courts;" he nicknamed most of us years ago. Besides the enormous gift-of-gab and nicknaming prowess, Jimmer was built like Charles Atlas, was simian strong and could get away with busting everyone's balls. I never saw Jimmer hit anyone; he just looked like he would.

My name was Tommy Frazier but Jimmer named me Dylan when I was 10, because he loved Bob Dylan. Since I was the polar opposite of the scraggly folk singer, he found that irony irresistible. Jimmer was a History major, felt compelled to show-off his education and sense of poetic irony whenever opportunity arose. I happened to be the convenient victim on a day he felt creative. Since he had just named Paul Becker, "Bulb," because "he's got a fuckin' (100) watt Sylvania on top of that scrawny chicken neck," I felt lucky with the Dylan handle.

I zoomed to a stop at my beloved courts. But none of my close buddies were there that day. I drove home; Mom was gathering the mail as I roared up the driveway. When she looked at me, I pretended to be out of control, about to crash into the azalea bushes. Before the feigned collision, I veered off, finished a harmless ride to the backyard. Mom stood, hands on her hips, shaking her head at my mischief. Despite her posture, I knew I'd made her laugh. She knew I was a knucklehead, liked that about me.

I wandered in the back door, found mom waiting in the kitchen. She had a horrible, troubled look on her face. Then mom started to tear-up as she handed me a fat envelope. It was an official-looking letter from the Department of The Army. I tore it open, weeded through a pile of forms. The cover letter delivered the punch line young American males dreaded. "Greetings," it told me,

"You've been selected to join the Armed Services." I
stopped reading, stood motionless.

BEN HOI

My reverie of home was broken as our truck pulled into the distribution center in Ben Hoi, Vietnam. The driver walked around back, yelled, "Okay newbies, pile out and find out where you're being sent. Say a prayer it aint north or west. Charlie likes those spots and can put you in a world a hurt. Pay attention, newbies, this place can really do you a job." Most of the Ben Hoi base was modern, meticulous: surprisingly nice. The roads were paved and clean. However, the distribution center was another story, on the edge of the base, it was very bleak.

The term distribution center was typical Army logic; from here you would be distributed, like a case of C rations, to your real base in Nam. A Staff Sgt marched us inside, told us we had nothing to do except show up for roll call at 9 am and 3 pm, to see if you had gotten assigned. There was a huge map of Vietnam in the center of the dirt field. Once someone got their assignment, they ran to the map to see the location. Word spread quickly about the unlucky ones; just as the driver warned, west and north were the worst. Those areas border the DMZ and the Ho Chi Minh Trail; Charlie considered that his turf.

Then the Drill Sgt shocked us, "There's a swimming pool, movies 4 times daily, athletic field and a PX. Enjoy yourself for a while newbies, The Dream Machine (I soon learned that was the Army) wants you to have fun before you ship out. Check it out. Don't miss roll call, newbies, or you'll be in a world of hurt."

I looked at Fleming, "Swimming pool?" Our positive impressions were soon deflated. The swimming pool was Olympic sized but jam-packed with soldiers in olive drab under shorts. A bunch of sardines squeezed into a can was the picture. The only way you could swim was going

underwater and slipping between the bathers sunless legs.
Not appealing.

As we were headed off to check out the athletic field,
our late-arriving MP walked up, introduced himself. Mike
McCarthy was a tall, red-haired, blue-eyed guy from
Oregon. He immediately told us he was married, had a
baby boy, Mike junior. I'd soon learn that McCarthy was
hardheaded, took no crap. He would flare up quickly;
laugh it off just as fast. He had a Master's Degree in
Biology, planned on being a Pediatrician. He missed his
wife and child, promptly displayed their pictures- cute wife
and kid. I liked Mike McCarthy right away. Someone to
trust?

The athletic field was a joke, a hard-packed tract of dirt
bordered by steaming latrines and barbed perimeter wire.
So we wandered over to where the giant map was haunting
the area. It was almost 3 pm, so we got ready for roll call.

Unlike stateside Army locations, there wasn't much spit
and polish discipline in Nam. The saying about discipline
was, "What are they gonna do, send you to Nam?" The
Drill Sgt called us to attention. I heard Callahan's name
first, then the rest of us got called; we were headed for the
3rd MP Division in Quang Tri. We would be shipped out
next morning.

Where the hell was Quang Tri? We looked all around
Saigon, then south before we worked our way midway up.
Then searched west. Good news, it wasn't anywhere
near the dreaded western border.

Nobody was saying much, so I said, "Quang Tri has a
nice ring to it, sounds a little like 'Christmas tree.' Maybe
it's a happy place." But then Fleming ruined my
lighthearted moment.

"Fuck a duck, I found it. You won't even believe this.
Quang Tri is the northernmost city on the map. It's
fucking closer to Hanoi than Saigon. You got to be shitting
me!"

We continued to stare at the map, retraced our search. We all hoped there was another Quang Tri, someplace less ominous. McCarthy took it badly, "I can't tell my wife where this is. She's become a maniac on South Vietnamese geography. When she sees its right on the DMZ, she'll flip. God damn it!" Mike got really flushed; I thought he might explode.

Then he screamed, "Fuck" at the top of his lungs. The nearby Drill Sgt seemed ready to say something, then turned, walked away. I remember shaking my head, silently mumbling, "Survive, Dylan, just survive."

No one said much. We worked our way back to the barracks, stowed our gear; laid around. After awhile, the gloom was driving me loony. I broke the silence, "Well, gentlemen, I've put this off as long as possible, but I can't avoid the issue any longer."

After a brief pause, McCarthy finally said, "Okay, Dylan, I'll bite, what the hell are you talking about?" I eyed my buddies.

"I've worked up the courage to take a crap in those latrines. This will be a first for me. Even as a kid, I needed the proper facilities to relieve myself. Now I have to brave the outhouses of Nam. If I'm not back in 15 minutes, send in the Green Berets."

Everybody was chuckling as I headed off. My worst impressions were fulfilled. I held my nose as I entered the rank, wooden outhouse. To my amazement, an older Vietnamese man was in there to do his business. The bizarre part was he was standing on the toilet set, with his pants in his hands, displaying uncanny aim as his pellets dropped into the dark void.

He smiled a black-toothed grin, said, "Papa-sahn take beaucoup no.1 shit." Then he hopped off, obviously not big on wiping afterwards, donned his garments, waved goodbye.

I stood there stunned, then climb the throne; did just as Papa-sahn did. It was my first crap standing up, it seemed unnatural but at least my aim was true. I laughed hysterically the whole time. Then I returned to my comrades, recited my experience. Even Callahan got red-faced from laughing so hard. Fleming said, straight-faced, "I'm going to try to hold it for 365 days, no way I'm shitting standing up." Picturing a constipated Fleming getting in a fouler mood each day struck us as hilarious. It lifted our spirits for the moment.

Before I went to sleep, I walked around the barracks, checked outside. I walked into a nearby bunker, looked around. It was empty. Then I noticed there were similar bunkers outside of each building. I could almost hear my inseparable childhood buddy Nut, now a Green Beret, telling me to carefully study my surroundings. Nut had always been something of a war skill prodigy.

As kids sleeping in our backyard, Nut's advice was, "Always plan your routes of evacuation and areas of defense." That struck me as really odd as a kid but now I was doing what he said. Where would I go if all hell broke loose? When I did fall to sleep, my recurring nightmare returned: I was trapped in a village, surrounded by angry Vietnamese, sensed imminent death. This identical dream haunted me through college. I shook it off as a fear of being drafted. Now I worried it was real.

It was about 2 am when the explosions woke me. Unlike the airport assault, these were farther away. I looked at my sleeping friends; no one was stirring except McCarthy.

He asked, "What's going on?" I shrugged but got up; we walked outside. McCarthy and I watched a dazzling display of fireworks in the distance. You saw the brilliant flashes; the detonation came soon afterwards. A jeep came by, slowed down when they saw us.

I asked, "What's going on guys? Is the base being attacked?"

Both soldiers laughed, "You must be new here, that action's 10 miles away. Get worried if it's 500 yards away. This shit happens every night."

They were still grinning as they road off. When we got inside, Fleming and Callahan were awake. We told them our conversation with the jeep driver. Again we walked outside, watched the distant fire fight. I said, "Kind of looks like the fireworks in Philly on the 4th of July. When I was a kid, we used to climb a huge tree in our backyard, watched the whole show."

Then Fleming added his dour perspective, "Ya, but in this fireworks, those little yellow bastards are killing Americans. Fucking gooks!"

Then pacifistic Callahan jumped in, "But we're killing innocent Vietnamese too. We invaded their country; they didn't ask us to come here. This whole war is bogus."

Then Fleming lost it, "Callahan, don't start that shit. Don't start that peace and love bullshit again. Asshole."

I told them both to shut up. "This argument isn't helping guys. No one's happy being here. Let's get off each other's back, stay cool. It's your nerves talking. Settle down."

Callahan was a physically strong guy but he never looked for a fight. Fleming was not a tough guy but always looked for a fight. I often ended up the mediator. As Callahan walked away, I thought about when we first met at Basic Training.

FT DIX

After another gourmet dinner at Ft Dix, the drill
sergeant announced, "Good news, shit heads, there's liver
left over." I looked around; saw a trainee rolling his eyes
the same way I was. That was Joe Callahan. Turned out
Joe lived near me growing up, in neighboring Highland
Park. He went to St Joseph College, majored in Sociology.

When he told me that I said, "Based on the characters
I've met so far, we might need your skill here." Joe
laughed. We soon become close friends.

Joe Callahan was short, heavily muscled from weight
training. His light brown hair was straight, beginning to
thin. His prominent nose was balanced by stern blue eyes;
a masculine face. You respected Callahan immediately. He
had a likeability that conflicted with his aloofness. Joe was
extremely strong but favored peace, a contradiction. He
was sincere to a fault. The idea of playing practical jokes
never occurred to him. He enjoyed my pranks immensely,
but he never got involved. "A waste of time," he told me
time after time. I set about trying loosen up Joe Callahan.
It was a difficult task because Callahan was very
compassionate, to everyone.

The poor performers got picked on in the Army. Curt
Warner was in our platoon, a prime example of Army
persecution. Warner was chunky, red haired and freckled.
His gray eyes enhanced a non-descript appearance. Along
with the other misfits, Warner ran extra laps after
breakfast. Warner never made it. He always fell to the
ground, puked and laid still. The drill sergeant berated him,
ordered him to run. Finally, Warner began to cry, but he
still never moved.

I watched this unfold with Joe Callahan from our barracks window. Never saw anything so pathetic. After 10 minutes, the drill sergeant literally kicked him in the ass, smacked him like a rag doll, forced him to his feet, watched him collapse to the ground again. Callahan looked at me, "That's bullshit, they can't do that. That's brutality."

Then Joe suddenly ran outside, but the MP's had already picked Warner up and dragged him off before Callahan got there.

When Callahan came back I asked, "What the hell were you going to do?" He looked puzzled.

Finally, "Stop them, what do you think?" Then it was my turn to look baffled.

"Joe, this isn't a democracy here. This is the Army. They can do whatever they want. All you would have accomplished was getting your silly ass kicked like Warner's." I'll never forget his response.

"That's the difference between you and me, Dylan. When I see something wrong, I jump in. You think about the consequences before you act."

The look on his face was not judgmental; he was stating what he thought was obvious. I didn't think he was right but didn't respond. Later that night, I kept thinking about what he said. Why did it bother me?

The only other guy I liked in Basic Training was Dominic Abreu. We met while shooting M-16's for the company championship. When I realized the winner had "Sniper School" waiting for him, I suddenly lost my aim. I finished a distant second. Abreu knew I threw it, but was happy because he wanted to be a sniper. Abreu was born in the Dominican Republic, but had lived in New York City since he was a little kid. He was short, wiry; was freakishly strong. Then there was his voice. It came from deep down, made you think of a foghorn on a dismal, foggy night. His singing was priceless. He loved Neil

Diamond, sang "Cracklin' Rosie" non-stop in his guttural, monotone voice. I still laugh every time I hear that song.

As I neared the end of Basic Training, I realized my early plan to stay inconspicuous had gone off-track. I found myself enjoying the physical challenges, trying to win every event. Callahan told me, "When you're serious for half a second, the platoon does whatever you say. You're a natural leader. Lately, you seem unable to restrain yourself and just take over. Better watch out, hot shot, they might make you an officer."

I knew he was only partially kidding. I did find myself jumping in to solve the myriad stupid dilemmas facing our platoon. Was it my insatiable craving to fix things? Or was it bucking authority when I knew they were wrong? I was that way as a kid. Most of my childhood friends were a little off. I found them more interesting, projects. But this enjoyment of the challenges of Basic Training surprised me.

The last week of Basic Training finally ended. I'd been selected to be a Military Policeman. Being a cop was the last thing I expected. Then I happily noted that Callahan would be joining me. Then I sadly noted Abreu's placement. He was being assigned to the Infantry Sniper School. When I went to console him, he looked happy. "I got my wish, Frazier, gonna be a sharpshooter. I get to be by myself mostly. I been takin' care of myself since maybe 6. I know how to do that."

BEN HOI

I was jolted awake from a fitful sleep that 1st night in Ben Hoi. A soldier was screaming to us that a helicopter would be here in 30 minutes to take us to Quang Tri. No one was saying anything. Not a morning person, I stayed quiet. We herded outside, walked to the athletic field as the chopper landed. A sandy-haired Staff Sgt yelled over the noise,"Are you the school-trained MP's going to Quang Tri?" When we nodded, he yelled, "Climb aboard." Staff Sgt Leonard Wilson advised us he would be our desk sergeant in Quang Tri. We looked at each other quizzically when he said, "It will be good having school-trained MP's that know what they're doing."

I noticed that Sgt Wilson had a slight Southern accent but seemed to hide it; unlike most of the southern soldiers I met who drawled relentlessly. I asked myself: Who cares? I did, I always noticed anything odd.

QUANG TRI

Sgt Wilson told us we'd spend some time in the orientation center before reporting for MP duty. The flight north was long and noisy. As we approached Quang Tri, I saw that the countryside was magnificent, lush and green. It seemed to be a farming area dotted with small villages of thatched huts. This very basic form of living didn't seem like a stage for war. No craters, burned forests or visible devastation. Maybe it wouldn't be so bad around here?

Sgt Wilson said orientation would only take a couple days. I was tired of being distributed and oriented but kept my mouth shut. It was pretty late, so we were shown where to stow our gear, given directions to the mess hall. Our first meal was surprisingly good; meatloaf, mashed potatoes, peas, and hot rolls, all covered with gravy. I looked at Fleming as I ate, "Fattening us up before the kill?"

He sneered, "Just like something these pricks would do."

After chow, I retrieved my stuff and inspected the barracks. I walked up and down, went outside to see what was nearby. We weren't too near the perimeter wire, but there was a manned bunker to the rear, about 50 yards away. McCarthy watched me curiously. Finally, I veered toward the back of the barracks with my stuff. "Why the back?" McCarthy asked.

"Might be safer if Charlie gets through the wire; he'd probably enter the front of our hooch, it's farther away from the bunker, harder to be be spotted." I smiled, "Plus there's more ventilation back here, it's hot as hell."

Fleming rolled his eyes, "You'll get used to Dylan; he thinks he's Davy Crockett." McCarthy shrugged, but he moved to the back with me.

Orientation was an eye opener. We were mixed with other new arrivals that were "non-infantry." The infantry group was very large; they were herded into a different room. Our orientation was done by Specialist 4th class Ivan McKinley. Ivan was a black Princeton grad who used his educational pedigree to get a cushy job; he lectured new arrivals on the perils of Quang Tri. Ivan was short and thin, sported the first beard I saw in the Army; affected a slight English accent.

He started his monologue like this, "Gentleman, Quang Tri is the most dangerous place on earth. After Charlie overran Quang Tri in '68, Uncle Sam dropped more bombs here than anywhere in the history of mankind. Statistics show that 10% of the ordinance just stuck in the ground, never exploded. So watch where you're walking when you leave the base, gentlemen." Ivan took a deep breath, "And then to make the place more unappealing, we sprayed Agent Orange liberally to really ruin Charlie's day. I wouldn't sample any of the local produce if outside our gates. Besides all that nastiness, watch out for mosquitoes, malaria, yellow fever and I haven't even mentioned the drugs and whores yet. Any questions so far?" I had a million but shut up.

Ivan continued, "Opium in Vietnam is the purest on earth. Grass is practically free here. Boredom can be filled with hours of pure high. Troubles will disappear. Days will pass by; life will be a blur. But as your tour comes to an end, the real difficulties appear. You're hopelessly hooked and Uncle Sam won't let you go home a junkie. Most guys re-up so they can keep getting the powder. If you do get rehabbed, you have a military record that you were a junkie. You're tainted for life; you have to ask yourself, gentleman, was it worth it? Why didn't anyone warn me about this? That, gentleman, is what I'm doing right now, stay away from drugs. It's more lethal than the VC."

Ivan paused, stepped out toward us; continued his cheerleading. "Now let me tell you about how to survive living on this base. More soldiers are killed within this camp's perimeter than in enemy action. Grunts coming back from the bush are so fried they can't see straight. Almost anything can set them off. If one of those guys tells you to go fuck yourself, I'd suggest you start planning a new way to fornicate. Don't fuck with the grunts; because that's the MP's job, and believe me, that is about as bad a job as you can have. Thank the Lord for MP's."

McCarthy looked at me with wide eyes. I could tell he was thinking about his wife and kid.

Ivan went on, "Then we have the fraggings, where people get caught in the wrong place at the wrong time. A grunt is pissed at his NCO or CO and decides he wants a new leader. He just tosses a government issued fragmentation grenade into the sleeping quarters late at night, and BANG, we got new leadership that doesn't bust their cojones. They hardly ever find the killer. Usually, there's a whole platoon of suspects. Who hated the Sarge the worst? Tough call, most times. More mess for the MP's."

By now I was wondering if Ivan knew we were MP's, was just trying to get our attention. From the looks on Callahan, Fleming and McCarthy's faces, I think he succeeded. I know I wasn't feeling so hot. Ivan continued on about taking malaria pills, "always on a full stomach or you'll shit a river." We had been vaccinated for all the other maladies of the jungle but malaria was a big problem in Nam. "Take those orange pills, gentleman, and everything will be copasetic. Don't forget to pick up your mosquito net before you leave today. They come in handy. Any questions yet?" He had succeeded in stunning the audience.

Mr. Joy Spreader continued. "Next I should warn you about the charms of the local ladies." Ivan made a dramatic pause. "They look like little dolls but they carry big girl bugs. Sanitation and personal hygiene are different in Nam. When you get the urge, make sure you use a condom. You'll hear rumors about the Black Syph, but there's no medical proof that we have a new strain in Nam. Believe me gentlemen; good old- fashioned syph is bad enough. You also need to worry if you get the clap. In Nam it's called "applause." When the doctor diagnoses your clap, they usually step back and give you a standing ovation. Who says there's no sense of humor in Nam? Be prudent, practice safe sexual habits or you may have an ignominious ending to your dalliance."

Then Ivan looked at us seriously, "Not exactly a Picasso I'm painting about your life in Quang Tri. Charlie overran this base in 1968 and still thinks he can take it back whenever he wants. The good news is that The Dream Machine took the loss personally and won't give it up easily. Although this place may look like one of Dante's rings of hell, it is heavily fortified. If you pay attention to what I just told you, chances are you'll walk away safely. Any questions?" The whole group was speechless.

We picked up our mosquito nets before we left the room. On the way to our hooch, McCarthy spotted a hut with ping pong and pool tables inside. "Anyone want to play?" I told McCarthy I would but Fleming and Callahan wanted to look around the orientation center.

"Good idea, Fleming, while you're wandering around, ask some of veterans if white guys can get the black syph."

Fleming mouthed, "Cretin," as he wandered off.

McCarthy was an incredible ping pong player. He said it was his father's favorite pastime; he grew up playing almost every day. "He never let me win, ever. I was 18 before I could beat him. I thought he'd be pissed but he hugged me, said he was proud of how hard I fought to whip him. I'll never forget the smile on his face. It was sort of like my rite of passage. Dad treated me differently after that day, like I was now a man."

I watched McCarthy thrash everyone that challenged him. He beat me 21-0 the first time we played. We then played 10 more games and finally I started getting a few points. "I'll be whipping your ass before we leave Nam, Mac." He answered by drilling the next shot off my chest. For some reason that cracked me up, I stood there, belly laughing, then McCarthy started laughing.

When we settled down, we walked over to get sodas, which were stocked in a tiny nearby refrigerator. "All kidding aside, McCarthy, if you don't mind, I'd like to keep playing. I never played ping pong much but its kind of fun. Made me forget Ivan's pep talk while you were hammering me. Man, was that depressing. I kept thinking of funny questions but figured he didn't have much of a sense of humor."

McCarthy, who I started calling Mac, nodded agreement, "Definitely not a funny guy."

Sgt Wilson picked us up the next day, drove us around the base before taking us to the 3rd Division, MP Company. There were no paved roads in Quang Tri; everything had a reddish yellow tinge to the soil, topped with a choking layer of dust. Wilson showed us the PX, ammo dump, chopper landing zone, and a large, fortified area he called "central command." I asked what the huge bunker was beside central command.

"That's where General Freeman lives, at least when he's here. He's gone a lot. You ought to see how nice it is inside, movie screen, stereo, great kitchen. War isn't hell for everybody." Sgt Wilson didn't look annoyed by this. He looked like: That's the way it should be.

The MP Company was surprisingly nice, considering how dreary the rest of the base was. Wilson first showed us the "front desk where I work." His desk area was elevated above floor level about 3 feet, surrounded by elaborate paneling and molding. It was huge. When Sgt Wilson got up there, he peered down at us.

"It's to intimidate the assholes you bring in. It makes them realize how powerful we are, what pissants they are.

It works, too." He smiled proudly. Then he took us to the motor pool area. "Sgt Burton runs the motor pool. The jeep's your best friend in Quang Tri. Sgt Burton makes sure we drive the best and nothing but."

The motor pool was enormous, jeeps were everywhere but I saw no activity. It was somewhat neat, but reminded me of a giant junkyard that someone kept shiny. "Where is everybody?"

Sgt Wilson smiled, "Burton runs a loose ship here, but somehow everything works. If you need a jeep, somehow he pulls one out of this pile. People don't mess with Burton, he's got lots of pull." Wilson grinned but also had a funny look I couldn't read. Was he sending us a message?

We then went to "The Club." I was astounded. It was a large hooch converted into a bar, pool, and ping pong area, with a TV that showed "what the Army thought was appropriate entertainment." The TV shows were mostly sports, comedies, sit-coms etc. that were reruns, but it was still a slice from the real world. "Sgt Burton runs this joint but also the base USO club. Once in awhile, he gets Korean acts to come in and put on a show. Pretty good stuff, really. Good-looking girls that sing perfect English. This one Korean girl just did "Stand by Your Man." You'd swear it was Tammy Wynette."

On the way to our new hooch, Sgt Wilson pointed to the mailroom, said, "Sgt Burton's the postmaster, too. If it runs, walks, drinks or writes, pretty much Burton's in charge of it. Other than the General or Provost Marshall, he's the most important man in your life. They call him "Gentle Ben" but don't be fooled. Most bears leave you be unless you mess with them. Old Ben's kind of the same, just do what he says and he won't bite."

Again I noticed the odd expression; Sgt Wilson was giving us important information.

We finally got to the hooch area. Wilson pointed Fleming to the CID section. Because of his legal background from college, Fleming had been assigned to the Criminal Investigation Division. They weren't MP's but they worked with us on unusual crimes, like murders or drug trafficking. "The CID's are in that area, Fleming. We work with you but mostly you keep to yourself. Like your shit is a much higher caliber than the MP's." Wilson wasn't pissed off; he seemed to be stating facts.

Fleming looked at me, "Now that you mention it, you do stink."

I pointed at him, "That's your breath."

As Fleming ambled off, I noticed that multiple layers of concertina wire surrounded the CID area. German shepherd dogs were tied-up near the gated entrance. The dogs growled fiercely but Fleming got by safely. The dogs probably sensed a kindred spirit. I yelled, "Those dogs are a good judge of character. They know another mean bastard when they see one."

Fleming turned, flipped me the bird. I'd miss rooming with him; he always thought everything was so lousy that, by comparison, my view of the situation seemed so much rosier. Hard to explain, but he made me feel better.

Wilson took McCarthy, Callahan and me to the nearby hooch. "Only one open bunk here, who's it gonna be?" McCarthy said he'd go. He knew Callahan and I had been together since Basic Training, assumed we would stay together.

Callahan spoke up, "No, I'll do it. I might as well get used to the new world. Catch you later."

He walked briskly into the hooch. McCarthy looked surprised but said nothing. As we kept walking to our new digs, I thought back to MP school at Ft Gordon, where I first met the irascible Fleming and how all the problems started with Callahan.

Ft Gordon, MP School

Callahan and I talked about our fate, as we flew from Basic Training to Ft Gordon. I looked at the lush green Georgia pines and rich clay soil as our plane landed. Would this be better or worse than Ft Dix? First impressions were favorable. The striking thing was how neat and orderly the base was compared to dreary Ft Dix. I noted that Ft Gordon was set on a plateau, with huge loblolly pines descending to the surrounding valley. We were trucked to C Company, Platoon 3, which had a great location on the edge of the base, peaceful views of the pine forests.

We scrambled out of the trucks and mosied into C Company, as 250 soldiers got called to attention. Sgt Dingle was a little guy, sandy haired, with a screechy, high-pitched voice. With a last name of Dingle, my vision of a macho MP leader burst. Dingle went on, "Now, soldiers, this can be pleasant or nasty. You choose. Being an MP is an honor; you are part of the Army elite. Only the best and brightest get chosen. Now remember, do what I say and we won't have no trouble."

We marched into the barracks alphabetically, standing next to me was a scowling guy named Fleming. Peter Fleming would become one of the funniest people I ever met, but he was rarely trying to be funny. Did you ever meet someone who was always pissed? Little things bothered him. For the next 8 weeks of AIT, I never heard Fleming say anything was good. He always felt lousy. He always wanted to be somewhere else. "This place blows," was his favorite saying.

Sgt Dingle walked through the barracks. I asked what we would be doing next. "Good question, er, is that Frazier? CID has been going through your background records.

Any security clearance problems will get you booted out. MP's got to be pure as the driven snow. They'll be here right soon."

He was correct. The CID sergeants assembled all 250 of us outside, called 140 names out, told them to get their duffle bags. When they were gone, I again asked Sgt Dingle what that was about. "Those are the unlucky bastards that got bad records. They're taking them to the airport and sendin' em to be grunts. Nobody cares if grunts are criminals." I thought: What does that mean?

As I watched the unfortunate 140 march off, I realized this was a defining moment in my military career, made me aware that little screw-ups got you sent to Infantry, any mistake could be fatal. I remembered after I got drafted, Nut telling me to watch everything; that I should never get complacent. Nut was already in the Green Berets, a born warrior, close friend since childhood. I understood his advice now. I had to stay alert, to learn the skills I'd need to somehow thrive in this shitty place. Like it or not, Dylan Frazier was going to be the best MP in Company C. My competitive juices were flowing; this was the biggest game of my life. Losing had a whole new meaning in the Army.

That night, I learned Fleming, a political science major, was accepted to Villanova Law School before he got drafted. When you coupled this legal background with Fleming's pissy personality, you had a nightmare for our first instructor the next day. Fleming argued every point, tried to trip-up the teacher by showing the differences of military and civilian law.

The instructor stared at Fleming when he ranted, "Take the lunacy of military law saying a felon 'was apprehended' rather than saying he 'was arrested,' makes it sound too soft, like you didn't want to hurt the felon's feelings. Let's call a spade a spade. Arrest the asshole and throw him in the slammer."

The instructor just grinned at Fleming, "First of all Fleming, shut the fuck up, speak only when I ask you to. Secondly, I'm apprehending you for guard duty tonight. Meet me at 7 pm outside your barracks. You'll get some on the job training about apprehension." Fleming turned beet red but kept quiet the rest of class.

That night he stumbled into his bunk, told me he guarded an empty building until 2 am. I frowned, "How do you know it was empty?"

Fleming mumbled, "Well, it did have a frog inside, so technically it wasn't empty. My job was to apprehend the frog for trespassing on Army property. Then I had to secure the frog and make sure it didn't escape."

When I saw he was serious, I laughed so hard that Callahan came over to see what was wrong. When I repeated the story, Callahan laughed louder, Fleming got furious. "You're just a couple of douche bags."

And that made us laugh even harder. But to his credit, he was no fool. Fleming dummied-up over the next few weeks of military law instruction.

The base library was next to our barracks, so I went over one night to do some research on Military Police, trying to get an edge on my competition. Callahan came with me but peeled-off when we got inside to look up background on "Conscientious Objectors." When I gave a concerned look, he waved his head, "Don't worry, I'm just checking it out." My buddy Joe had become very quiet since we'd gotten to Ft Gordon. I wondered what was going through that serious head of his.

While doing research, I was surprised to read that each branch of the military had their own version of MP's. The article said some bases had problems because of competing sets of priorities. For instance, on Ft Gordon, the Security Police of the Air Force might be hot to prevent drugs, but the Army MP's were cracking down on petty theft. The result was constant surprise inspections and pissed off troops who found all their gear tossed around when they returned from a full days work.

"Organized chaos" was how the article described the situation. As I read, it got even worse. Each Army division had their own MP's. Most bases had multiple divisions domiciled together, so you had multiple sets of MP's prowling around acting like they were in charge.

The list of duties was similar for all types of MP's:

- *Law enforcement for military personnel on military property*
- *Criminal investigation*
- *Protection of senior military officers*
- *Management of prisoners of war*
- *Management of military prisons*
- *Traffic control*
- *Route and re-supply management*
- *Antiterrorism activities*
- *Customs and drug activities*
- *Liaison with civilian law enforcement*

There were a myriad of smaller duties but the above were common denominators. The Army MP's reported to the Provost Marshall. If I read the article correctly, the Provost Marshall had a loose connection to the General in charge of the base, a looser connection to The Department of Defense. Apparently, this uncertain reporting structure had caused accountability problems and cries of corruption. There was a government committee studying the matter, charged with finding a solution. There was a sarcastic mention that this committee had "been pondering this issue for 8 years, with no end in sight."

As I was digesting this information about my Army assignment, Callahan walked up. I told Joe what I'd found, he smirked, "Maybe that makes my decision easier." When I asked "what decision" he told me he had been considering filing as a Conscientious Objector; that he wanted to make sure he knew the process before going forward.

Rather than scream "are you nuts," I reminded him about his family of military supporters, what that move would do to them. During our time at Ft Dix, he told me his dad and granddad had been decorated war veterans.

"That's what's eating me up. When I was thinking about this my senior year at St Joe's, there was a group of CO's on campus, offering advice. That's what I was looking up just now. Apparently, you can file for a CO status, but still fulfill your military duty. It's just that you won't bear arms or have any combatant role. I'd have to file for moral and ethical reasons; since I can't really say it's religious. I'm Catholic and they are generally okay with war. Anyway, that's what I've got to stew over."

I could see he was troubled. I asked that he talk it over with me before he took any action. "I'd like that," was all he said. I had a hard time sleeping that night.

Mail delivery was more regular at Ft Gordon. I got a surprise letter. My buddy Fran Philips had gotten drafted; had reported to Ft Dix a couple weeks ago. He filled me in on his anxieties, wanted advice on surviving Basic Training. I felt bad for him; he'd have trouble. Since he quit playing basketball, he was out of shape, would struggle with the grueling marches.

The closing part of his letter mentioned, "Maybe I can make the Army team, play ball rather than soldier." Fran had been a terrific college basketball player but I wondered what that meant.

MP classes were getting tougher; we were learning the "10 series" of radio communications that week. In the MP's, whenever you used the radio, especially in Nam, you had to use the 10 series code. The instructor passed out a long sheet of codes to memorize. The sheet had 150 codes but he said, "You only need to learn the 1st 50 for the test." I studied them relentlessly, enjoyed practicing.

That night I walked up to Fleming and noted, "I see you're 10-11 (in service) Private Fleming, how about we 10-35 (get chow). Am I 10-28 (loud and clear)?"
Fleming pondered that a bit, wasn't amused. He sneered, "Hey, Frazier, why don't you 10 fuck-off?"

Classes continued to be fairly interesting. "Observation is the greatest skill of a good MP," we were advised constantly. We were taught proper crime scene investigation and documentation that week. One of the tests was to review a crime scene where the PX had been robbed. Our task was to spot clues as to the culprit. Since we had to simulate a PX in our classroom, most of the exercise was reviewing sets of facts, spotting weaknesses in the evidence. When the instructor asked for ideas, I raised my hand. He looked at me skeptically, "Go ahead Frazier."
Since the facts stated, "No evidence of forced entry," I opined the obvious. "Inside job, Sgt Williams. I'd look at the soldier who ran the PX, see if there were any sudden large deposits in any of their bank accounts. If so, you got your man. If not, check if he's married, put it in his wife's name. After you eliminated the obvious suspects, I'd broaden the hunt to others that might have access to the building. That's what I'd do."
Sgt Williams raised his eyebrows during my monologue. "Bingo, Frazier, at least one of you cherries has his head outta his ass." While I feigned humility, Fleming was scribbling furiously, flashed "ass kisser" on his notepad.

As I chuckled, Sgt Williams glared at me, asked what was so funny. "Nothing, Sgt, I just swallowed down the wrong pipe." Fleming called me "Sherlock" for the rest of that week.

We started our "unarmed self-defense" courses the following week. My hometown Green Beret buddy Nut was a champion wrestler; used me to practice for our entire youth. Nut was a state champ since his sophomore year, so I ended up a decent wrestler by default. "You could be a damned good wrestler if you stopped that silly basketball stuff," Nut advised me frequently.

I just laughed at him, but this background allowed me to excel in the MP training. Sgt Grimm was our instructor; he took this training seriously.

I asked Callahan, "Do you think Sgt Grimm is related to the guy who wrote those famous fairy tales?"

Callahan gave me a rare chuckle, added, "More like the Grim Reaper clan, if you ask me." Maybe Callahan was snapping out of his funk; that was the first quip from him in a couple weeks. His gloomy mood seemed to be lifting.

I liked the unarmed self defense work; strangely, it reminded me of my basketball drills; and that reminded me of home. We did nothing but basic moves but Sgt Grimm made it clear that if you mastered these, anything else wasn't necessary. "Unarmed self-defense is about using your 'natural weapons' to survive. The goal isn't winning; it's survival. Remember, the primary objective is escape. Staying around 'to win' aint a good decision if Charlie's got buddies comin'."

That made sense to me but was not my natural inclination. If a psychiatrist pinned me down, I'd admit I liked to fight. Nut went out of his way to fight, loved it. I just let it happen, enjoying the challenge. If someone pushed me, I didn't back down. Once you pissed me off, I'd go after you hard. Other than to Nut, I'd never lost a fight. So, I paid attention to Sgt Grimm, he gave me some new weapons. I got good at the "spear hand" strikes to the ears, throat and solar plexus, but especially good with my feet. All that basketball work had given me good footwork.

As I kicked the practice dummy repeatedly, Sgt Grimm nodded, "That's as good as it gits, Frazier. Nice work." Fortunately, Fleming was out of range or I'd be in for more abuse.

After each test or physical event, your score got posted. Then they accumulated everything, listed the company aggregate leader. I thought the tests were simple, assumed most everyone aced them. Fleming was a nut about academic competition, informed me we were both near the top and "my Neanderthal abilities" allowed me to squeeze ahead of him in the physical events. I grinned, "Who gives a shit, Fleming? A pissant could pass these tests, its easy stuff." Without saying it out loud, I knew that Fleming gave a shit; he wanted to beat me.

Near the end of AIT, I got called into Sgt Dingle's office. "I got some news for you, Frazier. Captain Black got a letter asking if he'll send you to West Point to try out for the Army basketball team." I wanted to howl for joy but studied his face to see where the conversation was headed. Then he added, "I told the Captain that you might be the best MP candidate we ever had here, an that's a helluva lot more important than basketball. Dang, Frazier, I'd hate to lose ya. We got some sorry soldiers here; we need good school-trained MP's out there."

I decided to stay neutral, just shrugged. He told me Captain Black was, "thinkin' it over."

As I walked back to the barracks, I kept jumping in the air, slamming my fist in jubilation. "Playing hoops and not playing soldier," ran through my head. I guess my facial expression gave me away.

Fleming asked, "You look like you just took a two foot dump, Frazier. What are you so happy about?" I called to Callahan; he ambled over. I told them my good news. Callahan got a great grin on his face, hugged me. Then Fleming's face drooped mopier than normal, "Lucky son of a bitch." But then he grinned, slapped me on the shoulder. I asked them to keep it quiet since nothing was certain; I'd catch shit from everyone if they heard about my deal.

We got mail that night; I got an explanation for the incredible news. My buddy Fran Philips had arranged the basketball tryouts for both of us. The base CO, who was a basketball nut, had noticed Fran's star college career. Fran was headed to West Point after Basic Training. "I told them about you, that we'd be a formidable backcourt. The CO said it's a big deal to win the Armed Services tournament, huge bragging rights. I'll see you in a few weeks," was how he ended the letter.

Would my Army stint just be another basketball season? I knew I had to buckle down, make sure I didn't blow this.

We had a brush-up session on our recent unarmed defense training before we got to more advanced stuff. Callahan and I practiced the drills every night. I showed Joe the full nelson and half nelson holds that Nut and I had perfected since childhood. "The full nelson is supposed to be the perfect hold but Nut found a way to break it. Then he found a new variation of the full nelson that can't be broken."

I laughed when I thought how Nut would spend hours looking for loopholes in classic wrestling maneuvers. But he always did. Nut had a gift.

I showed Joe the full nelson. You got behind your opponent, wrapped both arms under their armpits and locked your hands behind their head. Then you would drop the enemy to the ground and wrap your legs around their waist. If you scissored your legs hard enough, you could cut off their breathing and knock them out. Fight over.

After Joe did it a few times he shook his head when I asked how to beat it. "No way," he offered. Then I showed him Nut's variation. If someone got the full nelson on you, you quickly backed into them to jar their balance, dropped down, and rolled them over your head. If you did it fast enough, you could reverse the hold, so that you could scissor the opponent and get their neck in a chokehold. I did it to Callahan 5 times in a row. "Shit, that's amazing," was Joe's praise for Nut's invention.

Then I showed him how Nut counteracted this maneuver. What Nut always did was as he wrapped his arms behind his enemy's head, he simultaneously jumped on the guy, hammered a scissor lock before the stunned victim had a chance to drop to the ground and roll him off. No one ever broke a full nelson hold on Nut during his undefeated reign as Pennsylvania State wrestling champ. Joe shook his head in disbelief. "That Nut must be one tough son-of a-bitch."

I just smiled at Joe, "You have no idea."

When we went to training the next morning, Sgt Grimm asked, "Does anyone know what a full nelson is?"

I raised my hand fast, loudly answered, "Yes, Sgt Grimm, that's what they call the full cast of the Ozzie and Harriet show." Only Callahan laughed, I added quickly, "Just kidding Sgt Grimm. Thought a little joke might wake the platoon up for you. The full nelson is the classic wrestling hold for subduing an enemy from behind."

Grimm liked me, so I knew I could get away with the joke. Grimm shook his head, "I'll decide if we need jokes Frazier. Knock out 50."

We marched back to the barracks afterwards, had a great meal; lounged around before lights out. Callahan asked to talk privately, so we wandered outside. It was a clear, chilly night; the sky was moonlit and dazzling. The full moon allowed me to read the serious look in my buddy's eyes.

"I wanted you to know first; I spoke to Dingle and Captain Black, I'm applying for CO status for moral reasons. I can't take this anymore. I can't fake my way through this, this war is wrong and I don't want to kill innocent people. Black was pretty cool about it after I told him I wanted to stay in the Army, do my duty, but just in a non-violent support position. There's a lot of paper work to file, but it's started. It's a load off my mind."

I wasn't surprised, just disappointed that my good buddy would probably be sent in a different direction. But I said, "I'm happy for you, Joe. I know it's been eating at you." I slept fitfully that night; Callahan had become part of my life, someone I could count on. Everything was about to change.

Training to shoot the legendary Colt 45 began the next morning after Callahan's bombshell. They trucked us to the remote pistol range. A bull-like Staff Sgt approached, addressed us. "I'm Sgt Snow, but ya might note I'm black as the ace of spades." A few of us chuckled. Sgt Snow continued, "Most times ya need a weapon, it seems to be too far away. That's why the Colt 45's so cool. MP's and General's the only ones get to strap it on legally. It there when ya need it most. Done 3 tours in Nam, the Colt 45 is gold over there. Truck drivers always lookin' for one. They git light up by Charlie and they run like hell to git from that truck. Then they notice they left the M-16 back in the cab. That's when they get that cravin for a Colt 45."

Sgt Snow loved his job. He showed us how to assemble, clean and load the legendary pistol. When you got that perfect, he let you shoot. "Packs a powerful kick, gentleman, so be ready. Once ya get used to the kick, ya don't notice it no more. Like riddin a horse, just go with the animal and all's good." I watched Sgt Snow put 5 rounds into a nearby target. Not much left of the target when he got done. "Puts a serious hurt on the bad guys," was how he always finished his shooting exhibition.

I was the first to pass the cleaning, assembly inspection, was allowed to start shooting. Sgt Snow took me into a small shooting shed, schooled me on what to do. He was right about the kick. First time it almost recoiled into my head. Sgt Snow laughed when he saw the expression on my face. "Some serious shit, huh, Frazier?" I did much better after a few tries, was soon able to hit the target dead on. After multiple attempts, the recoil just became part of the shot. The goal was to make a tight shot pattern in the chest area of the target, which was shaped like a man. "That's the fattest part of a shithead and easiest ta hit. If ya get lucky, ya clip the fucker in the heart. Ruin his whole fuckin' day," advised Sgt Snow.

Callahan was the second to pass muster, joined me in the shed. Callahan started shooting, got the hang quickly. His arm strength helped with the recoil. "That aint half bad Callahan. Let's see some tighter chest hits. Blow that fucker away, soldier." Then Callahan made a serious mistake.

"Sgt Snow, shouldn't we be shooting to disable, not kill him. It seems like we should be targeting the legs, just knock them down, and then disarm them. Shouldn't killing them be the last resort?"

At first Sgt Snow didn't react, he just looked at Callahan. Then I saw rage build into his face. His eyes bulged, red blushed his cheeks, his breathing got loud.

Then he exploded, "What are you, Callahan, the fuckin' tooth fairy. Ya wanta try the 'let's be nice' to Charlie and maybe he'll turn out to be our best pal shit? I lost buddies in Nam cuz they hesitated when they shoulda been shootin'. Any one pointing a gun at you better be getting ready to die. Now knock out a 100, an get that faggot ass back on line and blow that fucker away." Callahan did the push-ups easily, slowly walked over, put the pistol down.

"I'm done Sgt Snow; I already filed as a CO and won't be using a gun any way. This is a waste of time."

Without hesitation, a crazed Sgt Snow ran at Callahan and bowled him over. He got Joe in a chokehold, started banging his head on the ground. I ran over, grabbed Snow's shoulder, stopped him from pounding Callahan.

Sgt Snow looked straight at me, screamed, "Get outta here, Frazier, I'm gonna teach this pussy a lesson."

Then he started banging Joe against the floor. Joe had managed to shift his weight, so most of the force was on his shoulder. I could see Callahan was still breathing steadily but was losing strength. His face was contorted; I was worried he might lose consciousness. "Sgt Snow, let him up. You're gonna kill him. You gotta let him up." I started to pull at his arms to loosen the hold but he kicked at me to keep me away.

"Get the fuck outta here, Frazier or yer next." Then Snow started howling like a mad man, trying to hammer Joe to the ground. I squeezed my hand under Snow's arm, pulled fiercely to break the grip. Just as I got the arm free, Sgt Dingle ran into the room, looked shocked, but quickly helped me get Snow off Callahan. By then Joe was breathing better, rolled over, got into a sitting position. But Sgt Snow wasn't done. "I'm gonna kill that pussy Callahan. Ya can't assault an NCO in this man's Army. Yer gonna pay." Sgt Dingle managed to control him but yelled for me to get Callahan outside.

We got trucked back to our barracks; Callahan and I were separated, told to stay in our quarters. Sgt Dingle came up later, asked me what happened; I repeated the story. Dingle shook his head, "Same story as Callahan, this is some sorry business."

Then he left the room. By then Callahan had joined me, was fuming mad. "Snow's not getting away with this. He attacked me, like a madman. He's going to pay. Did you see the look in his eyes? Like he was totally crazy. He would have killed me if you weren't there. No question about it, he would have choked me to death."

And that's what Callahan told Captain Black, who called both of us in to retell the story. The Captain nodded to me, "Do you agree? Any other facts you'd like to add?"

I shook my head, "That's how it went. Sgt Snow went nuts when Joe put the pistol down. He charged him like a bull. I think he would have killed him."

Captain Black exhaled, shook his head, added, "Sgt Snow is a decorated war hero. Did 3 tours in Nam, has multiple Purple Hearts. Perhaps he was reliving a flashback." He paused for a second before saying softly, "We'll never know."

Before I could digest that, Callahan jumped in, "I don't care how many tours he did in Nam. Sgt Snow tried to kill me. He's not fit to work with young soldiers, and certainly not around pistols. I think he's lost his mind. The look on his face I'll never forget, he was in a blind rage, he would have killed me if Dylan wasn't there. I want him put behind bars. He should be off the street or it'll happen again." The look on Callahan's face told me a lot; he wouldn't back down until Snow got prosecuted.

The expression on Captain Black's face changed immediately. I'll never know but I think he was in our corner until Callahan insisted on jail time.

I could see him get his back up, "I decide what happens around here, Private Callahan. Until further notice, you are to talk to no one but me about this incident. Same for you Private Frazier. This is a serious matter and I'll deliberate, then get back to you. Dismissed."

Callahan and I left, walked back to the barracks. We were quiet most of the way; Joe broke the silence. "What do you think's going to happen, Dylan?"

I walked a bit further, turned to Joe; "I think he'll want to sweep it under the rug. Don't think that comment about Nam and Purple Hearts was for nothing. I think he was telling us the guy has paid his dues, is a war hero. No way they'll throw him in jail. They'll probably put him somewhere where he can't snap and hurt anybody. That's what I think."

Callahan looked at me, bit at his lips, puckered his cheeks, "Then he doesn't know me very well." That comment made me sick.

We went the entire week without hearing from Captain Black. I was hoping it would blow over but Callahan kept after Sgt Dingle for an update. There were only a few more days left in AIT. I was sitting in the barracks when Fleming walked in, "Guess who's got the top score in MP school? They just posted the final numbers."

I hadn't followed the weekly postings but imagined our squad leader, Bobby Joe Smith, was the leader. He worked like crazy, loved the gung-ho stuff. "Bobby Joe's my guess, Fleming." Callahan was nearby, chimed his agreement with my pick.

"Wrong to both of you. With his stupendous display of caveman skill, our own Dylan Frazier is the landslide winner." I thought he was busting my balls so we all trooped out to see. Fleming was right; I had beaten Bobby Joe by 90 overall points.

My reaction was sincere, "Holy shit, of all the things to be good in, it's my luck to be a natural born MP. Go figure, huh? "

My buddies congratulated me, Even Bobby Joe wandered over, shook my hand, "Nice competin' with ya, Frazier. Gotta admit, I thought I had a lock on this but you really have your shit together."

My joy was short-lived. That night Callahan and I got called into Captain Black's office and told, "After looking at the whole matter, I'm dropping the investigation. No one got hurt out of this unfortunate incident. Let's move on."

Callahan didn't hesitate, "I respectfully disagree with the decision. Who do I have to see to get another hearing? Sgt Snow is a menace and needs to be punished." Captain Black dropped his head, began to read something on his desk.

Without looking up, "Dismissed."

Callahan did make a big stink, got a hearing with the Provost Marshall. I was called to testify separately, was told, in careful words, to drop my support of Callahan's story or I'd regret it. The implied threat was, "We put trouble makers in the infantry."

I told Callahan what was said to me; he had gotten the same line. I looked at my resolute friend, "This is going nowhere, Joe. You made your point. They'll put Snow in some harmless position and let him retire with pay. No one wins by pushing this further." He just shook his head, walked away without saying a word.

They called Callahan in the next day, told him his Conscientious Objector petition was denied. "Anyone that fights with a decorated combat veteran like Sgt Snow, must be violent enough to bear arms," was the rationale. That knocked the wind from my stalwart friend. He wanted to keep pushing the matter but I told him I wanted it over.

"Joe, they already screwed you over with the CO verdict. Next step is they put you in the grunts. Give it up."

He put his hands on his hips, "Not me, I'm not quitting."

Nothing did come of his continued fight. I never had to drop my support of the story because Joe decided to go it alone. I told him I'd confirm what happened but he shook his head. He completely stopped talking to me, wouldn't even make eye contact. Fleming kept me updated on the last stages of his battle but Sgt Dingle finally told Callahan it was over. "Just shut your mouth, be a good MP, Callahan. That's my advice. Who knows, maybe Uncle Sam will send you someplace nice as payback for your trouble." Dingle chuckled as he walked off.

My last days in Ft Gordon were filled with disappointment. Dingle called me in, told me my request to try out for the Army basketball team was denied. "Captain Black says we don't do favors for troublemakers. Too bad ya got mixed up with Callahan, Frazier. Who knows, mighta gone a different path otherwise." I wanted to scream but took a deep breath, left quickly.

The worst came next morning. Our MP assignments were posted, only 3 MP's out of 120 got sent to Nam.

QUANG TRI

McCarthy broke my thoughts of Callahan and our unlucky assignment to Nam when he asked what bunk I wanted. I inhaled to recover my wits, "Let's see how things look outside, Mac." We walked around, noted the perimeter wire was to the rear of the building. No bunkers were nearby but a flat, dusty plain lay outside the wire. Not a likely spot for Charlie to pick for mischief, too easy to be spotted. "Let's take the front bunks, Mac."

He wrinkled his brow, "Why?"

I looked studious then answered, "Closer to the outhouse. Won't have to trip around in the dark going to take a piss at night."

Mac shook his head, grinned, "Fleming's right, you are a man possessed."

Mac and I got "CPO gate duty" next morning. The Civilian Personnel Only gate was the sole point of access for the Vietnamese onto the Quang Tri base.

When we asked Sgt Wilson what we had to do, he snickered, "You just guard the fucking gate so the locals don't steal our goods. First you check them when they enter the base, then again when they leave. If they come in a truck, search it. If they come on a bike, go through their bags. If they're walking, check them carefully. They steal everything not nailed down. Other than that, it's just boring as hell. Good way to start your time in Quang Tri. Get bored just like the rest of us."

Our shift was from 6 am till 6 pm. The CPO gate was a short walk from the MP Company, so we hoofed it there. The first thing I noticed was there wasn't any real gate, just a dusty road with an MP shack on the side. Trucks and bikes were lined up waiting for us as we walked up. They needed a pass from us to be allowed on base. If they were caught without one, they could get arrested, but the real punishment was getting banned from the base. Jobs on the base paid well, so that was a precious thing to lose.

Just as Mac and I were headed to begin the opening ceremonies, a jeep roared up, skidded to a halt before the line of Vietnamese. A cloud of yellowish dust engulfed the front of the crowd; they began choking for air, wiping the grit off their faces and clothes. A short, well-built soldier leaped from the jeep, strutted up to us. "Are you the hot-shot school-trained MP's?"

The way he pronounced "school-trained MP" was the same way most people said "asshole."

That was our introduction to Sgt Percy Price. His brown eyes were filmy; they seemed to look at the world from a stagnant pond. You could tell from his quick movements that he was athletic. He wasn't heavy but he exuded great strength. Kind of like a panther seems lithe, but then you look closer, see no fat, just solid muscle. He always had a grin on his face, showing teeth that looked ready to bite. When I described him later to a psychologist buddy back home, he diagnosed Price as a sociopath, someone who felt no guilt or remorse for any action.

Before I could say anything, Price continued, "I'm sure that cracker Wilson told ya what to look for, but I'll show ya how it's done. These yellow fuckers rob us blind; when I run a gate, I make them pay. Watch the master!"

Price pulled an old papa-sahn out of the front seat of his truck, began tearing things apart. When he found nothing, he jumped in the back of the truck, soon found a pack of cigarettes, Marlboros. Then he went nuts. "Where'd you get these smokes, mother fucker?" Papa-sahn said nothing, but moved back a step. Without hesitation, Price moved in, swept his right leg fiercely into the old man's shins, crushing his leg. The puny old man toppled to the hard ground.

Mac and I stood stunned, watching the man writhe in pain. Then Price jumped on the top of the truck, screamed at the rest of the crowd, "If I find any American goods in anybody's vehicle, you'll go ta the hospital, just like this piece of shit. Comprendez?"

Slowly, the whole line of people started moving backwards. Then Price jumped down, turned to Mac and me. "Now that's the way a field-trained MP does his job. Do what I show ya, you'll stay outta a body bag." Price spun around abruptly, drove off.

I moved in to help papa-sahn; he recoiled as I approached. The look in his eyes said, "Please don't hurt me." I lifted my hands, signaled that he had nothing to fear. He relaxed a bit but still was wary. Mac brought over some water, gave the guy a drink. We pulled up his black pajama-like pants, poured water over the damaged leg. He moaned in agony. As I was wondering what to do next, a Red Cross truck drove up, pulled a stretcher out.

The medics looked at me, "That crazy fucker Price called, said there'd been an accident. Said a papa-sahn fell outta his truck, broke his leg. Is that how it went?"

I looked at Mac. Before I answered the medic said, "Don't bother answering. If you tell me Price did this, then I gotta report it. Then he'll get suspended for a week or so and come looking for all of us. Price got booted outta the grunts cause he was too violent. That's how a lot of MP's got their jobs, too, too crazy to be in the field with other men. How's that make any sense?" I looked at the medic,

"Thanks for the advice. What will happen to papa-sahn?"

The medic shrugged, "We'll patch him up, he'll get three squares a day, maybe a little cash to shut him up. This shit don't even mean nothin'."

Mac and I spent the rest of the morning going through every truck, bike or scooter that came to the gate. By late morning, we'd collected 20 cartons of cigarettes, 2 bayonets and a Colt 45 pistol. When we asked where the stuff came from, each person said, "No bic."

We learned that meant, "I don't understand or I don't know." It was the universal response in Nam whenever you didn't want to answer a question. What a brilliant strategy.

When Mac asked me what to do with this stuff, I just shook my head, "No bic." We had our only laugh that day.

Just when I was starting to wonder about lunch, a jeep rolled up, a husky guy ambles out, hands us box lunches. "Names Ben Burton; wanted to meet the new guys, say hey."Ben Burton was about 5'8", weighed 250, easy. Had a big frame, wasn't all that fat, like a natural born lineman. We introduced ourselves, shot the shit a bit. We learned he was from Florida, had grown up on a farm, raising cattle and oranges. Ben seemed easy-going, had a great laugh. Like a deep chuckle that kept going. I liked him but remembered Sgt Wilson's caution.

After shooting the breeze a while, he got serious, "Heard ya'll met Price already. He's an uppity bastard but don't screw with him. He's got a black belt, almost killed a guy in his platoon when he thought he stole fruit cocktail from his C rations. That's why they dumped him to the P's. He don't fuck with me cause he knows I'll shoot him, but he likes to fuck with the new guys. If he starts with you, back away." He stared at us for a few seconds. "Fuckers got a loose connection."Then Ben switched topics, "What loot ya got so far?"

We showed him the stuff, he told us to bring it to him after the shift ended; he'd "stow it for redistribution."

Before he left he told us to drop over to the club after chow, he'd buy us a drink on the house. "I like you guys already. Think ya'll work out just fine. Just keep your head down, do your job; things'll be copacetic. But remember what I said, stay away from Price, he's like fuckin' snake, poison."

After the shift, we carried the loot to the motor pool, left it where Ben told us, behind his desk. There were other cigarettes there but Mac and I had a huge pile by comparison. "We must have the big gate, Mac. Wonder why they didn't find any pistols? We better check with Wilson, find out why our gate's so wild."

Mac looked at me, "Maybe the other guys don't care anymore. I'm beat. It's rough climbing in and out of those trucks. After awhile, they probably don't look so hard." I tucked that away, liked the way Mac thought.

We got our answer that night when we went to collect our free drink. Callahan was inside talking to his new bunk buddy, a big sandy-haired guy he introduced as Richard Clardy. "Just call me Clardy, who wants to be called Dick or Richard. Clardy suits me fine."

Clardy was from South Carolina, had a deep Southern accent; was immediately likeable. Plus he laughed all the time, seemed like he was having a blast. "Love the Army," he told us. "Pop served in WW II, talks about the Army as the best time a his life. Good pay, good grits, some pussy, what more could ya ask fer?"

He snorted a laugh when I said, "Agree with your list of perks, just wish we were someplace without the little yellow devils, rocket attacks, black syph, nasty shit like that."

We started talking about our first day as MP's. Clardy heard me mention all the loot we got on gate duty. He told us when he wasn't on village patrol; he worked for Ben in the motor pool. "Make sure ya keep most a that loot next time. Ben jus sells that shit, pockets the cash. He's already makin' a fortune with the jeeps an other shit he sells."

Mac and I chuckled when Clardy concluded, "Sweet deal, huh. You bust yer nuts crawlin' through the slopes shit an ol Ben makes a few hundred sellin' the shit. That ol boy's no dummy."

Then Clardy told us we could sell the pistols to truck drivers, get a couple bucks for the carton of cigs. "Gotta pay $2.50 at the PX, why pay more?" Now we knew why our pile was some much higher, Mac had been right.

Ben never showed up so we left the club, went looking for Fleming. I missed the sourpuss bastard, wanted to see how he spent his first day. Was looking forward to his litany of miserable things that happened to him. Somehow his misery would cheer me up. Big German Shepherds guarded the CID section; we approached cautiously. I leaned over the concertina wire, yelled for him. A few seconds later he peeked out, "What do you sorry ass, loser MP's want? Don't you know no self respecting CID hangs with your ilk?" Then he gave us a big grin, joined us.

I told him about Price, he shook his head, "I heard the same story, most MP's are burnt-out rejects from the grunts. There's big scuttle that the brass wants the MP's cleaned up. Colonel Mullen, he's the Provost Marshall, has me checking backgrounds, recent offenses, stuff like that. Says he's going to get rid of the trash. He mentioned you and McCarthy are part of the new breed; educated guys that enforce the law, do things right. He said the monkeys have been running the zoo too long. I told him I knew you guys well and he might be disappointed in Frazier, who's more machine than man. He's like a walking bag of muscle, but not too bright." Then Fleming burst out laughing. He loved his own jokes.

That night we soon learned what the mosquito nets were for. The previous day was cooler; the bugs must have been on R&R that first evening. About midnight, I started getting attacked. I hopped out of the bunk, tore through my duffle bag to find the net. Mac was just a step behind me as we draped our bunks and built a protective cocoon.

We turned on flashlights to kill the suckers that got under the net as we dived for protection. After a few minutes, we found peace. "Can you believe how big those suckers are, Mac? If you listen close, I swear I'm hearing landing instructions from the air traffic controller." Mac shook his head, chuckled.

Next day we were assigned the same CPO gate. We continued to find stashes of forbidden cigarettes, a few pistols. Mac and I decided to give Gentle Ben about 20% of the loot. "We better not piss him off too fast. Nobody likes new guys that don't know their places," Mac noted.

As he spoke, I watched three little girls wandering up the road, stopped outside the shack, grinned at us, all cute as a button. I walked out, said to Mac, "My eyes must be fooling me, I think I'm looking at three future movie stars. Shirley Temple better watch her back."

To my amazement, the girls burst into the sweetest giggles I ever heard. The tallest one looked at me, "You beaucoup funny MP."

That began my enjoyable relationship with Li, My, and Lin. I looked at them carefully. Li was slim, a dazzling smile, brown hair and Caucasian features. I wondered if her father was American. My was a classic Asian beauty, jet-black hair, round face and huge chocolate brown eyes that seemed to smile at you. Lin was tiny but with alert eyes that took everything in and electricity about her that exuded strength beyond her size. They were very different but instantly adorable. They were 10 years old, inseparable. "What are you young beauties doing hanging around this nasty Army base?"

My smiled at me with huge brown eyes, "We speak good English, so Viet trucks need us to sell, how say, ah, stuff."

Her English was almost perfect. I asked them if they had passes to get on the base.

Li said, "No have but you see soon, we beaucoup big help to MP's. Can help you with Viet. We stay and show."

Mac looked at me, "What do you think our pal Sgt Price would say?" At the mention of his name, My recoiled, almost like she'd been slapped.

"Sgt Price number 10. He come, we hide."

Then Lin piped in, "No, no, Sgt Price beaucoup number 10."

To my puzzled look, Li said, "Number 10 mean bad. Beaucoup number 10 even badder. Beaucoup fuckin' number 10 mean worst. Sgt Price beaucoup fuckin number 10!" The look on their young faces showed total fear.

Our new friends, true to their boast, proved invaluable. A rickety truck came up the road, Lin said, "Look under papa-sahn's seat, carry much drug. Steal much. You see."

Papa sahn exited the truck, gave me a big smile with blackish red teeth. He chewed away; spit a huge glob of reddish juice on the ground.

I smiled at papa-sahn, "You'd be a dental nightmare back in the States, buddy. Might be all right in a dugout at a baseball game, but that nasty juice wouldn't work with the ladies. Would be tough getting a date in my neighborhood, papa-sahn. Plus I'll bet you got some major assbreath." Mac laughed out loud, little Li laughed louder.

Papa-sahn stood there smiling as we looked over his paperwork, searched his truck. Mac pulled out a couple cartons of Kools from the rear seat. I found a huge bag of what looked like marijuana crammed between wooden boxes. When I smelled the contents, my guess was proven. "Planning to party tonight, papa-sahn?"

He continued grinning, "Beaucoup number 1," was his reply. Following My's advice, I pulled up the front seat, found a Colt 45 and ammo under some rags.It was my turn to grin. "You're a naughty boy, papa-sahn. Where'd you get this weapon? Last time I checked, they weren't letting Vietnamese in the U.S Army."

Papa-sahn kept grinning but went into his pocket, pulled out $20 in American money. He handed it to me; then reached for the Colt 45. I slapped his hand away, looked straight in his eyes, "Next time you try to pull this shit, I'm gonna put my boot up your bony ass and throw you in the slammer. Get the hell outta here."

I'm not sure he understood the words, but he got the message. I'm not sure why it pissed me off so much, but I was really angry. He left quickly. Mac looked at me funny.

"I thought you were gonna let him go from the way you joked around. Then I saw you were just making him relax. He thought it was going to be okay. Then when he saw the look on your face, I thought he was gonna poop his pajamas. Now that was a performance, Dylan."

I started to protest when the little girls walked close, smiled at me, said, "Beaucoup number 1," and patted my arms. For whatever reason, that made me feel good, like a dose of humanity.

After our shift, we dumped the Colt 45 and ammo on Gentle Ben's desk, but kept all the cigarettes. Mac found 20 cartons that day, was excited about the extra income. "If I can make $20-$40 a day selling these, I could pile-up a few hundred a month. Who knows, maybe this gate duty won't be so bad?"

Mac and I wandered around, found a beautiful basketball court on the other side of the motor pool. A couple black guys were shooting around when we ambled up. One of the guys yelled, "You play?"

We introduced ourselves to Jimmy Jones and Claude Nicholson. Mac and I stripped off our shirts, warmed up for awhile then played 2 on 2. I could tell from watching that Jones was a good player. Nicholson looked weak. The game started, I drained a long jump shot on our first possession.

Jones looked at me, cocked his head a little, "Huh, not bad."

It didn't surprise me much that McCarthy was a ferocious defender; he helped me with Jones. Nicholson was terrible but Jones was 6'4", could jump like a gazelle, I had a hard time if he drove to the hoop. Fortunately, Jones liked to shoot from outside but wasn't a good shooter. I had always been a good shooter, had one of those great nights; I rarely missed. Jones wanted to match me, foolishly stopped driving as we won easily 20-12. I could tell that Jones was puzzled by the loss, wanted more. Enjoying the bit of normalcy, "Another one?" I asked.

We had some great games, soon drew a small crowd. Jones was content to shoot jump shots most of the time, didn't capitalize on his size and jumping ability. I was 6'2", could dunk a ball easily but Jones flew over me. McCarthy was 6'3", lanky, but sneaky good, got every loose ball. If I missed, he usually beat Nicholson to the rebound, scored easily. After 4 games to 20, we still won handily; Jones saw the light. "I thought it was a mistake the first time but after 4 straight whoopins', guess you guys can play. How about tomorrow night?"

We put on our shirts, went back to the club for a drink. Sgt Wilson and Ben were at the bar, having what seemed like a jovial conversation, clapped when we walked in.

Wilson said, "Nice playing guys, nobody's beat Jones for months. We might have the makings of a team now. The MP's have gotten their ass whipped all season. We maybe have a shot now."

We learned there was an active basketball league on Quang Tri; bragging rights were a big deal. Other than Jones, the MP team wasn't too good. We learned Wilson was the coach. "Where did you learn to shoot like that Frazier? Jones is the best player on the base but you made him look bad. We never had a shooter before to let Jones work the boards. Plus McCarthy's like a pit bull out there.

This could be some fun." I noticed during Wilson's praise Ben never said a word, seemed to be studying us.

Then Percy Price walked in, yelled, "Who's the guys that beat my brothers? I heard we got some bad ass white guys."

Wilson responded, "Frazier's a stud and McCarthy boards like a madman. You finally got some help on defense Price. These guys can play." Percy stared at us, walked up to me, frowned; looked me over.

"I didn't realize you was that big Frazier. Ya got some meat on yer bones. I might have some help kickin' the fuck-ups around. I owe it to my body to get some rest." Then he walked around McCarthy, "You tall but kinda bony but got a big frame. Let's play tomorrow night after the shift. Jones and me gonna smoke ya." Then he walked off.

We learned that Percy was the self appointed captain of the team, took basketball seriously. Sgt Wilson said, "He isn't that big but makes up for it with mean. Most games end up in a fight. Percy hasn't lost a fight yet."

Then Ben added, "Percy always picks a fight when it's sure were gonna lose. He hits before the other guy even knows there's a problem. Ya got to be ready with Percy. If he gets a shot at ya, you're down. He loves to break legs. Gets ya lookin' at his hands then the foot comes callin'. That ol boy's lethal." Ben had a weird look on his face as he spoke. Approval?

McCarthy and I walked back to our hooch, went to sleep thinking about the game waiting for us. I thought it was a dream until I felt my bunk slam into the wall. The deafening blast and concussion left Mac and me staring at each other. Still muddled, "Explosion? And pretty close," I said. Mac scrambled up, yelled for me to head to the bunker with him.

"Be careful as you open the door, Mac. Let's see what's happening first." I peeked out; saw there was a mad scrambling in the Company area.

I saw our basketball buddy Nicholson running by, "Hey, Nicholson, what was that?"

Without breaking stride he yelled, "Nothin' good," and went into the bunker. Mac and I tore after him, got inside the sandbag shelter.

Nicholson looked at me, "Where's your boots, Frazier? There's usually snakes in here, crawl in here cause its cool and moist."

I looked at Nicholson, "What kinda place lets snakes in the bunker? So I get to choose whether to get blown up getting my boots or hope the snakes don't like white meat?"

Nicholson winked at me, "Snakes aren't picky eaters, Frazier. Any meat'll do." I moved over near the entrance, hoping any snakes were deeper inside. Mac cozied up beside me. We sat there listening; no one talked.

Finally, unable to stand the tension, "What happened?" I said to no one in particular.

"The ammo dump," someone responded from the darkness. "Happens all the time. They keep shifting the ammo site but the sappers find it sooner or later."

"What's a sapper?" I asked.

The hidden voice advised, "Just a small V.C. that sneaks through the wires, usually carries bombs or grenades. They usually just harass the base; try to keep us scared. Or, if they find the ammo site, try to ruin our whole day." I kept thinking: Will this happen every night? It got quiet.

We waited about 10 minutes, there were no more explosions. We left the bunker, walked back with Nicholson. He said, "I'm glad I'm not on night patrol. Those chumps gotta circle the perimeter lookin' for Charlie. Look all around the buildings makin' sure no unauthorized civilians are on base. Then pull the jeeps up to the wire and make sure no shits goin' down. How stupid, I aint even bull shittin'?"

I looked at Nicholson, "So, you're telling me the MP's drive around the base looking for a little yellow guy carrying grenades, then check to see if he has an appropriate pass to be on base?"

Nicholson gave a deep, throaty laugh, "You're a trip Frazier. Little yellow guy with a base pass, that a good one."

QUANG TRI

Next morning, Sgt Wilson told us a little history on
Quang Tri. It had been overrun in the Tet offensive of
1968; the Americans bombed Charlie mercilessly for
months before we regained control. "There's lots of
unexploded ordnance laying around. So watch where you
walk off the base; don't go off wandering. About 10% of
the bombs don't go off. But if you jostle them wrong, you
can be in a world of hurt. Plus the Agent Orange got
sprayed all over, killed anything that grew. That's why you
see it looks all yellow and dusty around parts of the city.
Ever since then, Charlie keeps poking at us, wants Quang
Tri back. This is a bad place."

With that jolly news, Mac and I went to our gates to do
our duty. Our young Vietnamese friends, My, Li, and Lin
were waiting for us. My looked at me with her huge brown
eyes, "We worry you no come. Worry you off gate, out in
village, do patrol." The girls told us that new guys did gate
duty for a while, and then got rotated to patrol either on
the base or around the villages. These little dolls knew
their stuff.

Li told us they lived in nearby Quang Tri City. When I
asked if their parents knew they were working on the base,
I got a funny answer. "Mama-sahn need money. Know we
speak good American. Make more money that her cleanin'
G.I. clothes." When I asked about their fathers, they
looked at me blankly, "Go back home. No see." They all
had American fathers, who had been sent home. "We
three friends. No one want us but mama–sahn."

I looked at Mac; saw he was exhaling deeply. How can
you walk away from your kid, he was wondering? Could

see he was thinking about his son back home, growing up
without him. Mac and I looked at each other, exchanged
the same thought: What a mess. But these beautiful little
kids were strong, resilient.

After they helped us get started with the truck line, we
let them hop the last truck, entered the base to help the
local traders make a fortune, at least by their standards. We
spent the rest of the day finding pilfered Army goods.

We ate chow after our shift, met Sgt Wilson as we were
leaving, "There's going be a crowd watching your game
tonight. Percy's been talking shit all day. He wants to show
the newbies how ball's played in Nam. Watch out Frazier,
he isn't exactly a finesse player."

I looked at Sgt Wilson, "I grew up playing ball in Philly.
Not many fouls got called. One of my best friends was
called "Nut", cause he was a bit intense. If Nut guarded
you, you got guarded close. We'll see how Percy measures
up." Wilson nodded; he liked the answer.

Percy was about 5'9", weighed maybe 165 pounds
dripping wet. He didn't have an ounce of fat on him, was
coiled in muscle. Plus he had those crazy, lifeless eyes. He
yelled, "I'll guard white bread, you take McCarthy, Jones."

I was 6'2", weighed 200 normally. The heat had melted
off a few pounds but my size helped me handle the beating
Percy gave me. He wasn't much of a player but he made
contact on every play. He held me to stay close, tried to
prevent me from getting the ball. If he got close enough,
he'd whack my wrist as I shot. When I did get free, I
caught the ball, shot quickly, that's how I was trained.
Most of the time they went in, we won the first game 20-
16.

Jones scored most of their hoops but Percy berated him
for playing soft. "If I wanted a weak nigger, I'd called
Nicholson. Play like a man, motherfucker."

Jones looked at him, said nothing, threw him the ball.

"Let's see how we do with you handlin' the load, brother."

Jones watched Percy take shot after shot, grinned as each ball clanged off the rim. Mac gobbled up the misses, scored easily. Percy got worn out playing so much offense, had a harder time hammering me. We won 20-5. Jones looked at Percy, "Who's the soft motherfucker, now?"

A crowd watched, a couple new faces popped up. I could see a small, older guy with full bird wings on his uniform. I wondered if that was the Provost Marshall. The other officer was a lieutenant, young and chubby with a gummy smile. When I spotted him, the word "doofus" popped to mind. All this flashed through my mind as Percy said, "Time to switch it up, Frazier and me'll play you. I'm feelin' generous, Jones, so you take it in first."

Percy guarded Jones, really went after him. Mac hounded me but I had no trouble getting open. Percy was content to watch me score; we took a 10-5 lead. Jones seemed to wake up, started going to the hoop every time. Percy almost road his back but Jones elevated, carried him to the rim for lay-ups. I tried to help but neither Percy nor I could stop him. The score was tied now 15-15. Mac had prevented me from getting the ball for the last few possessions but then I found my stride, scored on long jumpers to take an 18-16 lead. Jones fortunately got tired as Percy hacked him unmercifully. Percy scored the winning bucket as we won 20-17. "Check it out, motherfuckers," Percy crowed, strutted like he'd just won the NCAA tourney.

We headed to the club, once inside Ben Burton introduced us to the Provost Marshall Colonel Mullen. I saluted but Colonel Mullen smiled, "No need for that here. Out on the base, salute me but on company grounds, were a team. Private Fleming told me you're a hotshot, Frazier, came in 1st in MP school. After watching the pounding

Price gave you, no need to ask if you're tough." Then he turned to Mac, "I can see you're a team player, McCarthy. You did the dirty work; let Frazier shoot. But then you gobbled up the misses. That's good teamwork, McCarthy. You know how to use your strengths. Maybe you two can help me straighten out this place. Come see me before your shifts tomorrow." Then he walked out.

Callahan and Clardy were seated nearby, overheard the Colonel's comments. "Maybe basketball's going help you after all," the usually quiet Callahan said.

"Clardy says he's been playing for the team 3 months and Colonel Mullen never talked to him once."

Clardy looked at me, drawled, "Maybe cause I got a lard ass and suck has somethin' to do with it." Then he burst into a gigantic belly laugh, all of us chuckling along with him. We sat, yapped about gate duty and other mindless topics. I enjoyed being with my old buddy Callahan. Maybe our fences were starting to mend.

Mac and I got promoted to patrol duty the next day. Colonel Mullen was on the desk, Sgt Wilson nowhere to be seen. "It's time to let you see some of the local scenery," he advised. He showed Mac and I the duty roster. The bad news was I was on patrol with Percy; Mac was with Clardy. Colonel Mullen looked straight at me, "Price's a crazy bastard, but sometimes you need crazy in Nam. We've got a serious prostitution and drug problem on this base. I want you guys to keep your eyes open; report directly to me if you see anything that hints at something funny. There's a ring operating the whores and dope, I think both're connected. So far, none of your esteemed comrades have turned up rat shit. You ask me, they aren't looking too hard. If you see something, come right to me; say nothing to anybody else. Got me?" We nodded.

Then he switched topics. "I'm going to call my pal, Colonel Windsor at the 101st, challenge him to a little game. They've been beating our ass like a booby-trapped toilet seat; now's time for payback. I can't wait to watch that smug bastard gape when he sees you two de-balling his guys. Now that is a sweet thought, gentleman." Then he saluted us said, "Welcome to Quang Tri. Remember what I said. Something's rotten on this base. It's the MP's job to catch the bad guys. So far, the MP's have failed. I need you to help clean up the mess. Dismissed!"

Mac and I had no time to discuss what Colonel Mullen meant or why he'd asked two new guys to solve this problem because Percy was waiting right outside the office. "Been kissin' ass already, boys? No one likes it when the new pups get an audience with the Big Dog. Need to pay more dues 'fore you get that piece a chocolate. Come on, Frazier, lets' see if you can MP as good as you shoot."Mac looked at me as I left. His expression read: I feel sorry for you.

We jumped in the jeep; Percy floored it, roared off in a cloud of dust. Percy's eyes darted as he drove, almost like he sensed something about to happen. I began to do the same. I remembered what my buddy Nut used to say, "Expect the worst."

We drove so fast that even a skilled sniper could never hit us as we flew around the base. Then Percy took a hard right at the far end of a desolate road; we approached an MP gate. Nicholson and Jones were guarding this gate; they looked nervous as we drove up. Percy yelled, "You clowns stayin' awake? Don't let me catch any poontang sneakin' outta that shack. Talk to me if ya need a taste, hear?"

And then I got to see Nicholson in action. He was smooth, was one of the few blacks from his town that graduated from the mostly white University of Alabama, so you knew he handled himself well. I listened to him rap with Percy. He had a deep voice, kept his tongue to the side of his mouth. This produced a guttural sound that was oddly pleasant. He called himself 'Nick' when he referred to himself.

He was telling Percy, "Nick's been tellin' Jones, gonna stay on my toes. Ol Nick's gonna be vigilant. No sorry ass sapper's gonna ruin Nick's day."

Percy stared at him, "Keep talkin' so much about Nick, ya won't even notice Charlie sneakin up to blow your shit away. Dummy up, mother fucker."

Jones burst out laughing; Percy seemed proud of his wit. Then Nick started what turned out to be the strangest laugh I ever heard. It was a short, puffing sound, almost like he was slowly choking on a bone. He seemed to be in pain but eventually he gets a big grin on his face.

"Nick's got to remember that one, Sgt Price. I like a man with a sense of humor."

Price looked at them, "Remember what I said, I control any pussy on the base. If it aint Price's pussy, it aint belong here."

Then we peeled out leaving them choking on our dust. I recalled Colonel Mullen's comments on prostitution. Was Price the culprit?

We exited the base, drove down a decently paved road. "QL-1 runs from Hanoi to Saigon, Frazier. Slopes aint big on directions, so they made it easy. There's just one main road, north and south. If ya get lost, head east and you'll probably find QL-1 pretty quick. Hit the ocean, ya gone too far. That's yer first lesson, today."

I just nodded at Percy; he wasn't looking for a conversation. Then we approached a few shacks that turned into a small village. Although it was primitive, it struck me as neat, orderly. No junk or trash lying around, everything was in its place.

"Let's show the slopes the sheriff's in town," Percy said as he got out of the jeep. That left me feeling nervous.

I watched Percy stride up and down the village; his arrogance screamed, "I own the place."

Whenever a villager saw him, they lowered their eyes, turned the other direction. I stayed about 50 feet behind him, tried to smile at everyone. As I rounded a corner, I saw my little girl Lin, with the electric eyes, who hung out by the base gate. She waved, but ducked out of sight quickly. When I turned back, Percy was nowhere to be seen. I started getting nervous being cut off, headed to the jeep.

I sat there about 10 minutes, still no Percy. Then suddenly, from behind me I heard, "Hey, Dylan-sahn." Little Lin had worked her way up to the jeep without a sound.

"Hello Lin, do you know where Sgt Price is? I lost him back there."

Lin looked at me without expression, advised, "Sgt Price no lost. He boom-boom girl-sahn. He boom boom fast, so he want chop chop bo koc too. Take while. Me leave when I hear come. No want me chop chop." Then her eyes got big, she darted off.

Minutes later Percy rounded the corner, walked toward me. From behind the edge of a hooch, a scraggly dog came charging out, growled at Percy. The dog weighed about 25 pounds but was obviously a good judge of assholes; he disliked Percy, wanted to keep him away from his turf. Percy started talking softly, put his hand down in a gesture of friendliness. When the dog got close, Percy lashed his right foot into the dog's head, almost decapitated him. The stunned mutt staggered a couple steps but Percy finished the job with another shot to the ribs.

Then I saw the terrified villagers peeking from their windows, witnessing the brutality. My guess was something bad happened every time Percy visited. Percy was looking closely, seeing how I was reacting. "Gotta teach the slopes who's boss. That rangy mutt was headed for the stew pot anyway. Saved them the trouble of ringin' its neck. Just my way of helpin' the locals. Know what I mean Frazier?"

I looked at him blankly, "I was just thinking you're probably not a member of the SPCA, are you Percy?"

He shook his head, digesting my comment. "SPCA member? That's funny. Huh, I like that, Frazier."

That night I described my day with Percy; Mac winced. "He killed a dog, just like that. No reason whatever?"

Then I told him what I said about the SPCA, Mac shook his head, said that was quick thinking. "It's better not to show him you think he's nuts, Dylan. Who knows, maybe that's the way we'll be acting in a few weeks. Maybe you do need to be violent. I hope not."

I shook my head, "No way I'll be killing helpless dogs. I don't care how bad it gets."

Mac looked dejected, "I sure hope you're right."

We talked over what I saw and heard about prostitutes. "Do you think Percy's the guy Colonel Mullen's looking for? Seems too obvious to me, but what do I know?"

Mac nodded at me, "It can't be that easy." Then I said we should check with Callahan and Fleming to see if they got the same speech from the Provost Marshall.

We wandered around, found both at the club. Only a few guys were around, so we huddled in the corner; compared notes about our first days in Quang Tri. Callahan hadn't met Colonel Mullen yet; Fleming said he'd only had general discussions about "cleaning up the base."

Fleming was a skeptic, always looked for a person's angle, "I think he's keeping a tight lid on the problem, only wants you guys involved. He probably knows you aren't corrupted yet and can trust you. Maybe he read Callahan tried to be a CO, wouldn't be likely to mix with the sordid types. After seeing my PT scores, he probably thought I'd get killed if I messed with the tough guys. Who knows, maybe he finds me too charming for hazardous duty?" That made us howl; I could tell that Fleming was only partially kidding. He actually thought of himself as suave and debonair.

Before I left, I warned Callahan and Fleming about Percy, told them about the dog. "Jesus," was all Fleming said. Callahan got visibly angry, looked almost sick.

"I'm glad it wasn't me with him. Dylan's the only one who could have handled that right. Me, I'd probably have gone after Percy and I'd be lying by the road with a broken leg or worse. Wow."

I wasn't sure whether Callahan was complimenting me or rehashing our old wound of not jumping in without thinking first. He didn't look like he was taking a shot, so I just let it go.

As Mac and I headed back to our hooch, I imagined Callahan in my place, concluded he was right. He and Percy were not a couple made in heaven.

I mentioned this to Mac, he agreed, "Percy'd eat you up if you gave him any shit. I hope Callahan never has patrol with him. That wouldn't work. He's too nice a guy, doesn't have a lick of street smarts. This is Nam, it's not some peace and love protest march. He better learn to step back some. This isn't any place to act before you think."

It made me feel good to hear someone else read things my way.

One of my goals in Nam was to read a couple books each week. Mac was an avid reader, so we had started exchanging books, giving reviews afterwards. Mac was finishing "The Godfather" I gave him. I was anxious to see what he thought. He knew I loved it, wanted his

71

glowing review. He could tell I was waiting for him to finish, kept looking up, telling me to stop staring at him. "Stop bug-eyeing me, will you?" I gave him my best Peter Lorre impression as he turned to face the wall.

I went back to "The Count of Monte Cristo," left my sensitive buddy to read at his leisure. The hooch's were designed so no light leaked if you kept the doors shut. We read to keep our minds on something pleasant before nodding off. If you had a good read, most nights you forgot where you were. I heard Mac breathing deeply, knew his review would have to wait for tomorrow. I was tempted to steal "The Godfather" back, feign ignorance next morning. I always enjoyed pestering people. Tempting. Instead, I rolled over, dozed off.

The nightmare hit me like a thunderous missile attack! I was riding down Hwy 1; had entered a sleepy village. Screams from a nearby hut startled me. Callahan was with me; he bolted from the jeep before I came to a stop. The dead dog caught my attention but Callahan ignored it as he ran to the noisy hut. Villagers peered around corners and through windows. They seemed to be following Callahan's flight. I heard violent arguing and then a shriek of pain, then silence. Just as I neared the hut, the dog sprang to life and lunged at me…

"Wake up, Dylan, you're moaning like a madman. It's just a nightmare. Settle down." Through the mosquito net I saw Mac's concerned face. I was gasping for air, but soon calmed down. Then I told Mac about my recurring dream of being caught in a village, sensing imminent death.

I exhaled, "That incident with Percy must have set me off. Was hoping those were over. This place is bad enough without nightmares. Shit!" Mac looked upset, I told him I was okay.

"Gonna go take a pee, Mac. Go back to sleep. I'm okay. Thanks for waking me up. Who knows how long that dream would have kept going?"

As I was walking to the outhouses, I saw someone standing outside the club. Then I heard a grinding noise, so I moved quietly toward the prowler. As I got nearby, I recognized the familiar bulk, Ben Burton. He seemed to be looking around nervously, so I stopped, remained hidden in the darkness. What was he doing? There was a large metal object in his hand, which I recognized as the cash box from the club. I remembered watching him meticulously organizing the money every few minutes. Ben liked things neat. I was also anal, recognized the trait.

I decided to stay quiet, watched him walk off with the cash box and some bulky tool in his other hand. Keeping a safe distance, I saw him headed towards his hooch. His gait was more relaxed now. Whatever was bugging him must have passed. I reversed course, made my way back to the club door. As I got closer, I spotted the broken lock; it had been cut in half. After finishing my latrine visit, I went to my hooch, found Mac asleep, breathing peacefully. I resisted the urge to wake him, share what I'd seen. Thinking about that odd event, I nodded off dream free.

Mac and I were headed back from breakfast when I got called over by Sgt Wilson. "Frazier, report to Sgt Burton and fill out a burglary report. Someone broke into the club last night and got away with thousands of bucks. Bastard was smart, too. He must of known that the payroll run was tomorrow and Ben's would have a load of money to turn over. File the report to me then I'll send you out on patrol again. Percy says you carry yourself well, like a soldier." He blinked a couple times, continued, "High praise. Percy thinks most everybody is worthless."

I shook my head, "Will do."

I hadn't told Mac what I'd seen the night before; decided to keep my mouth shut till I met with Ben.

Ben missed his calling, was an Academy Award winner. He had a perplexed look. "Third time I been hit. Prick seems to know when the tills overflowin', then hits. I keep the door padlocked; hide the cash box different places. He sniffs it out, though. Unfuckin' believable." Then Ben walked me to the club; we inspected the door. "Musta used bolt cutters," Ben surmised.

We went inside, looked at the mess near the shelves. "I hid the box behind the pretzel tins. Didn't think anyone'd look there. Thought the cash box'd kinda blend in. Smart sum bitch," Ben said, shaking his head in admiration.

I filled out the report, learned that about $5,000 had been stolen. "We had a good month, what with the USO show and all. Too bad ya missed it. Korean group with some real lookers. Right before you got in country. Wonder if'n one of them slopes from the show was involved? Maybe ya outta check that out?"

I shook my head, said nothing. I also learned that this was the 3rd theft in less than a year. "Happenin' all over the base. Tell Wilson he's got a big problem. Might be a ring. Probably got the same leader, someone that knows the ropes. What aya think?" He wouldn't like my real answer.

Instead, "Sounds logical."

I gave the report to Wilson. "Ring, huh? That might be right. Check on the Korean troupe, too. Ben schedules them with the Korean guy, Park; he runs the barbershop, glasses place too. Park's a good guy but you never know."

I watched Wilson carefully to see if he was serious. Didn't he know that Ben was the thief? Was Wilson involved? Were they using me as the "school trained MP" who would do things by the book but not have a clue what was really going on? I nodded to Wilson but kept quiet. Needed more time to sift through this farce.

We had our basketball game that night, right after our shift. I never got a chance to tell Mac what was going on with the club robbery. We rushed to our jeeps, went to play the 101st MP's on their own court. While our basketball area was a nice half court set-up, the 101st had a gorgeous full court. Even had some stands and a shack for sodas and snacks, nice digs. But their game wasn't so great.

Apparently, they had been beating us routinely but Mac and I changed the dynamics. I scored 38 points as we won 105- 65. Jones and the relentless Mac ruled the boards. Jones was content to play around the hoop. If they guarded me tightly, I flipped the ball to Mac and Jones. The inside-out combination was too much for them. Pretty soon they gave up playing defense, just lofted shots. A good defensive player could control me. But if you didn't guard me, I'd score in my sleep. As the game ended, I saw Colonel Mullen collecting a wad of cash from his counterpart. The other Colonel looked really pissed.

We got a hero's welcome at the club that night. The team drank free; even Percy acted calm and relaxed. For a short time, I'd forgotten I was in Nam. As I sat there, it dawned on me I was adapting to my environment. A thought popped into my head.

It was Nut warning me, "Don't get too relaxed. That's when you make mistakes. Trust few people; keep them near your back. You never know."

I looked around, knew that Mac, Callahan and Fleming were on my team. Everyone else was suspect. I finished my beer, went off to read.

I had just finished telling Mac about "the mysterious club caper," when Percy barged into our hooch. "Wake up, boys. Got some serious tang in my quarters. Want my teammates to get early dibs. Check it out."

Then he was off. Sleepily, we stumbled outside; saw a light beaming from the supply room. There was a small line of MP's near the door. Percy and Lt Clep, the young chubby guy I had labeled a doofus, stood guard.

Clep yelled, "Frazier, you and McCarthy can move to the front. We don't want our stars losing too much sleep."

We walked ahead, peered in the room. There was a tiny girl, maybe 4"6", lying naked on a bunk. She was pretty, had the body of a 6th grade boy; was hairless where hair was expected. Clep looked at me, "She's a real looker, huh?"

I looked back at him, "I guess if you like the Tinker Toy type, Lieutenant. Me, I like a full-figured girl. Think I'll take a pass. She's more like McCarthy's type. Don't you think?"

Mac laughed, went with me, leaving Clep with a funny look on his face. Surprise? When we got a few steps, I spotted my basketball buddies, Jones and Nicholson. "You guys aren't really gonna tap that mongrel, are you?"

They looked at me for a while. "Just close your eyes, preten' she's Diana Ross," was Jones's reply.

Nicholson was more scientific, "I got me a serious case of semen back-up needin' attention, Frazier. You don't want to see your brother's skin break out do you?"

I shook my head, "That's why God invented Clearasil, Nick. I'd be more worried about a monster case of fungus amongus, guys." They chuckled, but I could tell they thought we were nuts.

Mac and I sat talking about the day. I filled him in on Ben's perfect robbery. We both agreed to keep it to ourselves. "Who knows who else is involved? If I figured this out in one day, don't you think others have? Why is this still going on? Maybe Clep or Sgt Wilson got their hands dirty, too. Either way, I'll just play dumb for now; I think that's what they really want, anyway." Then I added, "I am going to tell Callahan and Fleming, but not right now. Don't want them getting sucked into this. Knowing Fleming, he'd blurt out that Ben is the scam artist; end up a grunt. Can you imagine how pissed off he'd be?"I laughed just thinking about that. Then Mac started talking about his wife Mary, his kid, little Mike.

He looked at me intently, "I'm doing nothing to get in any trouble. Anytime I feel noble, I see those faces and I settle down. Mike McCarthy's no hero. I'm going to do my time and get out. No hero stuff in my future." I watched his set jaw; nothing would change his plan.

ABOUT LAURA

And that conversation started our nightly ritual of talking about home before going to sleep. Even after a grueling day, we alternated rambling about nice memories. Mac always talked of Mary and Little Mike, occasionally lapsing into crazy things he did as a kid. It was our way of staying normal, blocking out the insane situation.

When it was my turn, I told him about Laura Hartley, the girl I would marry. Mac smiled, "I didn't know you were engaged." It was my turn to grin.

"No, not engaged yet." He looked confused, so I continued. "In fact, we hadn't even dated before. Not till I got drafted and was headed for Basic."

Mac started to laugh, "Is this one of your jokes?"

So I told him of our weird relationship. "Been nuts about her since spotting her in church, I think she was in 6th grade. She had that amazing face, movie star beautiful, kind of a special glow." Mac was still looking at me funny, waiting for the punchline.

"Anyway, we stayed in touch over the years, always had this special bond, like we knew we were meant for each other but I was too busy with basketball, she was too busy doing meaningful stuff, being a great student, helping people, heart of gold stuff."

I looked at Mac, said seriously, "What I'm saying is, Laura is the exact opposite of me but somehow she sees through my shit, maybe spots something worthwhile." Mac was chuckling now as I added, "I didn't tell her how I felt until I was drafted." Mac calmed down some, asked me how I went about breaking the ice.

"I called her the night I got the draft notice. Told her my fun news. Asked if she wanted to go out for a burger and shake. On the ride there, I told her how I felt about her. That I had been crazy about her forever, that I knew we were friends, hoped it was more than that." I looked at Mac, "You'll never guess what she said." To his questioning look, "Laura said her brothers told her I was an asshole."

Mac grinned, broke into his funny chuckle. When he settled down, he choked out, "What did you say to that?"

I threw up my hands. "I asked if they meant being an asshole in a good way or a bad way; did they have a mean tone of voice or was there a tone of grudging respect. I knew I was okay when she started to smile." And when I added, "Your brothers aren't any prizes themselves," Laura laughed out loud, a sweet sound." Mac had a huge grin on his face. It was nice hearing stories of home.

QUANG TRI

I had patrol duty with Percy again next morning. He was a hyperactive guy, said whatever came into his head. Most times he just announced what he saw or heard. There was never any silence.

As we approached the PX, he yelled, "Look at that jeep over there Frazier. Some dumb bastard just left it out in the open. Let's play a little joke, huh? Watch this."

Percy jumped into the front seat, cranked it up; drove off. He waved at me to follow. He drove back to our barracks, pulled into the motor pool. Ben came ambling out. Percy crowed, "Got some new meat for ya, Ben. Another dumb fuck left this out in the open. You owe me, mo fo."

Then Percy pushed me over to the passenger side, drove off. Ben had never changed the expression on his face. He didn't seem surprised. I wondered why. We continued our rounds, Percy kept yelling about the dust, about how shitty the jeep handled, about the lousy breakfast, about being tired after banging the whore all night or whatever else popped up. I mostly sat, just nodded or confirmed what he was yapping about. "How come you got no pussy, last night, Frazier? You gettin' something on the side I don't know about?"

I knew this was coming. "No, Percy, it may be a long winter without rain, but I owe it to my body to wait for something special. Kind of like Christmas, build up the drama a little. Know what I mean?"

Percy chuckled, "Gotta remember that one, 'long winter without rain'."

We spent most of the day hunting for unguarded jeeps. Percy always roared up, leaped out; I followed him to the

MP motor pool. "Time to restock, Frazier. Can't be drivin' no sad ass pieces of shit. The P's gotta ride in style. Right?" I never saw Ben again, but each time we returned, the stolen jeeps were gone.

All Percy would say was, "P's gotta have the best rides. What those fuckers gonna do, call the police?"

Then he howled laughing. I'd just spent the whole day stealing jeeps and ¾ ton trucks. What kind of place was this? Should I tell Colonel Mullen?

Near the end of the day, we got a call to proceed to the USO club; there was a fight. Percy almost threw me out of the jeep when he took off so fast. He screamed, "Let's fuck somebody up, Frazier."

When we got there, we found a dozen MP's, including Mac, Clardy and Callahan, along with a bunch of police dogs. Standing ominously nearby was the MP's Armored Personnel Carrier, which was a modified tank with a big Thompson machine gun permanently mounted.

Clardy filled Percy in, "Bunch a black guys took over the club. Won't let any whites play pool, ping pong, shit like that. So far it's just a lot of yellin' but a couple a grunts got knives out. Might get bad fast." Percy just nodded, yelled to the dog handlers.

"Get behind me. When I say so, sic the dogs on the motherfuckers. Bring the APC up to the front door, point the Thompson inside. If I say fire, aim high, blow the shit outta the roof. Niggers hate dogs; think that'll work. If not, the Thompson'll get their attention. Spread out, don't clump up or you'll be an easy target. Frazier, you and Clardy follow me. I need some big guys with me." For once in my life, I wished I were a midget.

Percy stomped to the front doors, kicked them both open. He pulled his pistol, shot the Colt 45 into the roof; the place went dead silent. A hundred faces, stared at him. Then he waved the dog handlers in, 6 huge German Shepherds growled maniacally, straining their leashes. The dogs sent a signal: We're going to maul you to death. I stood still; watched the crowd, Percy had their attention.

He put his hands on his hips, "Gentleman," he bellowed, "someone told me we have a problem here. Some shit about not letting everybody have fun in the club. That can't be true, can it gentleman? Don't we got a war goin' on outside these wires? Why would some dumb motherfucker go and do that? Must be so dumb that he's gonna think my pets here (he pointed at the lunging Shepherds), won't tear the shit outta them when I give the signal." Then he moved further inside; the APC inched closer, the huge machine gun loomed its ugly head into the entrance. "Forgot to mention I brought some backup to deal with the motherfuckers when the dogs get their full. Your call, friends, clear the club ASAP or I start the party. I'm gonna count to 10. Here goes, I... 2...3" The club was empty by 5.

When Mac and I relived the event that night, we agreed on one thing, Percy was the right guy for that situation. He left no doubt he'd sic the dogs or blow the shit out of them with the Thompson.

I looked at Mac, "Now I know what Colonel Mullen meant when he said, 'sometimes you need crazy in Nam'."

Then Mac said, "All I could think about was Mary and little Mike. How would anybody explain that I got killed breaking up a fight in the USO club? That's the first racist stuff I've seen since getting drafted. Man, don't they all have to depend on each other out in the bush? That really bothers me. The more I think about it the more it makes me sick."

I nodded, stayed quiet for a while. After a long silence, we talked more about race, what we saw in Philly and Portland- two ends of the country. Mac said there were almost no black people in Oregon; he never saw any racism growing up.

"Most of the black guys I went to school with were middle class, like me. The Indians were the ones that got in most of the trouble. Once in awhile, they'd leave the reservation. Maybe get drunk, steal a car or something. Nothing too big; just once in awhile. I guess I lived in a cocoon out there." I filled Mac in on life in Philly.

"I never saw many problems but blacks and whites didn't mingle much, except in sports. Different neighborhoods, Italian, Irish or black, mostly stayed on their side of the boundaries, got funny looks when they didn't. When I used to thumb it into Philly to play ball at the black playgrounds, there'd only be Nut and me with white faces. After a few visits, nobody seemed to care. Especially since we could play, nobody gave us any shit. Got so we felt protected, like we were the crazy cousins come to visit." Then I told him I went to a high school with 1000 boys in my class, with maybe 2 or 3 blacks. "Philly wasn't what you'd call integrated."

We switched the topic to Nam, "Besides Jones, Nicholson and Percy, there weren't many black MP's, maybe 5 or 6," I guessed.

Mac nodded, "Driving around the base, I see mostly white faces here, some blacks or Puerto Ricans, but mostly white. That kind of surprised me. Based on what I'd read about the grunts, I thought there'd be more blacks here."

I went to sleep wondering if there was something odd about Quang Tri. Was that the cause for the USO problem that day? Something to watch out for?

I was on patrol with Clardy next day, used the opportunity to get more information on Ben. "How'd you get the job in the motor pool, Clardy? Based on what I see on the basketball court, you can't piss and chew gum. Don't tell me you're handy with cars."

Clardy grinned, "Yer a trip, Dylan. Aint never heard such funny talk afore. Where'd you get this shit?"

Clardy had a huge grin on his face, like a puppy dog with a bone. A hard guy not to like. I mixed basketball advice with my probes on Ben. "If you board like last game, Clardy, nobody's going to beat us. Don't pass so much after you get a rebound. Put them back up, otherwise they'll collapse on Jones. You're good around the hoop. Colonel Mullen might stop calling you 'that big, dopey guy' if you score some."

Clardy slapped his leg, howled in glee. Then I went after what I really wanted, what scams did Ben Burton have going on. Pretended like I was just curious.

Clardy rambled on with a series of facts. Ben had a Confederate flag in his hooch and "didn't like niggers too well." Ben hated Percy but they had reached a working relationship, despite his racist views. According to Clardy, "they needed each other." Then he told me, "Ben throws yer mail away if he don't like ya. When Percy pissed him off, he went weeks without mail."

Then he told me that between Ben and Percy, "they supply whores ta certain truck drivers ta make sure things arrive on schedule." Clardy looked at me, "Ben says everythin's a con in Nam, ya gotta take care of the right people and they'll take care of you. It be that simple."

I shook my head. "Why do we have to steal jeeps and trucks, Clardy? Doesn't make any sense to me. I mean, aren't we supposed to be the police?"

I learned from Clardy that stealing jeeps and trucks was big business in Nam. Every company had people out looking for unprotected vehicles.

"Ben's got deals with some other companies. He gets their stolen vehicles, files off the ID number, repaints 'em. He writes 'em new registration documents. Pretty slick, huh?"

I just nodded, trying not to look too interested. Even if you suspected a jeep or truck was stolen, you couldn't prove it because the motor block had been filed clean; it was impossible to figure out where's it came from. Perfect crimes. Ben and Percy were partners.

We had another ball game that night, against the 101st Airborne Infantry team. It was a much tougher match but we led 48-32 at half. Clardy took my advice, had 6 points and controlled the boards. When I missed, Jones and Mac scored easily. Even Percy was having a good game. The second half started well but quickly got ugly. The 101st figured that if I didn't get the ball, our team would stall. Every time I got the ball, I got hammered. The other guys had trouble scoring. The 3rd quarter ended with our lead whittled to 56-46.

Then the 101st made a big mistake. When I went up for a jumper, I got my feet knocked from under me; I fell hard. Before I could get up and defend myself, Percy came up behind the guy, kicked him in his hamstrings, dropping him like a sack of rocks. The referees were just other soldiers, really didn't know what to do. They called a double foul, but the 101st guys were enraged. Their guy had to be carried off, might have a broken leg.

Percy stood at half court, "Anybody fucks with Frazier, fucks with me." Although the 101st had a bunch of tough guys, they knew a maniac when they saw one. The game ended with no further problems, another win 75- 59.

Callahan was watching the game, came over to see if I was okay. I nodded, "Nothing too bad, can't say the same for the other guy. Percy isn't someone who takes a cheap shot well."

I told Callahan I needed to talk to him when we got back to our company area. We agreed to meet at my hooch.

I looked at him, "Don't bring Clardy, I need to talk to you alone." He looked puzzled but said okay. Before Callahan arrived, I told Mac what I'd learned from Clardy that day.

Mac put his hands on his hips, dejected, "This place is a mess." Callahan was shocked when I told him about the massive theft ring, gave him my opinion.

"I don't think Clardy's involved but I don't want him slipping, telling Ben I'm asking about him. Plus I'm puzzled with Ben's connection to Percy. That surprised me. From the way Ben talked, I thought he hated Percy. Now I find he's working with him sometimes." I looked at Mac and Callahan, "Who can we trust?" We kicked ideas around but no one had an answer.

Then I asked Callahan, "Keep an eye on Clardy to see if he's in tight with Ben or just a stooge. We need a pipeline to Ben; Clardy's got my vote if he's clean. The trouble is, we can't let Clardy know what we're doing. You're the only one that can do that easily, you live with him."

It was getting late, so we wandered over to the club, shot the breeze with Sgt Wilson, heard the word "monsoon season" for the first time. Sgt Wilson looked at me, "During monsoon season, even frogs wear raingear." I chuckled but he wasn't smiling. With that soggy vision, I headed back to catch some sleep.

I had guard duty next morning at a remote gate. From my previous experiences at this isolated spot, I learned to bring books, crossword puzzles and a miniature radio I bought at the PX. If you didn't occupy your mind, you went nuts. It was already 10 am, not one soul had approached my gate. The Stars and Stripes crossword puzzle was geared towards morons. Lots of questions about comic books; who is Batman's sidekick? US History; how many colors are in the American flag? And sports, what was George Herman Ruth's nickname? It took 5 minutes to complete the puzzle, as I wrote "Cowboys" to name the Dallas football team. Now I had 7 hours and 55 minutes to kill.

Finally, a few Vietnamese Army trucks came by, slowed down right away; showed me their papers. They were fine to go, hours passed without action. The only trouble I had later was an Army of the Republic of Vietnam (ARVN) Colonel who resented my demand for clearance. He looked like a Vietnamese Barney Fife, not too scary. I'm not sure what he called me, but I think it was something about my ancestry.

I finally looked at him, "My orders call for me to shoot anyone that runs the gate. I'm a pretty decent shot, so it's your call. I haven't shot anybody for a week or so."

I stepped away, put my hand on the Colt 45. His driver rapped at him, suddenly they backed up, roared off. I got on the radio, told Sgt Wilson what happened. He laughed so hard he dropped the mike; we lost our connection.

We continued to play b-ball, beat all the teams on Quang Tri soundly. Sgt Wilson loved coaching, delighted in each victory. I never saw a guy who loved sports more. He wasn't married, was a career soldier, seemed to have no ambition but was very bright. All his spare time was reading news magazines or watching sports. Trivia about anything but especially sports-related consumed him. "Frazier, did you know Red Grange's nickname was "Auburn'?"

I loved puzzles too so we got along well, I liked him a lot. Not a mean bone in his body, he had a unique way of handling people. Even Percy responded well to his coaching style. I mentally ruled him out of any involvement in the base shenanigans; he was too nice.

TRIP TO HUE

Wilson told us one night that we would play a team in Hue in a couple days. Hue was the ancient capital of Vietnam, was supposed to be a sacred place, mystically beautiful. The North Vietnamese Army captured Hue in a bloody battle in 1968 but, after a massive U.S. air assault, was quickly recaptured. We would lead a caravan of supply trucks to Hue to assure the trucks weren't harassed.

Wilson concluded, "Charlie likes to mess with Hue, really does a job on any traffic in and out. We'll have a Cobra leading the way, so it should go smooth. Cobra's can put a serious hurt on you."

The trip south to Hue was an eye opener. Clardy had done a lot of caravan duty, told me the worst spot was the front or the rear. Charlie could screw up the caravan if they hit the first vehicles, everthing stopped. Then they'd attack the stalled caravan, do as much damage as possible and then disappear. Sometimes, they did these sneak attacks a few times over the journey. If you were in the rear, because of driver hesitation and slow downs, you would have to drive 60 miles an hour just to stay close. Plus, you were a sitting duck in the back; Charlie could pick you off, nobody knew until the trek ended that you were missing.

Naturally, Mac and I got the caboose position, got to confirm Clardy's warning. I drove like a mad man to keep up. The road was mostly through farmland that wove between low mountains, but there were sections of lush forest. I gritted my teeth as I approached the first dense patch. Mac sat beside me with his M-16 poised. I had my Colt 45 holster unsnapped, ready if needed. I looked over at Mac; he was squeezing the rifle, tense.

"Hey Mac, did you hear the story about the dog with one eye, one leg amputated, no balls and smelled like a skunk?"

Mac looked over, puzzled. He shook his head, had no idea what I was talking about. "His name was 'Lucky'." I didn't get a big howl but his grin lightened the tension some.

We zoomed through the jungle area, soon entered a beautiful valley of rice paddies. The fields were a green I'd never seen before, a combination of gold, lime and mint green that dazzled me. Kids were riding water buffaloes through the paddies as their parents tended the fields. I thought about my college art courses, could picture Claude Monet pondering how to capture the beauty.

Mac was drinking in the scene, wondering aloud, "Why can't we leave these people alone. All they want is to farm, lead a simple life and raise their kids. What are we doing here?"

Before I could respond, the Cobra gunship tore overhead, obliterated a patch of woods bordering the fields. I'd seen pictures of what this horrific war machine could do, but the speed of devastation left me gasping. I stopped the jeep, watched as acre after acre was torched under a blizzard of bullets. We were told that Charlie was terrified of Cobras. Now I understood; it was like watching a pristine countryside being destroyed in seconds. I looked over at Mac, "Let's get the hell outta here!"

I pushed the jeep to the limit, quickly caught the caravan. I looked at Mac; he was dripping with sweat. Then I noticed my uniform was also drenched. We didn't talk the rest of the trip.

HUE

As we pulled into Hue, it was like walking back in time. For miles, everywhere I looked was temples, pagodas and palaces. The otherworldly feel was only marred by section after section destroyed by the 1968 assault. Next to an ancient tomb was a massive crater, thanks to a B-52 bomb that went off track. People looked at us, but didn't seem concerned with our presence. For decades, they'd gotten used to heavily armed soldiers walking amidst them. We were a common part of the daily life.

After getting the trucks settled, we headed to the majestic Thien Mu Pagoda. As usual, Sgt Wilson was the resident historian, told us "It was constructed by Emperor Thieu Tri in 1844. He was supposed to have seen a fairy woman who said this was a holy place and to build a pagoda. The fairy said this would bring prosperity to the kingdom."

I looked at Wilson, "Guess she was wrong, Sarge; this kingdom sucks the big one, don't you think?"

Wilson grinned, "You have a point, Frazier, she might have missed the call by a century or so."

Hue was built along the Perfume River, named, according to Wilson, for the fragrant odors it carried as it wound through a lushly flowered tropical jungle. I whiffed the air, noted, "Might change the name to Bull Dung River, based on my nose, huh Sgt Wilson?"

He grinned, "You're on a roll today, Frazier. I hope you save some of that energy for the game tonight. I hate to make this trip just to get our ass whipped."

My nerves were still jangled from the Cobra attack. I thought back to my way of handling pressure. The tougher things got, the more I kidded. So far, it hadn't worked.

We hadn't gotten an explanation for the Cobra action, so

I asked Lt Clep, the doofus, what happened. "One of the villagers tipped us that a few VC were camped near the road, waiting for a gap in the caravan. They had mines ready to plant for the unlucky stragglers following our caravan. Based on the noise I heard, it sounded like Claymores. We've been losing a lot of ordnance from the base. We've got to fix that fast. We can't be getting blown up with our own weapons."

Lt Clep had a pained look, he was usually laid-back, rolled with the punches; something was bothering him that went unspoken. He walked off mumbling to himself.

In typical Army fashion, they built a great basketball court right outside the royal Citadel of Hue. This magnificent Citadel was built in 1804, was mostly brick, and surrounded by a huge moat. When you looked at it you thought "fortress." The walls looked 20 feet thick, meant to withstand whatever the enemy had to throw at you. The court ran along one edge of the moat since it was the flattest area. I looked at Mac, "Can you believe they built a court right beside this beautiful place? Gotta really piss off the locals, us screwing up their history." Mac shook his head.

The game drew a big crowd of Vietnamese. We played a team from Chu Lai, the champion from that huge base. The locals cheered wildly but usually at the wrong time. For instance, when I stole a ball, clanged a dunk off the rim that shot 20 feet in the air, the place went nuts. They thought it was a nifty trick. I laughed out loud as I ran after the errant ball. The Chu Lai team was good, but our combination of Clardy, Jones, and McCarthy dominated the lane. Whenever they collapsed on the big guys, I just got uncontested shots. We won easily 90-68 but the crowd cheered like it went into sudden death overtime.

I had been in country a month, except for the Cobra artillery show on the caravan ride; it was the best day so far. We bunked inside the Citadel, in a section saved for visiting dignitaries. Sgt Wilson had coolers of chilled beer; we made a fire to grill burgers and hotdogs, my first since leaving the States. Percy drifted away after a couple beers; Wilson winked at me, "Now we can have some fun, Mr. Personality's off to charm the locals." Then he grimaced, "The crazy bastard will undo the good we did today. He'll beat up some poor papa-sahn or smack around some girl if she fights back. It happens too much. One day someone will catch him off guard. Fuck him up bad." I nodded, hoped he was right, sooner the better. I asked Wilson how Percy could get away with this. He hesitated, then seemed to catch himself; switched topics.

"How about that game? Those poor guys from Chu Lai never knew what hit them. Clardy, you're even pulling your head out of your ass. I think Frazier's a good influence on you." Clardy beamed like a puppy getting rubbed.

"I just cleanup the mess Jones don't want. Whenever they figure out that Dylan don't miss much, we get wide open. I aint even bullshittin."

After a few beers, everybody swapped stories of home. We learned that Sgt Wilson was on his 3rd tour in Nam. "I'm not too crazy about the war but the ladies are fine. Here I get the good-looking girls. You ought to see the honey I got in Quang Tri. I'm pretty sure that Frances might be the one. Back in the States I don't get much action with the lookers. Plus I get hazardous duty pay; all in all, I like it here." And then he added, "When I get enough money, I can find a way to get Frances back to the States. It takes some serious cash to grease all the right palms." I looked at Wilson; no doubt he was a plain-looking guy, probably got overlooked most of his life. But I kept thinking: Would I really go to a war zone, just to get babes?

As Wilson was talking, Clardy had wandered off, was taking a piss in the moat.

I couldn't help but comment to our relaxed group, "Can you imagine the dead Emperor looking down from the great beyond, shaking his head as he sees Clardy pissing in his moat? Talk about a comedown, one day the moat was there to resist Genghis Khan and now Dickie Clardy is debating whether to take a crap in it."

We were all howling as Dickie came back asking, "What's so funny?"

QUANG TRI

We began the ride back to Quang Tri after breakfast. For some reason, I was more relaxed as we began the ride. I could almost hear my buddy Nut whispering in my ear, "Don't relax." I took a few deep breaths, got fully alert. But the trip was uneventful. We didn't have duty that day, so I told Mac I was going for a jog around the base. My reheaded pal looked at me, waiting for the punch line. "Really," I said, "Even with the ball games, I still feel out of shape. Going to crack the whip, get my butt in shape. Want to come?"

I could still hear Mac taunting me as I went for my first running session in Nam. Wish I had a camera as I ran. Most of the looks were total amazement but some hoots and hollers followed me. I gave everyone the peace sign, worked myself into a strong gait. It took about a mile, but I finally got my wind. Running had always been easy for me. Part of the attraction to exercise was it gave me time to think. As I loped along the dusty roads, I thought about Ben and Percy's criminal activity. Should I just mind my own business kept running through my mind.

Mac and I had CPO gate duty again. The guiding rule at the gate was that Vietnamese could possess nothing "American." That was almost impossible since most locals came to the gate wearing Army fatigues, blue jeans, T-shirts: all from America. Soldiers were generous by nature, gave gifts to the locals in exchange for services, food or whatever. So the dilemma was that technically we'd have to strip everyone, repossess the goods to do our job correctly.

I told Mac, "If we enforce the rules too tight, we'll have hoards of naked yellow midgets walking back down the road. Are you up for that?" As usual, Mac ignored me.

Most of the Vietnamese people were gentle, dignified people. They would do anything for you if you treated them respectfully. I grew to like and admire them. Despite living in grass huts, they were amazingly neat, acted with quiet class. I had done some reading about their history of one war after another. Can you imagine living with generations of war? I watched my little friends My, Li, and Lin, who were working with us that day to make certain no weapons or drugs got onto our base. What hope did these beautiful little girls have?

My, Li, and Lin got all my stupid jokes; they always prodded me to do my favorite kill-the-boredom routines, which dealt mainly around negotiating with the locals. I learned quickly that the bartering system in Vietnam centered on the phrase "souvenir me." As an example, "I'll souvenir you a pack of cigarettes if you souvenir me fresh fruit."

This dialogue went on all day at the CPO gate. Haggling for deals was part of the culture; it was expected, understood. I got a kick out of this and spent hours persecuting Mac with my quips on souveniring. He'd run the other way if I started a monologue. But that never deterred me. So my little Vietnamese dolls became my prime audience.

A dusty papa-sahn drove up; got out of his truck, let me search him. Towards the end of the pat-down, he looked at our stash of cigarettes, "Souvenir me Kools?"

The three little girls started to giggle before I replied, "Okay, I'll souvenir you a carton of Kools if you souvenir me a water buffalo."

Papa-sahn stood perplexed, "No can do, water buffalo, no can do."

I raised my hands in bafflement, "No water buffalo, no Kools." Papa–sahn ambled off.

My redheaded buddy Mac shook his head, "You're so juvenile." But the girls burst into hysterics; that was the nicest sound I'd heard for awhile.

Later that day a truck loaded with Vietnamese workers came up. I found a Colt 45 hidden under a pile of bananas. Who do I arrest? I sent them off, threatening to lock them up next time. I sold my other confiscated pistols to truck drivers but decided to keep this one. Mac asked, "What for?"

I thought a moment, "Insurance."

He frowned, "Insurance for what?"

"Insurance if someone steals my other pistol."

Mac couldn't fault my logic. Vietnamese workers did our laundry, shined our shoes, cleaned the latrines etc. They had full access to our place while we worked. We paid them fairly but clothes got "lost" all the time. Jones had his radio stolen last week. So, if a radio can get lost, why not a pistol? After my shift I bought a huge lock to secure my stuff better. Maybe I was getting too relaxed. I could almost hear my childhood buddy Nut cautioning me to wake up.

Fleming and Callahan were at the club having a Bud, when I walked in after duty. "When are you guys going to stop drinking that rat piss? Miller's is so much better. It's the champagne of bottled beer, fellas."

They ignored me but Fleming asked, "Hey, Dylan, who's that buddy of yours you always talk about? I talked to a Green Beret Captain today named John O'Hanlon. He was asking if I knew where you were. I told him unfortunately you lived 100 yards from me but I'd make it worth his while if he got you transferred. That made him laugh. He said, "So he's bustin' your balls, too. Can you imagine growing up with that guy? Nothing was ever safe; he was always at us as kids. It kind of prepared me for my Chinese water torture training in the Berets." I was so startled; I didn't have a comeback.

After about 60 seconds I added, "You mean you were talking to Nut? He's here, nearby? Why the hell didn't you find me, numb nuts?"

Fleming grinned, "There's the Dylan we know and loathe. Take it easy, I told him where you were; he said to tell you he'd come by, check how you're doing."

I spent the next hour telling Nut stories. Like when Nut was in 6th grade and climbed the flagpole to retrieve a flag that got jammed. It was cold and pouring rain but Nut didn't want the flag desecrated. The nuns didn't know whether to punish or praise him. "The Nut had a flare," I concluded. Then it hit me, "Did you say Captain O'Hanlon?" Last time I talked to Nut he was just a Lieutenant. Fleming confirmed that Nut was a Captain in the Green Berets. "What was he doing calling you?" I could see Fleming started to fidget.

"Just checking out some stuff. Nothing special." I was about to press him when I noticed Ben was nearby, might be listening.

I played along, "Couldn't be too important if they had Nut involved. He's certifiably crazy." We switched to sports talk; Ben drifted away.

On the way to our hooch, I filled Fleming in on the Ben/Percy scams; told him to keep quiet till we thought it out better. "Son of a bitch," was all Fleming said. Then he told me that Nut was looking for drug arrest information.

"I think he's with some special unit of the Green Berets that's trying to stop the pipeline from Laos and Cambodia. He didn't say too much. He talked to Colonel Mullen first, got clearance to go through our records. It must be important because Mullen said give him whatever he wanted."

Then Fleming filled in some more of the puzzle, "It turns out most of the drug busts were whores that got caught on base. They had a stash on them, sold junk to the grunts after they road their tools for a while. Never any big busts though, no major dealer that supplied the whores or any connection to Army personnel. That's not the worst, though, seems that all the confiscated dope got lost. There's a big warehouse to store stolen or illegal goods. It's guarded round the clock by MP's from the 101st. Tons of shit in there but all the valuable stuff has vanished."

I kept thinking while Fleming talked: This gets worse and worse. No wonder Colonel Mullen wants to clean house.

Next morning I was on patrol with Clardy. He was rejoicing that he'd be on night patrol next month. "Mostly just tool 'round the base, answer calls on whores gettin' caught by some uptight grunt Captain, maybe some ruckus at the "steam and cream," shit like that. Most time you kin slip into the USO club, git decent burgers and dogs. It's a hoot. I aint even bullshittin'."

So far, I'd only worked day shift; that was okay with me. Things were mostly quiet during the day. Nam was a night war. The VC harassed the base and villages when it got dark. Slip in and slip out after wreaking havoc. Day shift suited me fine.

Sgt Wilson had other ideas. He called me in, said I would be on night shift with Percy next week. "Percy requested you. He said you deserved a break. Even though you're a new guy. He says you have your shit together."

I shrugged at Wilson, "Is that supposed to be a compliment?" He chuckled; told me to sleep in the day when night duty started, to meet Percy at Motor Pool around 6 pm.

Then Wilson added, "Watch yourself, Frazier. Percy's tough during the day but at night he's worse, gets damn intense. Keep your eyes open; be careful. Call in if something worries you."

Before I knew it, next week arrived. I slept later that 1st day, to kill time wandered over to CPO gate to visit Mac. Jones was working with him, already had a few cartons of Kools piled up. "Going to sell them Jones?"

He frowned, "Hell no. These'll keep me puffin' fer free. I can save my money fer some more potent shit. Take the edge off; know what I mean?" Unfortunately, I did. Jones had gotten more withdrawn over the past few weeks. While he still played ball well, he was slipping. Like some of the MP's I'd gotten to know, he was smoking dope regularly. Most nights he was wasted.

I liked Jones, "Better take care of that body, Jones. I need you pounding the boards, making me look good. Why not come over to the club, have a few beers with us?"

Jones smiled, "Ya'll never know, Frazier, never know."

Out of the corner of my eye, I noticed papa-sahn ambling up the road. Little Lin walked over to me, giggled. She was waiting for my routine. Papa-sahn was about 5' tall, weighed maybe 90 pounds. That was relevant since he was wearing Army boots and fatigues for a 6'4", 220 lb GI. He walked slowly because the boots were like small kayaks. The shirtsleeves dragged to the ground. I led with, "Papa-sahn, you're looking very dapper today. Got a hot date? But in all seriousness, I've got to tell you your tailor may be having some fun with you. What happened, did you beat him in the village 'toss the buffalo turd contest'?" I could hear little Lin laughing inside the guard shack.

Papa-sahn gave me a huge beetle nut smile. He didn't understand a word, but my smile conveyed friendliness. I asked him whom he favored in the Super Bowl, but the blackened teeth were all I got in reply. He had the correct paperwork, so I let him pass.

I looked over at Mac, "When you go home and become a doctor, make sure Mary never lets you go to your office dressed like papa-sahn, you'll scare the patients. I can see you slipping into these dress habits pretty easily."

Jones walked over, "You're a weird dude, Frazier." Little Lin walked over, hugged me. I could see Mac was thinking about his son as I hugged her back. As attached as I was getting to these little girls, how would it be with your own child?

PERCY

Fortunately, Percy was pretty quiet that night. He usually jabbered non-stop, so I just got to enjoy the silence as he roared around the base. Finally he said, "Got a letter from my aunt, my mom's dead. Aunt's yellin' that I never wrote or said shit. Don't that motherfucker know I'm in Nam? What the fuck?" Percy seemed more upset with his aunt bitching him out than that his mom died. When I told him I was sorry, he roared at me, "Fuck my mom. She never did nothin' fer me cept give me a fucked-up sissy name. Named me after some English jerk-off poet. Fuck she thinkin'?"

Over the next couple hours I learned that Percy's mom was from Jamaica. He never met his dad but said, "Was some piece o' shit who's part white, part Spic" Told me that since his father was American, his mom moved to Chicago trying to find him after he left Jamaica. Found some of his family but they were too poor to help. Never found his dad. Percy lived in the south side projects, got into boxing and jujitsu, fought to keep from getting the hell beat out of him. Dropped out of school, joined the Army.

Percy was no dummy. He finished his high school degree in the Army, used his natural violence to excel. Got into the Rangers, then into the Green Berets. "I was too bad-ass for the Berets, so they kicked me out. Signed up for Nam, killed every motherfucker in sight, then made Sergeant. Couldn't stand it when I got back to the states, so I came back to Nam. Killed a shit load more gooks. Made E-7 but got busted down when I tightened up some pussy. That's the Army. Want ya to be nasty but when ya step over the line, they come down hard. Check it out. Fuck ya gonna do?" I just shook my head, as if understanding the unfairness. Percy was only 26, had been in Nam almost 5 years. No wonder he was cracked. While he had his guard down, I asked him about his fighting skills. "I learned quick ya better hit first. Ya gotta make that first hit count. Put the guy down good. That's why I use my foot most. Ever get kicked by a horse? Guy taught me the legs'r heavier than the arms. Use that weight and power. Don't waste time using hands if the legs'r free."

I remembered that Percy always took a step toward the victim, looked down as if thinking; then pounded the guy. Something to keep in mind. I made every effort that night to know more about Percy, I never liked surprises.

STEAM AND CREAM

Next night, I was assigned to guard the "Quang Tri Massage Parlor." My puzzled look made Sgt Wilson laugh. "It's better known as the Steam and Cream, Frazier."

I heard stories about the place, but hadn't been there. Steam and Cream was the local name for the base massage parlor. This parlor was the Army's civilized effort at relieving a soldiers "sexual build-up." After weeks in the jungle, grunts would return to base mean and horny. Whores were illegal by Army law, so the massage scheme was the alternative. That way, the Army remained in control and the village women weren't harassed too much. In a weird way, it wasn't a bad idea.

Wilson told me my job was, "To make sure the GI's don't beat-up the ladies or get too violent. Sometimes they're not content with a massage; get nasty. Some of the gals provide special services, if you're willing to pay big bucks. But sometimes they aren't in the mood or just might not like the guy. There it is." Then Wilson added, "Turn your head if you see any brass in there. The top guys got personal arrangements, but some of them like the wild side. Know what I mean? There it is."

With that background, Clardy drove me to the Steam and Cream, kept mumbling about how lucky I was. "Only a few MP's git this duty. Wilson trusts ya; ya got yer shit together. Lucky bastard, I aint even bullshittin'." Clardy told me that Percy, Wilson and other E-5's from other MP Companies mostly rotated this guard duty. "Yer the only PFC I ever heard of got so lucky. I'll pick ya up at midnight; fill me in good. I want details, got a camera with ya?"

I told Clardy to relax; I'd give him the skinny on what I saw. He zoomed off, shaking his head excitedly.

I sauntered in, was shocked to see the sadistic Percy strutting around in a towel. "Hey, white bread, heard ya got the shift. Keep that pecker in yer pants, Frazier."

Then he disappeared around a corner. The place had a reception area decorated like a living room. There was a desk in the corner, with a lovely Vietnamese women flipping through magazines. She lifted her head, greeted me in perfect English.

"You must be Frazier-sahn. I am Frances; it is a pleasure to meet you. Leonard told me you are a gentleman and would treat us well." It struck me she knew Sgt Wilson very well if she called him Leonard.

Frances showed me around inside. The place was spotlessly clean. They had piped in music, stalls for each masseuse. The women were attractive but weren't local. Most were mixtures of French and Vietnamese blood. Vietnamese women were small and slender with tiny butts, no boobs. These girls were built to last, big guns, shapely tails. Along with the great bodies they spoke English well. Very few GI's would ever be touched in the real world by such beautiful women.

A massage costs 15 bucks and they never touched your weenie. The majority of the horny soldiers shot their load the second the masseuse dug into their lower back or got near their butt. I heard dreamy moaning as Frances finished the tour. She looked at me seriously, "Hand job $25, blow job $50, if girl-sahn willing. Some GI beaucoup crazy, get wild. You must help girls then."

She was telling me my real job was to protect them from the maniacs. I wondered if Wilson was doing me a favor. And then realized I could be on patrol with Percy. Easy choice.

I peeked outside, was shocked to see 50 soldiers lined up. As someone left, another was let inside. There was room for 10 customers at a time. After paying for the massage upfront at the desk, the massage seeker went to a locker area, got a shower, dressed in a white towel. Most guys weren't picky about who they had, but some wanted certain girls and had to wait. They'd talk to Frances about this preference, gave some extra cash, sat patiently. Once you entered the stall, you had 15 minutes, no exceptions. Occasionally, Frances asked me to go in, roust out a few loiterers. Frances made money based on volume; she didn't let anyone hang around. It was an interesting and overall quiet night. Wilson had done me a favor.

The next night Sgt Wilson walked in, chatted with me, disappeared with Frances. A stunning girl, introduced as Aimee', took her place at the desk. Aimee' was a no-nonsense type but had a nice way about her. She loved the United States, asked a million questions about our culture. "I marry hot-shot GI one day, go to America," she told me unabashedly.

I kept thinking, "Why would such a beautiful girl do this for a living?" I thought I knew the answer, based on my discussion with my little CPO girls. No choice.

I soon learned that Aimee's father was French, worked in Nam as a civilian engineer, but left after she was born.

She confirmed my theory about this sleazy work when she said, "My father French, no Vietnamese marry me. Village people hate. I go to Catholic school, learn French, English but no can get good job. Do this job or be prostitute. This is better, easy answer. I make lot of money. Maybe go to France, if no get to U.S." Just then, Frances came back, Aimee' got up, said goodbye.

As she left, Frances looked at me, "My number one girl. Beaucoup smart."

Most of the soldiers were friendly, just happy to be out of the bush. I took lots of shit about this "tough duty" but most was good-natured kidding.

My common response was, "They gave me a choice of this or be the company shit burner. Flipped a coin, took this job, smells better."

I saw many repeat customers that week; they were spending most of their meager paychecks for this moment of comfort. Who could blame them?

But there was one tense incident. A big Polish guy came in every day asking for Aimee'. Frances told him to wait, but each time Frances came back, told him Aimee' wasn't free, he needed to go to another girl. He moaned but moved on.

On night he got the same verdict from Frances, snapped, "Fuck that, she's hiding from me." He ran into the massage area, tore back the curtains looking for Aimee'. I was moving as Frances rose from her desk. I approached the enraged GI.

"Hey, friend, you can't do this, calm down, get back in the waiting area or I'll have to toss you out." He swung at me, grazing my head. When he came at me, I went into his stomach, lifted him off the ground; threw him backwards, hard to the floor. His breath exhaled forcefully, he lay stunned, trying to catch his breath. When he tried to get up, I told him to sit still or I'd rework his face. A couple soldiers from his platoon helped calm him down, got him dressed.

As he walked out, he turned, "Lucky yer an MP or I'd tighten you up. You was lucky this time, got me offguard." His buddies pushed him away. I yelled as he walked away,

"If I see you back here, I'll lock you up. No second chance next time."

Frances wiped my dripping brow, "You beaucoup number 1, Frazier-sahn." My adrenaline didn't settle for hours.

I saw Sgt Wilson next evening before my shift. "Frances said you're great, Frazier. That you're the only MP, other than me, not to chase the girls and make a fool of yourself."

I looked at Wilson, "Does that mean I've already been here too long and lost my mind?" Wilson smiled; he liked that kind of banter. I added, "Trust me, Sgt Wilson, I have dirty thoughts all day but I have someone special at home. Not going to mess that up. Plus I keep my eyes crossed, all the girls look start to look like Clardy."

It was my last night at the Steam and Cream. Frances and I had gotten along really well. As far as I could see, she didn't participate in any of the sexual shenanigans. Even when the higher-ranking officers came by, she just did her job efficiently. They had a private section for special visitors. Frances was a knockout, the officers flirted with her mercilessly but she deftly pushed them elsewhere.

When I mentioned her "good judgment for not messing with the low-life," she responded sincerely, "I am Leonard's woman. One day we marry after he save beaucoup money. It hard to get me to States." I just smiled, thinking Sgt Wilson a lucky guy, hoping that was true.

I wanted to say goodbye to Aimee' but Frances told me she already left. Aimee' had already thanked me solemnly for keeping the Polish guy from hurting her. "He is beaucoup number 10." I bet some lovesick soldier went berserk every week chasing these pretty girls. The week had flown by. I would miss kibitzing with Frances and Aimee'; besides being beautiful, they had a dignity I admired. Plus they thought I was funny, I enjoyed an audience.

BASE DUTY

Next week, I was still on night patrol. Nicholson was my partner all week. The first night, he told me Jones had moved out of their hooch, was "living with the dopers." Jones was an open, friendly guy but he had become silent, with a vacant look in his eye. The new Jones was a poor substitute for the happy guy I'd met a few weeks ago.

Nick shook his head, "The white powder's made Brother Jones a zombie." Nick liked to talk. He spent the week telling me his theories on life. "I almost joined the Black Panthers but decided Doctor King had the right approach. Black folks need to be more active politically. Use votes not weapons. My parents never went to college but they sent each of us kids. I'll send my kids to college. Build a future with our brains, no more cotton picking for us."

Nick said he was worried that Jones was going to re-up, stay in Nam. "He says he likes the pace here, everything's cool, no hassles. What he's saying is he likes the cheap dope. Some sad shit." I wondered what I could do to help Jones. Staying in Nam was nuts.

Other than the ball games, I saw little of Jones, but what I saw was a steady deterioration. He was a great athlete but slightly off now, missed plays he should have done easily. He became a constant problem for Sgt Wilson. He was always late for duty, falling asleep on guard duty, never completing his jobs. The only thing helping him was being in Nam. The standing joke about punishment was, "What are they gonna do, send me to Nam?" Only hell was a worse stop.

I finally got back on day duty, had CPO gate with Mac. We became an adept search team, found stolen stuff on every truck. Mac could find a hidden grain of sand on a gnat's ass. I marveled as he peddled confiscated goods to US or Vietnamese truck drivers. He'd sell the cigarettes to the Americans, trade food to the locals for handiwork. One local papa-sahn carved paperweights from teak. Mac traded cigarette lighters, socks, sunglasses, etc, for whatever he found useful. He was making $50 daily wheeling and dealing. It helped kill time, helped forget where he was.

I started calling him Shlomo McCarthy, claiming he was from the Irish section of Israel. I teased him non-stop, "Oy, what a kibitzer you are Shlomo."

He smiled back, "Stand back and learn something, Dylan. It comes from growing up poor. You learn everything has value. It might not be obvious but it's there. Poverty develops your eyesight. Amazing what you can see when you're hungry."

One thing was sure; Mac's wife and kid would never be hungry. Mac was driven; he'd be a successful doctor.

Mac wired all the trading money to his wife. The Army limited the amount of cash you could wire monthly, so he asked me, Fleming and Callahan to wire money for him. One day Callahan made an interesting comment to Mac. "Clardy told me Ben has a system for beating the monthly wire limit. Since he's the postmaster, he's not monitored. Maybe you ought to ask him for help, Mac?"

I jumped in immediately, "I wouldn't say boo to Ben about this. He'd want a share of your action. Don't trust him, Mac."

Callahan looked surprised but Mac nodded in agreement, "My lips are sealed." I could see Callahan thinking that over but he said nothing.

That night, Mac and I talked this over again. "Can you believe how naive Callahan is?" Mac said. "Hasn't he been listening to you talk about how Ben's ripping-off the club, stealing vehicles? Jesus!"

I really liked Callahan, offered another opinion, "Callahan isn't naïve; he's idealistic. He thinks people are basically nice, do the right thing. He's no pushover. If you push him too hard, he'll fight. He just doesn't expect the bad sides of people to pop-out so much. I like that about him. He's the most honest person I ever met. Sometimes that gets him in trouble."

I switched topics. "Mac, did you notice that no one on the base ever talks about the war? No rah-rah stuff about winning battles or defeating the Commies. You never hear jack. I mean we get rocketed all the time but then everyone just goes about their business. Kind of like having rockets shot at you is no big deal. Maybe it's different out in the bush, but on the base, the guys seem too loose. That bugs me. I'm trying to stay alert to everything but it's getting difficult. Know what I mean?"

Mac thought before answering. "Maybe the troops are so relieved to be out of the field that they blank everything out when they're here. Like the base is safe by comparison to what they just faced. Those guys look shocked when you see them return. Vacant looks on their faces, moving slowly, dirty as hell, flat-out beaten up. Maybe they just blank things out while they're here. They don't want to think about going back out."

Mac had reached the same conclusion as me. There was an eerie quietness on the base most times. Outside the wire, you entered the inferno.

Then Mac floored me. "I know it's dangerous here but so far it hasn't been too bad. The MP's stay on the base mostly, don't have it so rough. I'm making so much money trading that I might be able to save $10 grand if I play my cards right. That would give me the cash to buy a house right away. Sgt Wilson told me I could extend my tour 6 months if I wanted to be eligible for an early out. Maybe I'd just serve a few months then get released early, go right home from here. I've been thinking about it. What do you think, does that make sense?" That made me furious.

I looked at Mac, pointed my finger in his face, "What I think is that you're fucking nuts. I just read that more soldiers are killed on the base than in enemy action. Is

$10,000 worth that risk? All you ever talk about is Mary and little Mike. Snap out of it Mac, I think one of those rockets jarred your melon. If I hear you say that again, I'm going to give you a serious ass whooping. Got it?"

Mac looked stunned, then burst out laughing. "I guess that means you think it's a bad idea, huh?" Mac came over, hugged me, "Thanks. Maybe I am shellshocked."

Now that I talked Mac out of his lunacy, I headed to the shower area. Getting a shower became a highlight of my day. I grew up in a house that had no shower, just a bathtub. My thrifty dad washed all four of us kids in the same water each night. "Why waste new water for each kid when it's already dirty?"

My dad was a hoot. And hence began my love of showers. Having that warm water washing over me became almost a religious experience. The shower added dignity to my day, brought me back to a nicer world. Little pleasures were a big deal in Nam.

Next morning, My, Lin, and Li were waiting for us when we arrived at CPO gate. They were beautiful, dark-haired little dolls. I wished I could take them home with me. My was grinning ear to ear. "We hurry to beat mama-sahn. Wait till you see. We wait."

I could tell they were excited, wanted to see my reaction. Here came mama-sahn, riding a bike down the dusty road. She wore an enormous straw hat, like a small lawn umbrella. Her baggy black pajamas top dragged on the ground, her Army boots could fit me. Topping this splendid look was an enormous wad of tobacco, more like a bunched-up sweat-sock than a cigar, bulging in her mouth. As my little girls stared at me, I began.

"Mama-sahn, looking mighty fetching today. Judging from that giant sombrero, I'd guess you're headed for the beach? You could get Mac, the girls, and me under that lid, no problem. And I love the way you stuffed the pajamas bottoms into your boots. It highlights those shapely calves. Looking awfully winsome. Better watch out, papa-sahn's going to be chasing you around the hut tonight." I hesitated, "Well, maybe that monster cigar chaw might give him pause. Maybe you ought to lose that, a mood killer, so to speak."

Mac burst out laughing, then I lost it. Even though she spoke no English, mama-sahn was laughing along with us. The girls giggled uncontrollably. We looked like an audience at a Three Stooges movie. It was a fun break from the madness.

Clardy and I had patrol duty next day. We had another ball game that night; I used the opportunity to pump-up Clardy. "You need to step it up Clardy. Jones has been slipping, we need you to score more, don't shovel to Jones so much." Clardy got a funny look on his face, like he was thinking about what I said, wasn't sure if I was serious. He just nodded, never said a word. I was fond of Clardy. He wasn't the sharpest knife in the kitchen, but he had an easy manner I liked. Clardy had a nice game that night, outscored Jones for the first time. He apparently was paying attention.

Next day we were patrolling a village near Quang Tri, when I noticed little My getting out of a truck with a GI. My earned a nice living as an interpreter. As I drove up, the GI tensed-up. I spoke to My, "Whatya up to beautiful?"

She smiled, "Help GI get boom-boom."

The GI winced, said to me, "It's been a long time without a woman, My knows the ropes. She'll make sure I get a clean girl for a fair price. Any problem, sir?" That was the first time anyone called me sir, the soldier thought MP's were officers. I kind of liked that.

Before I could correct him, a young boy-sahn walked up to My.

"GI want my sister? She virgin, three times. Beaucoup, number 1 boom-boom." I loved that line. Being a virgin once wasn't enough salesmanship. This kid's sister was a virgin multiple times. My started rapping in Vietnamese, negotiated a good deal for the GI.

He handed My $5, walked off saying, "She just saved me $20 bucks."

My looked at me, "Me number 1 bargainer." I had no doubt. But then I thought that little My had probably seen more sex at age 10 than I would for the rest of my life. This would normally depress me but I could see she was immune to the perversity.

I mentioned this to My; she smiled, "GI beaucoup silly. Pay anything to spill milk. Then try to be romantic like American movie. Want girl-sahn to say 'really great' after. No understand why GI just don't enjoy, no pretend be like Clark Gable." It was easy to love this kid.

PATROL DUTY

Later that week, we were driving down QL-1, about 5 miles from the base. It was a beautiful, sunny day. The light reflected off the rice paddies, giving a golden hue to the fields. Clardy and I were enjoying the peaceful scene when Sgt Wilson called on the radio, asked our 10-14. I told him; he ordered us to 10-15 to 10-42 (suspicious gathering) near Loc Do village. I told him we were "beating feet."

Wilson laughed, "Use the 10 series on the radio, Frazier."

I spotted a small group of locals near the entrance to the village, staring upward. Hanging from a tall tree was a dead man, more like an older teenager. A rope was tied around his neck, lashed to a fat limb. The body was mutilated but appeared to be Viet Cong, based on his black outfit. Being this close to our base, villagers dealt savagely with any VC caught stirring things up. The locals didn't want trouble with the Americans, knew we would protect them. They might not like Americans but they hated the VC.

I didn't know what to do. No one said anything; they just stared at the grotesque sight. As I was making my way through the mob, Percy came roaring up, skidded to a halt. Percy reached under his front seat, pulled out a strange-looking rifle. He rammed his way through the crowd, nodded at me to follow; stood looking at the corpse. Suddenly he raised the weapon, riddled it with bullets. His last volley cut the rope; the body thudded to the ground.

He rattled off some pigeon Vietnamese words, the villagers proceeded to carry the body away. Then something weird happened, the people started to clap. Clardy and I looked at each other but didn't say anything.

Finally I asked, "What did you tell them, Percy?"

He smirked, "I told them to get rid of that piece of shit, burn it. Aint worth burying."

And then he turned, jumped into his jeep and road off; as if it was a normal day back on the farm. I was stunned but hit Clardy on the shoulder, told him we should go.

We didn't talk for about an hour. "What was that gun Percy used?"

Clardy cocked his head, "You really are new, Dylan. That's an AK-47. Probably got it off a dead gook when he was a grunt. Percy uses it when he don't want no proof that a GI was involved. If ya check wounds or shit, ya just think a VC lit em up. No proof. Pretty smart. Seen him use it a few times."

It didn't surprise me that Percy was smart enough to cover his tracks. He was crazy maybe; but not stupid.

Later that week it occurred to me I never followed Ben's suggestion that the Korean's were involved in the robberies. I had learned that many of the civilian businesses on base were Koreans. I knew the barber, Jung, so I started there.

When I walked in Jung greeted me, "I remember, make look like no haircut, right?"

My standard instruction to Jung was to make it look like I was clean cut but without really cutting any of my dark, wavy mane. The brass didn't hassle your haircuts like they did Stateside.

One time I put a baseball cap on, said, "Just trim what hangs out. I wear a helmet all day, so who's gonna know?"

Jung gave good haircuts, despite my antics.

I didn't want to alarm him, so I beat around the bush for a while. Jung told me that one Korean guy owned most of the businesses; they all worked for Chin Park. He said Park ran the eyeglass store, that I could find him there most of the time. So I dropped by, chatted aimlessly for a bit, found Mr. Park very cooperative. I told him I was interested in the traveling act that played on the base recently.

His answer was interesting, "All come through USO. Each company work with them, your Sgt Ben do. He nice guy, get me in to watch."

I shot the breeze some more, ended up ordering a pair of sunglasses. No way was Park involved; he was a nerdy, Don Knotts-looking guy who was already making a fortune. Why rob clubs, risk jail?

That night, Mac listened to my Korean findings; hit me with something unexpected.

"Why the hell are you poking around? What goods going to come from this? You're just stirring a pot that no one wants stirred. Just forget about it, ok? I don't want you getting in over your head, ok?"

I thought about what he said, realized I was getting good advice. Since the beginning, I questioned why I got picked, why I cared. Was it my hyper-competitive nature? Was it my insatiable sense of curiosity? Did they think I was a moron? Mac was worried that I was stepping into a shit storm.

I looked at Mac, "It pisses me off that they think I'm so dumb that I won't find out what's going on here. But then I say to myself, 'Who gives a shit?' And then I think about that pompous bastard Ben, and maybe Percy, ripping everybody off, laughing at us. But most of all, I'm curious about what's really going on here. If I find that out, maybe we can use the information somehow. You never know. I also wonder if CID's looking at these robberies, waiting to see when one of us is going stop it? Couldn't we get prosecuted if we knew this scam was happening and did nothing? I just want to get to the bottom of it, but still don't know what I'll do."

We continued to debate the merits of doing nothing, just playing ball with these assholes, leaving at the end of our tour. But we both came back to digging more, trying to reach some solid conclusions, and then making a decision about what to do. We would use the surly Fleming to monitor CID, to see if they were sniffing around. Colonel Mullen hadn't asked any questions since he sent us out to snoop. I thought that was odd, but Mac had a better view.

"There is a war going on, you know, maybe he's too busy for such small potatoes. And we keep hearing about a Tet offensive. That probably has him hopping."

I hadn't looked at it that way. These thefts were sort of chicken shit in the big picture. We did agree on one thing, being careful. I decided to let it sit for now.

A couple weeks later, Clardy and I were cruising around the base when we got called to report to the Steam and Cream. When I saw the look on Frances's face, I knew something was really wrong.

"Aimee's hurt bad, Frazier-sahn. GI snap neck when no boom-boom. Same GI you fight. He run out after. No sure where he be."

I went inside, saw Aimee' writhing in agony as the medics worked on her. I stood there, watching as they got her to a stretcher. The medics picked her up, carried her to the ambulance Sgt Wilson had dispatched.

As he shut the door, the medic confirmed my worries, "Probably won't walk again. Fucking maniac, hope you kick his ass but good."

You had to register when you entered the Steam and Cream. "Stan Jablonski, 3rd Calvary, I read. After calling Sgt Wilson for instruction, I went to the 3rd Cav area and waited for backup. Callahan and Jones pulled up; we went to the Company Commander's building, informed him what happened, who we were after. Major Gillen was a burly guy, about 40, loaded with medals.

He looked at me when I was done, "Any witnesses it was Jablonski? He's a good soldier, hard to believe he would do that."

When I told him that Frances had seen him with Aimee', and then running out afterward, he remained stone-faced.

He finally said, "Slopes don't count. Any soldiers witness this incident? Otherwise, I'm not interested."

I'm not sure what got into me; maybe it was delayed shock from seeing Aimee', her plans for a decent life crushed.

I walked right into his face, "Then I'll have to take you into custody for obstructing justice. You've got 5 seconds to decide, him or you. I'm not fucking around."

Then I added, "Sir."

Perhaps it was the crazed look on my face, or just dumb luck, but Major Gillen turned, hesitated a moment and then sent an orderly to get Jablonski. We loaded the ashen Jablonski into the back of our jeep, drove him back to the MP Company for questioning.

Sgt Wilson interrogated him. Jablonski said it was an accident, Aimee' fell off the massage table, he tried to catch her, her neck snapped as she hit the ground. Not his fault. Because she wasn't an eyewitness, Frances's comments were not taken as fact. Major Gillen came soon thereafter, filed a complaint about me. He had a heated discussion with Colonel Mullen, who backed me up, said I did everything right.

"We need more men like Frazier, he's helping make Quang Tri safer for your men."

Major Gillen stormed out with Jablonski close behind.

Colonel Mullen looked at me, smiled, "Damn, I wish I'd been there when you said you were gonna lock him up. Funniest thing I've heard in months. Gillen's a pompus ass." Then he dismissed us.

Sgt Wilson told me it was probably a hopeless case.

"The Army turns its head when grunts cause trouble with locals. Aimee' has no family here to raise hell, so it's just another shitty causality of war. Nothing we can do about it, Frazier. You did your best."

He thought for a few seconds. "Damn shame, Aimee' was a nice girl. She's the 3rd girl Frances lost this year. This place can really do you a job."

I was stunned. How could they let this guy get away with this brutality? Wilson seemed to be reading my thoughts, "Let it go, Frazier, nothing you can do."

The only good to come of this horrible incident was it brought Callahan and me a bit closer.

He came to our hootch that night, said, "That was a brave thing you did, standing up for the injured girl. I'm not sure you would have done that a few months ago. I just want you to know that was really good."

As I watched the short, muscular Callahan walking off, it left me thinking. Was he right, had I changed? Was I starting to go native? I wasn't sure Callahan had the right read. I think I would have done the same thing. Some things are too important to ponder.

TET

Sgt Wilson called us together next morning, said another Tet offensive was coming; we would be headed for Khe Sahn in a few days. We would rotate squads of MP's, a month at a time.

"Our jobs to keep the General safe, keep the roads open. Khe Sahn's a bad place. I was there for the '68 offensive. Shit really flew. I hope its better this time. I'll post the first shift out there tomorrow. Dismissed."

I saw Sgt Wilson at the club that night. "We got a few games left, Frazier, so none of the team guys will go on the first shift. Maybe I'll send Jones; maybe the shit storm will wake up his sorry ass. He's been about worthless the past couple games."

I was relieved but said nothing. When I read about the Tet offensive in the camp library, it mentioned Khe Sahn as the scene of some bloody battles. Funny how things change. A few weeks ago I thought Quang Tri was a hellhole; now it seemed okay. Like getting kicked in the nuts versus punched in the face.

Callahan was sent with the first group. A chopper approached the company area as I said goodbye to Callahan. I smiled at him, "Keep your powder dry, Joe. Don't go John Wayne on me, okay?"

Callahan had a grim look; I could tell he was nervous. Here was a guy that was a true Conscientious Objector being sent to the worst spot on earth. What sense did this make? Joe mounted the open doorway, sat in the chopper.

"See you in a few weeks."

Then I took a deep breath, exhaled. I felt a little guilty, if not for basketball I might be in that chopper.

My guilt eased that night when I got mail. A letter from Fran Philips explained that he was stationed at West Point, was a starting guard on the Army team; was headed for the Middle East to play overseas. "Too bad you got screwed out of a tryout, you'd have made the team easily," Fran wrote.

I don't know why but that made me feel better; I was just unlucky. Then I remembered what Nut used to say when we were growing up. "Dylan, you're the luckiest kid I know. Somehow you always win." I wondered what Nut would say now.

MONSIGNOR PUGH

That night, after Mac and I shot the shit before sacking out, I prayed. Growing up a staunch Catholic, I learned the power of prayer from a young age. As a kid, most of the time I prayed for horse shit stuff, like an English bike for Christmas, a girlfriend with big knockers. But I had many doubts about religion since High School. I used to persecute the nuns and priests with inane questions about Limbo, Purgatory, Archangels; whatever came to mind as a bit farfetched. Fortunately, we had a great parish priest, Monsignor Pugh. He was a regular guy, great sense of humor, had a way of explaining the oddities of faith that made more sense.

In my senior year he coached me through some serious trouble with my best friends, Nut and Truck. Monsignor Pugh had me pray daily for my buddy's problems to be resolved. Without mentioning it, I also prayed we would win the City Basketball championship, which we lost. But Nut and Truck pulled through their messes in flying colors, almost like miracles. When I complained to Monsignor Pugh in confession that the praying didn't work for the championship, he reminded me of what seemed like divine intervention that saved my closest friends.

He ended the confession with, "It seems to me that God heard your most important prayers and answered them. Maybe he did answer your basketball prayer. Maybe the answer is that wasn't really important."

I'd thought about that viewpoint a lot since then. That night I prayed that Callahan would survive Khe Sahn.

ETHICAL DILEMMA

Clardy and I were on patrol the next day, got a call to 10-24 to the 54th Infantry Company. I remembered that meant a "suspicious person." I wondered what that cryptic description really meant. When we drove up, two soldiers were holding a frantic, agitated Vietnamese girl. She was about 90 pounds but was giving the soldiers all they could handle.

"Number fuckin' 10," she kept screaming and suddenly lashed at them with her feet.

The staff sergeant told me, "She's a whore, she just freaked out. Almost bit my hand off when we tried to kick her outta the company area. I don't know any gook but it sounds like she's sayin an MP's gonna take care of her. Whatever that means."

I called Sgt Wilson, he told me to take the whore to the MP gate at the south end of base.

"They got female QC's there who can search her, find out what she's yapping about."

QC's were the Vietnamese version of MP's. Since being a QC was a prestigious position, most of them were smart, spoke English pretty well. We handed the ferocious little whore to the female QC, who took her into a shack to do a strip search.

I looked at Clardy, "Don't envy them; she smelled like my old sneakers, with a hunk of blue cheese inside that sat in the garage all summer. Bodacious nasty!" Clardy seemed to be enjoying this.

"We're lucky Percy's in Khe Sahn, he always gets whore patrol. Usually does it hisself. He likes ta tap the pretty ones. I was hopin' we'd get some action but thisn's a wildcat. I'm always horny, but even I aint inta this."

You had to like Clardy, he said stuff out loud that most of us kept hidden for fear of sounding moronic. Not a mean bone in his body, Clardy was having fun in Nam. I wish I were. Each day I woke up nervous.

My musing was interrupted as the QC exited the shack. She was holding a wad of money wrapped in some kind of plastic wrap. "Beaucoup money, she say belong to MP Sergeant. Say he fuck her up if no give. Say you let her go. What you do?"

I absorbed what she said, told her to escort the whore off the base, give me the money. Clardy looked at me, shrugged, "Must be one a Percy's bitches." He said it matter-of-factly, like everyone knew that. I counted the money, over $800.

"Holy shit, all this from one whore? That's 3 or 4 months pay." Clardy asked me something I hadn't thought through.

"Whatcha gonna do with it?" Maybe it was my Catholic brainwashing, it never occurred to me there were many options.

Quickly ruling out the temptation, "Take it to Sgt Wilson, there must be a way they'll recycle the money. He'll know what to do." Clardy started laughing hysterically. "What your problem Clardy?"

When he regained control, "Wilson'll think yer nuts."

He was right; Wilson looked at me like I was a 3-dicked dog. I think he was waiting for the punch line.

I stood there, then broke the silence, "Thought it was the right thing. Didn't know what else to do."

Wilson swallowed, "Sure, er that's right, Frazier. I just never had anyone turn in money before. Most times the whores ditch the money. Er, nice work." Clardy started laughing again, Wilson started to grin but shooshed him, "Settle down, Clardy. Dismissed."

I got a few steps out the door, told Clardy I'd forgotten something. I waved him on, went back to talk with Wilson. When he saw me he said, "Change your mind, Frazier?"

I shook my head. "Don't think I'm naïve, Sgt, that's just too much money for me to somehow lose. Not my way. But I wanted you to know that the whore talked about an MP that protects her. I think its Percy, just wanted you to know that. Kind of out of my league."

Wilson got a grim look, "Forget that Frazier. There's nothing but trouble down that road. Know what I mean?"

Then he got up, walked through the office door, carrying the wad of dirty money. I stood still, blinked a few times, thought as I walked off.

ABOUT KHE SAHN

That night at the club, trying to switch gears after the Percy warning, I sat beside Sgt Wilson, wanted to ask about Khe Sanh. He was chatting amiably with the conniving Sgt Ben Burton when I took my seat.

Ben looked at me funny, "Well if it isn't wonder cop himself. What can I git fer ya, Frazier?"

I wondered what that meant, decided to shrug it off. I got a Miller High Life, thanked Ben. Asked Wilson for a history lesson, telling him I wanted to know what awaited me.

He hit my shoulder, "Good to be prepared, Frazier, Khe Sahn's a bad place, I'm glad to see you're thinking." He sat back on his stool, began his lesson. While I listened, I noticed Ben watching me intently.

I learned Khe Sahn was southwest of Quang Tri, in a corner of Nam that bordered Laos. He informed me the Army of the Republic of Vietnam (ARVN), with aerial and ground support from the U.S., was trying to shut down the Ho Chi Minh trail.

Wilson added, "They're sending 50,000 ARVN's to shut the supply route. Without supplies, Charlie can't raise hell. We've got to do it now, before the rain starts." Then he explained that the MP's were there to keep the roads open and moving. "Calling it a road is kind of a compliment. Just dirt trails, really, cut out by the Army engineers. Khe Sahn sits on a plateau, perfect for an airfield. The grunts will set up around the base of the plateau; protect the airfield. Charlie will make it hot. We can fuck them up bad from that airstrip."

We hadn't gotten any word from our guys. I was nervous about Callahan, also apprehensive about my turn. I wanted to learn all I could before going. I kept drilling Wilson for detail. He shook his head.

"The Marines got their ass handed to them in '68. Charlie overran the place, booby-trapped the shit out of it. They didn't want us coming back too easy." Then Wilson added, "But our real job out there is guarding General Freeman. He'll be there most of the time. Wait to you see his bunker. It's like Fort Knox up there. And his sleeping trailer is like a pussy palace. If you get lucky, maybe you'll see it. He'd like you, Frazier, you've got your shit packed tight."

Later that night, I told Mac about my "tightly packed shit," he found that comical.

My redheaded amigo grinned, "If Wilson only knew what you were really thinking he might rescind the verdict. 'Loose and watery' might be the better description."

I looked at him, "Only after my malaria pill, Mac, otherwise I'm packed solid. Don't be questioning my shit packing, okay?"

We continued to kibitz about Khe Sahn, hoped we'd go together. "Sounds like a place where the more eyes the better," was our feeling. I didn't tell Mac about Wilson's warning on Percy. Wanted to chew on that more before getting him nervous. We had other things to worry about; Khe Sahn was coming at us.

RUEBEN QUILLEN

Sometimes fate steps in, deals you a good hand. You don't realize until afterwards that chance acquaintances could save your skin. My destiny was being steered when I got back from patrol the next day. I entered my hooch expecting to see Mac, found a stranger inside.

He stuck out his hand, "Name's Ruben Quillen, Sgt Wilson told me to bunk here." Reuben was a squirrelly looking guy- maybe 5'3', 130 pounds, wispy, sandy hair, pale skin, a failed attempt at a mustache, about half the normal number of teeth. Despite the un-commanding appearance, Quillen carried himself well, almost with jauntiness. I wondered how his shit was packed.

I showed Quillen around the company area, noticed an unusual patch on his sleeve, "Non gratum anus rodentum." Quillen told me that meant, "Not worth a rat's ass." I laughed but still didn't pick up the meaning. "I was a tunnel rat before coming here. The unwritten rule's if ya make 20 trips down the tunnels, then they recycle ya behind the lines. Kind a like a reward for not getting' yer shit blown away, know what I mean?"

I looked at Reuben with renewed respect. In our orientation, we learned Vietnam was pocketed with endless trails of underground tunnels. The tunnel rats had to crawl into these mazes, make certain they were empty and bomb free before the brass entered to reconnoiter for anything of strategic value. Charlie rarely left a tunnel without booby-trapping it. Tunnel rats were considered the bravest of the brave.

That night Mac and I introduced Ruben Quillen around.

Even Ben seem impressed, "Glad God made me a pullin' guard. No tunnels gonna handle this fat ass, huh Frazier?"

Being cautious, I added, "God was pushing the 'ample button' when he made you Ben. But as my mama used to say, 'more to love,' right?"

Ben gave me a gruff chuckle. You had to be careful with Gentle Ben, I remembered him studying me the night before; he reeked of controlled malice.

We sat in the club, listened to Quillen explain everything you wanted to know about Vietnamese tunnels. I bombarded him with questions, thinking my trip to Khe Sahn was coming soon. Can't know too much about the bush.

Quillen opined, "Nam's been full a tunnels since the French been here. Outside a Saigon, they say there's 200 miles a tunnels. Imagine that shit? Them holes full a giant crab spiders, fire ants, rats bigger'n cats. Seen shit down there that'd really do ya a job. Fuckin' rats fed on corpses; bred some other little monsters. I aint even bullshittin."

I looked at Rueben, "Why didn't they just bomb the tunnels or throw explosives down there? Why send a soldier down there? That's nuts."

Quillen scrunched up his brow, "Wouldn't a done no good. The slopes knew what they was doin. Some of the tunnels was like 5 different levels. Goes down 50 feet one direction, then turns 10 feet, goes another way. The levels was linked by trap doors ya couldn't see from 6 inches away sometimes. Just looked like a dead end. Sometimes it took me 3 passes before I spotted the entrance. Them slopes was sneaky. Check it out."

We learned that Quillen had been in the Army 6 years, but was still a corporal. "Hopin' the tunnel job'll get me another stripe. Gonna be a lifer, got me a family I gotta support now. I went on leave last year, met Sally at the USO club in Kansas City. She an her ma run the place, treated me nice. I asked her ta marry me an she done agreed. Been sending money to help her and ma, plus the baby. Sally had a kid by accident. Nice lil kid, Sally kept sayin' he kinda looks like me. Got responsibility now, no more tunnels for Ruben." Quillen had a proud look on his face, shook his head up and down.

It took all my control not to ask if Sally read the book "How to Hose a Homesick Hayseed." Then I looked at Quillen, pictured this burnt-out tunnel rat going on leave, meeting some desperate girl who was nice to him. Poor Quillen, he didn't have a chance.

I patted his shoulder, "Sounds nice."

Mac nodded his agreement, "Good for you Quillen, I've got a little guy waiting for me back home. Whenever I get down, thinking of my wife and kid keeps me going."

Rueben smiled a toothless grin.

I asked more questions about the tunnels. "Ever been to Khe Sanh, Rueben? Are the tunnels out in the jungle, or just near the cities?"

He shook his head, "Never been ta Khe Sanh, Dylan, but ya can bet they got tunnels. They put them lots a times down shafts vertical ta the jungle floor. Hard ta see even from a few inches away. Ya find most from falling in when grunts'er walkin' around. If yer lucky, they didn't booby-trap the entrance. Most a the slopes like to be tricky. Hide the pungi stick or mine where ya least expect. Most times they want ya ta crawl in way deep, then when ya think ya got it made, bang! There it is!"

I had a fitful sleep, woke abruptly. Rueben's stories were not a good balm for a peaceful night. I went outside to take a pee, stood admiring the beautiful night sky when I walked back from the pisser. There was a quarter moon; the stars were vivid, glittering brightly. The magnificent sight made me think about home. I thought of how much time I'd wasted in my life. Why didn't I look at the sky every night, drink in this magic? Things would change when I got home. I thought of Laura Hartley, how much I'd changed. Would she like the more serious Dylan? Would her brothers still give the asshole verdict? Probably yes.

As I pondered that, I saw the familiar pulling-guard shape of Sgt Burton walking from Sgt Wilson's quarters. I considered ignoring this but my damn curiosity got the better of my judgment. Ben was carrying some heavy boxes to a wheel barrel. He went in and out of Wilson's a few times before pushing the load towards the motor pool. I kept in the shadows, watched Ben unload the merchandise into his mail office. Why was he doing this at 1 am in the morning, not during normal hours? I resisted the urge to move in close enough to read the labels. Fighting my stupidity, I drifted away carefully. It took me awhile to get to sleep. But I had a plan.

I got up early, grabbed a quick breakfast; headed over to the mail office before my shift. Ben was not an early riser, didn't hit the floor till 9 am most days. I pushed the door open; Ben had not locked up. The boxes were still there. I pulled back a lid, inside was stereos, watches and cameras.

And then there was a noise behind me, "What the fuck er you doin, Frazier!" I almost jumped outta my skin. Ben had risen early.

"Er, sorry I surprised you Ben, was looking to get some advice on how to wire money. Won some cash playin' poker, knew there was a limit on what you could send. Any ideas?"

Ben hesitated, seemed to mull it over, then said, "How much we talkin' about?" When I told him $200, he laughed. "No big deal. I can fix that but it'll cost $20. Or maybe use the cash to buy watches, cameras, shit like that. Then ya just mail it to your home. The Army don't check on merchandise much. Your call. Let me know what ya wanna do."

I asked him if he was going to Khe Sanh. He belly laughed, "No fuckin' way. Hah, hah. No fuckin' way. Place is a hellhole. I already paid enough dues. Fuck that." He was still laughing as I left. As I walked: Did he buy my story?

When I walked back to my hooch, Mac was waiting.

"Wilson just left, said you're supposed to report to Colonel Mullen before going to duty. What are you going tell him? He's bound to ask what you think." Then I told Mac about seeing Ben coming out of his quarters last night. "Holy shit, do you think he saw you. That's kinda creepy." I truly didn't think I was seen.

"No way, just a coincidence. But I don't know what to make of Ben hauling away all that stuff. Maybe Wilson was away visiting Frances. Maybe they use Ben to get rid of the contraband MP's turn into Wilson. Who knows?" I thought about that as I trudged to see the Provost Marshall.

This was the first time I was inside Colonel Mullen's living quarters. If I didn't know I was in Nam, I'd swear I was in a swanky hotel. Nice furniture, a huge TV, more stereo equipment than I ever seen in one place, a coffee table that looked like it belonged in a museum.

Colonel Mullen caught my eye, "That's hand-made, solid teak but two different shades of wood. It's one of a kind. It will cost a fortune to ship to the States, weighs a ton. Go ahead, give it a lift." He was right. I had to struggle to budge it.

Then he changed gears, "What you got for me? Have you made any progress on the robberies? Wilson told me you talked to the Koreans. What do you think?" Colonel Mullen had close set eyes, bright blue; they seemed to drill into you. I was prepared for the question.

"I think it's an inside job. No way was it a random theft. Someone knew when the money would be collected by

Payroll, when it would be a nice, fat sum." Colonel Mullen blinked twice, real fast, took some time to absorb what I said.

Then he replied, "I've been thinking that myself. You're the first one to mention that possibility. Any ideas on the culprit?"

I was prepared for that too. "No idea, could be anyone who's around our company all the time. Might be a local, but I doubt it. I think it's an MP or someone at CID."

Colonel Mullen exhaled deeply. "Fucking lowlife. Stealing from the Army. I'm going to fry the fucker when I catch him. If it's an MP, I'll put him in jail to rot." He looked furious. Mullen paused for a minute or so, lost in thought. And then, "Keep your eyes open, let me know if you get any other ideas. That's some first rate work, soldier. Dismissed."

Mac was surprised I told Colonel Mullen it was an inside job. "Do you think that was smart, Dylan? I mean you don't have to be a rocket scientist to see that points at Ben or Percy. I thought we agreed to play it safe for now?" Mac looked worried. I didn't want him to think I'd reneged on our deal.

I exhaled, "At the last minute, I figured it was worse to play too dumb. Mullen knows were not pinheads. Thought he'd get suspicious if we gave him nothing. Sorry I didn't tell you before. I just made up my mind at the last second." Mac shook his head, concerned.

"I hope you're right."

BEN

Ben looked over the boxes of stereos, cameras and watches. The only time he worked hard was when money was involved. Wordlessy he summarized: This shit'll bring a tidy sum. But then his thoughts turned sour: That fuckin' Frazier might be trouble. He learned that Frazier suspected Percy was runnin' the whores on base. Don't take no wizard to a figered that but took some balls ta say it out loud. Percy Price aint one ta fuck with. Kid's got a sack on 'em. And then he remembered him looking into the boxes he was arranging. Pretended like he was just browsin'. Smart kid.

Ben turned on his radio. Marty Robbins was singing "El Paso." Ben whistled along to the sad tune about Rosa's Cantina, the black-eyed Felina's bewitching the lovesick cowboy. Ben's mind drifted to Khe Sahn. He chuckled thinking about Frazier asking if he would be going. No more jungle for this cowboy. Marty Robbins continued to sing in the background. Ben listened to the tragic end of the song, the cowboy dying in Felina's arms, soon to be forgotten. Ben closed the last box, leaned back and smiled broadly. Maybe Frazier was headed to his own El Paso.

Quang Tri

Clardy and I were on patrol next morning when we got a call to handle a disturbance on QL-1. Clardy had been very quiet, very unlike his happy-go-lucky self. As we sped to QL-1, I asked what was up.

"Ben tore me a new asshole last night. Said I'm done in the motor pool. Called me a sorry sack-a-shit. I'm not sure what I did. He never said what got the burr up his ass. I liked workin' with the vehicles. Reminded me a home, some. I never seen him so pissed. He had a real case a the red monkey ass."

As we drove, I wondered if Ben was worried Clardy was leaking information to Callahan and me. We were with him a lot, Clardy yapped non-stop. Maybe I screwed up asking Ben for advice on wiring extra money home. Probably wondered why I came to him. Must of figured Clardy tipped me that Ben had ways around the system. Maybe he even heard that Clardy told me the whores were run by Percy. I still didn't know whether Ben and Percy hated each other or were in cahoots.

I looked at Clardy, "You might be better off staying away from Ben. He might be bad news." Clardy was used to me clowning around so he looked to see if I was joking. When I didn't smile, he turned back to watch the road. I hoped he got my message.

THE WATER BUFFALO

There was a massive traffic jam ahead of us. As we pulled to a stop, I got out, asked a stalled truck driver what was up. "A soldier hit a water buffalo, killed it. The zipper-heads got him surrounded. They won't let anybody pass." I radioed Wilson who told us to be careful.

"Those critters are sacred to the slopes. I'm going to call CID, get an interpreter out there to help you. Fucking A, the Army's going to pay big. Call back after you investigate."

What we found was a 1 ton water buffalo lying in front of a 2 1/2 ton truck. I saw the truck drivers surrounded by about 50 villagers. As I moved in, I could see the soldiers were stripped of their weapons, had their hands tied behind them. One old papa-sahn, probably the village ruler, was screaming, gesticulating like a banshee. It didn't take Sherlock Holmes to see the truck drivers had been beaten up. Their uniforms were torn and dusty. I wondered where their weapons were.

Clardy had his M-16 drawn but I could see that wouldn't help. "Lower the rifle, Clardy. You're just going to piss them off." He did as I said but didn't like it. I draped my M-16 over my shoulder, put my hands in front of me as I moved into the crowd. As the locals noticed me, a louder din began. It was like an anxious football crowd, poised to explode for the home team. I wasn't sure what I was going to do next.

The village leader turned his tirade to Clardy and me. He mixed in a few recognizable words like, "pay beaucoup" and "fuckin number 10," to help me get the point. I tried my most sincere voice and facial expression to tell them it was an accident, the drivers were sorry, that we should all cool down, work this out like gentleman. One of the younger kids understood some of what I said, interpreted to papa-sahn. After listening to the leader, the kid turned to me. "No want forgive, want American dollar, didi mau!"

Then someone grabbed me from behind. I was surrounded by a gang; got stripped of my pistol and rifle. Clardy got the same treatment, gave me a look like, "Told ya we shoulda come in strong." At that moment, I was thinking he was right. I'd just screwed up. I got to my feet; adrenaline took over.

"You just made a big mistake papa-sahn." I pointed at my MP shield. "I'm a United States Military Policeman. We can play this your way or the right way."

Then I got knocked hard from behind, fell to the ground dazed. Clardy came to my aid but got worse treatment; he got clocked over the head, fell hard, out cold. From the ground, I heard familiar voices, was shocked to see my little buddies My, Li, and Lin shoving their way into the throng. They must have been on the stalled trucks outside the village. My was rapping non-stop, pointing at me then gesturing with her hand like they were shooting themselves in the head. Then Lin and Li jumped in, added more dramatics, ending with a slashing motion over their throats. If I wasn't so scared, I might have laughed, they were amazing little actresses.

We heard the chopper before it was visible. The village was surrounded by groves of banana trees that blocked our view. Helicopters have distinct sounds; I could tell this was a Light Observation Helicopter, called a LOCH in Nam. I was hoping it was a Cobra, which would seriously get their attention. The LOCH buzzed overhead like an angry bee. It circled over us; I could see 2 guys, one with a blow horn and a little guy with a huge rifle, strapped into in a swivel chair.

The big guy started yelling through the blow horn in Vietnamese. The LOCH didn't make that much noise so you could hear every word. I couldn't understand anything but the voice was familiar. I wondered if he was one of the CID guys from Quang Tri.

"What's he saying, Lin?" The Vietnamese doll looked at me with grave eyes.

"Say let you go or he won't be able to stop his friend from shooting. Say his friend kill VC everyday, no miss. Say back away now or no get pay for buffalo." Then I heard what sounded like a countdown.

The villagers slowly spread out a little, but not enough to satisfy the LOCH. The blow horn came on again; the big guy spoke in Vietnamese.

My looked at me, said, "He say watch." There was a little water tower that the GI's had built for the town. It had a banner sailing from the top, probably some town flag. The little guy in the LOCH started to aim, suddenly the banner got blown off the tower. The banner was mounted on a stick the size of my little finger. The marksman shot it dead center from a moving helicopter 200 feet away. Then he aimed at the banana trees and shot off huge bunches from one tree after another. They thudded to the ground like sacks of potatoes.

When I looked down, I noticed that the villagers had moved 100 feet from me. They wisely got the message. My rifle and pistol were lying beside me; their pitchforks and shovels were on the ground. No one wanted the little shooter to get a bad vibe. The guy bellowed from the blow horn, all the villagers took off.

The LOCH put down near me, I was shocked to see my childhood buddy Nut hop out with a huge grin, "I told you I'd keep an eye on you. You okay, Dylan?"

The surprises weren't over. I heard a deep baritone say, "Hey, Deelan, what you doin' in this shit place. Thought you was smarter than that." It was my little friend Dominic Abreu, who was the sharpshooter I got close to in Basic Training. Nut looked at me.

"You know each other?" I caught my breath a little.

And then, "Abreu could shoot the sweat off a squirrel's balls in Basic. They wisely picked the right guy to shoot banana trees."

Abreu laughed, shook his head, "Steel crazy, Deelan."
He un-strapped himself, came over, gave me a big bear
hug.

I couldn't stop grinning. Nut was one of my closest
friends since childhood. Seeing someone from home was a
shot of pure joy. We had been neighbors, teammates in
basketball, football and track. He was a huge guy when he
entered the Green Berets. But now a little slimmer than
the last time I saw him, but still formidable. This tropical
weather could wear you down. Then I heard Clardy moan,
I went to check him over. He had a big egg on his head
but otherwise seemed okay. The thick Southern melon of
his had probably saved him.

Nut checked him over, agreed with my diagnosis. "He'll
be fine, just a nasty headache. Friend of yours? Can you
trust him?" Odd questions but then Nut said, "We need to
talk in private. I don't have much time, let's move over
here." Nut explained that it wasn't an accident that he was
in Quang Tri. "I'm here to check on some dirty soldiers."

I interrupted, "I've seen the stolen trucks and jeep
myself. Plus I think one of the MP's is running the
prostitution ring. Pretty sure of that."

Nut nodded, "That's small potatoes, Dylan. I'm looking
for who's stealing ordnance and selling it to Charlie. That's
treason; I'm going to bury the fucker but can't get a good
lead. They made no mistakes so far. I can't figure how they
steal the stuff, get it off the base. I've got an wild ass idea,
though. You have too many ammo dump problems on this
base. Once a month, Charlie sneaks in, blows up the
dump. I think that's a cover. I think the guys steal the
ordnance, fake a sapper attack. And then blows up the
place to hide the theft. Then they truck it out during the
confusion."

Before I could answer, Nut said, "It wouldn't be smart
to say we met out here. For now it's best to forget you and
I know each other." Clardy started to revive enough to
move around, so Nut and Abreu headed to the chopper.

They didn't want to be seen being too chummy with me. I looked at Nut, "I think you're right about the ammo dump. They blow it up all the time. What you said makes sense. Want me to snoop around?"

Nut delayed before answering, "Yes, but be cautious. This is a shit storm. These guys know they'll hang if they get caught." I looked at my serious buddy, decided to tell what I already knew.

"Have you already heard about Sgt Percy Price? He's bad news, maybe crazy. I'll bet he's involved. He's definitely running the whore ring. The other guy is Ben Burton, runs the motor pool, controls the mail, never seems to work much. Plus, he's ripping off the club all the time. Steals the money and blames the Koreans. He's a bad guy. Nobody here wants to mess with them."

Nut thought before responding, "I don't know Burton, but I'll check that out. I do know about Price, doubt he's involved." He looked at me intently. "This is confidential information; say nothing to anyone. Price works undercover for the same people I do. I don't know him but heard he's a tough dude. He's trying to get into the drug gangs, find out who's the local supplier. Plus Price's specialty is questioning VC. He gets them talking when no one else can. And nobody seems to care how he does it. I've seen people like him before. Stay away from him, Dylan. Guys like him don't have a conscience. I gotta go."

As he got in the chopper, Nut said, "Remember, we don't know each other. I'll be in touch through your pal Fleming. I told him not to mention anything to Mullen yet; so far he's got tight lips. Mullen's a good Provost Marshall but I don't want anyone to know about my ammo dump theory until I get more facts. It's a small base, something like that can get around fast. The fewer people the better. I'll be in touch." I shook my head in agreement.

I looked at my sharp-shooting friend from Basic, "Take care, Abreu; hope to see you again under better circumstances. Wind at your back, okay?" They roared off, waving as they elevated. I didn't have time to tell him that Percy was playing them for fools.

I wandered over to the recovering Clardy. "Uh, what happened?" Clardy was on his feet, trying to get his bearings.

"We got lucky, Clardy, some Green Beret team heard the radio signal for help, stopped by. Scared the piss outta the villagers. You okay to walk? Let's get the hell outta here."

The traffic had started moving, My, Li, and Lin waved from their trucks as they sped by. They had scooted back to their trucks before I could thank them. I owed them big. I bowed to them, tipped my hat. Their big smiles stayed with me on the ride back.

I thought about how lucky I'd been. What were the odds that a high-powered, childhood friend would save my ass out in the middle of nowhere? That reminded me I'd gotten careless recently. Acting before I thought was not my style. Callahan might approve but my ass might be grass next time. My fortune card had been played. Clardy was still groggy, didn't talk at all. That gave me time to ponder what Nut had shared. Things were much worse than I'd thought.

Sgt Wilson greeted me as I returned. He looked at the dazed Clardy, "What the hell happened out there?"

Remembering Nut's caution, "It got bad, the zips pushed us around, knocked Clardy out. We got lucky, a Green Beret team heard our radio transmission, came in strong; blew the hell out of the village vegetation to show they meant business. The Green Beret Captain said he'd call CID; tell them to repay the village for the buffalo. Said it happens a lot. He was in a hurry, didn't stay around to shoot the shit. Think Clardy's okay, just shook up."

Clardy just nodded. "Need ta ice my noggin. Got a goose egg. It'll be okay."

THE PUZZLE

I filled Mac in that night; he couldn't believe what happened. Then I said, "Let's find Fleming, this is worse than we imagined. Stealing ordnance and selling it to the VC is treason. We have to figure these traitors will burn anybody that gets in their way. Got to be big bucks here. This is massive. How could these guys sell weapons to the enemy? That blows my mind."

Mac looked grim, "I'm not sure I want to get involved in this anymore, Dylan. It scares me. I keep thinking about some officer knocking on my door at home, telling Mary I'm MIA." I understood how he felt; I had doubts myself.

Fleming was playing cards with Nicholson in the club. Mac and I joined the poker game, shot the shit mindlessly. Fleming suddenly looked up, "Can you believe that we've been in this piss pot four months already? Time just flies when everything sucks."

That made me chuckle, "You have a real gift for cheering people up, Fleming." Even Mac's mood seemed to lift. Fleming was always so miserable that somehow he made you feel lucky you didn't walk in his shoes.

Ben was in the club, didn't seem to be paying attention to us. Clardy had just come in, sat at the bar with the new guy Quillen, the tunnel rat. He probably didn't want Ben seeing him hanging around with us. Might be a smart move. The poker game broke up early, I whispered to Fleming, "Gotta talk to you on the QT. See you in a few minutes outside our hooch." I didn't wait for an answer, just walked off quickly.

The usually deadpanned Fleming's jaw dropped when I explained what Nut said. "Fuckin' A!"

Then Mac jumped in, made it clear he didn't want to get involved any further. "This place is a cesspool, I just want to serve my time and get the hell out." I knew it wouldn't do any good to try to talk him out of his position, he was probably right; I had some thinking to do before I pushed anyone else.

No one said anything, so I added; "We've got to keep this mess with the four of us. No more questions to Clardy, Ben might drill him for information. Clardy isn't slick enough to withstand Ben. I'll fill Callahan in when he gets back." My buddies gawked, speechless.

Mac and I were on patrol that week. Since half the gang was in Khe Sanh, we were considered veterans, didn't get any time on CPO gate or any other remote gates. Mac was quiet. To make conversation, I said, "I gotta find those little girls; thank them for helping me during that buffalo fiasco. What kind of gift can I get them?" He didn't answer me. Mac was still nervous about the ordnance ring, hadn't said too much for a couple days. I was used to his companionship, so it was getting to me. Should I be an understanding friend, suffer in silence? I shook that off. Not my style.

Finally, "Mac, listen, I'm not going to do anything stupid, okay? I've been thinking about this non-stop; I want to poke around a little more. I think it's wrong to do nothing. Plus, I think that might be more dangerous. Follow my thinking; these assholes are selling grenades, mortars, Claymores and shit to Charlie. Then Charlie uses them to booby-trap the roads we're driving on, like right now. Or Charlie sneaks in the base at night, tosses grenades and mortars up our bungholes. Boom, were fucked! I can't get by the fact that we have to stop this. Where am I off?"

Mac was driving the jeep, glanced over and nodded, but said nothing. After a few minutes, he pulled over, slumped back. "I think you're right. I don't like it, but I think you're right. We can't let them get away with it; it's too dangerous for everyone. But we've got to be real careful. We're way over our heads. Less than five months ago, we were sitting on our duffs at Ft Gordon; today we're investigating a ring of traitors. What a cluster fuck!" Then Mac sat up straight, smiled, "What's your next move, Sherlock?"

I'd been thinking about that. "Let's go check out the ammo dump. We should figure out how they're stealing the ordnance. Got an idea about how they're sneaking it out but don't know the sequence. Do they steal it at night, hide it a few days; slip away? Or do they do everything at the same time? Do they fake the sapper attacks or do they somehow get Charlie to do their raids at a specific time? Maybe it'll be clearer once we scout out the dump. What do you think?"

Mac laughed, "I think you've been doing a lot of thinking about this. Maybe you are a born MP; maybe coming out first in MP school wasn't a fluke after all, like Fleming says." That gave me a chuckle.

The ammo dump was huge but nondescript. There were a series of massive bunkers, dug deep into the soil, piled high with sand bags. One bunker was for mortars, one Claymores, one grenades, one rockets etc. There was anywhere from 50 to a 100 yards between the bunkers. This massive dump was surrounded by 2 sets of 20 foot barbed wire fences, topped with spools of concertina wire. The dump was literally in the center of the base, so it took a smart sapper to maneuver through the outside perimeter defenses, walk a great distance through the base, and then get close enough to launch his attack. All that and no one saw you?

I could see Mac was still antsy. "Hey, Mac, did you hear about the dog with no teeth, one raggedy ear, most of his hair falling off, only one ball?"

Mac stared at me stone-faced, "You already told that one, his name's "Lucky."

I shook my head, "No, that's his brother; this dog's named "Pissed." It was good to see my pal laughing again.

I looked at the dump again. "Now back to reality, it would be almost impossible for a sapper to hit that place even once, doing it monthly is impossible. Got to be an inside job. Somehow they get into the dump, then take what they want, then fake the raids to cover the theft. Then truck it off the base to Charlie. Slick, huh?" I noticed the dump was full of ¾ ton and deuce and half trucks. They were either bringing ordnance in or taking it to choppers, to re-supply the grunts in the bush. Lots of activity. Lots of confusion.

We drove around the dump a few times then headed off to talk. Mac looked at me, "How come no one else has figured out this is a farce. It has to be an inside job. It has to be someone working in the dump, blowing it up afterwards. Thinking a sapper does this monthly is a joke. Jesus! There are three companies of MP's on this base and no one figured it was a rip-off? Maybe that's part of the genius of it. No one group is really in charge here. There's no real zookeeper."

Something else had occurred to me. "I wonder if those trucks we've been stealing are used to transport the ordnance. Think about it; untraceable vehicles, MP's get access everywhere in and out of the base, faking the paperwork wouldn't be too tough for someone like Ben. All he'd need is a contact at the dump. With that confusion all day, no one would notice a single truck doing what everyone else was doing. Brilliant." Mac shook his head, went back into a gloomy silence.

That night we briefed Fleming on our investigation. Fleming asked, "What do they do with the money?" Fleming continued to think out loud. "I checked, ordnance like that would be thousands of dollars for small amounts. Then I checked back; there's reports showing ammo dump attacks almost every month, going back over a year. If they do this monthly, were talking about millions of bucks.

Which leads me back to, 'What do they do with the money?' I've got to dig into that without raising eyebrows. Some serious shit here, boys." Fleming walked off, more morose than normal. Sleep was hard coming that night. Mac remained quieter than usual. I kept asking myself: What are you doing? Somehow I couldn't let it go.

Tom Faustman

THE GIRLS

I went early to CPO gate, found my little girls waiting for trucks. When I got close, I knelt down, pulled them in for a hug. I noticed they hugged me hard; they didn't get much affection at home. Looking at their adorable faces, "You three are like angels from heaven, you may have saved my life. I'll always remember you and thank you for that courage. I know you like music so I got a gift for my brave little sweethearts." I gave them small transistor radios that picked up the American radio channels. It would help with their English study; also give them some joy. This time I almost choked as they bear-hugged me. That was a nice way to start the day.

PERCY RETURNS

When I walking to the MP desk next morning, I was shocked to see Percy had returned from Khe Sanh. He was outside the MP station arguing with Wilson and Ben. Percy had his finger in Wilson's face, very agitated. Ben looked furious. I veered off before they spotted me. The nearby hooch had some brush by the side; I edged over, trying to stay inconspicuous, hoping to hear what was going on. No luck, they broke up as soon as I got in place.

I heard someone walking towards the hooch, so I stepped backward a few steps, then pretended to be walking the opposite direction. From behind I heard the dreaded voice. "Hey, hot shot, ready to get that sorry ass in the bush? Most pussies hate jungle duty. Me, I love it. Most er afraid Charlie's gonna ruin their whole day. For me it just like bein back in the ghetto. Every step can get ya killed. Eyes dartin' back and forth. Can't relax a minute. Survive, man, that's what life's about. Only the good or lucky make it. Me, I'm definitely good, so lucky don't matter. Percy be one bad dude." Then he laughed, walked away. What was that about?

I got to the MP desk; Sgt Wilson had a grim look on his face. "Pack your dufflebag, Frazier, you leave for Khe Sanh in an hour. Have you seen McCarthy, Quillen and Clardy?" I shook my head. "Go find them and tell them to see me. They're going with you."

The wind was knocked out of me. Quang Tri was bad enough, but it was the shitty place I knew. Damn, I'm headed to the jungle! As I walked to find the others, I had a premonition that I'd be okay, it might be terrible, but somehow I'd be okay. There was a certainty about the feeling. I wondered where that came from.

Wilson drove us to General Freeman's chopper pad. From there we would get airlifted to Khe Sanh. Mac was upset by the news. "Somehow, I really believed I'd never have to go. I don't know why, I just thought that. Pretty stupid, huh?"

Quillen looked over. "The bush aint so bad. Just gotta follow the rules. First one, the jungle always wins. Pay 'tention to that an you'll be okay." I looked at Mac; he didn't know what that meant either. Clardy was grinning, he seemed happy to be going.

When we reported to the MP desk later, Wilson gave us some details. We'd be out there a month or so. Then he said, "It might be shorter or longer, depending how long it takes the ARVN's to shut down the NVA's supply route on Ho Chi Minh." Then he dismissed us. As I walked off, he told me to come back. When the other guys got a few paces away, Wilson whispered, "Be careful out there, Frazier." When I shrugged okay, he looked funny. "I mean it Frazier, be careful. Charlie isn't the only danger out there. Watch out." Then he walked back, got in the jeep, drove off. I had begun to wonder if Wilson was somehow collaborating with Ben and Percy. Maybe trying to stash money away to buy Frances's way to the States? If so, why would he warn me? Trying to throw me off? Now I was more confused.

KHE SAHN

We stood around, shuffling from foot to foot. And then we heard it. A large transport helicopter thumped into view, landed nearby. We piled in, took off without a word. I watched the vegetation get denser, the low mountains closer. Forty minutes later we landed in what apparently was Khe Sanh. From above, you could see the flat airfield carved into the formerly lush plateau. On every side of the airfield, the jungle ruled. You could see pockets of clearings, where groups of soldiers were deployed. None of these encampments were too near the airfield. There were dirt roads connecting everything.

The scenery was spectacular. Thick patches of banana trees, tropical shrubs covered where the steam shovels hadn't dug roads or campsites. A crystal clear river wound through the mountain valley, disappeared into the green expanse. This was my first jungle but I had to admit it was impressive. Why did they have to ruin this pristine setting with a war? The chopper landed at the airfield, Callahan was there to greet us. He looked terrible, drawn, was almost gaunt. When I got out of the chopper, he came over, hugged us. "You're a sight for sore eyes, good luck out here. It's not so bad, really."

Before I could grill him, three other MP's piled in the chopper, yelled for Callahan to get in. "See you soon," was all he had time for. Then the chopper lifted off, taking them back to Quang Tri. My basketball buddy Jones was waiting in a nearby truck, ready to drive us to camp. Then we heard a low, howling noise; a mortar landed about 300 yards from us. I looked all around, not sure what to do. Then I remembered my first greeting to Nam, looked for cover. No bunkers in sight, so I rolled under Jones's truck, the others followed. From there, I heard the deadly Cobra gun ships lift off, hunting their prey. The second mortar hit closer this time, we moved deeper under the truck. Seconds later, the Cobra's obliterated the mountainside just west of the airfield. No more mortars came our way; I crawled near the front tire, gazed at the horrific display of firepower. Two more gun ships joined the fight; I watched the beautiful jungle being torn to shreds. The scenery I had just admired was now a smoking wasteland. The Cobras kept circling, like vultures making sure the prey was dead before coming in to eat. Mac was now beside me. I looked over, "I could have done without this greeting, how about you?" His eyes were glazed, thinking about his family. I just patted his shoulder.

We crawled out, got in the truck. Jones had sat inside the whole time. He looked calm, like nothing happened. "This happens a lot, Jones?"

He looked at me blankly; "Wha?" was all he said. His eyes were lifeless; he was stoned out of his mind. I smelled the grass before I saw the butt hanging in his left hand. He had smoked a joint during the battle.

"Let me drive, Jones, want to get used to roads. Move over." He didn't argue; we eventually found the MP camp. Bad start to Khe Sanh.

The MP area was primitive. A half-assed bunker was partially built on the edge of our clearing. Sgt Walter Davis was the NCO in charge. He was a lifer who had just transferred to our MP Company, went immediately to Khe Shan. I hadn't gotten to know him, so I went over, introduced myself. Davis nodded, said nothing. Mac had snapped out of it and joined me. Then Quillen and Clardy wandered over. We waited for Davis to fill us in or tell us what to do. Nothing. Whatever we asked or said, he'd answer, "Okay." My new leader in the most dangerous spot on earth was a mental dwarf.

Finally I said, "Think I'll go get settled, set up my sleeping bag and get some chow." I knew what was coming.

"Okay." Mac and I looked around the area, trying to figure out the safest spot.

As we were poking around, I whispered, "If I asked Davis if I could kick him in the nuts, do you think he'd say okay?" We both started laughing, Davis looked over at us. "Don't worry about us, Sarge, everything's okay." Mac howled even louder.

Jones sobered up a couple hours later; I asked him how often we got mortared. "Hardly ever, might a been one of our own guys launched that by accident. Ya know, smoked too much weed and got careless. Happens a lot." I wondered if that was what Wilson was trying to tell me before I left. Then Jones said, "We get rocketed every morning. Ya better get that bunker done right. They're goin' after the airfield but once in awhile the rockets fall short. There it is." Jones bobbed his head up and down, headed over to load sand bags. Mac and I joined the team. We finally got it done hours later, crawled into our sleepingbags after dark.

Jones was right. Soon as the sun was peaking over the mountain, a series of rockets sailed over our heads, toward the airfield. Mac and I had already followed Jones inside the bunker, watching the fireworks. Jones pointed at the explosions, "Check it out."

The phrases "there it is" and "check it out" could be used in any conversation in Nam, mean almost anything. I looked over at Mac, "There it is." Mac started to grin when I added, "or should I add, 'check it out'?" Jones looked at us but didn't get the joke. It wasn't worth explaining.

Sgt Davis came over after the rockets stopped. He had never left his sleeping bag. "Damn hard to get a good nights sleep 'round here." I waited for his grin but none came. "After chow, I'll show you new guys around." Then he walked away.

I looked at Mac, "There it is." We both choked down our laughs.

Mac finally said, "Please stop doing that, my stomachs killing me." Then we started chuckling again. Sgt Davis looked at us but must have decided we were just happy guys. When I started to say something, Mac put his hands up, "Enough!" and moved away.

I had my first C-ration meal in Nam that morning. We had C–rations in Basic Training but only once or twice, just to learn how to open them, use the sterno to heat them up. I watched Quillen and Clardy digging through the carton, taking parts from the C's they liked. Quillen was a pro; he combined cheese and crackers into his eggs and bacon bits for breakfast. He lit the sterno, stirred his meal as he waited. It smelled great. I followed his lead; it was quite good.

Later, Sgt Davis drove us around the base. Khe Sanh was a tropical rain forest that the Army decimated to make an airfield. Roads were being dug with gigantic earth moving equipment. The massive steam shovels literally plowed down anything in its way. Right behind them, grading equipment and steamrollers made the choppy earth into a decent road. The Army engineers were busy improving the roads down to valley floor level. The ARVN battalions would follow shortly to advance into Laos. The flatter areas would help the troops move faster, allow tanks and larger vehicles to keep them supplied and protected. The activity was furious.

One of the cleared roads led up to a small ravine packed with trailers and makeshift offices. When we got closer, I saw that the offices were metal cargo bins customized into work areas. Sgt Davis nodded at them, "Mission Control. General Freeman's trailer is tucked back there. Got him almost a perfect spot, notice all them bunkers, got some serious firepower in them. I aint even bullshittin." Then I saw a small landing site adjacent, with a chopper at rest but poised to leave quickly. The General wasn't about to take chances.

Then Davis drove inside the Mission Control area, showed us Freeman's trailer. It was jet black, spotlessly clean, loaded with antennas, surrounded by a thick wall of sand bags. Davis added, "Got plush carpet inside. I aint even bullshittin." You could see that it was situated to make it impossible to be hit by rockets. The only way to get at him was to maneuver through the hive of bunkers and toss some serious bombs inside. Davis looked back, "We guard him each night, right outside his door, so mem'rize how to get around. Quillen, you up tonight, sunset to sunrise."

Our main responsibility, besides guarding Freeman, was to keep the roads open and moving. With all the heavy equipment, ARVN vehicles scouting around, tanks providing protection, regular traffic, etc. the job was trying. Something always broke down; soldiers got antsy waiting for delays to clear. Whenever you got a radio message about a "Charlie Foxtrot," you knew there was a cluster fuck on the roads that needed clearing. I spent most of my first couple week untying Charlie Foxtrots. It was more dangerous than I thought. Most roads had steep drops on the edges; you had to make certain trucks and tanks didn't topple down the ravines. It was nerve-racking.

Every morning started the same way. We piled into the bunker before sunrise. As the sun rose, the rockets followed like clockwork, pummeled the airfield. Then the Cobras followed the trail, blasted the VC position. I sat myself near the entrance, watched the pyrotechnics. There was something awesome about that level of destruction. I found myself breathing like a distance runner, just seeing the devastation. At first it was terrifying, and then it became mesmerizing. Such power, it was frightening.

Then it was over, the daily routine started. I became an epicurean at C-ration cuisine. The trick was getting a stash of fruit cocktail, peanut butter, jelly and crackers. These mainstays were your back-up plan if your main course was a disaster. I never found a way to make beef and brussel sprouts taste human. Why didn't they use potatoes? The most edible food in the world, but the Dream Machine went for sprouts. Just part of the torture? I said to Mac as he spit out our concoction, "There it is."

I got night bunker duty the next week. A new MP, Tyrone Corbin, was a former grunt that got assigned with Mac and me. We walked over to the bunker, checked out our post for the night. That's when I noticed how close the bamboo and banana trees were to the bunker. I threw up my hands, "That's nuts, Charlie can walk right up and chuck a grenade into the middle of camp."
Tyrone looked at me, "Right on."
Mac walked closer and confirmed, "There can't be more than ten feet separating the bunker and jungle. That can't be right."
Tyrone again responded, "Right on." I looked at Corbin.
"Did you go to the same grammar school as Sgt Davis?" Mac spit out a laugh.
I learned the grunts used the phrase "right on" incessantly. It could mean anything you wanted it to. It could mean "yes" or "no." For instance, if I asked Tyrone, "Would you like to wear women's clothes?" Right on. Or, "Hey, Ty, is it true your mama wears hip boots?" Right on. It could also convey anger or joy, depending on inflection. The permutations were endless; I became adept at obscure usages. It soon became another way I could persecute Mac, make him laugh at inappropriate times.

We decided to ask Sgt Davis if he could get the jungle cleared out, make the perimeter more secure. He shrugged, "Guess so, never thought about it." I knew the conversation was going nowhere.

"When do you think you can check that out? We'd all be a lot safer if that jungle got pushed back. What do you say?"

I knew it was coming, "Okay." Then he walked away. I was sure he'd already forgotten the conversation.

Before dusk, we settled into position. We were to have two guys on duty while the third rested or slept. The theory was one guy might fall asleep but two wouldn't. Each bunker was connected by radio to Mission Control. The command center kept a grid that numbered each bunker geographically, so they'd know where you were if action occurred. We were bunker E-35. Our other instruction was to call in any movement in the wire, not to shoot until commanded to do so. The only exception was imminent danger. When I heard this, I looked at Mac, "Right on." He chuckled, but I added, "In all seriousness, if we see movement, let's blow the piss out of them, then call."

There was lots of chatter on the radio. You got a call every half hour, making certain all was well. I liked that, nothing to chance. The first night was quiet until around 3 am. Then we were jolted as huge spotlights illuminated the area south of us. I could hear lots of squawking, but no firepower. Someone must have seen something, called in; a magnificent light show began. I was impressed. Whatever light system they used really worked, it was like daytime.

You got to know people sitting for twelve hours in a bunker. Tyrone Corbin was a soft-spoken, nice guy from Savannah, Georgia. This was his 2nd tour in Nam, mostly as a grunt. I learned he was married with 3 kids. "My woman a simple farm girl. She stay with her mama while I gon. She likes it that way. I sends all my monies home, gonna buy a little farm, raise tobacco, corn, and the like. Gots me a couple more years till that comes together." He and Mac talked about kids while I watched. It was nice listening to them brag about their rug rats. That got me thinking about my Laura. Would we get married when I got back? What would our kids be like? Part of me worried they'd inherit my personality. Part of me thought that would be fun. Her beautiful face stayed with me all night. Thinking of Laura was my safe place.

We had one day left on bunker duty. Surprisingly, Sgt Davis came over after the morning rocket attack, told us he called Percy to ask about clearing the perimeter. "Sgt Price thinks that's a good idea. He says you, McCarthy and Clardy should do it, won't fuck it up. I'll get some machetes; get started after your shut-eye. Okay?"

With gusto, I blurted, "There it is!" Mac gulped, walked away shaking his head, muttering about someone being a pathetic asshole.

The banana trees fell like matchsticks. Clardy was more interested in getting a meal than platoon safety. He hacked down banana trees then rooted through them for ripe fruit. "Hey, Clardy, that fruits gonna tear you up. We're going to need bigger cat holes to shit in if you keep slamming them down. Lighten up, bro." Just as I finished admonishing Clardy on his digestive system, my machete clanged into something hard. I chopped down again, the machete bounced back. Thinking nothing of it, I moved a couple steps left and renewed my efforts. The cutting got easy again.

Mac yelled over, "I'm hitting something metallic, how about you? I can't make much progress here." I told Mac to move over, that I'd had the same problem. Then it occurred to me. I walked back to the tough spot, pushed away the brush. After a few minutes, I pulled up a long strand of wire. Following along the strand, I came to a steel pole, used to anchor the wire. I reached over the wire, hacked more of the brush and found more wire beneath. Was it old perimeter wire?

A bad thought hit me. "Hey guys, stop what you're doing. Right now!" My voice was loud enough that it caught their attention. "I think its perimeter wire. Weren't the Marines here in '68? Didn't they use the same airfield? Wouldn't they have set up a defensive perimeter?"

Clardy shook his head, "Dang it! Damn Marines was pretty sloppy. Not clearing out the wire and all. We might a cut ourselves." While Clardy rambled, I was thinking. Then my eyes got wide.

In a commanding tone, "Let's get the hell outta here. Back up slowly. Retrace the way you came in. Don't touch any more wire. Be careful." When we got inside the camp, Clardy looked at me, waiting for the joke. Then he noticed I was scared. "Clardy, if the Marines were sloppy enough to leave the perimeter wire here, do you think they went to the effort to clear out the mines?" Mac and Clardy gulped, I watched the blood drain from their faces.

I told Sgt Davis what I thought. He said the smartest thing since I'd met him. "Shit." He got on the radio, asked for a demolition team to check it out. They arrived quickly, confirmed my opinion. There were loads of active Claymores, rusty after laying in the rainforest for three years. They were too dangerous to handle, so the demo team called in special tanks to drive over and explode them harmlessly under the massive steel tracks. Mac had his head down, muttering in anger. I patted his shouder, signaled we needed to move.

We huddled in the bunker, listening to hundreds of explosions. The tank soon mowed down the jungle, pushed the perimeter out about 100 feet. I felt terrible; it was my idea to clear the area. What the hell was I trying to do? I didn't know shit, why was I butting in? My motive was right, but I'd almost caused a disaster. From that moment, Mac and Clardy became even more important to me. I put them in danger; I owed them. I just sat there quietly, thinking about Sgt Wilson's advice.

When the demo team was done, their Captain came to the bunker; Davis walked out. The Captain looked pissed. "Why did you mess with the perimeter? That was a live field out there! Why do you think we left the area un-cleared? We're trying to lure Charlie in, knowing this area was hot. Ruin their whole day. Now you cleared it out and fucked it up." Davis said nothing, took the dressing down. We watched the demo team set a new perimeter wire and mine field. "Fucking morons," was the Captain's parting words. I owed Sgt Davis thanks.

That night, guard duty was again uneventful. Charlie might have been out there earlier, watching all the explosions during the day, wondering what the hell we were doing. Probably figured not to fool with this part of the base, too crazy. No one said much that night. I waited till Corbin was snoring before telling Mac what bugged me. "Why did Percy okay the clearing? That Captain talked like we should have known not to mess with the perimeter." Mac looked puzzled, then pissed.

He finished my thought, "Why did Percy ask for us to do the job?"

I was amazed how much roadwork had been done during our week of bunker duty. Mac and I tooled around the base, trying to get the lay of the land. The new work had eased the traffic problems, not one Charlie Foxtrot. We drove down toward the river, admired the beautiful countryside. "It could be a resort," Mac noted.

I smiled, "Yea, except for that war shit. Might ruin the ambiance if you went for a dip and a sniper shot your sunglasses off."

Mac retorted, "Or if they told you to avoid the Claymore section of the beach." We went on like that for the next hour, killing time, distracting ourselves.

NATURE'S SHOWER AND FISHING HOLES

Little slices of humanity meant a lot. Staying clean became my obsession. I washed my feet and crotch each night, using the camp water truck. Hadn't had a shower for the few weeks we'd been here. Between the heat, bugs and sweat, I felt clammy. Corbin thought I was nuts, "You the cleanest dude I ever met, jus go wit it." Most of the guys took the same approach. While on patrol, I started looking for a way to bathe. When I told Mac my scheme, he looked incredulous. "You've got to be kidding?" I shook my head; "Watch me."

After an intense search, a week later I had found a rippling steam that fed into the river. There was a section of the stream that dropped sharply, creating a series of small waterfalls. My plan was simple; we brought soap and towel, stripped down, used the strong flow of water to wash the scum away. We hid the jeep off the road. Mac stood guard while I bathed. It was awesome, like you felt on a sweltering summer vacation when you first dove into the ocean. Exhilarating doesn't describe it adequately.

Carried away, I began to belt out, "Singing in the Rain," doing a weak Fred Astaire imitation. The water was ice cold but felt great. It was the best shower of my life. Mac had said he wasn't going to bathe, but soon started yelling at me to hurry.

"It's my turn!" he begged.

"You don't think I'm such a douche now, do you? Told you this was a good idea." As I dried off, Mac took his turn.

I belly-laughed as he sung, "When the moon hits your eye, like a big pizza pie, that's amore," by Dean Martin.

We repeated this ritual every other day for the next week. Then I made a mistake, telling Clardy and Quillen about the spa. Next time I went back for my shower, there was a load of grunts waiting their turn in the stream. Making it worse, there were two massive tanks guarding the area. Mac complained, "All we need is a giant neon sign announcing our location, with speakers blaring, 'Bring us your great unwashed!'"

I looked at Mac, "Right on." We both chuckled, spent the rest of the day looking for a new spot. We would keep this next site quiet.

There were numerous rivers and streams in the Khe Sanh region. The mountains were dripping with moisture, supplied abundant water to feed the rivers. Many of the vehicle trails wound near the rivers because of the flat terrain, perfect for roads and transportation. I was on patrol with Clardy this week, while Mac guarded General Freeman. As we passed by a trickling stream, Clardy said, "Let's check out that crick, Dylan."

I knew what he meant but replied, "Aint got no crick, Clardy, my necks fine. Thanks for asking, though." He scratched his head.

After a minute, "Why don't we go look at that creek, Clardy?" This time he scrunched his eyes but said nothing. It soon became more a river than a creek. The blue water was crystal clear, rushing towards the South China Sea, many miles away. As we edged closer, we found a sandy beach, sat on a log that washed up during the last monsoon season. "Slice of paradise, huh?"

Clardy grinned, "Sure is purty, betcha they got some big fish in there. Ya think there's some catfish?"

We yapped about fishing trips in the real world, how great it was to eat freshly caught trout. Clardy loved catfish, described in detail how his mama rolled the fillets in corn meal and seasoning; then fried them to perfection.

Never had catfish, but had to admit he made them sound delicious. And then he did something crazy. Before I knew it, Clardy tossed a grenade into the middle of the river. The explosion was muffled; a small hill of water rose, splashed water everywhere. "What the fuck, Clardy!"

He grinned, "Watch this." In a minute or so, a couple dozen dead fish rose to the surface. Clardy tore off his pistol and boots, waded into the water. He nabbed a few bigger fish, tossed them on the beach. After he got all he could, he came ashore, stripped off his wet clothes. "I'll dry them out some 'fore we head back, okay?" He walked around naked, stacked the fish together; carried them to the jeep. "Fish fry fer dinner, Dylan, fish fry fer dinner." In pure joy, he hooted his best Rebel howl. That night, Clardy showed he could cook. Sgt Davis never asked where the fish came from and enjoyed them more than anyone.

Mac got off General guard, we resumed our patrol duties. We roamed the base relentlessly that week. We now knew everything by heart. Other than the morning rockets, there were no other airfield assaults. There was always action somewhere at night. Charlie was trying to find a soft spot in the perimeter. We never got a sound sleep, some bunker always spotted motion; short firefights began. The floodlights were constantly moved, so Charlie couldn't chart their location. In almost a month, no one slept much. We all napped during the day.

We became preoccupied with Percy. After picking at it from every angle, Mac and I concluded that Sgt Davis had misunderstood when he talked with Percy. "Couldn't have told us to clear that mined area. Davis wasn't paying attention, or just messed it up. Or maybe Percy didn't even know it was mined. Who knows?" The more we were around Sgt Davis; the more we appreciated Sgt Wilson. "Guys so stupid, he's dangerous," was Mac's conclusion.

I looked pensively at Mac, couldn't resist, "There it is." He gave me the finger.

GENERAL FREEMAN

I finally got General guard, went to my post a little early. Wanted to check out the area, make sure I knew my turf. Charlie would have to come through the MP area of the perimeter, then weave his way through 9 bunker complexes that protected Mission Control. As I stood, outside the General's trailer, I thought about how I'd do the assault. I walked out again to take another look before the sun set. Wouldn't be easy, but was it possible? That's how I spent my first night. Never saw or heard the General. Wondered if he was even there.

By the third day, I found a weak point in the way the bunkers protected Mission Control. If Charlie got through the outer perimeter, there were patches of vegetation between the first 5 bunkers. Camouflaged and keeping low, Charlie could get that far without much trouble. Then it got trickier. A gutsy attacker might get through the next 2 bunkers by angling sideways, and then crawling under the front of both bunkers. If you were quiet, it would be hard to hear or see anyone crawling below the machine gun openings. Once Charlie made it that far, he was actually facing the rear entrances of the last 2 bunkers. Assuming the guards were looking forward, Charlie could walk right up to my station. Shit.

On my way down that night, I stopped at the nearest bunker, asked who was in charge of defending Mission Control. "Why ya wanta know?" was what I heard from the next couple bunkers. They laughed when I said I thought there might be a hole. "Fuck you know? Yer an MP, right. Go twiddle yer dick in a traffic jam." When I got near the bottom of the bunker formations, I found Sgt Brown who listened silently. I pointed at the patches of cover; then the angles going sideways, then the low crawl in front and behind the last 4 bunkers. "That leaves only me, Sgt Brown. Doubt you guys want me being the hero, right?"

His eyes brightened as he retraced my route. "Hells bells." Then he nodded, "I'll take care of that. Nice work, soldier."

When I reported to work that night, the area had been reconfigured. The brush was cleared, a couple new bunkers were built, and the angles of 4 bunkers were changed. As I walked by, Sgt Brown caught up to me. "Hey, it's Frazier, right? Take another look at what we done. See if ya can spot gaps. That was unfuckin' believable, what ya saw. Man, they're wastin' ya in the MP's. Want a man's job, come see me, huh?" I finished my walk, started thinking again about what I'd do to assault this new area.

Toward morning, I heard noise behind me. I drew my pistol, in reflex. Then I saw the door open; a bull of a man strode out. He stopped when he saw the pistol, then came forward as I holstered it. "A little jumpy soldier?" General Freeman was 6'6" and weighed about 240. He was built like a weight lifter, not an ounce of fat. The crew cut and intense eyes told me this was a born soldier.

I saluted, and then added, "We are in Nam, aren't we? Shouldn't I be jumpy, sir?" He didn't smile, but I could see he liked the answer. Not a wiseass, but not backing down, either.

Then he surprised me. "Are you the soldier that said we had a flaw in our layout here?" I couldn't tell whether he was pleased or pissed.

Thinking, Oh, what the hell, "Sir, I just told them what I'd do, if I had to assault. Not sure I was right, but I thought someone more qualified should check."

He looked at me for about 60 seconds. "Out-fucking standing work, soldier. There was definitely a blind spot between those top bunkers. We are in Nam, PFC Frazier, and yes, you better be jumpy."

The General asked me where I was from, how long I'd been in Quang Tri. Wanted to know what led me to looking for weaknesses in the defense layout. I gave him the real answer. "Sir, there's not much to do up here, so I did it to occupy my mind. I grew up a gym rat in Philly, always tried to spot soft defenses playing basketball. Did that everyday since I was ten, kind of a habit now. Sometimes you need an edge. Just the way I was raised, Sir. Nothing special, really."

Then General Freeman stepped back briskly, gave me a crisp salute. "Outstanding work, soldier. Carry on."

Being a bit of a smart-ass, I didn't care too much about military accolades. But I was pumped over the praise I got. The General was impressive. I felt like I'd met a man born to lead other men. Had never met anyone quite like that before. Came across serious, but with a sense of humor. Hoped I was right, my ass might depend on it. The rest of that night was uneventful, except for the periodic firefights and spotlight shows. After thinking that, I smacked myself on the head, muttered. "What was uneventful about firefights?"

I was sleeping peacefully, when Sgt Davis shook me next morning, said to get Mac, investigate an explosion down by the river. "I been calling Corbin and Clardy, but aint getting an answer, both er fuck-ups." Davis looked perturbed, wondered what set him off? We asked for more specifics on the location, but didn't get much. "Some grunts called it in, north side of base, by the river." There were a few rivers down that way, but I knew Davis wouldn't be helpful. He sat around the base camp all day, never got to know the base too well. With the constant roadwork being done, it changed some every week. He was useless.

We went down by our old shower site, saw the line of soldiers, chuckled. "Just think, Mac, years from now we can look back and say we helped keep our soldiers clean during the Khe Sanh invasion. Something to tell the grand kids, huh?" We rounded the corner; saw a tank parked near the river, by the entrance of where Clardy "fished" with grenades. Mac parked behind the tank. "That looks like our jeep, is that Clardy?"

I walked toward him, could see something was wrong. He was slumped in the seat, didn't respond when I yelled. "What are you doing, Clardy? Davis is pissed, why didn't you answer his call?"

A soldier came over from beside the tank; saw we were MP's, said, "I been called in to clear this beach. Been a problem here, Charlie's mined the area. Guy's been killed."

I looked at Clardy. "Where's Corbin, he checking it out?"

Clardy looked at me, his eyes red, teary. "Corbin's dead. Stepped on a mine. My fault; fuckin' fishin spot. Musta seen us here. Mined it." I exhaled deeply, letting it sink in. I turned to Mac; his head was down, taking shallow breaths.

We watched until the demo team cleared the beach. I called Sgt Davis, told him about Corbin. He was silent, then "Fuck." Corbin was wrapped up, so we never got to see anything, just the body bag. We got set to drive Clardy back to camp. The medic came over as we were about to leave, looked at Clardy.

"Get him a drink, that's the best thing for him. Keep him talking. It looks like he might be in shock. But, whisky'll help." We got back; Sgt Davis already had some beer and Bourbon ready. Maybe he wasn't so useless after all.

PERCY ARRIVES

The news got worse next morning. Sgt Davis asked me to drive him to the airfield. I learned he was headed back to Quang Tri. "Sgt Price's takin' over out here." We had been out here almost a month, I wondered if we'd be headed back soon. I wasn't happy to see Davis leave, mostly because Percy was the replacement. We had settled into a routine under Davis. It would change today; Percy would mix it up. I hoped I would stay on patrol with Mac. I knew Percy would hassle the truck drivers and ARVN's. My stomach started to rumble.

Sgt Davis got out of the jeep, never said a word, just ambled over and got in the chopper. Percy hopped out. I nodded, "Hey, Percy."

He surprised me with, "Proper address is Sgt Price, we aint on the basketball court no more." Then he added, "How ya like the bush, white bread? Great fun, huh. Pissin' in a cat hole aint as glamorous as ya thought, huh?" Then he laughed at his own wit. You could tell Percy was happy to be here. He liked danger; it got him hopped up.

I looked at Percy, "Isn't a problem anymore, Sgt Price, Clardy shits like a buffalo, we dug bigger holes. Been building wood seats to make it feel like home." Percy slapped me hard, grinned.

Modern war was not always hell. The convoys brought us beer periodically, even packed ice for storage. Not enough to get drunk, but enough to take the edge off. Percy introduced us to C-ration stew. I had my doubts when watching it prepared. A little of this C-ration can, a little of that can, would soon become the basis for our meal. Percy had connections. He had Worcestershire sauce, Tabasco, brown sugar, and dried mustard. Sounds terrible, but it was great. Sometimes beer was added to the mix. Each day was slightly different. I looked forward to it, helped with the cooking. It was a moment of civilization, made you feel normal for a few minutes.

No one talked about Corbin except Mac and me. I liked Corbin; he was planning on serving his country, then making a nice life for his family. Percy had been a grunt; saw death before, so I asked what he thought. "Remember I told ya about street smarts, Frazier? Stayin' on yer toes, watchin' fer who's gonna fuck ya over? Corbin was a fuck up. Fuck's he doin down by the river?" Not exactly sympathetic, but he had a point.

Percy didn't know about the fishing deal. I didn't expect a compassionate response, but he was colder than usual. He acted like Corbin deserved it. I guess my irritation showed. "Ya got a problem with that, Frazier?" Mac was nearby, he squirmed, nervous about what I might say.

"No one deserves that, Sgt Price. He was a good guy. Feel bad for his family. That's all I'm saying."

Percy ended with, "Nam's no place to go swimmin'. Fucks he doin?" I walked away thinking: Heartless bastard.

ARVN convoys started filling the roads. The South Vietnamese were the world's worst drivers. Made sense, I guess. They didn't grow up driving like us; never learned to operate vehicles until joining the Army. Then they put them in huge trucks, tanks and other behemoths. Not a good recipe for highway bliss. Whenever they faced a traffic decision, the ARVN's stopped driving. Making a mess worse, they usually turned off the vehicle, got out; started yapping about what to do.

For the past couple weeks, traffic was a nightmare. Percy switched Clardy as my partner. He knew Mac and I were best friends, seemed to be busting our balls on purpose. Wasn't sure what caused the change in his attitude. Just a random mood swing or intentional? Mac was on patrol with Quillen on the same roads, so we saw each other a lot. Most of the Charlie Foxtrots were huge, needing a few MP patrols to help unravel. We were on the road 12 hours a day. Covered with dust, you toweled clean at night, ate the hearty C-ration stew, had a rocket-blasting sleep, did it again the next day.

We learned the traffic pick-up was from 50,000 ARVN troops finally being sent to Laos to close down the Ho Chi Minh trail. This ploy hadn't worked in 1968, but this massive force, heavy American air support, and lessons learned from the past failure, made the ARVN's bullish on success. You could see the confidence in their faces, success was certain this time. Despite the screwy driving, I felt good about helping smooth the way. Truckloads of troops passed us daily, flashing the V sign. Their enthusiasm lifted our moods.

One day, traffic was worse than normal. There were more tanks than usual; they ate up the roads, made deep ruts that caused havoc with the following trucks. One big personnel carrier got stuck and blocked a convoy for miles. To make matters worse, seeing this wouldn't get cleared-up fast, the ARVN's got out of their vehicles, started making lunch, right in the middle of the road. Clardy was still jumpy after Corbin's death, got really agitated when he couldn't get the ARVN's moving.

"Fuckin' slopes, better git ther' asses in gear. Sittin' target right here. We got ta git them movin', Dylan. What'er we gonna do?" I felt bad for Clardy.

"Take it easy, Clardy. Can you blame them for cooling it? They're headed for war. Would you rush? War'll be there tomorrow. Let's let them enjoy their rice and chicken." Just then an ARVN soldier came scrambling up from a steep hill beside the road. He must have been taking a dump; something scared him. He was squawking like a lunatic. When I heard the words "VC", I got nervous. Went over to see what spooked him.

Quillen and Mac were also stuck nearby, had come over to see what the commotion was about. Quillen knew some Vietnamese, listened intently. After a few minutes, "Says ther's a big tunnel down ther', looks like VC. It's big enough to drive in, don't sound good; might be a base camp." Quillen was the expert on tunnels, so you took him seriously.

I looked at the tunnel rat, afraid of his answer to my next question, "What should we do?"

Quillen confirmed my worry. "Let's check it out."

We scrambled down the hill, Quillen leading the way. There was dense vegetation but suddenly it cleared. Quillen stayed in the brush, didn't approach the clearing, trying to see if there was activity. He turned to me, "Don't look live. No new footprints er signs of equipment movin' in er out. Musta been a major site one day. Musta been built fer the B-52 bombs. This place got shellacked back in '68. Wouldn't a bothered em too much, inside that hill. Maybe a headache; get ther' bell rung; nothing serious. Charlie just dug out the openin' a little, went back in binness."

I asked what we should do. "Leave it be," was Quillen's advice. "Might be nothin' but ya never know. If the zips plan ta come back, they mighta trapped it. Plan on it, was how I operated as a rat."

I looked at Mac, "Let's beat feet." Clardy hadn't gone down with us, too nervous. "Its okay, Clardy, it's dead. No activity for a long time. All overgrown. Nothing to worry about." Clardy exhaled, he was holding his breath.

Word spread of the VC tunnel, miraculously the Charlie Foxtrot had cleared; traffic was moving briskly. We resumed patrol; Clardy relaxed some. "Dad got a Purple Heart in WW II. It opened a lotta doors fer him back home. Big hero in our town, an such. Bank gave him a deal, got us a nice ol farm. Was hopin' I'd get wounded, jus like him. Nothin' too bad, mind ya, jus enough to be a big shot too." Then he was quiet a minute before adding, "Seein' Corbin changed my mind. No hero stuff fer me. Gittin' outta here in one piece." That was the smartest thing I'd heard him say yet.

Next morning, Quillen and I were a patrol team. As we drove along the camp road, I was surprised to see Percy driving General Freeman. There was an entourage protecting the General, tanks, Armored Personnel Carriers, Cobras overhead, the works. Other than the armada, it would be hard to pick who was the leader. He was wearing camouflage, just like everyone else. I saluted the General as he drove past. He didn't return the salute but smiled, I think he recognized me. Percy never acknowledged us. Quillen said, "Don't salute in the bush, gives Charlie a targit. Like ta pick-off officers, git me?"

I looked at my wily friend. "Good tip, thanks."

As we drove on, "Wonder where the General's headed?" Quillen asked. I wasn't sure but had an idea.

"Bet he's going toward the airfield. Maybe the ARVN's are attacking today. He might be going to observe. Just a guess, though." The traffic had dramatically dried up; we had the road to ourselves. I wondered how long the onslaught would take. Would it be a week or a month? I regretted not being more attentive in History classes. Now I cared, it affected me directly.

We circled the base a few times, found no traffic; it was dead quiet. Near the south edge of the base camp, I spotted a cloud of dust. Not big enough to be a truck or tank, so I waited to see what was coming. From a distance, I recognized a familiar, bulky figure. Then I saw the lean, older soldier beside him and put the names together, Ben Burton and Colonel Mullen were in Khe Sanh. Not knowing why, that made me uneasy.

I didn't salute but nodded sharply, Colonel Mullen returned the nod lazily. I liked that about him, not big on pomp. "How's it going, Frazier? I thought we'd come to see if you built a basketball court out here. It looks kind of bleak, makes Quang Tri look pretty swanky, huh?" Ben didn't say anything, just sat quietly, gazing all around. My bet was he was annoyed to be out here. In over 5 months, I had never seen him leave our company except to go to the USO club. Colonel Mullen asked to take him to our camp, followed closely as I led the way.

Percy returned to camp shortly therafter, greeted the Provost Marshall warmly. "Ya just missed General Freeman, he was askin' about ya. He was headed out to watch the ARVN's light-up The Trail. I hopes they do a better job this time. The slopes aint big on tough. They run when it gets bad, that's what I think." Mullen didn't show much expression, but seemed to agree with Percy. The battle in '68 had gone badly; would this avenge the loss? Mullen finally spoke.

"Time'll tell, Percy. They're much better prepared this time. Better air support, better equipped. We'll know pretty fast, these assaults tend to generate a fast response from Charlie."

Colonel Mullen said he was here to inspect the road conditions from Khe Sanh to Quang Tri. "I had to do it by jeep, to judge how the bigger vehicles would fare. Overall, the roads are tip-top. It shouldn't be any trouble if we need to exit fast. General Freeman'll be pleased." He paused, thinking, "In '68, that was a huge problem. Charlie had us like sitting ducks, because the roads were so bad. Nothing could move quickly. We can't repeat that again." He looked very somber.

We then learned that one of our patrols had to retrace the road daily towards Quang Tri; to make sure everything stayed clear. Mullen clarified, "Not all the way back; just far enough to get out of the mountains onto flat terrain. We'll have Cobra escort, but it'll still be hairy. Charlie knows that road is vital to re-supply and won't make it easy for us. We've got to be careful, gentleman. This is when MP's earn their money." Mac and I looked at each other, without saying a word. If we had this shitty duty, we hoped we'd be together, someone you could trust.

And then Mullen grinned. "Now I've got some good news, gentleman. It seems one of our MP's has impressed General Freeman enough to recommend a promotion." I thought of the smug look on Percy's face as he whizzed by us earlier that day. Driving the General had its privileges. Colonel Mullen turned toward me, "Step forward PFC Frazier. It is my distinct pleasure to award you a promotion to Specialist Fourth Class. General Freeman told me what you did. That was a piece of out-fucking standing work, soldier." I was speechless.

Then he shook my hand, laughed, "Surprised, huh, Frazier? I haven't seen you lost for words too often." All the guys congratulated me, asked about what I'd done to impress the General. I downplayed it, but I could see they were excited, not jealous at all. Ben walked over, slapped me on the back.

"Not bad fer a Yankee, Frazier. That was A-1 work. You might work out after all." In a few minutes, we broke up; Percy wandered over when I was alone. He looked at me with his dead eyes, said in a whisper.

"No one likes an ass kisser, boy. Stay away from the General. Hear me?" As he walked away, I got chills down my spine.

Before I had time to worry, Colonel Mullen yelled, told me to drive him to Mission Control. "I've got to check in, advise Freeman the roads clear. He'll be worried. He doesn't like loose ends." We drove up slowly, Colonel Mullen asked about what I spotted as weak points, nodded as I showed the changes they made. "I'm not sure I could have seen those and I've been doing this work 30 years, Frazier. That's an amazing piece of observation." I don't know why, but that didn't make me feel better.

My day then went downhill fast as Mullen said, "I've been thinking about what you said about those robberies being inside jobs. I've been thinking it might be someone with enough knowledge and access to pull it off. I ruled out Wilson, he's too dumb. That leaves Burton and Price as suspects. What's your thought? I've seen how perceptive you are, what do you think?" I was caught off-guard, hadn't thought through an answer. I dropped my eyes, hesitated.

"Uh, I can't believe those guys would be, er, involved. They're good soldiers. Uh, must be someone else."

The blue eyes drilled in closer. I sensed he didn't buy my answer, too clumsy. I was starting to sweat when he shrugged. "I hope your right but I'm going to keep my eyes on them. I want you to do the same. Anything funny, get to me asap. Clear?" I relaxed some; maybe I had sold it. After a few minutes of small talk, Colonel Mullen delivered another punch. "Did you tell anybody else about your theories, Frazier? I know you and McCarthy are close. Does he know about this, too?"

I lost my breath, whispered weakly, "Ah, no one else. McCarthy isn't interested. Just wants to get home. Doesn't want trouble."

He looked at me without blinking. "It's better to keep that opinion to yourself, Frazier. Let's keep the circle tight. If they are rotten apples, best not to tip them off." I knew he didn't buy my answer. Now he knew Mac was involved; he didn't want anyone else to know my suspicions. What had I gotten Mac into? Colonel Mullen again switched topics, steered the conversation to Khe Sanh. He asked me to drive him around the base, mentioned the roads were better than expected. He was here in '68, didn't want another disaster. "Charlie whipped our tail that time. The ARVN's can't afford another loss like that. This offensive might determine the course of the war." He seemed very worried. Then he sat back, didn't say much. I knew this place had suddenly become more dangerous.

Next morning I got another surprise from Mullen. "Frazier, McCarthy, after chow, we're going to the border of Laos. I want you two to know the way. We'll be taking reporters there tomorrow and for a few weeks or so, we need MP's to accompany them. Let's roll." Clardy drove Colonel Mullen, Mac and I followed in our jeep. That made three of us that could escort the press.

Mac whispered to me, "How'd we get so lucky?" I hadn't told him about my conversation with Mullen. I planned to do it that morning. He wouldn't be happy.

LAOS

The US government promised not to violate the border into Laos. Our job was back-up support. Mullen made it clear that reporters would be dropped at the border. "There'll be no cowboy shit fellas, drop them and head home. Got that?" It had rained that night; the roads were slippery. Some of the ruts were deep, hidden by pools of muddy water. It was a bumpy ride; we had to pay attention every second. The only good thing was it distracted us from the fact we were driving through dense jungle on the way to Laos. Now Khe Sanh looked like a safe place.

As the road got quieter, I unloaded my bad news. Mac took the Mullen conversation well. "I already figured he knew I was involved. He knows we're tight. He might believe I know what's going on but aren't interested in being involved. That's not far from the truth. Who knows? Doesn't change anything. We've got to cover for each other and get the hell out of here. This invasion probably screwed up their little operation anyway. Ben and Percy are out here. They don't have time to rob the club, run whores or steal ordnance. Maybe it'll settle down?"

Suddenly we stopped. Mullen waved us up. He pointed to a shabby, wooden sign. "Beware, no Americans beyond this point." I'm not sure what I expected but not this.

"If you blinked, you could miss that sign, Colonel Mullen."

He nodded, "That's why I'm taking you myself, to study the area, it's easy to miss. I don't want anything happening to my team." I looked around for distinguishing signs. There weren't any, just jungle. Clardy hopped out, hacked more brush from around the sign, making it more visible. Mullen directed him to pile the sign up higher, make it pop out more. It helped but not much.

I looked at Mac, "There it is." Even Colonel Mullen grinned.

KHE SANH

Mac and I wandered from camp that night to discuss Ben and Percy. "Do you think they know we suspect something?" Mac asked.

I nodded, "We need to play it like they do. Based on the way Mullen blindsided me, he may have done the same to them. You know, he'd just say it looked like an inside job and that they were logical suspects. Then he'd tell them he knew they weren't that type of lowlife scumbags. Laugh it off, maybe. But he'd sent them a signal. It worked with me, I wasn't prepared." I looked at Mac, "Won't happen again, though. Fool me once."

Mac thought awhile. "They seem to hate each other. It's hard to believe they're working together. I mean they never talk unless forced to. Like when Mullen gets them together and wants input on something. That gets me to whether they operate independently, Ben with stolen vehicles and Percy with whores. But that leaves the ordnance. Could there be another explanation we overlooked? I keep running that around, but get nowhere. Are we missing something?"

I told Mac about Percy's change with me. "Used to kinda like me; at least as much as Percy could like anyone. Then, bang, he's hostile as hell. You should have seen the look on his face after I got the Spec 4 promo. Like he wanted to kill me. Same look as when he killed the dog, no animation, just dead eyes." Mac said what I suspected.

"It sounds like he thinks you ratted him out. That maybe Mullen did spring that trick on him about being a logical suspect. I can't come up with anything else. Well, maybe he resents the General taking a liking to you, getting you promoted. Maybe that set him off."

I told Mac my verdict, "I think it's both."

Trips to Laos

We always picked up the reporters at Mission Control. We'd wait for an hour after the rocket attack on the airfield, then head out. Mac and I did the first few runs together. Usually, there was a reporter and cameraman. Most were from the big magazines, like *Time* and *Life*, but lately, newspaperman started showing up. The reporter from the *New York Times* spent the night at the airfield, so he could experience the rockets, get a few pictures, see the havoc up close. That impressed me, lotta guts. That also told me he was mostly nuts.

Each reporter looked different, but each had common traits, they asked a million questions, were curious about everything. To amuse myself, I began exaggerating answers to the silly, repetitive questions. It became my new favorite game. Mac occasionally joined in, but was mostly the straight man. He was good at that. He'd nod at the reporter as I recited preposterous stories. It kept us amused that first week of limo driving the road to Laos. We would howl like hyenas on our way back to camp.

The *Times* reporter asked me about snakes. I gave my best look of awe and disbelief. "You won't believe some of these suckers. Huge anacondas here; can knock over banana trees when they climb up. Even the gorillas are scared of them. Seen silverbacks wet themselves when those snakes drop out of trees."

The reporter looked at me dubiously, "Aren't anacondas in South America? I never heard about any in Nam."

I threw up my hands in amazement, "That's what they tell everybody when they land here. Probably don't want to scare you any worse. Maybe the VC brought them in as new guerilla weapons. Vietnam is supposed to be a unique microclimate for animals and reptiles. No place like it; is what they say. Who's to know?"

Every reporter asked, "Have you killed anyone?"

I always gave the same response, "Many people." When they probed for gory detail, they got the same answer. "Too painful to think about. I just want to go home and play basketball."

The *New York Times* reporter was relentless. Finally, I pointed at Mac, "That red-haired dude driving has killed tens more than me. Loves it, he's one sick dude. That why they paired him up with me, trying to rehabilitate him. Think it's starting to work; aint killed no one in a week or so. He still looks kinda crazy though, don't he?"

The merriment ended the next week. Colonel Mullen left the previous day. He put Ben in charge, as Percy drove him back to Quang Tri. Ben called Mac and me over next morning "Splittin' you two up. Don't like those numb nuts Clardy and Quillen ridin' together. 'Bout half a brain between em. Frazier, go with Clardy. There's some hot shots from the Pentagon need ta go ta Laos. Got ta git em near the line. So, ya'll gonna need ta go past the border. Just follow the road. The noise'll tell ya the right way. Take my jeep; it's the best. Questions?"

I told Ben that Mullen was adamant about not crossing the border. He got a funny look on his face, lowered his eyes; mumbled as he walked away. "New orders. Git goin'" We picked up two civilians later that day at Mission Control. They weren't too talkative, never told us their names. I thought that was odd. Most people were nervous out here, yapped to quell their jitters. Not these two, sat in the back, talked softly to each other. It was plain they didn't want us listening.

As we approached the warning sign, I stopped and told them this was the border for Laos. They started to get out, grabbed their gear. "What are you doing?" I asked.

The taller guy said, "You can't go past here, can you?" I told them Ben had told us to get them near the line of battle. They turned to each other; then looked at me.

"Great. Better than we thought. Let's go." It was obvious they were surprised. I wondered who gave Ben the go ahead to break protocol. No use discussing it with Clardy, Ben was right about him. Good guy, not much savvy.

I was getting nervous. We were now about 5 miles over the border, heard no signs of action. Just squealing birds and what sounded like monkeys yakking at each other. It was another 10 miles till we saw troops. I slowed down, tried to make it obvious we were the good guys. One guy walked up, "Don't see many MP's out here, you lost?" The Pentagon hotshots jumped out; asked to see the company commander.

Then the tall guy looked at us, "Well, get out here. Thanks. Been real." I wasn't about to argue, it was late afternoon, we wanted to get back before dark, when the action got hot.

Clardy was driving fast but did a good job avoiding the ruts. We whizzed by the DO NOT ENTER sign when the jeep started to sputter. I looked at Clardy, who was a grease monkey. Talking to himself, "Sounds like she's outta gas. Gauge says half full." Then we came to a dead stop. Clardy jumped out, popped the hood, poked around. He checked the spark plugs, oil, water and all the wires. He looked perplexed. "Don't see nothin' wrong." Then he went to the gas tank, stared into the tube. He got a flashlight from the glove box and peered down. "Sheeiitt, Dylan, she's dryer'n an ole whore. How comes the gauge say half full?"

I went to the radio to call for assistance. The transmitter normally crackled when you picked it up, but today was silent. I clicked the transmit button, waited for a signal. Nothing! I looked at Clardy, "It's dead. Do you know anything about radios?" Clardy played with it some, pushing all the buttons, but I could tell he was just guessing.

He looked at me, scared, "This is some shit, what'er we gonna do? Gonna be dark in less'n a couple hours." I could tell Clardy was looking to me for an answer. How should I know? I'm just a dumb ass kid from Philly.

Clardy played with the radio for about 15 minutes but couldn't get a peep. I used the time to think. We were about equidistant from Khe Sanh and the front line in Laos. The idea of heading toward the battle wasn't appealing. It was about 15 miles to the base camp. Even running without our gear, it would take about 4-5 hours. My guess was we had an hour or so of daylight. The thought of approaching camp in darkness was dangerous. The perimeter guards would be jumpy, would shoot at any movement. Maybe we could yell out as we got near the camp, hope they heard us and wouldn't fire. I didn't like those odds.

Clardy was looking at me like a puppy waiting for dinner, antsy but knowing he had to wait patiently. "Here's the deal, Clardy. Let's make our way toward Khe Sanh but plan to camp out when we get nearby. We'll get our butts lite-up if we hit the perimeter in the dark. Don't see any way to do it safely. Then we walk in tomorrow after sunrise. Wait till after 8 or 9 so everyone's wideawake. Stay in the middle of the road, so we're out there easy to see. Any other ideas?" He had none. And then I added, "Maybe Ben will send a patrol out for us when we don't show." Even Clardy didn't believe that.

We pushed the jeep to the side of the path, just in case there was some US traffic at night. Doubted there would be but who knows. Didn't want the MP's blamed for another screw-up, ditching our jeep was bad enough. Had to make a decision on the Thompson machine gun. Couldn't leave it with the jeep but it was heavy as hell. "Got to bring the Thompson, Clardy. We can take turns carrying it. Should bring some ammo, too. Might need it, hope not, but good to have just in case." Clardy nodded, grabbed the machine gun, ammo box.

Without the jeep noise, it was spooky walking through the jungle. The bird and animal sounds were deafening. I remembered at orientation training the sergeant said, "Get nervous if the jungle gets quiet. It means Charlie's snoopin' around. Stay still till you hear the critters yappin' agin. Got that?" It was loud as hell, so I took comfort in that advice. Hoped that sergeant knew what he was talking about. Clardy hadn't said a word since we left the jeep. People talked when they were nervous. I wasn't sure what Clardy was feeling, but I didn't think it was anything good. "Hey, Clardy, did you ever hear about the dog with no teeth, two glass eyes, a scraggly tail, most of his fur droppin' off, and no legs?"

Clardy was in a stupor, "Huh, what're ya sayin'?" I repeated the dog's problem, asked what they called him.

Clardy perked up a little, "Heard this one already. LUCKY, right?"

I shook my head, "No that's his cousin, this guy's called, TOTALLY FUCKED." I laughed at my own joke so hard that Clardy began to chuckle.

We walked a little further, Clardy leaned toward me, "Hope we aint like that dog, Dylan."

My guess was we were about 8 miles from Khe Sanh. It was getting dusky, so we looked for a place to camp. "Let's stay near the road, but far enough away that someone trailing the road won't bump into us. Find a spot that seems untouched, like no one's ever been there." We settled on a spot about 100 yards from the trail. It was beside a banana grove, dense with vegetation. We cleared a little camp, piled the shrubs underneath us, to keep the moisture out. It was hot but not unbearable. There was a steady breeze, so the insects weren't a problem. Lucky so far.

We sat back to back, planning to stay awake all night. I spent the first hour wondering about our jeep and radio trouble. Colossal bad luck or cleverly planned? It would take someone expert with jeeps and how to manipulate the gauges. Didn't know if Ben was an expert with radios but my bet was yes. The more I thought about it the more I knew it was a set-up. I remembered the way he averted his eyes when I questioned the order to drive past the border. He wanted to make certain we were deep in the jungle when the gas ran out. Had to be Ben. What did he think would happen to us?

I couldn't discuss this with Clardy, so I thought about what to do about it when I got back safely. Then I heard a low growl, maybe 500 yards to my right. Clardy grabbed my shoulder, "Fuck's that? Sounds like a tiger. Thought that was bullshit, just ta scare us. Sheeiitt." From orientation I learned there were leopards and tigers in Vietnam.

"Don't worry, we were told in orientation, 'nobody ever sees them'. They'll avoid humans." Most of us thought that was propaganda to yank our chains. Not me, I looked it up in the Quang Tri library. There were lots of big cats in Nam, including tigers.

I could feel Clardy shaking. So, I said softly, "Where's the Thompson? Let's get it ready. If we hear the growls getting closer, maybe we fire off a few rounds. Make him look elsewhere." Clardy was good with guns, so he got the tripod set in the direction of the noise, put the Thompson in place. I got my M-16 ready, faced the opposite direction. I whispered to Clardy, "Don't fire unless you hear something close. Don't want Charlie to know we're here. Okay?"

I felt him nod agreement but within seconds, he was shooting the Thompson recklessly. Must have fired 50 rounds. Utter stillness followed. I wondered what spooked him. We sat quietly without hearing a peep. After about 5 minutes, I asked why he shot. He mumbled, "Got scared is all. Sorry." I was pissed but kept it to myself. Dumb ass had announced our presence. If Charlie was in the area, he knew there were visitors. Clardy finally whispered, "Think the tigers gone, don' you?" I leaned over again, "Maybe you scared him away when you shit your pants." He didn't laugh.

I began to relax a little but told Clardy to keep the Thompson ready. Apparently Clardy relaxed too much, because I soon heard deep breathing, he slumped against me dead asleep. The jungle continued its cacophony of sound. I remembered it got quiet before the tiger growl. The bedlam of birds and monkey howls meant that the predator had passed. At least, that's what I hoped. The only critter I saw all night was a huge toad that hoped up beside Clardy as he slept. The toad looked at me for a long time before moving. He seemed to be thinking, "What the hell are you doing out here?"

My dad had given me a luminescent watch before I left for Nam. "You might need this sometime," was all he said. My dad was man of few words, but whenever he talked, it was worthwhile. I silently thanked him for his insight. I watched that glowing dial, thought of home. How would I describe this night when I returned? I was more jacked up on adrenaline than scared. Time moved slowly.

Then I heard different noise, human voices. Now I was scared. It sounded like a large group of soldiers moving near the road. The voices were muffled but the words were clearly Vietnamese. I put my hand over Clardy's mouth, gently woke him. Before he got freaked about my hand, I whispered, "We got company, stay quiet. Think they're out by the road; we're probably okay. Stay still." I looked at my watch, 5 am. Charlie was probably moving toward Khe Sanh, getting ready to launch mortars or rockets.

The voices were suddenly closer. I was worried Clardy would unload another burst from the Thompson, but couldn't risk talking to him. I saw movement on the edge of the banana grove. Two small soldiers were looking at the ground closely. Were they tracking us? They continued to circle the grove, chattered to each other. I got my M-16 ready. Clardy hadn't moved, I didn't hear him breathing but could sense his panic. My hope was if we had to shoot, an American squad would come to investigate. We'd need to hold out for an hour or so. I thought: This is it.

But the tiger changed everything. He came crashing from above, pounced on the shocked soldiers. Their AK 47's went flying as the huge cat raked his massive paws at their puny chests. Both guys screamed, began rolling, hoping to get away from the claws. The cat finally settled on one target; that gave the other soldier time to grab his rifle. He shot aimlessly. The tiger turned on him, seemed ready to spring, but vanished into the brush. Within seconds, other soldiers came, started yelling. They quickly picked up their wounded comrade, carried him off. The jungle got quiet again. I looked over; Clardy had passed out.

We heard truck and jeep activity around 7 am, so we moved closer to the road. "Let's sit here a while, make certain it's our guys are the ones driving around, okay?" Clardy didn't answer, still dazed from fright. A few minutes later, we saw a familiar shape roar by. Ben Burton was by himself, flying down the trail. Clardy perked up, "Bet he's lookin' fer us. Must be worried as hell." I just shook my head but said nothing. My bet was he wasn't worried at all. Bet he was hoping Charlie cooked our ass.

We got out on the road, flagged down the next jeep. "Do us a favor guys, call the perimeter bunkers, tell them were walking in. Don't want to surprise anybody." While we waited, Clardy looked at me sheepishly.

"Dylan, you gonna tell anybody I fucked up? Might go bad fer me if they think I'm a coward. First time I been in that sorta spot. Sure I'll do good next time. Alright?" I assured Clardy it was our secret. Didn't blame him, wasn't sure why I held up. Maybe too stunned to do anything but watch.

KHE SANH

Mac spotted us walking up toward camp, came running to meet us. "What the hell happened to you guys? We've been scared out of our minds. Ben left a while ago to find you. He's been calling around all night. Trying to see if anyone saw you. But nobody saw squat. Where have you been?" We told the story of our run of bad luck but left out the Clardy mishaps. "Man, that's unbelievable. What are the odds of that happening?" Pretty slim, but kept that to myself. I'd fill Mac in later when alone.

We radioed Ben from camp; he acted surprised. "Scared the piss outta us, Frazier. Shoulda called." I explained about the gas and radio. He stayed quiet, "I aint found the jeep yet. Check it out when I git there. Don't sound right." It didn't sound right to me either. When alone, I explained to Mac what I thought really happened, his jaw dropped.

"You think Ben messed with the gas tank and radio?" When I said yes, he got flushed with anger. "You could have been killed out there."

I grabbed his shoulder, "I think that was the plan. He figured Charlie or the tigers would get us. Solves his problem. Mullen must have talked to him about the inside job theory. This is getting bad. Might have to go to Mullen if something else happens." Macs eyes were piercing.

Ben returned a couple hours later, told Mac and me to get in his jeep. "I found the jeep, had gas in it. Not sure why you couldn't git it goin. Maybe ya flooded it. Radio had a loose wire. Not sure why Clardy couldn't fix that. Dumb-ass cracker." I noticed that Ben had 2 gas tins in the back of his jeep. As I got in the back seat, I pushed them gently. Empty. We had a quiet ride back into Laos. Mac sat in front, small-talked with Ben about our bad luck. I could hear the edge in Mac's tone with Ben. I nudged him in the right shoulder, signaling him to settle down.

Ben was especially nice to Clardy and me that day. Said he felt really bad about what happened. "I shoulda checked that radio better. Glad you guys got back safe." He gave us that night off, told us to sleep in. "Least I can do fer ya." If Ben was acting, he deserved the Academy Award. He seemed legitimately sorry. Maybe I was getting paranoid. It was quiet the rest of the week. That all changed when Percy arrived to relieve Ben. I drove Ben to the chopper. "Back ta beautiful Quang Tri, Frazier. Stay safe. See ya in the funny papers."

Percy was all wound up. He got all over Clardy. "I heard ya flooded the engine an left the jeep in Laos. What are ya, a fuckin' retard?" When Clardy started to defend himself, Percy got up in his face. "This aint a conversation, Clardy. You do the listenin', I do the talkin'. Yer a fuck-up waitin' to happen. Next times the last time. Follow me, boy?" Clardy withered. As Percy turned away, he spun and smacked Clardy hard in the temple with his open palm. Blood trickled from the edge of his eyebrow.

Mac and I had patrol next day; we were dead tired. Besides the unease at camp, it had been a wild night. Charlie messed with the perimeter non-stop. Every hour there were grenades exploding, AK shots, blinding light shows. I sat there, wondered what it was like to sleep peacefully. Would I ever take that for granted? During one of the firefights, I looked over at Mac, "Too bad Fleming isn't here to share the experience. Can you imagine how pissy he'd be?"

He didn't laugh, but added, "I can hear him now.'This place blows.'" Mac was good under pressure, but we were both beginning to fray. My prayers that night were for Mac. I got him involved in this; he needed to get home safely. He was a born husband and father. I felt the weight. Sleep never came.

So next day on patrol, I asked him how he was doing. Mac stared at me, shook his head. "I think this mess has escalated. Scaring us into shutting up is one thing, getting us killed is another. There's no way those jeep problems were an accident. Then Percy comes in here like a ton of bricks. The guy's a psycho. He's trying to push our buttons. We've got to figure this out. Find a way to make them think we dropped the whole thing. It won't be safe till we do. That's what's bugging me. I know what to do; just don't know how to do it." I agreed with his thinking but had no clue either. Told Mac I would get to Nut when we got back to Quang Tri. We needed help.

Traffic had been slow for weeks, but suddenly got busy. Now the vehicles were moving toward Quang Tri, not away from it. A steady stream of ARVN trucks drove by. Most were carrying dusty soldiers who looked beaten and shell shocked. Just a few weeks ago, these same troops were pounding their chests with confidence. Mac looked at me, "Why are they headed back to Quang Tri?" I was thinking of rats leaving a sinking ship, but shrugged instead. Mac already knew the answer.

We had a wet week, so the roads got worse. The more the trucks struggled, the bigger the ruts. Add steady rain to the equation and trouble followed. Percy was on the road 12 hours a day. He became more brutal as the jams got worse. If he caught an ARVN out of his truck, having a leisurely lunch, he'd get a big grin. He'd ask the driver in a low, calm voice, "So you're gonna take it easy, have a little snack, huh pap-sahn? Not on my watch, motherfucker." Then he'd kicked the driver's food all over the road. If the driver resisted, he'd sweep his legs, drop him to the ground; draw his Colt 45. With the gun in his ear, the driver would get back in the truck and beat feet.

One day, Mac and I were helping an ARVN get his truck out of a monster rut. The driver grinned at me, "Beaucoup fuck up." The guy was maybe 18; like many young Vietnamese, spoke English well. We put wooden planks into the rut, helped the wheels get better traction. Most times it worked after a few adjustments. During the process, I asked the driver how the fight was going in Laos. He pointed at the truck, "Same same road, beaucoup number fuckin' 10." He said it matter-of-factly, like it was inevitable. Charlie was creaming them.

Most days it rained some. I knew the invasion strategy was to close the Ho Chi Minh trail before monsoon season. The wet season in this part of Vietnam was supposed to be a couple months away but had started early. But today was brilliantly clear; our moods soared with the weather. I was on patrol with Quillen. We gabbed about how beautiful it was in Khe Sanh, what a waste this war was. Quillen scrunched up his nose and eyebrows. "Gonna come back one day and do some fishin'. Bring my gal and show her around. Bet they make it a resort er somethin'." I agreed with Quillen, it was wondrously beautiful, a paradise, even with the war.

The radio broke our pleasant thoughts. Percy asked to talk to me. "Got a situation, Frazier. ARVN's found a big cave near the road about 2 clicks from you. Might be a VC outpost. Go check it out and call back with a status. Out." We stopped when we saw the ARVN truck, with a few soldiers milling around. They seemed agitated. This part of road had been difficult to clear. It was a flatter, rocky section near the middle of a steep hill. If you got stuck here, you were fully exposed, good place for an ambush. Quillen said matter-of-factly, "Perfect spot for a tunnel."

He was right. The ARVN's showed us where the tunnel was, seemed anxious to leave. "What's yer hurry, boys?" Quillen asked pleasantly.

The last soldier turned, "Bad place, number 10. We didi maw." Then Quillen asked something interesting.

"How'd ya find this place?" The ARVN looked surprised by the question, "From GI, like you, he say we look. Make sure no VC."

I asked, "What GI?" But the ARVN never turned or answered.

Quillen looked at me, "Strange shit, huh?"

We got to the bottom of the hill; saw a beaten down path. Quillen was leading and suddenly put his hand out, "Stay off the path, try ta walk in the brush. Should play it safe. Best way." We veered off the trail, followed it from about 20 yards away. It was tough going but I liked Quillen's caution, he knew his stuff. After moving about 100 yards back toward the hillside, a clearing popped up. The opening to the tunnel was huge; you could drive a tank inside.

Quillen confirmed my impression. "This'n looks active. Ya see the tracks. Looks new, past couple days, maybe. Let's check er out. Stay behind me." We stayed in the jungle but veered closer to the opening. "Don't see no tire tracks, just some boot prints. Might be one guy, tracks look the same size. Aint been a lotta activity. Maybe it aint recent action, can't be sure." I looked at Quillen.

"Let's get outta here. Call Percy to get a demo patrol in here to check it further." We circled back to the jeep.

I called Percy, heard something I didn't expect. "What do you mean, we should check it out?" Percy was telling me to enter the tunnel to determine if it was active. I couldn't believe it!

"Got a hearin' problem, Frazier? Get your sorry ass in the tunnel and make sure Charlie aint waitin' to light up the troop traffic." I took a deep breath, tried to reason with him. I argued we needed some firepower and support. "Move, Frazier. Ya argue any more, I'm wrtiin' ya up for disobeyin' a direct order. Ever hear of court martial, Frazier? Get yer ass in motion."

I told Quillen what he said. He looked stunned. "That's fuckin' crazy. That aint how its dun. Ya always need backup when ya enter a tunnel. Need a grunt patrol, er demo team." I told him about the court martial threat. "He said he's on his way here and we better be in the tunnel or he'll relieve us of duty; march our asses to lock-up. That's a direct quote." We headed back to the tunnel, talked about how to approach the job.

Fortunately Quillen said, "I'll lead the way. You stay 'bout 50 feet behind me. Play it by ear from there." He stood before the opening, stooped down to study the ground. He was deciding which side of the tunnel to enter. "If it's active, they usually don't mine it. Sometimes, but not most. This side looks clean. Make sure ya crawl where I been. Don't wander." I told him there was no chance I'd move an inch out of his path.

Quillen picked the right side, crawled slowly. He got down low, looked to see if there were trip wires or buried pressure gauges. If he had a doubt, he used a sprig of brush to sweep aside the mound of earth that concerned him. He had gone about 50 feet, so far. I entered the cave, followed Quillen's trail. We went another 50 feet when Quillen said the last thing I wanted to hear. "Think I got somethin'."

I hugged the ground, closed my eyes. After a few minutes, he said, "Just a rat hole. Must be a big fucker, judgin' by the hole." Only then did I realize I'd stopped breathing. I gulped in some fresh air, tried to relax my shoulders. Felt like I'd just scaled Mt Everest. Quillen always carried a flashlight, a habit from his tunnel rat days. That proved to be a valuable routine because we had gotten far enough from the opening that the light was bad. Quillen had stopped; lay motionless.

After a few minutes, I asked what he was doing. "Listenin' and smellin'." The cave was dead still, smelled damp. "Don't think nobodys here. If people been here, ya can smell things. Even when ya piss in a cat hole, stink hangs on. Getting' nothin'. How about you?" I had a good nose, had been sniffing along with Quillen.

"Smells like animals have been here, maybe rats but nothing else. Hope we're right."

Quillen said he'd go a little further; then we'd head back; meet with Percy. We were about 125 feet inside the tunnel when it suddenly split. Quillen shined his flashlight in both directions. "Don't see no foot prints either side. Right looks bigger, they'd use that to live. Gonna go there a little more then scoot back left. He was very careful, was gone for a few minutes as I waited. "Nothin' here," I soon heard.

I watched Quillen crawl out of the right side, suddenly heard him yell, "Run." He was on his feet, in full stride in a second. I leaped up, sprinted toward the entrance. I hit the opening as the explosion thundered. When the noise stopped, I lay on the ground, rolled over to look at my hands and feet. Didn't see any blood. I wondered if my back was hit. Ran my hands over my shoulders and lower back. No blood. Felt my face, neck and head. Seemed like I was okay. Ears hurt some.

Quillen? Dust was belching from the cave entrance. I got my Colt 45 ready, went inside. There was a pungent smell in the air. Gunpowder? I rubbed the dust from my eyes, stayed low. After about 20 feet, I heard, "That you, Frazier?"

I wanted to shout but said softly, "I'm coming for you. You okay?"

Quillen coughed, "Think my legs hit. Not too bad. Can't walk on it." I got to Quillen, still couldn't see much, too dusty. I thought about carrying him, but decided I better drag him, not jostle the leg too much.

Quillen's leg was shredded with shrapnel. It wasn't bleeding too badly, but I used my t-shirt as a tourniquet, just in case. "Think you can handle it if I carry you back to the jeep?"

He smiled, 'Aint stayin' here. Let's didi maw." As I carried him through the bush, Quillen said, "Think it were a US weapon. Heard they was testin' motion devices. Remember they said in trainin' ya see a red light if it's triggered. Got seconds after that. Was lucky the mine was blocked by the turn there or I'd a been in a world a hurt. Charlie aint got them weapons. Musta stole em."

I got to the jeep, called camp. Was told Percy was on his way to us. Seconds later, Percy drives up. When he spotted us he looked surprised. He stood still, seemed to assess the situation. Snapping out of it, he stormed up, "Fuck happened here? Quillen okay?"

I filled him in, Quillen added before I could stop him, "Think it was a US weapon. Thought they was just in testing. Damndest thing Charlie gettin' em."

Percy didn't respond, thought for a bit. "Take Quillen back, Frazier, get him to the airstrip. They got medics there; maybe have to evac him to Quang Tri. I'll check the tunnel. See if I can find what Quillen's talkin' about. Git goin." Percy took off toward the tunnel. He never asked me for directions.

I drove to the airstrip, stayed with Quillen as the medics attended him. His leg was torn up pretty bad. "It's not life threatening. But enough to get you a ticket back to The World," was how the doc diagnosed the situation. I helped load Quillen into the chopper. "Thanks fer helpin' me, Frazier. Ya got yer shit together. 'Preciate it." I watched the chopper leave Khe Sanh, thought how lucky I was to have been with Rueben Quillen. I shuddered as I thought about being in that tunnel without his skill.

I was surprised to see Lt Clep in camp when I returned from the airstrip. As I was walking over to find out why he was here, Percy came up to me abruptly. I had made up my mind to restrain my anger, act like nothing happened. There was no value in letting him suspect I was wise to him. Percy blathered out just what I expected. "No sign a

195

secret weapons in that tunnel. Just yer basic mine. Think Quillen was in shock or somethin'. He's a dumb ass anyway, ya know?"

Seeing the smug look on his face, listening to him malign a kid that just about got killed set me off. I stepped right into his face, yelled, "What I know is you should never have sent us in that tunnel! What I know is that a demo team should have been called in! What I know is you almost got us killed! What I know is that was about as stupid a move as it gets! What I know is I won't be following any more of your God damned orders. That's what I know!"

Although I had studied his move, I was too slow. Percy leaned in, lashed out his right foot. Too late, I veered right but the boot glanced off my shin and dropped me to the ground. Percy kicked me in the hip, but I remembered years of wrestling with Nut, rolled into his legs. I grabbed his left leg, which knocked him off balance. Percy was fast but was surprised when I grabbed his legs. I curled up, held tight. He karate chopped at my back a few times before Mac and Lt Clep pulled us apart. Percy was fit to be tied, bellowed about disrespecting a senior NCO, putting me in jail. I regained my cool, told Lt Clep that he better get all the facts before he sided with Percy. When Percy started railing again, Lt Clep surprised me with a piercing stare before saying firmly, "Back down, Sgt Price, that's an order!" I could tell Percy was shocked by the command.

I rattled off what had happened, shockingly watched Percy calm down. It was like a switch had gone off inside him; he lost power. His face was drained of tension. Weirdest thing I ever saw. Suddenly he was saying, "Don't blame Frazier for getttin' upset. Almost lost it down there. Woulda done the same thing. Glad youse allright and Quillen aint too bad. Check it out." And then Percy walked off, like he was without a care in the world, got in his jeep and left..

Before I got a word out, Lt Clep told us why he was here. "We're leaving Khe Sanh asap. The ARVN's are in retreat. They hit a shit storm from the NVA. We've got to run convoys back to Quang Tri before this place's a world of hurt. We probably got a days lead at most. We've got to get out of here before 50,000 ARVN's and their equipment gum up the roads too bad. Frazier, you and McCarthy are going to take the lead. I'll take the middle; Clardy and Percy will ride rear. Be prepared to get started tomorrow after sunrise. Start cleaning up your gear. Get everything packed. Questions?"

My left leg was sore as hell but nothing was broken. My hip hurt but not too bad. I was lucky. Most people left an encounter with Percy with broken bones. When Clep left, I told Mac about the tunnel, he got quiet. "So you think he was trying to kill you?" I told him I didn't know but it seemed too coincidental.

"Why would he ask us to enter the tunnel? Far as he knew, we had no training. He didn't know Quillen was a tunnel rat. I asked Quillen, said he never told anybody but me. Doesn't make any sense."

Mac then said something I hadn't considered. "Clep just said the ARVN's are in retreat. Maybe Percy was making sure they didn't get ambushed. All the grunt units are providing support, might not have any demo teams here. Maybe that was the right call. Maybe Quillen was wrong about the new type of mine. It might have been a reflection from the flashlight." For the first time in a few hours, I relaxed.

"That's what I like about you Mac, you always find a way to make me seem like a paranoid knucklehead. Are my boys at the courts back home giving you coaching?" I started to calm down.

CONVOY

I had never been in the front of a convoy. Lt Clep told me to man the Thompson, while Mac drove. As I had heard before, "You got your shit together, Frazier, I need a calm hand on the Thompson. Don't shoot unless you're sure. Once you start shooting, the whole convoy's going to panic." While he blathered on, I thought about the Army fixation with terminology related to the anal passage. A bad soldier has his head up his ass. A weak soldier's shit is loose.

All this ran through my mind, but I answered Clep, "Glad you're confident in my fecal tightness, Sir." Mac chuckled but Clep just shook his head. Maybe he was reevaluating my packing.

I quickly discovered that riding upfront was the worst spot. You had to drive 10 mph to make certain you didn't get gaps in the convoy. The road was lousy; the rain had taken its toll. Mac was busy avoiding the potholes while I scanned the countryside. For much of the road, there was a steep drop to the right. But on the left, the rain forest loomed. There was a Cobra gunship overhead, but we felt alone at the front of this huge caravan. We knew the Cobra would take over after the first shots. But the first shots would be at Mac and me. Stop us the whole convoy stops. Easy pickings.

For the first few hours, I fixated on the jungle to the left. It suddenly occurred to me that the lower side of the road might be more dangerous. If I were attacking us, I'd find a spot that gave a clear look at our convoy and mortar the front and the back simultaneously. Maybe I'd have a small strike force from above, one that could hit us and move quickly. That would draw our attention away from the dangerous valley and perhaps confuse the Cobra enough

198

to allow escape. Those pleasant thoughts percolated as I studied the terrain.

There was so much noise from the convoy, that I got no feedback from the jungle. From my tiger incident, I knew the birds and animals would be quiet if predators were about. Mac was doing a great job driving, missed the ruts, kept a steady pace. I was happy to be returning to Quang Tri. Our buddy Fleming could contact Nut; help us figure a way out of this mess. I was relieved to see we were gradually leaving the highlands; it would be easy once we hit flat ground.

I was dead wrong about the attack. The snipers were scattered above us and picked off a half dozen soldiers at the center before anyone knew what happened. The convoy sounds masked the noise, prevented the Cobra from seeing the action. I learned later that Lt Clep saw a truck veer into the jungle, realized the driver was shot. He radioed the gunship; I watched it hover, waiting for a target. When the sniper shot, the Cobra obliterated that area. Rather than wait for more shots, the death machine went along the ridge, wiped out all terrain above the convoy.

It was over in minutes. We were trained to keep moving during an ambush but we had slowed to a stop, mesmerized by the devastation. But Clep radioed Mac, told him to gun it. "Get the hell outta here!" were the orders. Not taking any chances, the Cobra fired random shots into the jungle that followed the road ahead of us. I watched spellbound as the trees and bush were torn to shreds. We reached flat ground in 20 minutes, huddled with the rest of the convoy to assess damage.

I realized I'd been wrong about Clep. He looked, sometimes acted like a doofus, but he stepped up big during the attack. No hesitation, he acted. Perhaps he had tighter stool packing than I thought. It took 15 minutes before all the trucks and jeeps were accounted for. Lt Clep had called for a chopper to evac the dead and wounded soldiers. Feeling both sick and angry, I watched as two were loaded into body bags and four flown back for treatment. I remember thinking: We were leaving Khe Sanh, why did Charlie screw with us?

Callahan and Fleming were waiting for us when we pulled into the company area around midday. The taciturn Callahan was visibly glad we returned safely. Even the surly Fleming was happy to see us. When I told him to give me a hug, he reverted to form, "Fucking homo." That cracked me up.

"That's my boy, Fleming, don't get all mushy on me." But Callahan came up, hugged us intently. The relief was on his face.

I told them we needed to talk later; I had avoided giving Callahan too much detail about the ordnance thefts but he needed to know. If they were trying to kill us, Callahan might also have a target on his back. Ben and Percy knew he was our friend, would assume we had him in the loop. Fleming pressed me but I shook my head, "Too many ears, let's wait till its dark." While Fleming was gabbing, my thoughts had raced. During the trek from Khe Sahn, I relived the jeep problems and tunnel incidents. I was back to trusting my instinct. Percy and Ben tried to kill us. No question about it.

With that premise whirling around my mind, I changed topics, "What's new around here?" Fleming floored me with the reply.

"I guess you heard Sgt Wilson went AWOL?"

Callahan added, "He fell in love with some Vietnamese girl, rumor is he ran off with her. We haven't seen him for a week. Crazy." I thought about the beautiful Frances at the Steam and Cream. I remembered she said they were going to be married one day.

Fleming added, "He'd been acting weird, seemed on edge. That surprised me though; it's got to be dangerous living in the village."

As Mac and I got settled, I mentioned my surprise at Wilson going AWOL. He agreed, "It makes no sense, he could see her every day. Why split?" I liked Wilson; he'd been good to us. When I mentioned what he'd said to me before I got on the chopper to Khe Sanh, Mac exhaled deeply. He looked at me seriously, "Do you think he knew Ben and Percy were after you? Was trying to warn you? Maybe he was involved in the ring but drew the line when it came to killing his own guys?" I nodded at my astute friend, that's exactly what I thought.

When I walked in the Steam and Cream that afternoon, I didn't expect to see Frances, but there she was. I got a big smile but she turned serious. "You hear Len disappear? No hear in week. Beaucoup worry, Frazier-sahn." I asked about the AWOL theory, Sgt Wilson running off with her. Her look told me all I needed. There was no way Frances was lying; she looked terrified. I told her I would check around, drop by every day to let her know what I found. As I turned, Frances said, "Len would never leave me." I saw them together, recalled the affection. He wouldn't walk away from Frances unless he had no choice. Was he worried about getting caught for treason? Split?

Callahan was shaken when we filled him in on our ordnance thinking. "You really think they're stealing weapons and selling them to Charlie? I know they're mean guys but selling weapons to use against their own people? There's got to be another explanation. I just can't believe that." No matter what we said, Callahan didn't budge. He kept insisting we were misreading the circumstances. I wished he was right, but I didn't think so.

I looked him square in the eyes, "Joe, even if you don't believe us, I want you to act like its true. Keep your eyes open, don't let them put you in a dangerous spot. What happened to me at Khe Sanh wasn't an accident. Someone wants me dead. And after me, I think they'll go after you guys. We need to close ranks, watch each others back." I could see Mac wanted to smack Callahan on the head, say "Wake up!" He didn't have my history with Callahan; I didn't want his idealism to get him killed.

Tom Faustman

Moving South

Our world got turned upside down next morning at assembly. Colonel Mullen addressed us, "We're shutting Quang Tri down ASAP. The base has become too difficult to defend. With the retreat from Khe Sanh, the ARVN's have left this area with a huge target on it. Charlie wants it back; it's become the prime objective. The ARVN's aren't willing to deploy the troops and the Army isn't willing to leave us hanging out to dry. Get your gear packed, we'll be leaving tomorrow after sunup."

I don't know why but I was elated. Quang Tri had become too dangerous for reasons other than Charlie. We hadn't been given any detail of our next assignment. The only thing we heard was "south." That sounded good to me. I remembered looking at that map in Ben Hoi, that first day in country. South was good. As we were packing that last night, I thought about Nut, Sgt Wilson, Frances, and the little girls I'd befriended on the CPO gate. Fleming would help me get in touch with Nut, but the others?

I never did get to say goodbye to the beautiful little girls. I never had the chance to see Frances. She would know soon that the base was being evacuated. I hoped she understood that I had no way to visit her. In Nam, you developed strong bonds with people quickly. Whether it happened from the constant sense of danger, I'm not sure. You just clicked with certain people, they became important. As I drove away from Quang Tri, I had a sense of dread. Nothing good awaited Sgt Wilson, Frances, or my sweet little girls.

The rumor was we were headed for Da Nang. Based on what I heard, being stationed in Da Nang was the best it got. It was a huge base with perhaps the best airport in Nam. Most of the bombing missions in the north were launched from there. During a stop on the drive, Clardy told us he went to Da Nang on leave, raved about the beautiful beaches, movie theatres, and celebrity tours. "Got ta see Pasty Cline singin'. That ole gal can plain bring it. Had a boner fer a week after."

I raised my hands, "Clardy, you had a nice image going with your story till the boner part. You just killed it for me. Bad, bad image there." We continued the relentless convoy south.

Chu Lai

It turned out our pleasant thoughts of Da Nang didn't matter. We drove past the turn off for Da Nang, kept heading south on QL-1. After a couple hours, we pulled into the Chu Lai base, looked at the paved roads, quickly realized this was a big step up. The south part of the base was a massive airstrip. There were numerous hangars scattered about, none close to each other. Hangars were prime targets; they housed the bombers, choppers and other ships of destruction. The north part of base was a steep, rocky peninsula that jutted out into the South China Sea.

As I neared the hill approaching the north base, I looked at the gorgeous aquamarine colors of the South China Sea, yelled to Mac, "Let's go swimming after dinner?"

He grinned at me, "Make sure you bring the Coppertone, I'd hate to get my milky skin burned." Then, as we climbed the hill, we spotted the swanky USO club nestled on the beach. You could see lifeguard stands, sandy beaches. Mac smiled, "I thought we were joking; it looks like we really can hit the surf. Wow!"

Our MP campsite was enormous. Chu Lai was the American Division Headquarters; we would be merged into their MP unit. Lt Clep had come with us but Ben and Percy were to depart Quang Tri a day or so after us. "I hope they get stationed elsewhere," Mac said. "Maybe we can serve our last few months without looking over our shoulder." I walked over, asked Clep when they'd get here.

"I'm not sure about them. Colonel Mullen's got to work out who's going to run this operation. He's got seniority but American wants their guy. Burton and Price'll probably stay with him if he runs this place. We have to see who wins."

Clep told us to hang loose, he'd figure out where we'd bunk. We wandered around, were pleased to see a beautiful basketball court set on a flat part of the camp. Much of the MP area was hilly, with hootches built side by side, like row homes in South Philly. I noticed ruts in the ground outside most of the buildings. Mac saw me staring at the rutted pathway. "What're you looking at?"

I squinted, "Looks like they got a lot of rain. See how the water run-off dug out the dirt? We ought to find a place on higher ground, might be messy here when monsoon hits."

Mac shook his head, quipped, "So now you're a weatherman and geologist?"

Lt Clep came over shortly, told us to bunk in any open hootch. "I'll be stationed here with you guys. Get set up, then come into the MP station and meet the new desk sergeant. I fought off the urge to ask about Sgt Wilson, would save that for later. After we found a place to dump our gear temporarily, we wandered to the MP station. We introduced ourselves to Sgt John Stroh, our new leader. Stroh was a big guy with straight brown hair, thick glasses. He wasn't handsome but had a nice face, masculine in a way the ladies would like. I soon learned he loved to talk, told stories "of home." No matter what you asked, he'd respond, "Back home, we did…." You never got away from Sgt Stroh without a long tale of life in Missouri. There was never a quick conversation. Despite the longwindedness, everybody liked Sgt Stroh.

Besides the beautiful setting on the South China Sea, Chu Lai was modern and clean. Quang Tri was incredibly primitive by comparison. There were even shrubs planted here and there. Sgt Stroh told us they wanted things "to be cheery, just like home." I made a mental note to read the street carefully. Was this place really this nice? Where were the dangerous spots? I mentioned my thinking to Mac; he smiled, "You never let up, do you?" I hoped he was right. It might look nice, but it was Vietnam.

Sgt Stroh told us that Chu Lai was built to provide relief for the busy Da Nang Air field. "We gits all the traffic here. Biggin's and littlins'. See a lotta F4 Phantoms flyin' around. Charlie noticed we done got big. Fusses with us. Most of the stuffs at night, so we spends the days makin' sure Charlie don't get too close. When ya patrol the airfields, keep yer eyes open fer mortars. If ya patrol the roads, make sure the papa-sanhs er out in the fields workin'. Ya see papa-sahns hangin' in the village; we might got us a VC. I'll show ya around tomorrow." As Sgt Stroh talked, I pictured Andy Griffith telling us how to maneuver around Mayberry.

We spent the whole next day exploring the base with Sgt Stroh. As we drove around the airfields, I noticed Cobra gun ships circling. Sgt Stroh noticed me watching. "Lettin' Charlie know he's gonna pay if he fusses. The grunts patrol the hills; call in the big bird if they spot somethin'. Been quiet lately." During the trip, I saw that Chu Lai was built in a flat valley bordering the South China Sea. Not too far away were low mountains, reminded me some of Khe Sanh. Lots of places to hide. Lots of tunnels to run to when the gunship came after them. That made me think of Quillen; hoped he was okay. His skill had saved my life.

There was a large naval docking area, full of big ships at the north end of Chu Lai. Stroh told us, "Gotta guard the coastline ta keep Charlie from hittin' us from sea. Don't take much ta float a sampan out there an launch some rockets." I didn't know anything about the Navy, but I could see these were serious ships. We drove near the water's edge. I saw at least 3 ships cruising within sight, big guns sticking out, ready to pummel anyone who screwed with us. There were tons of Vietnamese sampans fishing the water off the base. Stroh concluded his briefing, "Most troubles at night." To myself: Same pattern as Quang Tri and Khe Sahn.

Next day we patrolled the highway QL-1 outside the base. Sgt Stroh was driving, Lt Clep sat beside him. We learned that the CID headquarters wasn't far from the main entrance to the base. Clep told us that Colonel Mullen, Percy, and Ben were domiciled there till the "who's in charge" issue was resolved. Fleming was also there, so I made a note to drop by when I had a chance. Clep nodded when I said, "Hope Mullen forgets to bring Ben and Percy with him." Then he added, "I don't know what the Colonel sees in them, they seem like bad news to me." Lt Clep was growing in my eyes.

Going south on QL-1, there were endless pristine fields. Rice paddies and gardens lined the highway, dirt roads led to quaint villages. The people worked all day tending their crops. Kids sat on water buffaloes that grazed peacefully. The pleasant scene was broken as we came to a fortified area, teeming with tanks and heavily bunkered large guns. I never saw such enormous weapons. Stroh pointed, "Those bad boys back up the Cobras and Phantoms. If Charlie thinks he's gonna waltz up ta Chu Lai, he's gonna have his balls rearranged." He told us this was our last stop on the route south.

North of Chu Lai was quite different. There were series of small islands off the tip of the base. Ky Xuan was the largest island and had a bridge connecting to the mainland. It was heavily fortified, no easy way for Charlie to set up a camp there to harass Chu Lai. We were told to patrol the island, watch for anything "funny." I looked at Sgt Stroh, "You mean like a team of little yellow guys wearing can't-see-me clothes carrying bazookas?"

Stroh nodded seriously, "Yea, stuff like that." Lt Clep chuckled, shook his head in mild amusement.

When we returned, Mac and I settled into a hootch, smack in the middle of the pack, on high ground. "We back up to another hootch, so no access that way. Plus, at night, it will be hard for anybody to find us. If someone wants to screw with us, lots of people around as witness. Know what I mean?"

Mac normally would have jabbed at my paranoia but simply said, "I'm in." We padlocked the hootch when we left on patrol. At night, we locked ourselves up tight. I was a light sleeper, could hear anyone walking outside. This noise sensitivity freaked Mac at first but now he liked my bat ears. We settled into a routine of heightened awareness.

The first week was peaceful. Stroh paired Mac and me with guys experienced with Chu Lai. My partner was Spec 4 Lou Simpson. Lou was 33, explained he would retire from the Army at 38. "Then I'm gonna join the Post Office and retire at 58. Live off both pensions and fish." I found that Lou was fairly bright and funny, he just had no ambition; didn't want promotions or accolades. Do the time, get out; collect the pay. He spent all his time reading about the best place to retire that offered fresh and saltwater fishing. Plus cheap beer.

Lou was an expert on Chu Lai. From the MP site, it took 20 minutes driving flat-out to reach the end of the lengthy airstrip. I asked Lou how far it was. He had an interesting reply. "Don't know in miles but I can smoke 3 cigarettes if I don't gun it." Today I was driving, Lou told me to follow the road to a patch of scrubby trees. When we got into the shade, he pulls out a satchel, fiddles inside, pops open a beer. "Want a brewski, Frazier?"

It was 7 am, so I told him, "I normally wait till 8 am before my first beer." He shrugged, then belched like a gorilla.

He smiled at me, "Mama!"

As we sat at the end of the base, I was surprised by the scarceness of bunkers surrounding the field. They had cleared the area of all brush, built tall cyclone fences topped with concertina wires, but that was it When I asked Lou who was supposed to be guarding the airfield, he said, "Whattaya think we're doin? We're supposed to look for any breaks in the fences and investigate. At night, the bunkers use the new breed of night vision binoculars to watch the fence. If they see anything, they shine those monster spotlights on them. But not much happens around here."

Suddenly, the radio popped, "All units respond, action in the wire near Armor Division. Please advise your 10-14." I grabbed the mike but got nothing but crackle as I tried to answer.

Lou took another slug of his beer, said, "No use responding. There's not good reception down here. It's why I like hanging here. No use being a hero, probably a false alarm; happens all the time." Then he belched. I kept trying to respond but Lou was right, I couldn't reach Sgt Stroh.

When I started the engine, Lou asked what I was doing. "Show me how to get to the Armor Division, beer breaks over."

Lou was right. When I got in range, I radioed Stroh, told him we were 10-11, had radio trouble. "Yer with Simpson, right? He has lots of trouble." Lou Simpson shrugged at the radio in response. Stroh added, "False alarm, Frazier, proceed on patrol. Out." Our next stop was the USO club. We drove into a paved parking area, lined with palm trees and blooming hibiscus bushes. The club was painted gray, had fringes of blue to make it seem beachy, like an old Victorian in Cape May. It worked on me; it was very appealing. Lou said he'd show me around, so we parked, headed inside.

The first thing I noticed was the women- real American females. I flashed my best smile, said hello. They waved back, but seemed surprised by my gestures, like I'd caught them off guard. Lou advised, "Navy and Air Force got some nice gals. Don't get any ideas; they only like the officers. I tried before, waste of time. It's like I got the plague or something." I thought silently: Bet Lou gets that response in the states. Offering a date beer for breakfast wouldn't open many doors.

Everything was free, so I got a Coke and potato chips. We moseyed to the beach area, blue umbrellas and lounge chairs dotted the white sand. I noticed a few guys wading on the edge, no higher than their knees. It was hot as hell so I wondered aloud why no one was swimming. "Sharks," was the answer I never expected. "They got shark nets out there but every once in awhile, one of the big ones busts through."

He wasn't kidding; I noticed the sign "Shark nets- swim at your own risk!" I learned the sharks were natural protection against VC divers swimming in to mine the dock area. "Every once in awhile, some cowboys swim past the nets, try to prove how tough they are. It isn't good duty when you gotta pull the mangled bodies out. The worst I've seen is 4 guys got chewed up, only 1 died. We couldn't swim for days. Them sharks kept smelling the blood." Len told me this matter-of-factly, like it was part of his daily routine. I looked at the inviting, incredibly green water. Were there any safe places in South Vietnam?

We left USO, headed to the north side of Chu Lai, which was dominated by the Navy. All the buildings and accommodations were plush, the nicest I'd seen in Nam. The Navy had the best of the best. Lou told me we should stop at the Navy mess for lunch, "Best in Chu Lai," was all he said. Lou told me the MP's could eat wherever they wanted. "They give you the snake eye but nothing they can do about it. We got hand." He was right about the chow. I had the finest meal since I'd been to Nam, real roast beef, baked potatoes, carrots, green beans and thick gravy.

Washed it down with moist corn bread and ice-cold chocolate milk. That became my regular lunch stop when I had base patrol. Lou had shown me one thing worthwhile.

"I'm going to show you the beach gate, Frazier. That's where the whores come in. You got to have pull to get that gate duty. MP's make a fortune there, charge whores without ID's big bucks. You can make something from the regulars, too, mostly getting souvenired watches and such." I thought silently: Just like Quang Tri. We drove near the gate; Lou introduced me to the MP's. I was surprised by their looks: older, grizzled and beat-up, like they smoked and drank hard. There were also Vietnamese MP's, called QC's, in an adjoining gate. I asked Lou what they did. "Same shit as us. Everyone wants a cut, don't you know?"

I looked at the surrounding area; saw a pathway leading to the water. Most people arrived by sampans, which they docked while they did business on base. The water was teeming with boats. Most had older people sitting in them, tending to the craft while the younger Vietnamese did commerce. Out of the corner of my eye, I saw someone approaching. I felt a smack on my helmet, turned to see an annoyed Percy. "What the fuck you doin' here? This is my post. Don't need no horny white breads pokin' around. Get the fuck outta here."

I hadn't seen Percy since our tussle. He had left Quang Tri after most of us. It had been a peaceful week without him. Seeing the malignant bastard brought me back to full alert. "Nice to see you, too, Sgt Price." Percy didn't smile. I put the jeep in gear, waved goodbye. As we got some distance, Lou asked about Percy. "He wasn't kidding around, Lou. He's a bad guy. Stay away from him. Rumor was he ran the whores on Quang Tri. Looks as if he's moving into business here. Based on what I see at that gate, he's going to be busy as hell."

Mac topped my Percy episode that night. "I ran into him and Ben at the main gate, going out for village patrol. I never saw him; he came up, surprised me. Hit me hard on the arm, told me, 'I aint fergot ya put yer hands on me, red head. When you was helpin' Frazier in Khe Sahn. Yer gonna hear from me when ya don't suspect. Just like that, yer gonna turn an find me there. Then we'll have some fun'. He walked off and jumped into a jeep with Ben, left the base, headed north. I have to tell you he scared me. I don't think he's screwing with me. He likes to frighten people, but I think he's serious, he's coming after me."

I agreed on that conclusion. "Best to avoid him, hope he doesn't get assigned back here. Maybe he'll get too busy with his new business." And then I added, "Maybe we ought to mention this to Clep. He isn't the pushover I thought; he really put Percy in his place back in Khe Sanh. So, if we got Clep to tell him to back off, we might get by. What do you think?"

Mac thought before answering. "I think we should go to Mullen. If both of us tell him Percy's threatening us, he's got to do something. At least Percy would know he'd get fingered if he got too rough."

That was the problem I'd been wrestling with. Mullen seemed to like Mac and me but he'd worked with Percy and Ben for a lot longer. He knew what they were like but still tolerated them. He probably viewed them as the devils he knew. If we ratted on them, why would he suddenly side with us? I remembered that Nut told me Percy was working undercover for his special intelligence outfit. Mullen had to know that. Was Percy just acting like a lunatic to keep his cover? Did that mean that Ben might also be helping Percy? Mac heard me out, concluded, "He's one great actor if he's playing crazy." But Mac agreed to bypass Mullen for now, that I would approach Clep when the moment was right.

After chow that night, we drove to the CID location, found the irascible Fleming. "It's nice of you homos to slum it and pay me a visit. I've been going crazy since I got here. This place's worse than Quang Tri. The good news is they're putting Colonel Mullen in charge of CID on this base. Americal still wanted their guy to run the MP's. First time they've split control. Most Provost Marshals run both. From what I hear, that's like the fox guarding the henhouse. Balance of power is what they taught in law classes. I guess the Army has another view."

I hoped that meant Ben and Percy would become part of CID. I didn't wish Fleming bad luck, I just knew he wasn't on their radar screen, would leave him alone. I told Fleming we would be discreet when we visited, not get him on their shit list. "Don't worry, Frazier, I'll pretend I don't like you, won't be too hard a part for me. You can be a world-class jackass." Mac chuckled, so Fleming added, "Don't get cocky, McCarthy. You got yourself a major dose of horse's ass, too." Then we all laughed.

When I asked Fleming to get in touch with Nut, I got bad news. "I talked to him the other day, said he's got to stay in Quang Tri for awhile. It's been pretty hot there since we left." The news got worse. "He had a setback checking the records. Ben's truck got hit coming here, had all our records from Quang Tri; had to abandon the vehicle. We went back with some firepower but lost all our paperwork, gooks ransacked the truck." I waited for Fleming to mention the obvious. When I got nothing,

"Sounds like covering your tracks to me. I'll bet Ben and Percy were the only witnesses to this attack." Mac had gotten to the same conclusion but Fleming look shocked.

"God damn."

I remained on patrol with Lou Simpson. "Maybe you'll be a good influence on him," Sgt Stroh told me. "He's a sorry sack a cow pies. Laziest sumbitch I ever met." Stroh was right; Lou wasn't dumb, just Olympic gold lazy. As I drove with him, he told me he'd been engaged for 8 years. "Every time we go to get married, I get cleaned out in a card game, gotta postpone." When I asked why he played cards, risked losing his wedding money, he had a priceless answer. "I can't afford to get married unless I make a killing in poker. Between my beer and Jim Beam, each paycheck gets pretty cleaned out. I just need some luck is all." I tried to picture the girl who would marry Lou but that made my head hurt.

Lou was thrilled we had village patrol. "Stroh must like you. He's never let me out here before. Most guys gotta pay him off to get this duty." That made me worry, was Stroh on the take too? I asked Lou why he wanted village duty. "Total freedom is all. We can zoom up and down the road, eat gook food, drink gook beer and such. Maybe get some poontang if we're lucky." I guessed Stroh figured I wouldn't abuse the villagers was why I was out here. He was correct, these people had it rough enough; I would treat them right.

Mac was on patrol with Clardy that week. "Percy paid him a visit, too. Scared the hell out of him. He put a 45 pistol up near his head and shot into the air. Clardy almost shit his pants. He can't figure out what he did to piss off Percy." I knew it was as simple as leaking that Ben ran the stolen vehicle ring and Percy the whores. It wouldn't do Clardy any good to know what was going on, might put him in more danger.

"Nothing we can do for him," Mac agreed. "Just steer clear of the maniac."

While on base patrol one day, I asked Lou about the ammo dump. "It's down at the end of the airfield, towards the USO club. Kinda hard to find, they got it tucked away off the road." He was right; I had passed by it every day, never noticed it. We drove up closer, got stopped by the MP's, a couple guys Lou knew. They let us in to look around.

"Ever have any problems here? Like sappers getting in, trying to blow it up?"

Lou laughed, "Man, you're paranoid. There's no way they get past all that security. Nothing like that happened since I've been here."

He was right; the dump was disguised to look like part of the hill that rose toward the north end of the base. Complete with palm trees and sand dunes. If you drove by it you wouldn't look twice, perfectly harmless. Even the MP gate was inconspicuous. There were 2 other layers of security outside the dump. Again, they blended in with the surroundings. If Percy and Ben tried to run a scam here, it would be much harder than Quang Tri. Those two crooks would be out of their league in Chu Lai. Mac would be happy with my findings.

Lou and I continued on village patrol, passed the village of Ly Tin, soon got about 10 miles north of base. "Wanna do some shooting?" Lou said over the jeep noise. He pointed at his satchel. "I got a 100 rounds of ammo. Aint shot for awhile, need some practice." Normally, I'd say no, but it been ages since I shot my weapons, needed practice myself. We veered off the road, got out of the jeep, looked around to make certain the area was deserted. Lou even brought some empty cans of beer for targets. For the next hour, we shot the cans into smithereens. Primitive as hell, but I loved it. All I could do was laugh when Lou reached for another sack, pulled out a beer and asked, "Want a brewski?"

On our way back, we got a radio call from Stroh to investigate a disturbance in Khuong Hiep, a little village near the base. There was a gang of locals staring into a tree. We smelled it before we saw anything. The putrid odor was overpowering. A naked, mutilated body, hung by the hands in a pose of humiliation. The crowd seemed nervous but not afraid. The battered body was Vietnamese, I couldn't tell anything else. I called Stroh and told him what we found. He told us to keep our distance; he would send a detail to remove the body. A boy-sahn walked over, pointed at the corpse, "VC see number 10 to fuck with Chu Lai."

LT CLEP

After patrol, I was shooting hoops, spotted Lt Clep walking toward me. No one was around. "Want to play 21?" he asked. To my surprise, he was a good shooter.

"Why didn't you play for the Quang Tri team?"

He smiled, "It would have blown my cover. You guys all thought I was a douche bag, right? Once you saw I could play, things might have changed." And then he knocked the air out of me. "Your buddy, Captain O'Hanlon said to say hello. He told me to keep an eye on you. He says you have a habit of getting your nose dirty." I stood with my eyes wide.

Lt Clep was a special intelligence operative assigned to find who was stealing ordnance and selling it to the enemy. "I didn't want to get you exposed, but you took care of that yourself. Captain O'Hanlon says you'd make a good agent for our outfit, that you're a natural." All I could do was shake my head.

"First of all, your Captain O'Hanlon has been known as Nut to me since I was 10. That name might give you a clue to his judgment of character. Secondly, despite my gift for mayhem, I don't want to do this for a living; I get into enough trouble by accident."

Clep looked amused but said nothing else about recruitment. He asked me to fill him in on all my suspicions. He seemed surprised by my ammo dump theory, but shook his head after a few seconds. "Damned if I don't think you're right. I can see Ben arranging that. He plays it like a good ol boy, but he went to Vanderbilt, majored in Economics. He got high marks; he's real intelligent. Worked for a big-time bank before he got in the Army. I don't think Percy's involved, though. I know he's working for our drug unit, trying to flush out the heroin pipeline. I'm not sure if his crazy is an act or it's

218

how he really is. He has a good rep for getting things done." He stayed quiet for a few seconds, "But Percy's a lot smarter than he appears. He aced his GED marks in the Army. They gave him an IQ test because of his high marks, got a 122. A very bright guy." He shook his head, "His file also mentioned 'a violent temper that made him unfit for Officer Candidate School'."

I smiled at Clep, "That's an understatement, Percy's flat-out crazy, it isn't an act."

When I told him about my episode in Khe Sanh, he hesitated. "I asked Percy about that, said he had to make certain that wasn't a live tunnel. With 50,000 ARVN's retreating, he couldn't take a chance of an ambush, needed to act fast. He says you're a hothead."

I laughed, "He might be right about that but I'm playing it like he might be involved. Can't hurt. I'll say it again, he's not faking that violence, Lieutenant, he's really a psycho."

Clep nodded, "That's fine with me, by the way, Percy doesn't know I'm a plant. Most of the special intelligence outfits operate anonymously, don't interact much. Captain O'Hanlon, er Nut as you call him, gave me the information about Percy. O'Hanlon still thinks he's not involved, just playing it tough to maintain the undercover role. So, what I'm saying about Percy is he thinks I'm just a regular MP. He tolerates me; thinks I'm just another worthless officer. So, don't blow my cover."

I asked what he thought about Colonel Mullen. "He's the first place we checked. Mullen's record is squeaky clean, a lifer. He's a decorated hero, Purple Hearts, the whole show. He's got a stellar arrest record as a Provost Marshall, considered one of the best. He'll probably get promoted to General before the year's over. Plus he lives in a simple house outside of Augusta, Georgia. He loves golf. He just wants to retire when his time is up and hit that silly ball. There's no signs of secret bank accounts, girlfriends, or changes in lifestyle. He's been married to the same woman for 25 years, just a regular guy. By the way, he knows I'm in special intelligence, but no one else does. I'm not telling him I'm confiding in you, so keep it to yourself. I don't want him treating you differently, someone might notice." That made a lot of sense.

I told him McCarthy and Fleming should know about him. He didn't like it at first but soon agreed we needed more eyes. "Meet here same time tomorrow. Pretend we're playing hoops. We'll talk strategy after we play. " We continued to shoot for awhile, completed the game of 21. He asked me a few questions about Nut, seemed to enjoy the story of him climbing the school flagpole during recess in 6th grade.

"The flag was stuck and Nut didn't like that. Thought it was disrespectful. You should have seen the nuns when they saw him 40 feet in the air. I can still picture their faces, almost had a cow. Still makes me laugh." Clep was chuckling as he wandered off.

I rounded up Mac, told him about Clep. I could see Mac tense up as I blathered. He was quiet as we drove to visit Fleming. I wanted to fill them in before we met with Clep, get our own thoughts together. Fleming asked if we should include Callahan but agreed that wouldn't work. "He's got no poker face," was how Mac saw it. "Plus he still wouldn't believe they were capable of treason. Callahan's too gullible. He can't see that some people are just rotten." I felt bad leaving him in the dark but also thought that might protect him. We were about to up the ante, jump fully into the boiling pot.

We met with Clep after patrol, played hoops before we talked. As we rested, Clep filled us in on his plan. "I'll see to it that one of us is near the ammo dump each day. I've got cameras with telescopic lenses. If you see Ben in there, take pictures. I want to see who he's talking to, see if it's the same guy each time. We need to see if he's got an inside contact already. He'd need that to steal the ordnance and fake the sapper attack to cover his tracks. If we're lucky, we'll catch them stealing the explosives. We need pictures as proof. I've got an ARVN contact who's pretending to be a buyer. He's starting to ask around. Maybe we'll get proof both ways. Other ideas?"

I acted as spokesman. "Lt Clep, we think you're wrong about Percy. Somehow he's involved. We smell it; he's a rotten apple. Maybe he's not involved in the thefts, but he's too sadistic to be playing a role. I'll bet he's running drugs, playing you guys as suckers. What better way to con the government than to be the thief and get assigned to catch yourself. Bet he laughs about that every night. We want to keep an eye on him too but don't know how to pull if off. We need your help."

Clep rubbed his chin with his left hand. "I doubt you're right about Percy but I'll keep an open mind. I'll think about it some, let you know if there's a way to tail him. That's going to be tough. He's a wily character. That's why he's so good at his job." Before I could react Clep added, "By the way, Percy also does interrogations for our unit. I checked around, he's the best. To do that job, you have to be tough. It's not something most people can stomach. He's broken some hard characters, saved American lives from the intel. The brass thinks highly of him, don't questions his tactics. I want you to know that; I'll have a hard time selling him as a traitor. They think he's a patriot."

Fleming was assigned to do more background checks on Ben and Percy. Were they living beyond their means? Extravagant purchases? Fleming would also be our contact point if we needed to reach Clep quickly. That way we'd bypass the MP radio band, not hint at what we were doing or leak private communications. Clep had a portable radio that he kept with him at all times. Just in case we'd need him fast. We agreed to meet each week at the same time, play ball and debrief as we appeared to rest after a tough game. Clep asked, "Any questions?"

I raised my hand, "Just one, can I have you or Mac as my partner next week? Fleming sucks."

That night Sgt Stroh gave us some good news as Mac and I walked back the mess hall. "Just heard that yer old pal Sgt Wilson showed up in Quang Tri. He's okay. Said he got loaded one night, woke up, got loaded agin and kept at it." He looked at us sincerely, "This place'll do ya a job sometimes. They kicked his ass some but he's gonna go back ta work with Colonel Mullen." Stroh shook his head up and down. "That sumbitch Mullen must be some damn nice guy ta work fer. Some Provost Marshalls'd fry his nuts." My first thought was: Did he bring Frances with him?

Mac was pretty tense that night, the conversation with Clep got him to thinking about the shit storm we walked into. To break his mood, "Hey, Mac, let's wrestle some, practice some of those moves we learned in AIT. Don't want to lose our edge, huh?" He was a bright guy, saw through my plan." Grinned his big Irish grin.
"I have been kind of pissy, haven't I? It couldn't hurt to practice some violence." We went outside our hootch; I refreshed him on all the tricks Nut had tortured me with over the years. Funny how they all came back; muscle memory, I guess. After I did the full nelson escape on Mac and pinned him to the ground, he looked at me. "Now I know how you feel after we play ping pong." We slept well that night.

CHU LAI

When Lou and I patrolled the ammo dump next day, I was surprised to see my old teammate Jones manning the entrance gate. I gave Jones a big greeting, got a muted response. He looked higher than a kite, slurred his words. I asked, "How'd you get this duty, Jones?" It took him awhile to answer.

"Aint for sure; think Sgt Burton put in a good word. Sgt Price's been on my ass some, so's its nice ta have some help. Sgt Burton always be nice." It was sad to see this terrific athletic specimen so wasted. It was also interesting that Ben had an inside contact at the dump. It wasn't a coincidence.

As we were driving from the dump, Lou asked to borrow $5. I wrinkled my brow, "We just got paid yesterday, why do you need money?"

Lou shrugged, "I lost it all in a poker game last night, need a few bucks to get back in the game. My fiancé will kill me if I don't send her some cash for the house we're gonna buy. She'll think I'm being irresponsible again. What with postponing our wedding again and all, I'm up shits'crick in a leaky raft. Get my drift?"

I smiled at Lou, "Can't help you buddy, I give all my money to the church back home, my way of helping the poor people. Don't tell anyone, I don't like showing off." Lou nodded in admiration.

Just then, Sgt Stroh radioed, said to return to base. He had "a special assignment for me." When we arrived, Stroh dismissed Lou, pulled me into his office. "This is gonna sound weird, Frazier. I got word there's a shipment of Korean noodles stashed near the Navy mess hall. I want you to swipe em. We aint had noodles fer months, Navy keeps stealin' our requisition. Aint fair, so we're gonna strike back. Follow me?" I repeated what he wanted, waited for the punchline; this had to be a joke. None came. He gave me exact directions to the steel cargo container, handed me a pair of bolt cutters.

As I drove toward my destination, I realized that Stroh was right; I hadn't had any noodles or any form of pasta since I'd been in Chu Lai. When I asked Stroh why I got picked for the robbery, he answered, "Cause you got yer shit together, won't fuck it up." I chuckled as I drove. All these years of Catholic school and disciplined physical training had prepared me as the ideal thief. Since my shit was tight, I was the perfect noodle bandit. What a place.

I ate at a nearby Navy mess hall, afterwards cased the noodle hideout. Apparently, this was a storage location for the north side of the island, serviced all the Navy mess operations. Stroh got me a ¾ ton truck to haul the load. The only instructions were, "Git as many as ya can, then high-tail it." I waited till dusk, then boldly drove to the huge storage container, looked around casually, cut the lock, loaded the truck as fast as I could. There were stacks of noodles, so it was easy to fill the truck. When that was done, I closed the container, put the broken lock back in place. I hated being sloppy. My throat hurt that night from laughing so hard. When I told Mac of the caper, he rolled his eyes. I don't think he believed me.

Next day, Stroh radioed, again called me back to base. With a straight face, he told Lou and I to investigate a theft from the Navy mess halls. "Some scallywag stole ther' noodles. Ther's shit to pay." Lou stared at Stroh and me as we howled like hyenas. The Navy mess sergeant glared when I asked him to describe the noodles.

"What er you a retard? There just fuckin noodles. Same as always."

I don't know why but I added, "What I mean is, do the noodles have any distinguishing characteristics? Are they curly, or long, or shaped like little tubes. Like that." When I told that story afterward, Sgt Stroh told me he laughed till his eyes got bloodshot, "Any distinguishing characteristics?"

My day of harmless pilfering was ruined as an explosion rocked me from a sound sleep. I looked at Mac, he said what I was thinking, "Ammo dump?"

I nodded, "Those clowns don't waste any time, do they?" In a few minutes, Clep came to our hootch, told us to get to the dump to see if we could find any evidence.

Then he added, "I'll be out there too, but won't interact with you much, in case someone's watching. Play it like it's a routine investigation. Interview the guards; see what they think happened. And get their comments in writing; we need objective opinions, a paper trail."

As we approached the dump, I noted the bright moonlit night. "If I'm a sapper, would I pick a full moon as the day to hit Chu Lai for the first time? Must be a cocky son-of-a-bitch, huh?"

There was bedlam at the dump. Fire trucks were hosing down the smoldering corner of the compound. That was the side closest to the ocean. Again, does that make any sense if it was a sapper? Where is the escape route? Clep told us when we came to Chu Lai that the Navy had new radar that could monitor small craft activity. That made it virtually impossible to approach the base by water. But somehow this sapper slipped through?

At the last MP post, I was surprised to see Nicholson, my loquacious friend from Quang Tri. He was very agitated while he talked to Clep. Nicholson and Jones had been assigned to the CID headquarters with Ben and Percy. I wondered if Ben was trying to play Nicholson like he was Jones. Mac interviewed the firemen, got their input. The lead sergeant said, "Damndest thing I ever saw, Charlie found the bunker with the heaviest firepower. It'll take over a week to replace all the rockets and mortars."

When I asked if the explosion was consistent with all the munitions in that bunker, he gave a slow, troubled reply. "I didn't think about that; now that you mention it, no way. Maybe we had a slew of duds. Guess we got lucky. Shoulda been much worse. Woulda had more casualties if the thing had blown full tilt." I asked if there was any threat that unexploded weapons were still left. "None, we checked that first. Clean as a whistle." I then asked if it was clean, where did the duds go. He looked at me for a while, then, "Shit if I know." I got his comments in writing, got him to sign the bottom with name and rank. I agreed with Clep, we needed a trail.

Next we interviewed the front guard post. As expected, no vehicles had entered the dump since dark; nothing unusual was spotted. I mentioned the full moon, got another funny look. "Charlie's got a major set of buffalo balls to hit us when it's this bright. Check it out!" Again I got a signed statement, mentioning the bright night but leaving out the colorful description of Charlie's cojones.

As we walked out of earshot, "They must have stolen the munitions earlier, set the explosion to cover the theft. I wonder if Clep's camera's could pick up any of that action?"

Mac shook his head, "Based on all the loading and unloading that goes on all day, it will be tough to spot the theft." I agreed with Mac, the dump was crazy busy.

Nicholson was manning the last guard post. Clep had left, so Mac and I asked Nicholson what he thought. "I told Lt Clep that one minute I'm out looking at the Big Dipper, next minute the sky's like the 4th of July. Bout scared the Bejesus outta ol Nick. I think that fuck-up Jones is one lucky motherfucker. He's supposed to be on duty with me but got sick and left early, before the show started. Wasted is what he was, was jumpy all night. Finally called in sick, got taken back to base. I could a been killed.

We're supposed to walk the perimeter every 15 minutes but I stayed put with Jones gone, couldn't leave the post unguarded."

That comment got me thinking. "Who made the last perimeter check before Jones left?" Nick told me Jones had, came back moaning about a bad stomach.

"Jones called Sgt Price, he came for him about 10 minutes later. Surprised me some, Percy usually has no time for Jones. Thinks he's like tits on a bull. Percy said he'd get some one out to replace Jones but then the attack came. Think Nick'll be going solo tonight."

Trying not to act too obvious, I told Nick that Clep wanted everything in writing so I'd need him to help me with an accurate statement. As he recalled the events, Nick mentioned that Jones had done the final patrol before the explosion. I assumed that Jones had been the one to set up the explosion using a time-delayed detonation. How had he gotten the bomb inside the dump? I looked around, noticed the jeep. "That yours, Nick?" He told me Jones and he had driven together, but since Percy took Jones back, he was on his own. I looked inside; saw a big, empty knapsack. "What's that for, Nick?"

He looked puzzled, "Damned if I know." I didn't ask any more questions. Nick was bright; I didn't want him mentioning my inquisitiveness to Jones or Percy.

We debriefed Clep, who was waiting for us as we left the dump. He raised his eyebrows when I mentioned Jones making the final patrol around the dump, left claiming sickness. I added, "Probably didn't want his sorry ass near the fireworks."

When I told him about the empty knapsack, Clep shook his head, "Bastard." I asked if we had enough to bring Jones in for questioning. "Maybe, but I want to wait. Let him think he fooled us; try to catch him off balance. It would help if we can get him on film with Ben, show Jones the pictures, sweat him; get him to spill. We can't wait too long, who knows what the bastards'll do next." I asked if they had any pictures of the dump from earlier that day, got the answer I expected. "I never got out there today, I didn't think they'd act that fast." Now we knew.

I told Clep I was worried about Nicholson being involved. "Nick's smart, hope I didn't tip my hand with all the questions about Jones." As I thought about it more, I changed my mind, "My gut says Nick's not involved. He's a pretty good guy, likes to smack his gums too much, but overall a decent guy; I like him. He seemed upset with Jones; don't think he was playing possum. I wonder if Jones thought the guard post might get knocked out with the explosion, might explain why he left." We headed back to the MP base agreeing to proceed with our original plan, keep our eyes open, try to get pictures, hope someone screwed up.

With only a couple hours of sleep, Lou and I headed off base for village patrol next day. I let Lou ramble about more gambling losses and worry about what his fiancé would think. He looked at me seriously, "I hate for her to think I'm a fuck-up, know what I mean?" I almost laughed out loud.

I said with deadpan, "Lou, I don't think you need to worry about her wondering if you're a fuck-up. My bet is she already solved that riddle- she KNOWS you're a fuck-up. She's probably working on the remaining part of the puzzle. Are you fucked up beyond all recognition? You know, the ultimate FUBAR." Lou wasn't a morning person, wasn't into irony; took my comments as advice.

He turned back at the steering wheel, "Maybe you're right. I guess there's still hope."

I was really tired from my late night ammo detail, was glad we had patrol off base. We took our time messing around in the villages, stopped for lunch at a restaurant we knew was good. Vietnamese food was great, very spicy, a pleasant break from Army chow. Naturally, Lou washed the food down with Tsingtao beer. Lou turned, belched like a summa wrestler. "Ah, the beer that made Beijing the king." The food revived me; we continued our trek back to Chu Lai, only a few more hours till sleep.

About 15 miles from base, we spotted a cart pulled to the side of the road, with a papa-sahn kneeling over a body. I told Lou to pull over but to approach cautiously. Was this a VC trick? "Lou, stay back, draw your Colt. Call Stroh, tell him what we're doing and where we are. Stay sharp." Lou seemed surprised but knew I wasn't fooling. He was calling as I walked up, my pistol drawn.

I heard the moans before I saw the rounded shape of a pregnant woman. Papa-sahn was much older than her, perhaps her father. It wasn't unusual to see young married women living with parents as their husband fought for the ARVN. Dad looked troubled, "Baby-sahn beaucoup number 10." Mom suddenly groaned then belted out a piercing howl. She rolled to her back, screamed.

"Baby come, baby come. Yaahhh! Yaahh! Yaahh! Yaahh!"

Before I could react, she lifted her legs, pulled up her pajamas; I spotted the crown of a baby's tiny head. Papa-sahn started babbling incoherently; without thinking, I dropped to the ground, put their blanket under the emerging child. Mom calmed briefly while the pain subsided. But then the wave of misery returned, the yelling started anew. I couldn't believe such noise came from this tiny woman. That mystery remained unanswered as I instinctively reached to support the child, now half way out. Mom started deep breathing then pushed for the stars, popping out a beautiful, slimy child into my awaiting hands. And then she delivered a bucket of goop that I wasn't sure how to describe. The baby started to wiggle in my hands; I could tell it was gasping to start breathing. I used my sleeve to wash away the moosh, heard the magic sound of a baby's first cry. Then I noticed the anatomy, a baby girl.

Lou had wandered over, saw me holding the baby, "Holy shit, Dylan, you just delivered a baby!" I continued to clean up the baby girl, got to the serpentine umbilical cord. Now what do I do? Cut it or what? We had no training on delivering babies. I knew the cord had to be cut but didn't know if there was a specific way to do it. If I did it wrong, what would happen? As I pondered, mom reached toward me asking for her child. The baby girl was still and breathing quietly, it was a sweet sound.

Lou kept babbling "Holy shit" and walking in circles.

I looked up, "Lou, watch your mouth in front of my child." He started apologizing as I stopped him. "Just kidding, Lou, let's get mom and baby to the nearest hospital. I'm not going to cut that umbilical cord unless I have to. Chu Lai's only 15 minutes away. Let's get going. I'll carry mom and baby; you drive. Hustle!" Mom understood a little English; I told her what I planned.

"Number 1, beaucoup number 1," was her way of agreeing.

The closest hospital was the Air Force facility at the edge of the airfield. Most of the action these doctors got was treating wounded GI's that were air-evacs from the bush. As I burst into the emergency room carrying my new family, I was greeted by shocked looks. A male medic listened to my hectic explanation, wagged his head sharply, "Army protocol, we don't treat gooks here. You gotta take her to the local facility, south of here."

Still carrying the young mother and child, I got up to the medic's face, replied, "Listen, asshole, I'm not asking permission. Treat them or I'm gonna shove Army protocol up your ass, then I'll drag you outta here and put your your sorry ass under arrest. Now move!" The medic stopped breathing.

Fortunately, a doctor walked up, brushed the medic aside. "Put her over here. We'll take care of them, deal with protocol later." I told the doc about the umbilical cord needing attention, he laughed. "Not a problem. You did a good job with the delivery. I hope they know how lucky they are. Most people would have walked away." I stayed until the operation was over, was told all was well. I told the doc I'd be back next morning to visit. It was my message that I'd be checking on them. The doctor smiled, "We'll be here waiting for you."

It took an hour in the shower to get the stink off. Afterwards, I went to the MP desk, told Sgt Stroh what happened, warned him a complaint might be coming from the Air Force hospital. Stroh laughed, "You can be a cowboy sometimes, Frazier. That temper might git ya in trouble one day. Don't worry, though, I got yer back." As Stroh kidded me about my temper, I recalled how my pal Callahan criticized me for being too thoughtful before acting. I wondered what he'd think now. As I thought over my actions, I concluded my behavior wasn't really hotheaded. That little baby didn't have the luxury of following Army rules.

Mac and I had base patrol next day. This was the first time we'd worked together since arriving in Chu Lai. "The only thing I miss about working with Lou is having a cold Budweiser after breakfast. You don't have a knapsack of beer, do you?"

Mac shrugged, "I always wait till noon before pounding them down. Rum and Cokes work?" It was fun catching up. We talked every night but now we could yap all day, snoop around the ammo dump without calling suspicion to us. Lou always bitched about any break in his endless quest for new places to eat. The ammo dump wasn't noted for fine cuisine.

I didn't know any of the MP's guarding the dump; so we just waved, did a brief look around, saw nothing peculiar. I snapped a few pictures, getting all the different angles; it might be good for a reference point later. As we exited the dump, we got a call from Stroh to investigate a drug incident at the CID station. "Hope it's not Fleming," I kidded Mac. We entered the CID area, spotted a small crowd.

I didn't recognize anyone but one soldier pointed at the hootch, "In there, it aint pretty."

The hootch was dim, so as I looked at the naked body sprawled on the floor; it took awhile before I saw it was Jones. Needles were scattered on the floor along with other dope paraphernalia. His eyes were wide open, almost looked surprised. His arms had needle marks at the crook in his arm. If someone was tempted to use heroin, a look at Jones might deter him. He looked pathetic, completely forlorn. I looked at Mac, he looked the way I felt, sick and helpless.

I got the camera Lt Clep gave me for ammo dump reconnaissance. Before disturbing the scene, I took multiple pictures of Jones, some close-ups of his arm and face. The medics arrived shortly, waiting to take the body away. As they lifted Jones, I noticed a goose egg on the back of his head. "Guys, hold up, let me get a picture of that welt." I took a couple shots, asked the medic how he got the bump.

"Maybe he fell out of bed as he passed out, who knows?"

I took a closer look, "Looks pretty severe for a short fall? Could the floor cause that much damage?" The medic shrugged.

They carried Jones away, Mac and I stayed inside. Mac looked at me funny, "What are you thinking?"

Just then, Nicholson walked in, looked about to cry, "Damn shame, Jones was a good man, got hooked on this shit, never been the same."

We explained what we'd found; then Nick said something interesting, "It don't make no sense, Jones was scared of needles. He never gave blood, said needles made him pass out. Big dude like that, imagine that."

I patted Nick's shoulder, asked, "So, as far as you knew, Jones never mainlined?"

Nick shook his head, "Never, just smoked mostly."

As we were leaving CID, I spotted Ben Burton walking toward a jeep. From my basketball days, I studied body language closely. If my opponent bent over on breaks or put hands on his hips, I knew he was tired. If he started to move or dribble faster than normal, he was nervous. If he smiled and had a spring in his step, I knew he was ready for battle. As I watched Ben walk, I saw that same bouncy gait of confidence. Why was he so elated?

As we were driving away from CID, we spotted Sgt Wilson. I waved; he stood still, no wave back. Mac turned the jeep around so we could say hello. The first thing I noticed was the look on Wilson's face. Anguish? Normally, he was happy-go-lucky. Talked sports non-stop. I told him I was glad he got away from Quang Tri. He nodded, "The place will get lit up pretty soon. Charlie wants it back." I asked about Frances. He got a hollow look, didn't say anything. Finally, "I've got to run, fellas, nice to see you. Colonel Mullen's waiting." He hustled off. Mac looked at me.

"That was peculiar. Did you see the look on his face when you asked about Frances?" I did. Embarassment? We started to drive, not saying anything.

After a few minutes, I called in that we completed the investigation, Sgt Stroh told us to return to camp, debrief with Lt Clep. As we drove up, Clep waved us to follow him to the basketball courts. As we shot hoops, we filled him in; he was happy I got pictures of Jones, stopped dribbling when Mac told him about the welt on Jones's head. "I'm going to go over and check that myself. Maybe he hit the edge of the bunk, then hit the ground; could happen that way." He stopped dribbling again when I told him about the drug stuff on the floor. I added, "Should have been on the bunk. Why would it be on the floor? And then there's him being afraid of needles. Too many loose ends."

Clep said he would check with the medic about the time of death; ask about the head injury. "I won't push him too much; see if he offers that something looks suspicious. Even then, it will be hard to get much interest in this one. Jones was a known drug user. Unless there's an eyewitness that puts Ben in Jones hootch, we've got nothing." We continued to shoot some more when Mac suddenly threw the ball at the backboard in anger.

"There out there killing people and we can't do anything about it. When are they going to come after us?"

As we walked back to our jeep to resume patrol, I told Mac I had an idea about our safety. The Company area was meant to house about 100 people. There were only 45 MP's using the space so many of the hootches were empty. "Let's set up bunks in a couple other buildings, rotate where we sleep. We'll keep our stuff where it is, but move around when it's time to crash. What you said down there was right; they'll be after us soon. My guess is they'll do something when we're on village patrol, but you never know."

Mac smiled, "I'm glad you read all those James Bond books." The idea of rotating bunks seemed to give Mac some peace. I hoped it worked.

Next morning I had village patrol with Clardy. We had seen little of Clardy since leaving Quang Tri. "What have you been doing with yourself, Clardy? Haven't seen your sad ass since we've been here. Is it my deodorant or did you get yourself a girlfriend?" Clardy told me he'd been guarding the beach gate on the north side of base, where the Vietnamese merchants (and whores) entered the base.

"Told Sgt Stroh ya kin leave me there forever. Sweet stuff, I aint even bullshittin'."

I filled him in on Jones, could tell he was upset. "Flat-out waste. Good guy, Jones, but aint been the same since gittin' on the powder." I asked if he saw much of Ben since we got here. "Not hide ner hair. Don't think he wants ta see Ole Clardy. Turned on me fer some reason. See more'n I want a Percy. He's pretty much the pussy king already. The MP that was runnin' it afore, came up lame one day. Took a short ride on Percy's boot, won't ever walk the same."

I told Clardy we played ball after duty; that he should drop by. He shook his head, "I'll probably drop down ta the gate, always some poontang ta be had. Beats playin' hoops, know what I mean?" We went through the main gate, began village patrol. We went north; Clardy had never been off the base since arriving. It was a hot, sunny day so the breeze felt great as we meandered aimlessly. Clardy was rambling on about the local prostitutes, how "they really seem ta like me." That made me laugh out loud but Clardy took it as agreement.

As we drove toward Da Nang, a thought popped into my head. One of the things that puzzled Nut, Clep, and Fleming was how Ben wired large amounts of money to the States. A trace of all activity in Quang Tri came up with nothing. Some money sent home but nothing exceptional. I thought about our ride south to Chu Lai when we evacuated Quang Tri. And the ride from Quang Tri to Hue was even shorter. And Hue to Da Nang was also just a couple hours. Did Ben wire money from other locations? Had he avoided detection by using multiple sites under multiple names?

I radioed Fleming, told him to come over to play hoops after he got off duty. Mac and Clep played Fleming and I, it was a feisty match. Mac was having a great night; he took out his nerves on me as he fought for every loose ball. For an hour, we forgot about our dicey situation. Even though I lost, it was a blast. Puffing hard, we sat down and I unloaded my theory on wiring money. Clep's eyes got wide. "God damn, why didn't I think of that?"

Fleming smirked, "Cause you're not Sherlock Frazier, he thinks of weird stuff all day. Sometimes he comes up with something half decent. Most times, it's just whacked-out and super paranoid."

Mac laughed harder than anyone, added, "Can you imagine living with Frazier? He's now bringing his pistol when he takes a dump. Now that's crazy."

I turned to the crew, "Have you ever seen the flies in our shitter? Monsters! I'd bring a Thompson, if it fit through the door."

We brainstormed for the next hour. I mentioned that we saw Sgt Wilson, that he acted odd. "Maybe we should take a harder look at him?" Clep didn't say anything right away.

Then he shook his head, "It would make sense that he's involved. I know he's smart; he's wellspoken but plays down how sharp he is. Maybe a good cover?"

Mac said, "I hope that's a wild goose chase. I like Sgt Wilson." I nodded my agreement with that. Since no one added anything else, Clep said he'd debrief Colonel Mullen, get him to send Fleming to Hue and Da Nang to check for unusual wire accounts being sent from there. Clep still wouldn't mention Wilson, Percy, or Ben as being our prime suspects.

"Still too soon to point fingers. We only have hunches and circumstantial evidence. Mullen likes those guys;

they've been loyal to him, so he won't buy our weak evidence yet. Plus Mullen might start acting funny around them and blow it."

Fleming piped in, "I've had to do research on Swiss bank accounts. If you have enough cash, you can set up a private account where you wire money using a number only, no names. Most of the drug king pins in Nam do that, no traces of money in country. When they get enough money or are close to getting caught, they disappear to Switzerland, learn to yodel and tend cows. If they're doing that, it'll be hard to pin a conviction without names on the transfer wire. Or maybe they get careless and send money home, that kind of thing." I didn't think Ben was the careless kind, but Percy might be. We'd see.

For the next week, Clardy and I got reacquainted. He bunked with Callahan, filled me in on my taciturn friend from Basic Training. "Callahan sticks ta himelf mostly. Aint even drinkin' anymore. Reads mostly, goes ta sleep early. Just biddin' time till his DEROS." I learned that was the magical moment we dreamed of: Date for Estimated Return from Overseas. Going home! That made me realize I'd been in Nam almost 9 months, only 3 more to go. Hard to believe, time flies when it sucks. But that realization tempted me to leave this hornet's nest alone. What was I getting from this? I bet Mac was already thinking: Let's just get out.

We awoke next morning to torrential rainfall. So far, the dread monsoon season had been mild. It was now October, today the storm gods got even. We had slept that night in one of our alternate locations, had a short walk to our real hootch. I looked out the door, turned to Mac, "We'll need our flippers and wet suits, buddy. It's lucky we're getting so short, maybe the rain won't touch us, cause we're so microscopic. Just kind of fall around us, like we aren't even there. Know what I mean?"

When you were approaching the end of your tour in Nam, they called it "being short." Once you got within 90 days of leaving, you were allowed to start using "short jokes." With my warped sense of humor, I knew my pals were dreading this. I had been preparing a medley of short jokes for months; Mac had been the unfortunate tester. He looked over at me, "Don't start, I'm begging you."

I couldn't help myself. "Mac, I'm so short I need a stepladder to climb up a gnat's ass." Mac screamed as he ran toward our hootch. I guess he didn't like that one.

Later the next day, Clardy and I made our way through the soggy roads towards the village of Ky Phu. We had driven up and down the mostly deserted roads, decided to stop for lunch. The local restaurant was Lou's favorite, I wanted a dry place where we could kill time, eat great food. When Clardy ate his first bite he howled in delight, "Fuckin' A Tweetie, this is some good shit."

Papa-sahn, the cook and owner, was standing nearby, asked what Clardy said. He spoke a little English but was puzzled by the phrase. "Tweetie Bird is a cartoon character that Clardy fantasizes about, almost a mythical figure to him. When Clardy evokes Tweetie as a comparison, that's high praise." I omitted any mention of the shit comparison to his his food. Papa-sahn gave me a huge grin; he understood hardly a word but liked my exuberant delivery. Clardy started to belly laugh, which made papa-sahn join in the fun. Pretty soon, I jumped in; we stood there laughing like mental patients. It was a great lunch.

We got bad news next morning from Lt Clep. "Colonel Mullen won out, he's now Provost Marshall of the whole base, including CID. They'll be moving over here shortly, Ben and Percy will be part of our happy family." The distance between our camps had given us some sense of security. Now, the enemy was among us. I could see Mac tense up. He was thinking about the little time we had left in Nam. He was thinking about why this had to happen now. I remembered the old axiom, "Keep your friends close, but your enemies closer." We'd get to test that one. I mentioned that to console Mac.

He looked glum. "To me, the farther away the better." His shoulders sagged.

Ben set up a new motor pool on the edge of camp, got Clardy back working for him, just like the old days in Quang Tri. Hadn't seen Percy at all, Clardy said he saw Percy move near the MP station, had a place to himself. Fleming and the other CID guys moved into a corner of camp near the basketball courts. The rain had stopped, so we continued to meet at the courts when off duty. Clep said Sgt Wilson would stay working with CID; he wasn't sure where he was bunking yet. Then he filled us in on Percy's whereabouts. "He works at night, spends most of his time at the beach gate, watching his minions come and go. Any luck, we won't see him much."

Clep was worried about being seen with us, so he would only play ball occasionally. I noticed that he returned to his douche bag imitation, kept tripping over himself. "You never know who's looking, Frazier." We agreed to continue using Fleming as our go-between, to meet in his hootch after dark, when Percy was gone and Ben was at the USO club. There was no excuse for Ben to have a club in our camp, since the plush USO facility was a short walk down the hill. I bet Ben was sitting there now, wondering how to rob it.

I saw Callahan walking from the outhouse as I left the courts. I noticed he had a book with him. "Doing some deep thinking as you rid yourself of the excretory demons, Callahan?" He chuckled; we compared notes on how fast time had passed.

"Only 11 weeks or so left, Dylan, maybe they'll let us out for Christmas. I hear they do that a lot. They get the newspapers involved, get a lot of publicity to show how humane the Army is." Thinking about Clardy saying he was becoming a recluse, I asked if he wanted to have a drink at the USO club that night. To my surprise he agreed.

Later, over a beer at the USO club, I warned Callahan this place was suddenly more dangerous with Ben and Percy moving in. Mac soon joined us; we drank beer mindlessly before telling Callahan the gory details on our investigations. "You really think Ben killed Jones? That's nuts." I let Mac explain the unusual crime scene, the unexplained knot on Jones's head. Callahan listened intently, again surprised me, "I think you're right, it does sound like someone killed him. But what you don't know is if it was Ben or Percy. Or maybe Jones owed some druggie money and wouldn't pay. Who knows what trouble he was in?" Before I answered, Callahan said what had been on Mac's mind, "You're too short to be getting involved in this. You should forget about it and just go home." Callahan had a solemn look as he said that.

Mac turned to me, "I agree with Callahan, I'm done with this. I'm so nervous I can't sleep. I keep thinking about Ben and Percy flipping a frag under our hootch, blowing our shit away. How's Mary going to get by if I'm gone? How will she explain to our son that his Daddy got killed by another American who was selling weapons to the VC. Its been eating me up, I just want to go home and I want you to do the same thing. I'll feel guilty if you keep going and something happens. I can't live with that either. You have to stop, Dylan. I'm asking you to stop."

I'll never forget the look on Mac's face. The combination of concern and fear made him swell up, like he was about to explode. I could tell that he wanted an answer right away. This tension was suddenly overwhelming him. I think the realization that we were finally "short" had tipped him over the edge. And then

Callahan looked at me, said, "Just forget it, Dylan. I know you're driven to stop this. What I don't know is what set you off. What made you change so much? Whatever it is, it isn't healthy. Let's go home and get out of this nightmare." They both stared at me.

My shoulders slumped, I said, "Okay, I'm done. Let's go home." I felt great relief. I hadn't realized how the stress has eaten at me. Callahan was right, something was driving me to solve this, to put those bastards away. I'd never been able to figure exactly what it was. I'd never been so intent on doing good, for good's sake. Most times I avoided fights, went my own way. But one thing was a constant in my life. If you pushed me, I'd push back. And fight hard once I started. My fuse burned slowly, but burst when pushed to a certain point. Somehow, these gutless bastards had set me off. Now I needed to reel it back.

Mac kept looking to see if I was busting his balls. Callahan also looked skeptical. Finally I said, "I mean it. Stop looking at me like a pair of numb nuts. Let's play some ping pong." Unfortunately, Mac hadn't lost a thing in his game; he whipped our ass like a nun punishing mortal sinners. Callahan was pretty good, gave Mac a run for his money, but Mac always upped his game, crushed him when it counted. I enjoyed Mac seeing the good side of Callahan. We needed all the friends we could muster to get out in one piece.

Now I had to tell Clep we were backing out. Next day I wandered to his hootch, unloaded. He listened, didn't look surprised or pissed. "I can't say as I blame you, would probably do the same thing if I was in your place. This is my job. I volunteered and trained for this. This is what I want to do as a career. It's in my blood. I think you're making the right decision." The air left my clenched stomach. Before I left, Clep turned to me. "Do me a favor, Frazier, still keep your eyes open. These guys are dangerous. They won't know you're out of this. And if you see anything funny, let me know."

I got about 20 steps away before Clep yelled, waved me back. "I've got to be careful what I say to Colonel Mullen. He's high on you and McCarthy, trusts your judgment. He thinks you are capable of solving this, he told me that. So, I can't say you're refusing to help, after all, you are MP's and this is a military crime. So, as far as he's concerned, you're still engaged. Got that?" I understood his point.

"Got it. By the way, I'll keep in touch; keep my eyes open. If I think of something useful, I'll yell."

Walking away, I thought about what he said. Deciding to back off wasn't going to keep us safe. He also had a good point about being an MP. Chasing bad guys was my job. I was feeling some remorse about leaving Clep on his own. I wondered what he'd tell Nut. I started to think of ways to help without jeopardizing our safety. It wouldn't be easy hiding anything from Mac; he'd pick up on it if I acted strange, at least stranger than normal. And then I remembered that Clep was right, we were still in the line of fire. The bad guys wouldn't know we had retreated to a passive role. Was it actually making it worse by disengaging?

I saw Fleming at the USO club next night. He reacted with surprise when I told him our change of plans. Fleming smirked. "I don't think you can pull that off, Frazier. You're in too deep already. Plus that aggressive personality you're afflicted with won't let you stop. I give it a couple days and you'll be back digging." When I started to explain, he interrupted, "By the way, wait till you hear what I dug up on Ben. I got something interesting on Percy too. Let's go outside."

Mac and Callahan weren't off duty yet, so I got to hear the news without worrying them. Fleming had recently started to smoke, lit up as he began his update. I pointed at him, "Fleming, before you start, what's the deal with smoking? And stop blowing it in my face; you're annoying enough without the fire breath."

Fleming smirked, "It makes me look like the Marlboro Man, don't you think?" That cracked me up.

"More like the Marshmellow Man, Fleming. You're goofy enough, lose the weed, okay?" After a brief pause, he exhaled deeply into my face.

He had some interesting news. "Old Ben had an unusual job before he entered the Army. He worked for The Royal bank of Scotland in Tampa. And guess what he did there? He ran the international wire transfers; I'll bet he got to be rather expert at that, huh" Before I could answer, "And Percy? It turns out he's married, lied about that on his forms. His wife lives in Charleston, has a different last name than him, Smith. I haven't found any direct link to her getting money, yet. There's lots of Smiths in that area, it's going to be tough hunting."

I saw Mac and Callahan walking down the hill from the MP base. They had finally become friendly; that made me happy. Last night Mac told me, "I see what you mean about Callahan, pretty good guy. I was wrong about him; not such a wuss after all, he just isn't looking for a fight." That Callahan was a good ping pong player didn't hurt either. He was the only one who gave Mac competition. Thinking about my agreement to drop out of this,

"Fleming, keep this between us. I don't want those guys involved, right?" Fleming nodded agreement.

Mac trounced everybody in the club that night. When I got close to him, he'd start jabbering while we played. "This one's coming at your belt buckle, Dylan." Then he'd bounce it off my chest, howl with joy.

"No one likes an irritating winner, Mac. Keep fat-mouthing like that and I might get serious about the game, whip your Irish ass." The next shot bounced off my forehead. Callahan almost choked with laughter. Fleming quipped, "I love seeing Frazier getting thrashed. Finally, he's not great in something." Then he blew a huge smoke ring at me. It was a fun night.

It was raining cats and dogs when we woke next morning. Water was ankle deep as we trudged to the MP desk to see what our duties where that day. Stroh looked up, "Typhoon's coming, boys. Sit tight while we figure out what to do"

Clardy waddled in, "It's wetter'n a frog's asshole out there, Sarge. We goin' out in that shit?"

Stroh never looked up, "Dummy up, Clardy, and wait like the other guys. Aint got patience fer yer country charm right now, kinda busy."

Stroh worked the radio but was having trouble with reception. I looked outside, the rain was in sheets, couldn't see more than a foot or so. This building was on flat ground so the water started to gather as it ran off higher areas. There was now over a foot of water flooding over the front steps. Stroh turned from the radio, "They say this sucker's gonna last all day, should clear by dinner. I'm sending word out for any trucks or convoys to hunker down, wait it out 'for goin anywheres. Seems people shoulda figured that out thimselves but I can't chance it."

Before we could respond, Percy came flying in, sopping wet. He looked at Stroh, "We need patrols out by the hill; make sure nobody tries to go up or down. Someone does that they'll be washed to China. Frazier, McCarthy, you get to the bottom. Clardy, you and Callahan stay up top. Move it."

Stroh stares at him, "I give the assignments round here, Price. Stay put fellas." Percy pointed to his stripes; he was suddenly an E-6, outranked Stroh.

"I got promoted Stroh, I'm in charge now. Check with Clep if ya got any beef." He growled at us, "Now, git it!"

Stroh was furious but he waved at us to do as ordered. As we headed out, Stroh cautioned, "Don't do anything stupid, boys, it's dangerous out there." I opened the door;

rain pelted me. Before the tumult drowned all sound out, I heard Stroh tell Percy, "I am gonna check with Clep, this is flat stupid. No one should be out there, it's suicide."

Mac heard this, looked at me, "What are we doing? This can't be happening."

I looked at the water, now to our knees, "I got some thoughts, let's get out of sight first."

The four of us got to our jeeps, vainly tried to start them. Not even a spark of life, stone dead. We moved to a nearby hootch. I looked at my dripping companions.

"Anybody thinks it makes sense to get to our posts?"

Callahan answered quickly, "If we get near that hill, we'll be washed over. There's no chance you and Mac can make the bottom. No chance."

Clardy looked nervous, "But we got orders. Orders is orders. Be an article 15 if we don't go. That aint good, know what I mean?"

Mac weighed in, "Fuck the article 15, Percy's trying to get us killed."

I started to laugh; Mac looked at me like I was a lunatic. "This isn't funny, Dylan." I could see he was about to smack me so I put up my hand.

"Listen to me. Didn't Stroh say this was supposed to end by dinner? And I never heard Percy say exactly when we had to man these posts. He just said we had to go. So, let's wait out the storm in this dry hootch, maybe play some cards, then head out when the water starts to drop. No one will be out there checking on us. We'll do our duty, just a little later than Percy had in mind."

Clardy started to chuckle, "Damn, that's slick."

And that's what we did. We took turns going outside to monitor the weather. Torrents of water flooded any flat area. Winds were vicious; I guessed over 100 mph. Many of the buildings in our company were flattened. Tin roofing flew everywhere. You couldn't see more than a couple feet, not a sole stirred outside. If the water was this high at the top of the base, what must it be at the bottom, a lake? I didn't want to talk about Percy in front of Clardy, so we let it sit. The look on Mac's face told me what he was thinking. I poked him as his face got redder and redder, "Let it go, Mac."

Around 4 pm the storm stopped suddenly. It became utterly quiet, like a crowd that just witnessed a spectacular performance, stunned to silence. The sun peeked through the clouds, the wind stilled, almost a dead calm. I looked outside, the water was gushing down the path but you could now see clearly. We had discussed strategy for reaching our posts. We would stagger our departure, walk in different directions before heading to the road. Guessed we probably had an hour or so before activity started.

I left first, waded around camp, avoiding the MP station, not wanting to get spotted. It was amazing how fast the water was draining off. As I got near the road, I saw the area Mac and I would have been guarding, it was still a torrent of flooding water. The USO club was on higher ground, was the only building left undamaged. Most of the airport was underwater. The big hangars were half submerged but were draining rapidly, like a big stopper had been pulled from a tub, water rushing down the pipe.

I looked at the South China Sea; it was a chaotic mess of debris. Where sampans usually huddled, now it teemed with trees, rooftops, and what was left of the buildings. Monkeys and birds sat listlessly on the detritus, waiting for the right time to head back to their former homes. I turned as I heard Mac sloshing towards me. Pointing at the stranded creatures, "If we survived Percy's assignment, we be perched there with them." Mac sneered, "If there was any doubt that he wanted us dead, it's gone now."

Clardy and Callahan joined us shortly. We watched the base begin to drain. My guess was half of Chu Lai was gone. Still no movement anywhere, I looked around trying to concoct a plausible story. I pointed at a hill on the west side of the road, "Callahan, that's where you and Clardy stood. See that big power pole? You both hung on that, okay? Mac and me got washed down the hill but made it to the USO club. We watched the road from there, right?"

To authenticate the story, Mac and I slogged our way downhill. After standing there for a few minutes, we went in the USO, casually played ping pong; told a few grunts our story of being outside for the deluge. When the NCO running the club asked who sent us out in this mess, he gave a perfect reaction, "That Price is one crazy fucker. Didn't he know ya mighta been killed?" We turned down free beer as his gesture of sympathy. He laughed when I said, "Can I get a rain check?"

Within an hour, the base was a beehive of activity. Mac and I trudged uphill, walked into the MP station, sopping wet. Stroh looked up, grinned, "Ya'll are a sight fer sore eyes. Wasn't sure I'd see ya again." We told Stroh the tale of our survival; he shook his head. "Lucky sumbitches ta survive that. Worst storm I ever seen. I aint even bullshittin."

As I walked out, I turned, "Sgt Stroh, did you have a chance to talk with Clep?" Stroh's face got grim as he nodded, "He said he never talked to Percy about patrols. But he did confirm the damned promotion." I could tell by Stroh's look he was puzzled about that.

The base was a mess. Everyone would have to spend weeks cleaning up. Mac and I patrolled the airport area next morning, watched massive planes landing, unloading special equipment to help the base recover. Huge fans were deployed to dry the interior of the hangars. We drove up, chatted with a civilian engineer running the show. The deeply tanned guy laughed when I asked whom he pissed off to get sent to Nam. "This place is like the land of milk and honey, son. I make a fortune every monsoon season. When I get lucky, more than a typhoon or two pops up."

That caught me offguard. I asked a ton of questions. We learned that civilians made a fortune in Nam, doing jobs the Army deemed inappropriate for the military. The talkative engineer said he spent 6 months a year in Nam, made enough to buy a nice house in Houston. "I'm gonna get me a Cadillac this tour, maybe a nice wagon for the wife. I hope this war lasts awhile, need me a vacation home on the Gulf." He told us most of the civilians lived with the Air Force and Navy, in custom built trailers. "They got all the trimmings" was how he described his living conditions.

We cruised back to the Navy section, noted a dozen trailers with antennas and heavy wiring. "Never noticed them before, how about you Mac?"

He shook his head, added, "I still think they're nuts. No way I'd work in Nam just for a big paycheck."

I smiled, "That's cause you love your wife and kid. What if your wife beefed up to a deuce and a half after the honeymoon? Maybe sprouted a moustache after popping out a couple kids. Started chewing tobacco, spitting like a baseball player. Nam might look pretty good, huh?"

Mac laughed, "Where do you come up with this stuff?"

When we got back to camp that night, I spotted Percy Price leaving the MP station. Mac was still steaming about getting sent out in the typhoon, was about to call him out as we passed by. I yelled quickly, "Hey, Sgt Price, thanks for sending us out in that typhoon. It was really cool riding the rapids down the hill, felt like I was back in Boy Scouts camp again. You should have seen Mac and me taking turns hanging on the flagpole at the USO club. The wind blew us horizontal. What a blast."

Then I walked a few more steps, added, "At first I thought you were out to get us, but then I realized you were just trying to protect the other soldiers. You know, just doing your duty. Oh, and by the way, we checked with Lt Clep, he never gave any orders to send out patrols. That's how I know it was just your instinct that the base needed extra help." Mac looked at me, not sure what was I doing. As he was processing,

Percy called back, "Got my eye on you Frazier. Don't forget that."

I smiled at Percy, "Believe me, Sgt Price, I know that and you know what? I'll be watching you too." Percy arched his brow, wandered off.

Before Mac could say anything, "I'm trying to keep you from going after Percy. I know you're pissed and might go ballistic. Plus I wanted him to know we talked with Clep, might make him more cautious. Anything happens to us unexpectedly, it would point at him. Made a judgment, it's better to go after Percy than wait for his move. Sorry, it just popped outta my big mouth.

Then Mac started chuckling, "Hanging on the flagpole, blowing horizontal…"

Sgt Stroh continued to run the MP station. Apparently, Percy just got involved when he thought he could bust our balls. I had patrol with Lou next day, got caught up on his latest capers. "I found a new restaurant out near Dong My, got a good-lookin' gal too. You should see her, class A poontang. I almost forget to eat, lookin' at her." I knew Lou had low standards, but thought good chow sounded worth the trip. It was good to have a destination, made the day go faster.

Before our lunch excursion, however, we had a nasty assignment. Sgt Stroh told us that morning to drop by each company on Chu Lai; start tallying how many people were killed or lost. I looked at Stroh stoned faced, "Sounds like a bad job, Sarge. What's second prize, shit burner?"

Stroh grinned, "Perfect job fer you, Frazier, don't let Simpson do any of the talkin'. That fucker could screw up a wet dream. Sumbitch is bout half a shit hook, know what I mean?" Lou heard Stroh, but just grinned. He didn't mind being the butt of jokes.

We started at the north of camp, made the rounds. Most of the company clerks had the details typed out, knowing we'd be asking for it. I was expecting a grim reception, but the clerks seemed to take it in stride, like any other day of reporting casualties in Vietnam. My list grew to 87 dead by the time I got done this section of Chu Lai. Some of the clerks joked about the missing, "They're probably laying low for a few days. Know they can get away without being charged AWOL. Not in a rush to get back in the bush." Over 200 men were missing.

There were mostly Air Force units to visit as we descended toward southern Chu Lai. Many of the aircraft and personnel had departed before the typhoon hit so casualties were relatively light, only 6 confirmed dead, 42 missing. One of he clerks summed it up best, "Lucky that equipment is expensive or we'd a been in a world of hurt. I seen a shitter in the South China Sea yesterday. It would a been those planes floatin' out there otherwise. That typhoon would a really done us a job." Final tally, 93 dead and almost 250 unaccounted for. I was percolating that dismal news as Lou blabbed about lunch.

I had to give Lou credit. This restaurant in Dong My served the best food I'd had in months. What looked like a sleepy village was surging with activity. Just west of the tip of Chu Lai, many merchants stopped here for food and supplies as they came to and fro. I ordered what I thought was chicken, snow peas and rice. What I got was far better, thick and spicy, drop-dead delicious and puckery. The old mama-sahn who served us was broken down, sporting a scraggly set of whiskers on her chin. I looked at Lou, "If that's your idea of a major babe, my bet is you also love braided armpits on your women."

Lou grinned, "Aint her, just wait."

We did wait but nothing happened. "Let's go back tomorrow, Frazier, maybe she's off today." The food was so good I didn't need any encouragement to return.

We had another mindless ping pong session at the USO that night. As usual, Mac killed all comers. He was becoming a minor star; everybody wanted a shot at him. If he liked you, he'd toy with you then pour it on at the end. If you talked shit, he'd bury you. I knew when he really disliked someone when he bounced a smash off the end of the table into his nuts. That always made me laugh; he was getting more like me, a wise-ass.

Fleming came wandering over as Mac was thrashing another poor sap. He watched Mac play for a while. "It's too bad McCarthy isn't smart enough to make money playing ping pong, he's like a circus freak, people might pay to watch him. You know what I mean, like looking at Jo-Jo the Dog Faced Boy for a buck. He's too naïve to figure that out himself, maybe I could be his manager."

Thinking back to my whiskered mama-sahn lunch maid that day, I responded, "Any interest in a bearded lady for your freak show? Know where I can find one; maybe pair her up with McCarthy as a two-for-one deal." I could see Fleming thinking it over.

We kibitzed for a while, busting loudly on Mac- but it never broke his concentration. The balls kept bouncing away for winners. Fleming told me the trip to Hue and Da Nang hadn't produced any proof that Ben was wire transferring large sums of money. "If he is, he's doing it under an assumed identity. Only people I found sending big bucks back were some high-ranking brass and civilian contractors. I spoke to your buddy Nut; he said that was normal procedure. And none of the brass was sending huge amounts, nothing irregular. The contractors make a ton, so that wasn't unusual. I gave Nut the list; he said he'd dig some more. Then he ran to his chopper and took off; he's a spooky guy, Dylan. He makes you look almost normal." We had hit another dead end. What was I missing?

Lou and I had village patrol next morning, so we had a good excuse to visit our new lunch spot. As I moved through the beaded curtain, I spotted her. This stunningly beautiful girl moved to greet us, "Ah, my favorite people, the MP's. I know we will have a safe meal today. Welcome, follow me." Lenore was tall, slender, had raven hair hanging to her waist. When she moved, the hair acted like a fan, wafting a sweet flowery smell in its wake. She spoke perfect English, the best I'd heard in Vietnam. I'd forgotten how much I missed talking to women.

Lenore was maybe 20, was married to the older papa-sahn who owned the restaurant. Business had been moderate until Lenore took over. Her husband was now the wealthiest man in the village. Lenore was part French, had been shunned by her village. Like many of these deserted children, she ended up in a Catholic mission school, raised by nuns. She learned to cook at the mission, soon showed she had a great gift. The nuns spotted this unique talent, got her a job cooking for the restaurant she now co-owned. Part of her agreement to marry papa-sahn included half share in the business. This was a smart young lady.

I learned all this background as we lunched there over the next couple weeks. Lenore reminded me of my girlfriend Laura, stunningly feminine; a thought I quickly subdued. Too painful thinking of how much I missed her. Jabbering with Lenore made me feel relaxed, almost like home. You nearly forgot her beauty she was so funny, so comfortable to be with. One day she said to me, "You are very handsome, for a GI."

I pretended offense, "What do you mean 'for a GI?' Are you saying that Americans are more ugly than your little rascals? Are you serious?"

She didn't flinch. "Most Americans are hairy like dog, fat like water buffalo. Most are sloppy, not so good to look at. Vietnamese men slim. Have hair only where it belong. Don't wear perfume like they trying to catch bees. You,

Frazier, not so bad, is all I say." Lou almost fell out of his chair laughing.

"She got you good, Frazier, got you good." Lenore treated all customers the same; we got no preferred treatment. If you walked in her restaurant, you felt special. The fact that she was gorgeous didn't hurt. Lunchtime was a little slice of paradise.

Lou and I talked up Lenore's restaurant. Pretty soon, all the MP patrols became regular customers. She thanked us for the publicity, confirmed she liked having MP's around. "Like insurance," she said, "VC go somewhere else, leave us alone. People eat more when safe, not nervous. Come every day, good for business." As she said that, I thought she was right. The village was bustling; it didn't look like the VC would have much luck selling their hatred around here. Capitalism was alive in Dong My.

The post typhoon cleanup of Chu Lai was going well. All the mess had been removed; some reconstruction was underway. All this repair work didn't jibe with the persistent rumor that Chu Lai might be shut down; merged with Da Nang. "It looks like business as usual," was Mac's view.

I agreed, "Fine with me to end our tour right here, who knows what Da Nang would be like. The only thing that intrigues me is there might be someone there to smack your ass in ping pong. You are definitely getting on my nerves." Mac just shrugged. I knew a ball would bounce off my head when we played later that night.

I hadn't seen Lt Clep for a few weeks, was surprised when he called me to his office that morning. "I talked to Captain O'Hanlon or Nut as you call him, said he wants to meet with you tonight. Just you, he's worried about you backing away from this investigation. He understands your loyalty to McCarthy, but wants your eyes and ears on this. At first, I argued with him, but now I think he's right.

We've hit a blank wall here, and need your help." Clep smiled at me, "It's probably not what you wanted to hear."

Not knowing what else to say; "See you tonight." I couldn't turn my back on Nut.

I was supposed to have patrol with Lou but he left with Clardy because of my delay. Callahan was my new partner for the more tedious base patrol. As we drove off, he chuckled when I bet that Lou and Clardy were already headed to Lenore's for a second breakfast. We talked about how much time we had left before heading home. "I'm so short that my balls have rug burns," drew a cringe from Joe. It was fun shooting the breeze with my old buddy. Callahan was back to his normal self, I think knowing this tour was ending had loosened him up. It was a quiet day on Chu Lai; that allowed me to prepare for meeting Nut.

I told Callahan I'd meet him at the USO club later on, I had some letters to write. He walked off, I reversed course, headed for Clep's office. Nut loomed in the doorway as I approached. "Better get your large Neanderthal frame inside or rumors will start." Nut backed away; let me get inside.

"You didn't get any better looking, Dylan, but you're still a sight for sore eyes." I hugged my muscular buddy but noted he'd gotten thinner, not quite as imposing.

"You eating okay, Nut? I might be able to whip your ass now; might be able to lock that full Nelson on you without getting tossed." Nut grinned a rare grin.

Before Nut started his pitch, I told him what was on my mind. I had less than 2 months left, didn't plan on making a career in the Army. Besides my unnatural curiosity and aggressiveness, why would I put my ass on the line? He came back with something I hadn't considered. "Because I need your help." He stood in front of me, said nothing more. I looked at Nut, remembered he was like a brother; the guy that was always there for me growing up. How many times had he stepped up for me during our lifetime? Exhaling deeply,

"Okay, Nut I'm in." And then I added, "But just me, I don't want the other guys involved. I'd never forgive myself if they got hurt."

Nut told me this was one of the most grievous cases of treason he'd ever seen. "Whoever is doing this has to be stopped. They assigned me to stop the bleeding. I've hit a blank wall." Lt Clep knocked on the door, Nut waived him inside. We spent the next hour comparing notes, seeing if we had overlooked anything. We seemed to be getting nowhere.

I mused, "There has to be a way they're hiding the money. We just haven't found it. Maybe we should expand the circle for Fleming. Let him go to Saigon. It's such a big city; it would be the perfect spot to vanish. Know what I mean?" Nut squinted, seemed to consider my suggestion.

Then I told Clep I needed to be working solo, needed an excuse. Otherwise Mac would see I was still snooping around. Clep scratched his chin, "That's not a problem, I'll assign you as Colonel Mullen's driver. He'll only need you once a day or so, but you always have to be on call. You and I can spend all the other time poking around. Stir things up some, see if anything shakes out." We agreed to watch the ammo dump daily, see if we'd missed any patterns.

"That reminds me, has Nicholson been on night duty at the dump?" Clep didn't know but would check. "If he is, my guess is he's the guy they use next. Hope not, but it's worth a look."

Nut got up, said he had to scoot before it got dark. Something popped into my head. "Is there any truth to the rumor about shutting down Chu Lai?" I could see Nut puzzling how to answer me. "Cool it, Nut. I don't want confidential information. My point is, if they are going to shut the base down, then they might try another attack before that happens. We should assume they heard the same rumors. It might be a lot harder to pull off this scam in Da Nang, so Chu Lai could be a target any day now. I think we should patrol the dump at night, watch for something funny.

Nut smiled again. Pointing at me, "Bingo!"

Nut left, I sat with Clep for a few minutes. "I'll get you assigned to Mullen tomorrow. He knows were meeting with Nut, so I'll brief him on what we plan. He likes you anyway, so he'll he happy you're his new driver. Percy used to drive him around but hasn't been around much lately, he's busy at the gates, trying to keep prostitution in check."

I looked at Clep, "You've got to be kidding. Percy's only concerned about one part of the whore problem, making sure he gets first dibs and collects the money."

Clep shook his head, "I can't convince the old man; he thinks Percy's done a good job infiltrating the local gangs, says he made great busts."

It was my turn to shake my head, "The old 'use a thief to catch a thief' trick, huh lieutenant? I don't believe that for a second. He's making a monkey out of Colonel Mullen. He'll regret it; trust me. I've got a good nose for smelling bullshit. Percy's a bullshit artist, par excellance." I could tell Clep had his doubts about Percy, but he kept quiet.

I was keyed-up, so I ambled over to the USO club. It was almost 8:30; the place was buzzing. Mac was holding court at the ping pong table. About 20 soldiers were gathered to see him put on a show. I watched carefully, trying to spot some weakness to exploit when we played again. Most players are better with forehands, using the backhand for defense only. Mac could smash you either way, it made no difference. Even high bouncers gave him no trouble, the ball came flying back higher than you sent it. He always grinned while he played, like he was listening to a Jonathan Winters monologue. I gave up on the weakness study; Mac was a force.

Out of the corner of my eye, I spotted Sgt Stroh barge into the club. I saw him scanning the place, agitated, looking for somebody. He locked on me, rushed over. "We might got a problem, Frazier. Clardy and Simpson aint checked in, don't answer their radio. Hoped they was here. Ya seen'em?" We wandered through the bar, didn't find them.

"Maybe a poker game going on, Sarge? You know how Lou is with poker. Maybe he's due to get married again, needs to lose his stash. That seems to be his M.O."

Stroh seemed to calm down, "Maybe you're right, let's go poke around."

We walked all over the MP camp, not a trace of Lou or Clardy. "Lou can sniff out a poker game anywhere. He plays with the Navy and Air Force guys all the time. My bet is he just dropped by on his way in, got suckered into a game. Clardy would just hang around, mooch on the free beer. Lou plays with the pilots all the time, he's really a good player, wins most of the time. Only seems to lose his mojo when wedding dates get set. That's when Lou suddenly gets beat like an old mule."

Stroh strode off muttering, "Gonna kick their ass tomorrow."

As I walked in to the MP desk next morning, I saw Stroh arguing with Lt Clep. "Takin' my best man, Lieutenant." Stroh was upset about my new job driving the Provost Marshall. "Those dumb fuckers Simpson and Clardy is missing; need Frazier to find them." Stroh explained what happened.

Clep responded, "I'll go with Frazier, we'll take care of it." As we drove around base looking for the AWOL MP's, I explained Lou's gambling habits but that Clardy didn't gamble much. That puzzled me. Figured Clardy would have gotten bored with the poker, wandered back. We were near the south end of base, when Stroh radioed us that an MP jeep was found abandoned near the village of Dong My, the one Clardy and Lou had used. We headed there at full speed.

There was no trace of either guy when we found the jeep, pulled into a thicket outside the village. A local farmer found the vehicle as he went to tend his rice paddy. He was waiting for us, probably expecting a reward. Using pigeon English, we asked if he knew where the MP's were. We were getting nowhere but then Clep slipped him $5, hoping to improve his memory. Papa-sahn looked at the jeep, then us sheepishly, "Beaucoup boom boom."

I looked at Clep, "Fuck." After a few seconds I started to think: Did papa-sahn mean an explosion or prostitutes? When I turned back to clarify, Papa-sahn had already vanished.

We called Stroh, asked for a chopper to surveil the area. It would take us hours to circle the meandering roads, so the chopper would be vital. I looked more carefully at the jeep. There were no signs of violence but I noticed that Lou's usual knapsack of suds was missing. It wasn't like Lou to leave his beer behind. I surmised, "Maybe he and Clardy had eaten at Lenore's, decided to have a few brewskis, got lost coming back?"

Clep nodded, "Based on what you've told me about Simpson, that doesn't sound far fetched." We radioed the chopper, told them we'd be in Dong My following a lead.

The village was very quiet as we approached the restaurant. "Something's not right, lieutenant. This place is normally a madhouse by now." I drew my pistol, chambered a round. As we cautiously entered Lenore's dining area, I was stunned to see Lou and Clardy lying on the floor.

Before I could worry if they were dead, Lou lets out a huge fart, a drowsy Clardy slurs, "You fuckin' pig Simpson." Clep looked really annoyed but I burst into laughter, the poor bastards were blind drunk.

Papa-sahn entered the room, pointed at the drunken slobs, "Beaucoup number fuckin' 10." It took another $20 to get papa-sahn to settle down. He finally made some potent green tea, said it would help. Clep started tearing them a new asshole. When he paused, I pulled him aside.

"Lieutenant, I know they're flaming assholes but I'm asking a favor, look the other way on this one. Let's just say they had food poisoning, got violently sick, couldn't even move. That isn't farfetched anyway. I'm calling in a favor for helping on the ordnance problems."

Clep exhaled deeply, "Fuckin' assholes." But he agreed to look the other way.

Apparently Lou had eaten lunch at Lenore's, got engaged with some local sharps into a game of Chinese poker. Being new to the rules and less than fluent in Vietnamese, Lou and Clardy lost their shirts. Not being a sensible loser, Lou began wagering his Colt 45 and whatever wasn't tied down. He even bet his jeep, which he ultimately lost. Sipping beer non-stop, both guys were shit-faced by nightfall, got into a big fight. Fortunately, Lenore intervened but not before they tore up her place. They decided to have a few more drinks to salve their wounds, soon passed out.

The locals knew they couldn't keep the jeep but decided to drive it around the village raising hell. To have the last laugh, they drove the jeep out of the village, hid it in the thicket. We got all this background when Lenore came walking in to help her husband clean up. She looked at me, "Tell Lou, he no come back. He play with bad people, lucky not dead." She pointed at her husband, "Beaucoup upset, no want MP's back. I try to talk but he no listen. Say MP's bad news."

Lt Clep looked at her, "I'll make certain you get reimbursed. No problems. Your place will now be off limits to our guys."

I was amazed how different Clep looked and acted when in action. Gone was the soft, slumping officer I'd met months ago, who seemed to be a punching bag. When things got tough, he stood tall, became a commanding presence, barked orders. As we escorted Lou and Clardy to their jeep, I was thankful Clep was in my corner. We probably had some scary days ahead of us. Thinking about having Nut as my buddy growing up, always there for me, I knew how important a tough friend could be. Now I was in Vietnam looking for traitors, I needed a strong partner.

Colonel Mullen called while we were driving back, Clep dropped me off to begin my chauffeur duty. We drove around the base; Mullen said he just wanted to see how the reconstruction was going after the typhoon. "This place took quite a punch, I'm not so sure it's worth all this clean-up effort. The newspaper's say the war is being lost, that we're out of here before too long. If that's true, what a waste of time, huh Frazier?"

I hoped that was true but kept my comments neutral, "After Quang Tri, this place still looks pretty nice. That place, Colonel, gave ugly a bad name."

Mullen chuckled, "You've got a point there, son, got a point."

We spent a silent hour or so, but Mullen killed that when he asked, "So, you think Burton and Price are dirty MP's, huh, Frazier?" I wasn't sure what Clep had told him recently but I was prepared for the question this time, decided to stir things up. Mullen had no expression on his face, like he was trying to avoid giving away his viewpoint.

"Sir, I know you've been with them a long time, but maybe this place has turned them, you know, made them snap. Based on what I've seen, has to be one or both of them. There's too many coincidences for any other conclusion. Having said that, sir, I admit I'm just a dumb-ass kid from Philly. Maybe, I'm way out in left field." Mullen chuckled again but said nothing. Had I pissed him off?

The rest of the ride was uneventful, chitchat about sports, what I was going to do when I got out of the Army. He listened to my ramblings about coaching basketball, or teaching or maybe being a writer. Mullen smiled, "You should think about the Army, Frazier. You're a natural, maybe the best MP I've seen here. I can get you in Military Intelligence in a snap. It's not just your smarts; you've got guts; that's what you need to be good. Based on what I've seen and heard, not much rattles you. You should think about it; just say the word and I'll get you to MI school in a week. I hate to see you throw that gift away coaching basketball or babysitting some rich kids." I thanked him, said I'd consider it, but thought how wrong he was. I wanted out. And fast.

It had been a weird day, I was anxious to catch up with Mac, trade some mindless chatter. He'd get a kick out of Mullen's pitch to get me to re-up. I could almost hear Mac's chuckle. Our hootch was empty but I could see that Mac had already been there. He was probably at chow, so I walked over to eat. Callahan was sitting by himself, advised that Mac had just left. "He's heading to the USO to annihilate the ping pongers again. He said he'd meet you there, if I saw you."

We walked to USO; Callahan told me Clardy had spilled the news about his all-night poker game. "He said he owes you big, Dylan. He said Clep was really pissed, that you talked him out of making it a Charlie Foxtrot."

I laughed, "Clardy's too dumb to just shut up and let it die. Bet he tells Stroh next. Can you imagine Stroh listening about them losing their guns and jeep? He'd shit a brick then kick their ass to Hanoi."

Lt Clep drove up just as we were about to walk into the club. "I need you for a while, Frazier, Club's gotta wait." I said goodbye to Callahan, joined Clep. Before I could ask, "Let's do an ammo dump drive-by. I think you're right, I bet they're going to hit it soon." When I looked puzzled, he added, "Colonel Mullen just got the word, they are shutting down Chu Lai. It could be as fast as a couple weeks." I wondered if the shutdown was good news or bad. I hoped it meant things would settle down, have a few quiet weeks before probably heading to Da Nang. After that, home! I liked that thought but quickly asked myself: Or would it get nuts?

I was relieved to see Nicholson was not manning the dump post. We had a few new MP's, these unfortunate bastards had recently landed in Chu Lai, were now on dump detail. The two newbies saluted Clep as we drove up. "Keep alert, soldiers, this place has a habit of getting blown up. Make sure you report any unusual activity. If you see anybody carrying a knapsack, stop them and search it. It doesn't matter what rank. If it's an officer and he bitches, tell them you're under direct orders from the Provost Marshall. Understand?" The rookies' eyes got big; no one had mentioned the recent bombing to them. Now they knew this wasn't such a schlock duty.

I told Clep about my discussion with Mullen. "So you told him directly you thought Ben and Percy were involved?"

I nodded, "Seemed like he'd already gotten that idea from you, I decided to stop beating around the bush, call a rat a rat." Clep surprised me when he said that he went out of his way to avoid mentioning Ben or Percy as clear suspects. I was quiet awhile, "Maybe you weren't as subtle as you thought, Mullen's a wily bird; he put two and two together."

Now Clep was quiet, "I wonder why he never asked me directly?"

I looked at him, "Maybe he was testing me, see if I'd bullshit him." I told him about the MI school discussion.

Clep nodded, "I think you're right, he was testing to see if you're as good as he thinks." Clep grinned, "I wonder if you passed?"

Mac was walking back from the shower when I got back. "Well if it isn't the carrot-topped ping pong potentate. Haven't seen your scrawny ass for a couple days."

Mac chuckled, "You're too busy driving limousines to mingle with the little people anymore." I told him about Chu Lai shutting down but that he needed to keep it quiet. Mac looked thrilled, "Damn, that's good news. The faster we get to Da Nang the more I like it. From what I hear, the place is a little city, has the best of the best. I hope I can find some decent ping pong competition there. I'm getting tired of spanking the local talent."

We talked for hours. Mac had heard a rumor we'd be home before Christmas. "Sgt Stroh said they never keep you over Christmas if your DEROS is around New Year's. If that's so, we got a month left in this shit hole." I looked at Mac.

"My only worry is I'm so short they might not be able to find me to send me home." He chuckled and we talked about what we'd do when we landed in the States. Mac and I agreed, "Going to run off that plane and kiss the ground, no question."

Early next morning, I met Clep and road over to see Fleming. He'd gotten back from Saigon; we wanted to see if he'd gotten any useful information. I asked him about the trip. Fleming had a combination smirk and smile on his face. "Before I get into that, I got to tell you about Da Nang. I stopped there for a couple days and got to see the whole base. Talk about your ocean resorts. That place is too cool to believe. I ate at a mess that served huge steaks, cooked on an outdoor grill. Then I got a lobster tail to keep it company. Fuck a duck, it was friggin' great."

Clep stared at him, "Let's put a hold on the cuisine tour and tell us what you found. I've been to Da Nang many times; I already know it's not the real war there. Anything useful in Saigon?" Fleming was wound up but he saw that Clep was in no mood for dicking around.

"I never saw so much money being wired all over the world. The civilian contractors are making a killing. Some of those guys are wiring hundreds of thousands dollars home every month. The guys that supply the PX's and do engineering work are millionaires. Fucking astounding!"

Clep drilled in, "Did you tie any of that loot to Burton, Price, or anybody interesting?" Fleming shook his head,

"Squat. Then I figured they might be using a fake name or ID. I tried to find names that had some connection. You know, like Mr. Percy or Mr. Ben, stuff like that. I still got no hits." And that got me thinking.

I looked at Clep, "Is it possible they got a contractor's ID? If so, they could shoot loads of money stateside without it looking abnormal. Or maybe they work with a contractor to fence the money, that kind of thing."

The look on Clep and Fleming's faces read: "Shit, that might be it."

Clep said he'd talk to Colonel Mullen; send Fleming back for more digging. I added, "Get a list of all the contractors that worked in Quang Tri, then see if any work here in Chu Lai. If nothing comes up, get a list of contractors in Da Nang and Saigon; see if any of them spent time in Quang Tri. There has to be some connection if the fake contractor is the way they're doing this." The more I thought about it the more it made sense. If I was a treasonous bastard, that would be my approach.

It was a beautiful day in South Vietnam. Clep and I tooled around base, went to the ammo dump a half dozen times. On our first trip, we saw Sgt Wilson there but he was driving a jeep, no way to hide stolen goods. I waved to him but got nothing back. Clep said, "I don't think he saw you." I wasn't so sure. I kept thinking: What had changed his attitude so drastically? Had Nam gotten to him? Had there been some disagreement with Frances that soured him? Was Wilson doing reconnaissance at the dump, letting the truck driver know if it was safe? I hoped he wasn't involved in this treason. I had to remind myself not to be fooled.

But other than seeing Wilson once, we saw nothing abnormal. We knew they'd steal the ordnance during the day, try to blend in with the other trucks loading up to re-supply the field troops. Clep was very quiet; you could almost see the fury building. "What's bugging you Lieutenent? You haven't said a word in an hour."

Clep exhaled deeply, "I can smell we're close. But I also think they might get away with this. It just drives me nuts. These fuckers are killing our soldiers to make a buck. It makes me so mad I want to shoot somebody." I understood how he felt; we drove wordlessly the rest of the day.

After chow, Mac and I walked to the USO, waited our turn for winners at the ping pong table. Although not in Mac's league, I had gotten much better. Mac let me play other guys for a while before he challenged me. He wanted me warmed-up, ready to give him a match. My serve had gotten good, a topspin forehand that could occasionally give Mac trouble. If I did it perfectly, it dipped quickly. If I got it deep enough, Mac couldn't smash at will. We usually went neck and neck till mid-game but then Mac would adjust to my angles, drill it back harder and harder. Although I lost every time, my only satisfaction was Mac could no longer pound balls off my head.

Clardy, Fleming, and Callahan joined us; we cheered Mac while yapping about being short. Clardy shocked us when he said he was considering re-upping for another tour in Nam. "I'm still in fer another 2 years, think I might as well spend it here. I know the deal, plus I kin make more money." We took turns trying to tell him what a bad idea that was but he had one reason we couldn't counter, "I kinda like it here. I still worry some about what happen' ta Corbin, but the war's windin' down, might be okay ta spend time in Da Nang or Ben Hoi. Them bases is kinda like the States, but no spit and polish. Know what I mean?"

While we were arguing with Clardy, Percy had wandered in, was waiting his turn against Mac. Percy rarely came in here, spent most of the time at the adjoining NCO section of the club. I wondered what brought him in. Percy started taunting Mac's opponents. "None a you motherfuckers gonna beat McCarthy. He's the second best player on the base. Don't fuck with the MP's, we beat your ass in basketball and now we rule in pong. Some sorry motherfuckers is what I'm lookin' at. Drill their ass McCarthy. Show em what the P's can do."

Percy had about 5 guys ahead of him but most of them wandered off without playing. Losing to Mac was bad enough. No one wanted to listen to Percy berate them too. Percy was next up. It started off okay. Percy was really good, Mac had to break a mild sweat to beat him 20-15. Percy glared at the line of guys waiting for winners, "Fuck if I'm done yet. Just warming up. Gonna show McCarthy my A game next. Any problem with that?" Percy's reputation preceded him; the line of guys just shook their heads.

Mac got more serious, won the next few games by wider margins; Percy was getting pissed. "Fuckin' pussy shots is all you got, McCarthy. Play straight up, like a man. No pussy shit." Mac drilled the next shot off the table, into Percy's forehead.

I looked at Callahan, "Oh, shit." Percy didn't seem to notice this was intentional, kept yapping. But whenever Percy got too personal or called Mac a pussy, the ball caromed off Percy's unsuspecting body parts. That made me nervous.

Finally, Percy realized Mac was toying with him, amped-up the taunts. I tried to get Mac's attention; he was headed down a dangerous road. I didn't want him to tank, but he had to stop pelting Percy. He was the wrong guy to screw with. Fortunately, Mac seemed to sense that already,

backed off some; he just swatted the ball for winners.
Percy wasn't grateful for the gesture. "Give me your best
stuff, you red-headed dick head or I'm gonna fuck your
woman next time I'm home on leave. Show her how a real
man fucks. Not some pussy ping pong faggot." Mac
answered by hammering the ball into Percy's crotch.

Percy didn't hesitate. He threw the paddle down,
screamed how he was gonna show Mrs. McCarthy his
manly style of fornication. Just as Percy hoped, Mac
charged, Percy dodged sideways and crushed Mac's left leg
with his deadly move. It all happened in seconds. As Percy
pivoted to give Mac another kick, I ran at him, tried to
tackle him. Just like a wild animal, he sensed me coming,
ducked low and shoved me over his back. I saw Mac
writhing as I crashed down beside him. Percy hadn't
connected cleanly with me; I was unhurt.

I knew I didn't have much time. I rolled to my feet,
faced Percy. He did something I wasn't expecting, he
laughed maniacally, "Must be my lucky day, get to whoop
my two favorite pussies in one night. Get ready to be
fucked up, Frazier." Before Percy could move, Callahan
fell in beside me.

He looked at Percy, "You better make that a double
dose, Sergeant. I'm with Frazier." Then I felt Fleming on
my other side.

"Make that a trifecta, Price. You're going to have three
of us." It got even better as Clardy joined us.

"Make that 'me too'; don't know no fancy words like
Fleming."

Percy started blinking rapidly, like a hawk confused by
his prey fighting back. Then oddly, he shrugged, turned
quickly and walked out the door. He yelled behind him.
"This aint over, Frazier. A world a hurt's comin at ya."

Mac moaned, that snapped us out of our defensive
huddle. I ran to my buddy; saw bone protruding from his
bleeding left shin. Callahan got the bartender to call the

medics; we tried to calm Mac while we waited. Finally I came up with something that made Mac smile. "You're headed home, buddy. No way they'll let you hang around here with that injury."

The medics arrived quickly. They lifted Mac carefully but he groaned in agony. "Where are you taking him?" I asked.

"Closest hospital is the Air Force base, down by the runway. We'll head there; hope it aint a bad night in the bush. Most times it's quiet. Mostly just crazy cowboy shit like this."

I looked at the lead guy, "I'm going with you, make sure they don't give you any shit. He's my buddy, they're going to fix him fast, it isn't a request, Get me?"

The medic saw the look on my face, "Yes, sir."

Callahan, Fleming, and Clardy went back to the MP station, told Sgt Stroh what happened. "Fuckin' lunatic, that Price. He's gonna kill somebody one day. Take the jeep, I'll tell Lt Clep what happened. We'll see what he wants to do with Price." Callahan and Fleming told me this when they arrived about 15 minutes later.

I looked at Callahan, "They won't do dick. He's tight with Colonel Mullen. Just like what happened to you in Basic, they'll sweep this under the rug." Fleming nodded; Callahan didn't answer but I knew he agreed. The Army way, keep bad news within the family.

While we waited for news on Mac's condition, we talked about Percy. I told Callahan that I'd been privately helping Clep investigate the ordnance thefts. He looked troubled but I added quickly, "With Mac going home now, nothings going to hold me back. I want those fuckers to swing. In fact, if we can't pin anything on him, I'm going to kick Percy's ass before I leave. That's a promise."

Now Fleming jumped in, "That's a real bad idea, Dylan. Percy is crazy. Guys like that don't live long. Let someone else do the dirty work. You're going to end up like Mac, hobbling around on a bum leg."

The medic interrupted us, "Your buddy's doing fine. We can't set the bone till the swelling goes down. I've got him pumped up with painkillers and stabilized the leg. We're going to medevac him to Da Nang tomorrow. They'll cast the leg when they can, wait a day or so then send his lucky ass to Ft Ord for rehab. He'll be sipping those California wines in no time. Maybe walk on the beach to strengthen his leg, all in all not so bad." That news made me relax; Mac would probably be seeing his wife and kid in a few days. I forced myself not to think about Percy, didn't want to do anything stupid.

Mac was sleeping, so we asked when he'd be sent to Da Nang, was told mid-day. We planned to be back first thing, to say our goodbyes before he took off. I stopped in to see Stroh, found Clep with him. "Bad news on McCarthy, Frazier. By the way, don't do anything dumb with Price, we'll take care of him. I already filled Mullen in; he's really pissed off. He wants to talk to you first thing tomorrow to get the facts. Price's in trouble; I haven't seen the Colonel like this before."

I got up early, drove to see Mac before duty started. He had an ice bag on his leg but pulled it up when I walked in. He had a huge shit-eating grin on his face. "Swelling's almost gone, might be able to get the cast on today. Did you hear they're sending me home? If I knew that I'd have baited Percy before. Holy shit, I'm going home!" It was hard not to laugh.

I looked at him, "Mac, that crazy bastard busts your leg and all you do is talk about home. Where's your sense of revenge? Maybe, Percy's right, you are a pansy ping ponger."

We both laughed, talked about his going home. "The Doc said I'd probably get an early out if I wanted. I only have 7 months left on my duty, probably the Army won't want to pay me during rehab, so they'll let me go if I want. What a silly question, I'm history." While he was jabbering,

I realized I might not see him for a long time, maybe ever. He lived in Portland, me in Philly. During our time in Nam, we had gotten really close, almost like brothers. I was happy for him but would miss him.

He seemed to sense my mood. "Don't worry, Dylan, you'll be getting out soon. I want you to come to Portland, meet Mary and little Mike. Mary says she feels like she already knows you, from my letters. She says she's glad you're so paranoid, maybe it kept me alive." And then he looked serious, "By the way, thanks for stepping in last night, that asshole would have broken the other leg if you hadn't charged him. I owe you big." He got a sheepish look as he said. "If I haven't mentioned it, I don't make friends too easily. I consider you my best friend, I hope we stay buddies forever, grow old together, and can reminisce about our fun in Nam someday."

The medics walked in before I could answer. "Good news McCarthy, your leg's looking good, so we'll get you to Da Nang right away, a planes leaving in 30 minutes. Time to get you ready to travel." The Doc started to wheel him out, I only had a few seconds to grab his hand, wish him luck.

"See you in the Real World, Mac. When I get back, I'll make a side trip to Portland, make sure you're really married to that beautiful girl. My bet is that picture came with your wallet. Why would that babe marry you?" Even the medic chuckled. Then my good friend was gone.

I got back to the MP station; Stroh said Clep and Mullen were waiting for me. The Colonel listened to my story, asked detailed questions. I could tell from his queries that he wanted to know who actually made the first aggressive move. Anticipating his conclusion, I added, "Percy threw his paddle then taunted him about his wife. He baited him, knowing his wife was his hot button. Percy started it, no question." Mullen had a solemn look; I could see he had another viewpoint.

"When McCarthy charged Price, he lost his advantage. We're in Nam, Frazier; you can't attack somebody and then claim it was his fault when you get hurt. No military court will touch Price."

As I was about to argue, Percy walked in, saluted Mullen. "You wanted to see me, sir?" Mullen asked his version of the incident; he corroborated the sequence of events but forgot to mention slurs on Mac's wife. To my surprise, Mullen brought that oversight up, Percy grinned, "Just talkin' shit, sir, you know how boys talk trash. Nothing big." Mullen surprised me again. He tore Percy a new rear end; that if there were another incident he'd personally throw him in jail, get him dishonorably discharged. No pension. He'd burn him. Mullen was flushed with anger as he stopped, fought to compose himself.

Percy remained stoic throughout the harangue. He never flinched or said a word. He looked as if he was listening to a priest on Sunday morning, attentive but mildly bored. I tried to figure what was running through his mind. Was he so insane that he just didn't care about anything? Colonel Mullen continued to blast him about injuring one of his best men, how he hurt the unit. Percy continued his strange silence. When Mullen was finally done and asked if Price understood the gravity of this situation. Percy came to attention and said, "Yes, sir," saluted and walked out. Mullen narrowed his eyes.

And after taking a deep breath, Mullen switched topics, asked Clep what our next move was with the ordnance thefts. I could see Clep was puzzled by the sudden switch but he shook it off, said we were closely monitoring the dump, looking for unusual activity, that we expected something would happen in the next week or so. Mullen nodded, said we should watch the dump even closer. "Maybe do 24 hour surveillance. We've got stop these thefts. I'm taking a lot of flak already from MI. Let's get this settled. Dismissed."

When we got outside I asked Clep his read on the Price discussion. "The Colonel knows Price is losing it. He told me he'd take care of Price 'The Army way'." Clep gave me a little background on how hard it is to get decorated war veterans court-martialed. That didn't make me feel a lot better and I said that. Clep nodded, "I'm not saying I agree with Mullen but it's his call. Let's concentrate on catching the ordnance thief, maybe we get Percy in the same trap." We visited the dump a dozen times before nightfall, made plans to go again around 9 pm. Nothing unusual was happening. Maybe we misjudged their greed. Why risk another hit? They already had a fortune.

I ate chow with Callahan; he asked if I wanted to move in with him and Clardy. I grinned, "Not sure I could take seeing Clardy without his make-up on in the morning. The guy's scary enough all dressed up. Plus, maybe I'd see him nude by accident and lose my cookies. Thanks anyway, Joe."

Callahan smiled, replied, "Now that you mention it, maybe I'll move in with you. I've gotten used to seeing Clardy naked and that's not a good thing." That was funny.

I bid him goodnight, made my way to the hootch. My practice of switching different sleeping accommodations would continue. Percy warned me things weren't over; I didn't count on Colonel Mullen's tongue-lashing having a long impact. My mind wandered to how Mac was doing as I rounded the corner near the MP station. I hoped he was okay after his procedure. My thoughts were jolted as I spotted Colonel Mullen and Percy in the midst of an animated discussion. Mullen has his finger in Percy's face. The usually cocky Percy looked stunned. What was going on here? Was Mullen delivering a stronger message?

I met Clep early next morning for an ammo dump patrol. Clep had no answer to the heated exchange I witnessed. "Mullen's a cagey guy, Frazier, he lures you then pop, he's all over you. He and Percy have some history, he's going to deal with him in his own way. He'll probably get hm assigned Stateside as a Drill Instructor. If Price tries any of that caveman stuff in the real world, they'll force him out. There's no use throwing salt in the wound while he's in Nam, that's what I think." I let that sink. I had experienced Mullen's sudden intensity. We rode in silence. We got to the ammo dump, just like before, nothing odd going on. I stewed in my anger till we got back to base.

Mac and I spent hours fortifying the various places we slept. Most of our effort went into adding layers of plywood under our bunks. We figured that Percy and Ben would try to frag us, so we closed any openings in the hootch, also piled a couple mattresses under our bunks. Even if the grenade went off right beneath us, all the padding and wood would absorb the impact. Since it was only me now, I dragged Mac's mattresses over, added more protection under my bunk. Mac still was helping me out.

I was deep asleep when the deafening explosion rocked the night. My first reaction, "Grenade?" But hazy night vision showed my hootch was intact. The blast was not here. Then it hit me, "The dump." I dressed quickly, darted towards Clep's quarters. He was running out as I neared.

"Let's get a jeep, check this out. Maybe the fucker's are still on the base. Let's get to the gate." The base was suddenly alive. We had to dodge some curiosity traffic as we tooled to the base entrance. As we roared up, Clep shouted to the MP on duty, "Any big trucks come through here lately?"

We learned a 2 ½ ton had recently left but the guard wasn't sure in what direction. Clep looked at him and yelled, "Guess. Think back, what's your best guess. North or south?" The guy was shook by Clep's hostile mood.

"I'm not sure, lieutenant. Maybe south? I was too busy watching the fire at the dump." Clep pointed at him,

"Next time, pay attention. Your job's to watch the traffic, not fucking star gaze. Got that?" I had never seen Clep this intense. He was furious.

We drove south but soon realized this wasn't a good idea. It was pitch dark, we had no machine gun, were in Vietnam chasing who knew how many thieves. I slowed down some, told Clep I thought this was a wild goose chase. He clenched his jaw, "I just wanted to do something. I just wanted to move." Then he sat back, "I think you're right, this isn't smart."

I looked at him, "Let's go back; see if that MP remembered what the guy looked like. Might get something there."

It was another dead end. The MP said the driver had a valid pass, that he was delivering ammo to re-supply the grunts. Nothing unusual. "What did he look like? Big guy, little guy, was he black or white? Was he wiry or a linebacker type?" I could tell by his blank look that he had no clue.

"Just average lookin', it's pretty dark and the lights was shining in my eyes." The only thing he could say for certain was the guy was white. Clep looked at the poor sap,

"You got no future in law enforcement, son. A fucking useless piece of work tonight. Get your head out of your ass next time. Got that?" I felt sorry for the MP; he was shaking as we left.

We drove to the dump, but it was a crazy. Fire trucks had controlled the blaze some but we had to park and walk inside. Clep drilled the guard but nobody saw anything. Trucks were always loading or unloading ammo, but the protocol was if the dump got hit, trucks got out fast. There was no chance the guards would note any particular driver or their actions. All the drivers got the hell outta there in seconds. Clep remained dour, prowled around the dump, hoping something would surface. I stayed close by, kept quiet and thought. I believed this was our last chance to nab these guys in the act. But instead, we had another failure.

As we were driving back, I told Clep we should check Ben and Percy's hootchs to see if they were there. Clep banged on their doors but we got no answers. Both of them were gone. I got excited but Clep doused my enthusiasm. "It doesn't prove anything, Frazier. Most guys got up to check on the explosion. All they have to say is they were checking out all the action." I tried to talk him into waiting for them, confronting them when they returned, maybe catch them off guard. Clep chuckled the first time all night. "I like your guts, Frazier but these two are tough bastards. There's no way they fall for that. Plus that crazy fuck Percy might shoot us if he sees someone waiting for him in the dark. Bad odds. Go to bed. We'll go at it tomorrow."

I slept fitfully. Had visions of the exploding ammo, Percy and Ben laughing as they drove to their rendezvous, Clep stomping mad. Then I realized that I wasn't dreaming, another explosion had rocked me awake. What the hell? As I scanned my hootch, I was relieved the explosion wasn't near me. I got half dressed, wandered to the MP station. I saw Stroh bolt out the door. He just stood there, looking wildly left and right. When he spotted me, he called me over. His eyes were wild. "It's been another bad day, Frazier. I need ya to come with me." Clardy was standing outside looking left and right, said someone fragged Ben Burton's hootch. I recoiled, was stunned.

Clardy and Callahan were standing outside Ben's smoking hootch. Stroh had a couple flashlights, started inspecting the half shattered front door. "We gotta be careful 'fore we enter. Ya never know if there's more'n one grenade. Sometimes they don't all go off. So spread out a little." Stroh stayed low, edged open what was left of the bottom part of the door. He peered inside, flashed on the bloody carcass laying half off the bunk. Stroh pushed open the door fully, slowly illuminated each section of the room. He turned to me, "It looks okay. I'll go in first, go to the left. Follow me, you go right. Don't touch the body. Sometimes they leave frags underneath to fuck up whoever tries ta help." He handed me the other flashlight.

I entered slowly, methodically flashed every area I moved into. Lots of dust, ripped bedding but nothing seemed unusual. I realized I was holding my breath, so I exhaled, felt better immediately. That got my nerves under control. I looked at Ben quickly, knew instantly he was no longer a threat. His torso was torn to shreds but his face was untouched. He had a startled look, like "What the hell's happening." But his eyes were vacant; his mouth was puckered up, totally still. Ben Burton was stone dead.

Stroh confirmed my diagnosis. "Ben Burton done stole his last truck." Then he looked at me. "What the fuck's going on here?" I thought I knew the answer to that before but now Ben's death threw a monkey wrench into my theory. I still caught myself holding my breath, like my expanding diaphragm might put me in danger. I took another deep breath, got oriented again. As I silently gulped air, it occurred to me what was happening: Percy was covering his tracks, had decided splitting the profits was no longer good enough.

There was now a big crowd outside Ben's hootch. I spotted Sgt Wilson standing quietly on the fringes. Just then Colonel Mullen came to investigate. Stroh and I walked over to him, gave him the bad news. When he heard Ben was dead, he stared blankly. Then his eyes got wild. He grinded his teethed, muttered: "Fuck! This makes no God damned sense. Who the fuck would frag Ben? I'm tired of losing good men. We're shutting this God forsaken place down." He turned suddenly to Stroh. "Why in the world would anyone kill Ben?" He wanted no answers. He just wanted to vent. This was the first time I'd ever seen Colonel Mullen lose control. He walked away muttering, angry, shaking his head.

On the walk back, I remembered I'd forgotten to lock my hootch when I ran out to see what was happening. When I returned, I had a sense that someone had been inside. There was a smell I couldn't place. Was it smoke? I still had Stroh's flashlight, so I backed to the door, shined the light around to see if anything had been tampered with or moved. Nothing seemed out of place. Was I imagining this? Just a heightened dose of adrenaline? Maybe I just smelled the aromas my cloths picked up in Ben's hootch. Just as I talked myself into dismissing my fears, I remembered Nut's advice: Never let your guard down. I locked my hootch, shut off my flashlight, silently moved to one of my other locations.

Next morning we got official word that Chu Lai was shutting down. Mullen stood before the assembled company of MP's, said we'd be some of the last to go but that in two weeks the base would be turned over to the ARVN's. Mullen looked at us with a resigned expression: "Next stop Da Nang, gentleman." I looked over; saw Percy. He had a subdued grin on that smug face. He turned toward me, caught my eye. The grin disappeared; a look of pure malevolence filled those cloudy eyes. Then he shook his head just a little. His look said, "This isn't over." I'm not sure what came over me but I lifted my right index finger, pointed as if to say: "I'm ready." Percy didn't react, turned his head, walked off. He had an animal spring in his step.

Mullen would be busy all day planning the orderly downsizing of Chu Lai, so my chauffeur duty was over. Clardy took over Ben's role in the Motor Pool, Callahan and I became partners. Clep said he was meeting with Nut to discuss the next course of action. "Ben was our best lead, that's now a dead end." I looked at Clep.

"If that's a pun, even I wouldn't stoop that low." Clep shook his head, said he'd pretend I hadn't said that.

Then added, "I think we have to follow the paper trail now. Nothing's going to happen around here. Maybe it all dies with Burton. Either way, I'll get back to you."

Callahan didn't have Mac's sense of humor or feistiness, but I liked him a lot. We fell into our old routine, reminisced how far we've come since Basic Training. "For a Conscientious Objector, Joe, you turned out to be one slam bam fightin' man."

Joe laughed, "It's hard to figure isn't it. Most of the things I've done here don't seem to have anything to do with fighting Communism. Just crazy everyday stuff, watching for something to happen and then fixing the mess." Then Joe pointed at me, "You on the other hand have blossomed from reluctant leader to pride of the unit. It's like you were born for this." When he saw my quizzical look, he added, "That's a compliment."

Over the course of that patrol, I filled Joe in on all the behind the scenes investigations. I wanted his logical brain to help spot what I must be missing. Joe listened to the wire transfer and false identity theory, shook his head. "That's a big leap of logic but I can't say it's wrong." I watched Joe mulling this idea some more before he hit the heart of the puzzle. "If Ben was the brains of the outfit, why frag him? Greed?" We road quietly, thinking, looking for answers.

Joe had frequently eaten at Lenore's restaurant in Dong My, so suggested that as our destination for lunch. I hadn't been there since Lou and Clardy got soused and screwed our already mediocre reputations. I told Joe I thought MPs were banned. He got a shy look. "Not me." I thought: Interesting. Dong My was noticeably quiet, no longer the throbbing bustle at lunchtime. I walked in the restaurant, spotted Lenore and her husband packing chairs and tables. When she saw Joe she gave him a huge smile. When her husband saw me he grumbled. She rapped at him in Vietnamese, turned back at us.

"I told papa-sahn you MP who help clean up mess, not crazy man, puke on floor, drunk card player." That made me belly laugh, pretty soon even papa-sahn was chuckling.

Over a delicious meal, we learned Lenore was moving; with Chu Lai shutting down their business would dwindle. She looked at Joe, "We move to Hoa Xuan. I go mission school there, so know it good. Not far from Da Nang. Near road so we get traffic. Soon we build business like here." Lenore gave us her serene smile, "You spread word we beaucoup best. Okay?" That wouldn't be too much to ask, her food was amazing. We bid her farewell, told her we'd look her up in a few weeks.

After she left, Callahan turned, "That's the most beautiful girl I've ever seen." He kept shaking his head.

On the ride back, I told Joe I was thinking of following Percy that night to check his patterns. He looked at me funny, "You think he's still after you?"

I nodded, "He told me it wasn't over, I believe him. Whatever I have to do to avoid being ambushed should give me an edge. Agree?" Joe thought a second then nodded.

"I'll come with you, two eyes are better than one." That caught me off guard but I did need the help.

"Are you sure Joe, he's not on your case. If he sees you with me, he'll widen his vengeance."

Joe nodded, "I owe you from back in Basic when you kept that crazy Sgt Snow from strangling me. I never really thanked you. I got too busy with my crusade for truth and justice. It seems like a million years ago. Boy, was I naive. I was lucky they didn't send me to the grunts." It did seem like a million years ago but it was also fresh in my memory. Our relationship had been nearly ruined. I shook my head.

"Forget about it, Joe. We've both changed a lot since then. Maybe we were better off as two simple numb nuts from Philly. As they say in the Nam, 'This place can do you a job'."

I told Lt Clep what I planned; he seemed anxious. "I'm not sure that's a great plan, Frazier. Since Ben got fragged, we aren't sure what we're dealing with. This might be a bigger gang than we thought. It seems like it's more complicated than a couple burned-out NCO's running a scam. You only have a few weeks left. You might want to let it be. I can handle it from here. The paper will tell a tale. We just have to find the right lead. With Ben gone, maybe they'll get careless."

I thanked him but told him I wanted to stay on the offensive. "Never been one to wait too long. That's why your boss Nut and I got along so well. We'd knock each other over trying to get an edge. I won a lot. He might be more aggressive but I was faster. Even he'll admit that."

Clep grinned, "He already did. He said you were the real crazy one but you were smoother than him. That he always got the blame." I chuckled.

"Perhaps there's a grain of truth in that. But don't tell him I said so."

Percy went to the USO after chow, stayed there till around 9 pm. Then he went to the north gate, kibitzed with the guards till the whores showed up. We had parked our jeep around the bend, hid in the brush watching. The gate was illuminated so it was easy to spot him strutting around, like an emperor inspecting his harem. He grabbed a couple lovelies then zoomed toward the Air Force quarters near the main entrance to Chu Lai. He unloaded the girls, disappeared inside.

Percy stayed on the airbase till about 11 pm, headed back toward the MP camp. We let him get a big lead then drove with our lights out. There was a full moon that reflected off the South China Sea, gave us a clear target. We were fairly certain that Percy never saw us. He was as arrogant

as ever, acted like he owned the road. Once we saw him
pull into the MP camp, we drove past the entrance, waited
5 minutes and then drove back to the Motor Pool. With
Clardy running things there, we had no trouble getting
wheels.

Callahan and I split up but agreed to pass by Percy's
hootch separately, a few minutes apart. Joe had gotten
there first; whispered as I passed him, "He's in there. It
looks like he's headed to bed." I nodded, went to look for
myself. Lights shone under his door, loud music pierced
the quiet. I was surprised to hear Cat Stevens familiar voice
lulling Percy to sleep. "Moon Shadow" followed me as I
made my way to rendezvous with Callahan. I knocked
three times, with a delayed fourth, signaling it was me. Joe
opened the door. I threw my hands apart, exhaled.

"Looks like the lion isn't hunting tonight. See you
tomorrow."

DA NANG

I got some good news next day from Sgt Stroh. "We're moving out tomorrow. Colonel Mullen's leaving Price and a few others as a stand down team to help the ARVN's. I won't miss seeing that crazy fucker fer a few weeks, huh?" I looked at Stroh.

"It's like being a kid and told the Dentist isn't going to drill anymore. Kind of like the dull pains finally gonna end." Stroh bobbed his head up and down.

"I know what ya mean. Price could fuck up a wet dream."

We spent the day gathering our meager stuff. The plan was to caravan to Da Nang. Lt Clep was in charge, put Callahan and me at the rear. When he saw my reaction to this position, Clep laughed. "I need someone who knows the drill, Frazier. Plus you drive like a bat outta hell normally, so this should be a piece of cake." I raised my hands over my head, in the surrender position.

"I remain a helpless victim of air-tight fecal matter. But don't worry about it, I've gotten to love swallowing dust from a 100 trucks. Just another chance to live the dream."

Clep saluted me, "You're welcome, soldier!" It was good to hear Callahan belly laugh again.

The road was mostly lowland, dotted with farms and small forests. I drove, did my normal evaluation of where the Charlie would pull a surprise attack. I yelled my theories to Callahan as he manned the Thompson machine gun. The noise was deafening so Joe mostly nodded, said nothing. I wasn't sure whether he was ignoring me, couldn't hear me, didn't want to be creeped-out or some combination thereof. Somehow it made me feel better jabbering warnings, so the one-way conversation took place the whole trip before our uneventful arrival at the magnificent Da Nang base.

They called Da Nang the "Saigon of the North." We drove on the outskirts of town; I was surprised to see a bustling but featureless city. Most of the trees and vegetation were obliterated. People were everywhere. The noise was deafening, clouds of dust followed us as we headed toward our nearby base. In contrast to the drab city, the American base was immaculate, pristine. Roads were paved and spotless, low vegetation and palm trees gave it a resort feel. I thought about my first days in Quang Tri, silently cheered spending my final weeks in such splendor. Plus Percy wasn't there.

Once the caravan got safely inside, we stopped, awaited directions to our new home. Lt Clep drove up, took one look at me before laughing. "Wipe that grin off your face, Frazier. Just because you made it to paradise doesn't mean you're going to get to fuck off. I still have work for you. I need that devious mind of yours to help me setttle a few loose ends. Follow me, we'll head to our new digs, then go to CID to hook up with Fleming. Even that sad sack chuckled when he saw his new home. "

The MP camp was huge. It was set in a dip of the low hill leading up to Marble Mountain. From that vantage point, it overlooked the natural harbor that made Da Nang an ideal military location. There were over a hundred hootches in our new camp, a huge club and the nicest basketball court I'd seen in Nam. When Clep spotted my awed look he agreed. "This is the biggest location of MP's in Nam. We'll be small potatoes here; we just have to blend in. Colonel Mullen told me he'd have no shot at Provost Marshall here. He'd probably just wait to be reassigned or maybe sent back to the States, retire to his golfing life in Augusta. He didn't seem too upset; he says he wants to get his handicap back to single digits. I think he wants to get out. Seeing Ben fragged did him in."

We reported to the MP desk, were told where to bunk. Callahan, Clardy, and I wandered into our hootch, were amazed to see individual bunks and sleeping areas. Although walls didn't separate the areas, low paneling made it feel you had some privacy. Clardy described it best, "Holy Shitoly. This is some fancy smancy place!" The previous residents had left paperbacks on the top shelf in my area. I picked the first one up, grinned.

"This one's for you Clardy." I showed him the cover: "Nude on the Moon." Callahan chuckled, Clardy looked excited.

"Sounds like some damn fine readin' ta me."

Chow that night was a whole new experience in fine dining. The desk sergeant gave us directions to the mess hall on a nearby hill. Trudging up, we were again amazed. The place was enormous. We entered the front; saw the place was divided into inside and outside dining areas. The cooking was done in a semi-enclosed, outside kitchen. Most of the meat selections were cooked on the biggest barbecue grill I ever saw. Did we want chicken, pork, steak or burgers and dogs? I looked at my buddies, "Holy Shitoly!"

Clardy took some of each. Rather than get two plates and appear a hog, he piled his stuff about 8 inches high. Callahan and I stood in awe. "Buck says you can't eat all that, Clardy."

He arched his sandy eyebrows, "Ya'll are on." I ate the best steak of my life. Maybe it was the atmosphere of civilization but I savored every bite. The baked potato and sour cream melted in my mouth. Callahan sat next to me silently, except for an occasional moan as he slowly devoured the slab of beef. We never heard a word from

Clardy as he tore through his feast. Finally he threw his hands up, belched like a trumpet. "Where's my buck?"

I grinned, "Double or nothing you puke in an hour."

Clardy never hesitated, "Yer on." An hour later I gave him two dollars when he pulled out a giant pack of M&M's to wash down his feast.

We decided to ride around some, let our stomachs settle, explore the base before it got too dark. I spotted a huge outdoor amphitheatre, wondered out loud if that's where Bob Hope and the other stars entertained the troops. Before Callahan could answer, Clardy blasted out a prodigious fart. "Jesus, Clardy, don't shit your pants and ruin the ambiance. This is my first night in paradise."

Clardy grinned, "Think that steak got things percolatin'." We continued the tour but had to turn back quickly as Clardy's call to nature wouldn't be denied.

Next morning, Clep wandered into our hootch, told me to meet him after chow. He looked at our new accommodations. "Nice digs, huh? You ought to see the officer's quarters. So nice it's almost embarrassing. See you in a bit." Breakfast was as sumptuous as dinner the night before. Callahan spied my overflowing plate.

"Better watch it Dylan, you're going to get fat if you keep that up." I never looked up but replied.

"Following Clardy's lead. Don't want the system getting jammed. Got to start things percolatin'." Callahan grimaced. It was the best breakfast I'd had in months. I thought about Callahan's jab. This place could put meat on your bones.

I met Clep; we drove to CID headquarters, which was farther up the road to Marble Mountain. Although smaller than the MP camp, it was immaculate, packed with small buildings loaded with radio antennas. I looked at Clep, "What is this place, Mission Control?"

He nodded, "You're not far off. They have the A Teams in Da Nang. Fleming was a hot shot in Quang Tri and Chu Lai. Here, he's just a gnat on the A Team's ass." That thought perked me up. Fleming wouldn't like being a stooge. He'd be pissier than ever and that would be hysterical.

I was right on. The look on Fleming's face said it all. "Now that's one sour puss if I ever saw one, Fleming. Old Noah Webster might put your picture in his next dictionary update. Right after, "discontented." Before he could flip me off, another guy walked around the cubicle, introduced himself as Captain Ruger. He was almost my height but not as heavy, closer to lanky in build. He exuded confidence, like he was thinking what you were about to say, already had an answer. I looked at his pale blue eyes, blond crew cut; thought of the ideal Aryan race Hitler had envisioned. Then I wondered if he knew why we were here.

On cue, "You must be Frazier. Lieutenant Clep filled me in on the weapons thefts you've been tracking. I like some of your ideas. I think we can crack this with an experienced auditor."

I looked at Fleming. He knew he was viewed as "the inexperienced auditor" and didn't like it.

He said, "Captain Ruger, I'm just warming up," when Ruger cut him off.

"Not relevant, Fleming. You'll stay on the team. I just need people involved that do this for a living. We've got to ratchet up this investigation. These traitors have gotten away with literal murder and will pay. Count on it. Frazier, follow me. I want to talk to you and Lt Clep privately. This way." I couldn't look at Fleming, might bust out and spoil my good reputation with Ruger. Didn't think he would get my sense of humor.

We spent the next hour filling Ruger in on all the details. He wrote voluminous notes and then wheeled in a big blackboard when we were done the debriefing. "Let's file these facts by categories." He then proceeded to list all the assumptions and wild-ass guesses. Ruger turned abruptly, got on a radio, called for Fleming and a name I never heard before. A pencil-necked geek came in with Fleming a few minutes later. "Gentleman, meet Sgt Peake. He's the best snooper we have in Vietnam. If he can't sniff it out it doesn't smell. Let's get to work, gentlemen."

Peake asked questions about the facts, had Fleming fill us in on what he'd already investigated about wire transfers. I told him my thoughts on using a fake contractor's ID. Peake looked at me sharply. "I like that idea. Tell me more." I expounded on my view that a Swiss account may have been used, that they were numbered accounts that could be falsified with fictitious names. Based on what Nut had told us before, false SSN's and driver's licenses were child's play to get in Nam.

Peake closed his eyes for a few minutes, seemed almost in a trance, then said, "It could be done. The only problem is that would require a personal visit to withdraw large amounts. Small wire withdrawals can be made but even those amounts are capped. You can't game the system by making numerous small withdrawals. That would pop-up on a report. It would also be expensive to travel to Zurich each time you wanted big money. And there's tight scrutiny as the normal protocol whenever large sums are withdrawn in person. ID's are carefully checked. It could be done, just much tougher hiding a paper trail. We'll start with the wires; see where it leads."

We started to break up when I had another question. "What would you do, Sgt Peake?" He looked at me, puzzled. "I mean, if you were stealing the money and wanted to do it anonymously, what would you do?" Captain Ruger looked at me funny but then settled back awaiting Peake's response. Again the eyes closed, this time for about 2-3 minutes. I wondered if he'd fallen asleep.

His eyes opened suddenly, "I'd wire it to the Caymans or maybe Bermuda. Then whenever I ran short, I'd take a vacation, like a million other people do, and get enough to live on for a while. Then come back and do it again. I'd stay under the radar. Plus there's better weather for reliable flights and it is much closer to the USA."

Ruger perked up. "Check those locations, too. Any others you can think of? I like that angle. Whoever this is has thought it through carefully. They don't seem like the type to rush. Also, look for smaller deposits, but done more frequently."

I jumped in, "Look for the same names, maybe sending money to both the Caymans and Bermuda. That way he could alter his trips, withdraw smaller amounts, stay even more invisible." I paused again, added, "Add Len Wilson to the search list." Lt Clep looked at me skeptically. I added, "I don't think he's involved but maybe he's playing us."

Again Ruger gave me an odd look before adding, "Are you sure you haven't done this before, Frazier?"

I shrugged, "The nuns always said I had the devil in me." He blinked a few times, didn't grin, just nodded.

Fleming was totally silent the whole time. He normally looked flushed and disturbed but he now looked explosive. I wished Mac had been there to see him. We'd have laughed for hours. As we were walking out, I heard Peake ordering him around. I had to deep breathe to prevent losing it. Lt Clep and I walked toward the door, suddenly Fleming appeared around the corner. He looked at me in anger, mumbled, "Fuckin' ass-kisser!" Clep and I chuckled all the way back to camp.

The life of leisure ended next morning. Callahan and I got patrol duty. Sgt Stroh had been given desk duty, handed us a map. "Get ta know Da Nang, boys. Can't hep ya much, don't know my ass from lef field either." We spent the morning riding around the massive base. All the roads were paved and clean- like the real world. I spotted a sign that said, "Movie Theater."

I looked at Callahan, "Gotta see this." The theater was gigantic, much nicer than the Waverly Theater back home in Drexel Heights. My mind flashed to one of the Waverly ushers who looked like Shemp Howard of The Three Stooges. Shemp threw me out a few times for making too much noise. I wondered if this theater had weird ushers? I mentioned my reminicience to Callahan. He just shook his head, not wanting me going off on that tangent.

We parked outside, walked into the lobby. It even had carpeted floors, satiny railings to help manage the crowds. I smelled it before I saw it- popcorn! A soldier was standing behind a counter loaded with candy, soda and popcorn. I asked the soldier for a large bag, was further surprised to hear, "It's free."

Being a wise-ass, I inquired, "Any butter on that?" The soldier never hesitated as he scooped a dripping load over my huge bag. We grabbed a large Coke, walked contentedly to our jeep. I was tempted to go back for a box of Goobers but refrained, not wanting to act like a newbie.

Da Nang city was disappointing. As we noted on our arrival, the streets were chaotic, dingy. Kids screamed at us as we drove by, "MP's beaucoup number 1!" Some ran bedside us, asked if we wanted, "Boom boom."

Although I was incredibly horny, I shook my head, "Not today, boy-sahn, I'm so short I'd need Oscar Meyer to find my wiener." Callahan giggled as we drove off. I watched the filthy place vanish and lush lowland farms appear. Without saying why, Callahan suddenly pulled over.

He looked at the map, tried to find Hoa Xuan, the village where Lenore was moving to start her new restaurant. "Do you think she's there yet?" Callahan wondered. Then he got a big smile on his puss. "She said she was leaving the next day after we had our final lunch.

She should be there by now. Lenore isn't one to dawdle. That girl's driven. She wants to make a fortune and get the hell out of Nam. I like her plan. She could make a killing with a restaurant in Philly." I just nodded, knowing he had more on his mind about Lenore.

Callahan continued his out-loud musing. "I think she'll wait till papa-sahn kicks off. She'll own the whole deal and can then make all the decisions. I wouldn't mind staying in touch with her." My friend Joe was smitten. Couldn't blame him, Lenore was special. I decided to stir things up.

"Let's check it out. Still have a couple hours. Let's pay her a visit, see if we can get you two to become pen pals. Maybe she'll start feeding papa-sahn some funky mushroom soup if she knows you're interested." Callahan had a moonstruck look on his face as we drove.

Hoa Xuan was about 20 miles south. The village was as charming as Da Nang was bleak. The people were used to American soldiers, paid us no heed as we circled, looking for traces of a restaurant. We had no luck, began to lose hope when Callahan had an idea. "Let's go real slow and smell. I'll never forget that aroma." I asked whether he meant Lenore or her cooking but Callahan scoffed, "Don't be a pervert."

It didn't take us long. On the backside of the village, we smelled that haunting aroma. The elegant Lenore was shuffling people inside when she spotted Callahan. He got his reward, a huge smile from his secret sweetheart. She held her breath as she looked at Callahan. Maybe Joe wasn't overestimating the mutual attraction. Then she noticed me, returned to her more business-like manner before saying, "Callahan-sahn, Frazier-sahn, so good to see you. It must be lucky day, see my favorite MP's to help business. You stay?" It visibly broke Callahan's heart he couldn't stay; he told Lenore we were checking to see if she made it safely, would be back soon. She looked truly sad but smiled demurely, "So sorry. Maybe not my lucky day." She stared at Callahan without saying a word, then bowed, turned and guided the straggling customers inside.

Callahan couldn't wipe the grin off his face the whole ride home. "Joe, I know you like me a lot and think I'm cute, but you really don't have to smile at me so much."

He finally laughed, "Is it that obvious? Jesus, is she something or what?" I promised we'd make it back tomorrow but that he'd better go slowly.

"Even though her marriage was one of convenience, papa-sahn might not like you being too obvious. She's his meal ticket. Better check things out some." I watched that silly grin the rest of the night.

Sgt Stroh assigned us to base patrol the rest of that week, so Callahan was stymied in his Lenore pursuits for a while. But we did get a nice break a couple days after that. We got sent to do guard duty in My Khe, which was better known as China Beach. This gorgeous stretch of sandy beach was a few miles outside Da Nang. It became an R&R location for US and Australian soldiers during the war. Naturally, it was heavily protected; our duty that day was patrolling the beach club. Sometimes soldiers got blind drunk, cooked by the sun, and wanted to kick someone's ass to salve the pain.

The other source of trouble- American girls. Lots of nurses and female soldiers, mostly Navy and Air Force were also lounging at the beach. Put together shell-shocked soldiers who are drunk, world-class horny, and trouble isn't a big leap away. Since I was big, looked mildly crazy, Stroh must have thought I'd be effective preventing damage. Callahan was small but well built, came across confident. The fact that Joe was a former Conscientious Objector seemed to skip Stroh's mind.

Regardless, we arrived at China Beach, had a mostly uneventful day in the sun. Navy cruisers patrolled offshore, but other than that, we could have been at a beach in Ocean City, N.J. Big umbrellas, lounge chairs and cabañas gave the battle weary soldiers a dose of relaxation. The USO had tiki huts every few hundred yards that offered burgers, dogs, soda, and near-beer. You had to drink a load of this watered-down brew to get a buzz. But never underestimate American ingenuity, crafty soldiers smuggled in the hard stuff, and gave their Coke's some personality.

Most of the guys on the beach were hooting and hollering in joy or blissfully drunk and unconscious. There was some friendly flirting with the ladies; everybody seemed content to savor a dose of normalcy. There was lots of reminiscing about which beach back home was best. "Youse outta see Wildwood. Them rides is skyscrapers. Not rinky dinky like Atlantic City." Then the pro Atlantic City guy would bust on how tacky Wildwood was and new taunts would start. Occasionally the girls had to ward off some unwanted advances, but nothing too dicey.

Toward the end of the day, Callahan said, "Looks like we won't need any of the wrestling moves we practiced in Basic, huh, Dylan?" I remembered how we constantly practiced half and full nelsons. Callahan started to grin. "I wrote my mom that you told the Drill Instructor that the full nelson was the entire cast of Ozzie and Harriet. She said she wants to meet you when we get back home, she liked that quip a lot."

I turned to Joe, shook my head, "Funny how even Basic Training, which sucked big time, is now the good old days. Better watch ourselves, Joe, we're losing our standards."

Our reverie was jolted by a curdling scream. About 50 yards behind us, a small crowd had gathered. We moved quickly to investigate, found a couple soldiers had a girl pinned to the ground. The third buddy had pulled off her bathing suit top, was fondling her exposed breasts. The one guy kept yelling, "Ya been teasing us with those titties all day, bitch. Now's time ta get ta business. Jus shut up an enjoy it." The frightened girl just struggled and moaned.

Typical of Callahan, he barreled through the crowd, pulled the molester away. The other guys jumped up, went for Joe. I came from behind, grabbed both around the necks and pulled them down hard into my outstretched knees as we spilled to the sand. The air shot from their chests as we hit the ground; both were dazed. I got upright, turned to see if Joe was okay. He seemed fine but then I sensed someone charging from behind. The new knucklehead hit me on the right side but I rolled with impact, tossed him over my shoulder; quickly regained my footing.

As he started to rise, I kicked him flush in the stomach. His eyes bugged from his sockets, stunned by the blow. I spun in a circle to make certain no one else was attacking. I moved toward Joe, keeping my back to his. I looked at my sneak attacker; he was vomiting on the ground. Apparently a couple gallons of beer and my boot weren't good for digestion. No one else seemed a threat, so we moved to make certain the girl was okay. Her friends had her covered up, were trying to calm her down. "You okay?" I asked.

She looked up meekly, "I just want to get out of here."

I thought I knew the answer but asked, "Do you want to press charges?"

She looked confused but soon added, "I just want to leave." She and her friends drifted away.

The other soldiers had gotten to their feet, seemed to regain their wits. One walked over, "Sorry, we're just fucked up. In the bush yesterday, drinking beer on the beach today, seeing pretty titties bouncing around. Fucked us up, is all. Don't want no more trouble." They were a sorry looking group of guys, maybe 18 or 19 years old. But I couldn't let down, "Get out of here NOW! If I see you here again, I'm going to put you where the sun don't shine, understand me? Move out!" As they trudged off, I took a huge breath, got my wits together. Thinking as I walked with Joe to the USO club: So much for easy duty at China Beach.

Riding back to base, Joe was quiet. To break the tension, I smacked his shoulder. "You jinxed us with that wrestling comment, Joe. It's not out of your mouth a minute and I'm doing a reverse nelson on China Beach. Next time, internalize your thoughts, okay? Didn't they teach you anything in psychology class?" Joe didn't answer.

A few minutes later he muttered solemnly, "We've got to get outta here, Dylan. This place is like a time bomb. Things go along smoothly, but you know the bomb's ticking. Just when you think things have settled down, it explodes." He looked at me sadly, "I hate this place."

And then it got worse. Who else but the demonic Percy Price is chatting with Clardy as we turned in our jeep at the Motor Pool? Percy didn't skip a beat, "Well look who it is. Captain America and his sidekick, needle-dick the bug fucker. Aint seen such sorry motherfuckers since I left Chu Lai. Thought you two candy asses'd be ushers at the movies or some shit. Don't tell me they let you two pussies outta the base?"

I smiled at Percy, "We were out warning the locals you were coming. Better lock up the women and children, is what I told them. You're just like a typhoon on its way, better stay indoors." I thought that might provoke him but he surprised me by laughing.

"Yer a smart one, Frazier, yer a smart one, all right." He turned, clicked his heels together, gave a mock salute and left.

Lt Clep came over after chow to tell me Percy was back in town. I frowned, "Already had the pleasure of a visit. Did say something useful, though. Said Callahan and I should be ushers at the movies. I like that idea. You must have some pull. When can we start?"

Clep grinned but added, "Stay clear of him." I told him I would but thought Percy would be back to goad me. He wanted a piece of me. Clep nodded again, "We've got more important stuff to do- like putting him in prison. But I'll head over tonight; tell him I'll hold him accountable if he starts anything with you. I hope he tries something. I would enjoy letting him see my ugly side."

His other reason for visiting came out next. "Let's head up to see Capt Ruger and Sgt Peake. I think they have something already." We drove over, Ruger got right to the point.

"We have some leads. I'm not sure they're solid hits but wanted to talk them over, see if something strikes you as familiar." Peake then rattled off the names he'd uncovered. Flanagan Engineering, Masters Protection, Nortek and Melzen Manufacturing have employees in country that earn big bucks. Most of these employees wire money to the States but a few send it offshore. I got a list of names wiring to Bermuda, the Caymans or elsewhere, have it broken down by company.

He handed lists to Clep, Fleming, and me. I looked at the names quickly. Nothing was familiar. But then I thought they could be using fake names; something might pop later. I looked up from the list, was caught off-guard when Fleming smiled at me. Not like him to be happy. Wondered what was up. Someone died and left him money? The answer came out quickly from Peake. "I've got to give credit to Corporal Fleming. He ran a report that summarized monthly activity, not just single entries. We got blanks till he did that. I leaned over, whispered to Fleming who was sitting nearby.

"Welcome to the ass-kisser club." I didn't wait for his retort, just started plugging through my lists.

Melzen Manufacturing was a company based in Connecticut. I asked about them. Ruger said, "A supplier for Sikorsky Helicopter. It's a crackerjack company that maintains the choppers, but mostly the Cobras. They want the A-team working on them. Guys who do that make a fortune." Then I asked about Masters Protection.

Peake answered, "Based in Atlanta, specialize in light weight flak jackets and new protective gear. They do testing for us and the ARVNS. It's supposed to be state-of-the-art material. Soldiers rave about the gear. They get serious praise from the brass."

Nortek was a west coast firm that built the latest weapon's system for the tanks. According to Ruger, "They had lots of trouble with the accuracy when the tanks got jostled around too much. They had a slew of the engineers trying to keep everything working. The engineers made a fortune because they mostly worked in the field, close to the shit storm." Peake told us that Flanagan Engineering was in Groton, Connecticut.

"There's lots of subs patrolling the South China Sea. The Flanagan firm does exclusive contracting for Electric Boat. They fix unique problems with oxygen systems." Then Peake added with deadpan expression, "You can't be running out of air when Charlies's dumping depth charges on you."

Clep spoke before me. "It looks as if all these firms are legitimate. Where do we go from here? How do we get these names checked out to see if they're clean?"

Ruger nodded, "Already underway."

Then I asked the obvious, "What if the source you check with is part of the rotten deal?" I could see Ruger didn't like the question.

"We're thorough at this base. Not seat-of-the pants operations like Quang Tri. We'll also check and double-check our sources. We go right to the CEO if necessary."

I asked if I could keep my list. "Something might pop into my head later. Want to stew on these names awhile." Ruger ok'd that but said to keep it with me.

He looked at me sternly, "Loose lips, as they say in the Navy." We agreed to huddle again when more background checking was done. As we were leaving I asked, "Can you get a report that summarizes these transfers by individuals, going back a couple years? Let's see who the big winners are, how much money we're talking about. Again Ruger looked annoyed, "We obviously would have done that, Frazier." I guessed Ruger was never taught by nuns who told you: There's no dumb question. And then I asked about Sgt Wilson.

"Not a trace yet," said the meticulous Sgt Peake.

As Fleming walked us out, I said, "Congratulations on graduation from 'B Team Academy,' Fleming. Now you made it to, 'A Stick–Up-Your-Ass University.' Way to go!" Fleming didn't even flinch.

"You know what, Frazier? I actually like this work. Ruger's a jerk off but Peake's teaching me a lot. I've been thinking about how I can use this training back in the real world. Naturally, I'd charge mega-bucks for my expertise. See you in the funny papers, dick-head" It was rare to see Fleming so happy.

Next morning I got a big surprise when I reported to Sgt Stroh. "I got movie star duty fer you and Callahan. Bob Hope's comin' in today with his all-stars. I need someone presentable. Work base patrol till around noon, then hit the airfield and look fer a big plane coming in. They stagger the flights, so as not too many hot shots 'er together, in case the shit flies. You'll shuttle them to General Headquarters. Supposed ta be bout 2 flights worth a stars. Ann Margaret's suppose ta be on one. She's some hot dish! Wouldn't mind escortin' her myself. Put in a good word fer me, huh?"

Callahan and I killed the morning rehearsing being suave and debonair. I practiced a few lines on Callahan for when

I met Bob Hope. "Joe, how about this one? 'So Bob, what's a guy named Hope doing visiting the Land of Mayhem and Hopelessness?' Think he'll dig my wry sense of irony? Maybe take me on as a writer after I leave this shitbox?" Callahan shook his head.

"It might get your tour extended if you try that one. I think the strong silent approach might be the way to play it. You have the kind of personality that's an acquired taste. No offense, my friend." I practiced the rest of my routine silently.

We stopped back to base around 11 am, got cleaned up; changed into fresh uniforms. I had lost some weight, only a couple of my fatigues fit well. While I dug for my better duds, I watched Callahan actually wetting his eyebrows. "Joe, when you polish a turd, it's still a turd no matter how hard you rub. Give it up." Joe grinned but brushed his teeth for the third time, finally announced he was ready. As we walked out I added, "Between those greasy eyebrows and peppermint breath, I don't think Ann Margaret's going to even notice me. Lookin' good, buddy."

Callahan got to drive Bob Hope, Ann Margaret, Frankie Avalon, and Annette Funicello. I did meet the great man; he was as nice and engaging as billed. When Bob shook my hand he asked me how I was doing. "It's another great day in Vietnam, Mr. Hope. Welcome to Camp Sunshine." He laughed but quickly introduced me to the other stars. Frankie Avalon was really tiny, barely bigger than the ladies. Ann and Annette were more gorgeous than on TV. As they walked off with Callahan I yelled, "If you smell anything strange, it's only Corporal Callahan's peppermint breath. He chewed a whole plant before you arrived." I could see Joe explaining my "acquired sense of humor" as they drove off.

The next plane arrived 15 minutes later. As luck would ordain, I didn't recognize any of the stars as they deplaned. Plus, all were men. I would have settled for a beautiful unknown but I approached the male visitors, introduced myself. The older guy said, "Hello, I'm Ben Hogan." He said it was nice to meet me, shook my hand. Then he introduced Arnold Palmer and Jack Nicklaus. Then it hit me; these were the best golfers in the world. Bob Hope was a golfing nut. He brought these superstars to pal around with as well as to remind us that better things, like golf, awaited us in the real world. If I got the chance, I'd tell Bob that bringing Annette and Ann was a better idea.

Arnold was really chatty, perked up when he learned I was from Philadelphia. He told me he was born and raised in Latrobe, Pennsylvania. Talked about how beautiful the countryside was there. Asked me if I was excited to get back to the City of Brotherly Love. He grinned a little, probably knowing that Philly would boo Santa Claus if late with the presents. I shrugged my shoulders, "Tough call. Nam or Philly in the winter." Jack Nicklaus then jabbed Arnold that Ohio was really God's Country; that Pennsylvania was for the Amish, Mummers, and other bumpkins. They continued the good-natured banter as we completed the ride. I waved goodbye, silently cursed Callahan's good luck.

That night we attended the Bob Hope extravaganza in the outdoor amphitheatre. Thousands of soldiers cheered Frankie and Annette as they reprised their beach movie songs. Ann Margaret did her numbers from Bye Bye Birdie; all was right with the world. Fleming sat beside me enthralled. "Hey, Fleming, hate to ruin the mood, but Annette can't sing worth a lick. And Ann Margaret is almost as bad. Like nails on a chalkboard, know what I mean?" Fleming glared at me.

"Shut up, Frazier. Just look at those knockers and shut up." He turned, grinned like a baboon. It was disorienting to see Fleming happy twice in the same week.

I lay in bed that night, pondered all the chaos of the past 12 months. With some luck, I'd be home in a few weeks; all this would be just a lurid dream. Most of the time, I subdued thoughts of home and loved ones. I was not only worried about being distracted and careless, I also knew that homesickness, dread, and self-pity would set in. Being alert, taking what good I found in the moment was what got me through. Nam was deadly. Little mistakes could get you killed. This was when I missed Mac the most. Not having him there to talk with, trade ideas, laugh at the silliness. I shook that off, it wasn't helping my mood.

But as I thought about the treason case, something nagged me. What was I missing? Why did something seem to elude me? The more I thought about the facts, the more I knew some illusive connection was there. I knew Ben Burton was smart enough to pull off this scam. But was he a traitor? Percy was a sociopath, but was he sharp enough to plan this slick con? The only thing that made sense was that the two had collaborated. It bugged me that Ben seemed to hate Percy. Would he put aside his loathing to make a fortune? Probably, but it still didn't feel right. And how did the affable Wilson play into this? He seemed such a nice guy. Or was he just a great con man? Was he the true mastermind? Sleep eluded me.

Big Changes

Sgt Stroh was grinning when Callahan and I walked into the station next morning. "What's got you so happy, Sgt Stroh? Did Ann Margaret pay you a nocturnal visit by accident, thinking it was the ladies latrine?" Stroh shook his head slowly.

"I got some good news fer you two." He waved some papers back and forth. "Here's your DEROS orders. You lucky sacks a shit is goin' home the end a next week. How bout that for a way ta start the day? Better'n flap jacks and sausage, huh?"

We waited for the "just shittin ya" comment but none came. Stroh realized we didn't believe him so he mosied over, put the papers in our hands. Joe and I read like zombies. "Your DEROS date is December 18th. Report for outprocessing in the Da Nang Center on December 16th. You will have drug testing and a reorientation session before going stateside. See your company commander for any questions. Congratulations!"

I looked at Stroh, "Not sure I can leave that soon, Sarge. Annette and I seem to have made a connection. She wants to talk over a part for me in "Beach Blanket Bad Boy." She'll be devastated if I have to scoot so soon. Any chance I can delay this?"

Before Stroh could answer, Callahan grabbed me and we ran out of the station screaming for joy. We hopped around like our pants were on fire. "We're finally getting out of this hell hole," Joe bellowed. "I can finally get on with my life and bury this as just a black hole of despair. Do you think this even happened to us, Dylan? Was it all some horrible dream?" I looked around at the pristine surroundings that Da Nang had become. I bet in the beginning it was as nasty as Quang Tri. Over time, the

American spirit had transformed this place into a model of civilized war. I looked at Joe.

"The nightmare was real, Joe. But now we're going home."

Stroh wandered out after we exhausted our euphoria. "I'm glad someone's happy 'round here. Tell ya what I'm gonna do boys. You was already scheduled for village patrol today, but I'll assign ya ta base duty after that. Try ta find ya some easy stuff. Least I can do. Gonna miss ya, though. Aint got many I kin trust. Mostly boneheads and burned-out grunts left. By the way, make sure ya see Lt Clep tonight. Wants ta say congrats about ya leavin'. He left early with Colonel Mullen to inspect Chu Lai's turnover to the ARVNS. Lucky sumbitch Mullen is getting' sent home too. Says he's getting' out fer good. Best Provost Marshall I ever served under. This war aint been the best for a lifer's morale. Whole country hates our guts. Glad he's leavin'. Too good a man ta take that shit no more."

We exited the base, drove aimlessly, still pumped-up over our big news. But then I thought about never catching the bastards who played with our lives the past few months. But I had to move on. Shook my head, said, "Let's drive to China Beach, make certain the surfs not too rough, huh Joe? Hate to see our boys having trouble riding the waves." And that's how we spent the morning. Not wanting any more wrestling matches with horny soldiers, we never went out on the beach, just surveyed the action from inside the USO club.

As we watched a lovely nurse walk by, Joe said. "That reminds me. Let's head over to Lenore's for lunch. I want to tell her the news. I already have her address so I can write after I get home. This might be my last chance if Stroh doesn't let us off base after today."

My boy Joe was really lovesick. Since I wasn't the most mature guy around, I didn't feel right giving him courting advice. Here I was a knucklehead that was in love with a girl for 8 years but never mentioned it to her until the night before I left for Basic Training. But I knew enough not to mess with a married woman, how difficult it would be to marry a Vietnamese. Lenore's husband was ancient but it might be years before she was widowed. So, I gave Joe my spiel, dispensed sage advice. He listened politely, smiled. "I know you mean well, Dylan, but I don't care. Lenore's amazing. No matter how long it takes, I'll wait." He seemed to assess that, "I haven't told you but Lenore and I have talked. She feels the same about me." Callahan had a huge grin on his face.

We were a few miles from Hoa Xuan when our radio erupted. Stroh sounded serious, "Patrol 1, report your 14!" Joe got the radio, told Stroh where we were. "Good, yer close. There's been a serious incident; I think a local got killed. Got a garbled call, but I think it was a gook but aint sure, saying somethin' bout a body. Better git there quick and investigate. Be careful. I'll send in backup. U'sally hell ta pay if a local gits killed. Don't know no more than that. Stay in touch. Call when ya git there and let me know what's goin on. Don't do anythin' foolish, yer too short."

The look on Joe's face mirrored mine: Why today? How about letting us cruise to the finish line? As I drove to Hoa Xuan, I cautioned Joe. "Let's take this easy. Last time I dealt with a dead local I got clocked by the villagers. We'll just mosey in there, case the situation, call Stroh with the skinny, wait for the back-up team. Both of us tend to get too exuberant. We're too short to be heroes. In fact, Joe, you're so short I can't even see who I'm talking too." His nervous laugh didn't help our anxiety.

We entered Hoa Xuan, the first thing we noticed was the quiet. The normally buzzing town was empty. I wove through the dusty streets, watched the people duck inside when they saw us coming. Something had them spooked.

Was it Viet Cong? I called Sgt Stroh, told him what was going on. "Be careful, VC don't come out much in the day but ya never know. Backup should be there in 15 minutes. Keep the signal open, tell me if ya see somethin'."

When we rounded the corner near Lenore's restaurant, we spotted the body. I grabbed Joe's arm, "Go slow. Sometimes they rig the bodies with booby traps. Don't go Superman on me." Joe nodded, too nervous to speak. I looked around, still didn't see anyone loitering. Where was everyone? Why didn't anyone try to help this guy? "Let's circle slowly, see if we can spot any clue to what happened here." Again Joe said nothing. I punched him, "Breath." He finally did; I stopped the jeep, but kept it running. I looked at Callahan, "Just in case we need to bolt."

Again I scanned the area but still no movement. Weird, I thought. "Joe, I'll look at the guy from the back, you take the front. See if we can make any sense of this." I picked up the radio, told Stroh were were reconnoitering, still no idea what happened.

"Keep the radio open," was all he said. I approached slowly, spotted the blood pooled under his leg. I looked further; saw more near his shoulder. Gun shot? Knife wound?

I remembered some earlier advice, "Don't move him, Joe. They put the grenades under them. Move them and the pin releases."

Joe didn't answer but stooped near the face, looked up quickly, shock on his face. "Dylan, I think it's Lenore's husband. His eyes are closed but I'm pretty sure it's him." I came around to take a closer look.

"Think you're right. Looks like him." We both almost jumped out of our skin when the radio started squealing. "Probably just Stroh getting antsy cause he hasn't heard for us. I'll fill him in." I wanderd over to the jeep, about 100 feet away, updated him.

I told Stroh who we thought it was; that we hadn't touched the body. "Pretty sure he's dead. Not breathing, no movement at all." I watched Joe move away from the dead papa-sahn, begin to scan the nearby huts. I guessed he was worried, didn't want any surprises. Stroh had stopped talking, probably thinking it over before he told me what to do. Before he could respond, a blood-chilling scream shattered the stillness. I felt shivers run down my spine. Stroh hollered, "What the fuck?"

As I was about to answer, I saw Joe take off around the nearest hut. Stroh yelled for an update, I said, "Gotta go, Callahan just took off. Gotta help him." I dropped the mike, sprinted after Joe. I got around the corner, couldn't see him. I yelled for him but got nothing. I exhaled deeply, yelled, "God damn it!" I went into a slow trot, swiveling my head in every direction, tried to guess where he went. The ground was all beat up, no tracks that could help. I got near the next corner, heard loud voices, then a dull thud, like someone had been hit with a club.

I went where I thought the noise came from, stopped to listen. There were low mewling sounds, like someone in agony, coming from the hut beside me. I drew my pistol, approached the door cautiously, peered inside. When I saw Joe writhing on the floor, I burst in. I spotted Lenore next, naked, tied to the bed. That was when my wrist got tomahawked, arms pinned from behind. Percy whispered in my ear. "Like a dream come true. Get to fuck-up the wonder boys on the same day. Then I get me back to some pussy. Baby that's sweet."

He tightened his lock; I felt the blood drain from my head. Before I passed out, instinct took over. Nut had me in this position a million times before; I knew what to do. I breathed in deeply, exhaled, relaxed my body as I felt Percy's grip loosen. Then I dropped to the ground, pulled him over my head. He hit hard, I scrambled over, got a scissor lock around his stomach. Percy tried to hop up but that allowed me to get a solid full nelson around his arms. He hammered his head back but my hands cushioned the blow. I regained my grip, tightened my legs. I could feel him losing air; weakening.

From experience wrestling with Nut all my life, I knew if you squeezed long enough, your opponent would pass out. The only way I could escape this was to wait for Percy to go unconciosus. I took a deep breath, crushed my legs together. I heard bones snap, Percy sagged. Still not sure, I gulped again, got more energy, pulled his arms back as hard as I could, heard another crunch, felt him quiver, go dead still. Afraid to let go, I held him as long as I could, then rolled over. Still cautious, I moved away, found my gun. Percy lay still. Was he dead?

Callahan jarred me. "Get Lenore, Dylan." Keeping my eye on Percy, I untied her, helped her cover up. Still worried about Percy, I went to Joe; saw he had a broken leg, courtesy of Percy's lethal kick. Otherwise, he seemed okay, fully alert. He saw me staring at Percy every few seconds. "He's gone, Dylan." I helped Joe to the bed; he and Lenore hugged each other as she wept. I took another deep breath.

"If you're okay, Joe, I better get to the jeep, call Stroh.This is going to be messy."

The village had suddenly revived. As I rounded the corner, there was a mob around my jeep. It was a cloudy day, felt like rain. The dark clouds made it seem like night. As I passed Lenore's dead husband, I noticed the looks of hatred on the villager's faces. I knew something was familiar, terribly wrong, and then it hit me. This was the recurring nightmare I had for the past few years. The people moved closer, slowly surrounded me. Did they think I killed papa-sahn? And then I felt the heavy pole snap over my helmet and shoulders as I passed out.

Most of the next hour or so is still a blur. When I awoke, I was inside a make shift cell. I could hear arguing outside. Was that Clep's voice? I shook my aching head, moved toward the door. I tried to pull it open but felt resistance.

It was barred from outside. Listening closely, I picked out Clep's voice, what I thought was Colonel Mullen. I yelled like a banshee, heard Clep's reply. "You all right, Frazier?"

I yelled back, "Got a bad headache. Where's Callahan?"

Mullen answered, "On the way to base, got a broken leg needs fixing. He's okay. Sit tight."

My head was pounding; I sat on the ground near the door. The debate continued, with Clep's voice getting louder and louder. I could hear Mullen telling him to settle down. It took a few minutes but I figured they were talking about a ransom for me. Why me? Wasn't I the good guy that saved Lenore from that psychopath Percy? And then I looked at it from their perspective. A bunch of MP's come to the village, killed papa-sahn, almost raped a woman. They probably thought we were a team. I kept thinking: What about Percy?

It was starting to get dark; the arguing seemed to ease. There was movement outside my cell but the door stayed shut. I remembered the last time I was in this mess; Nut and Abreu swooped from the sky to save me. Would my bigger-than-life buddy pull another dramatic entrance? I listened for chopper sounds. Nothing. I didn't think Nut was coming to save the day this time. What had I gotten myself into? My eyes were getting drowsy when the door rattled open, Clep rushed in. "Can you walk? Let's get outta here before they change their minds."

On the ride back to Da Nang, Colonel Mullen filled me in on the negotiation. "They wanted $10,000. They said MP's killed one of their leading businessmen. It didn't matter that you were the one that saved the girl. They hold the MP's accountable. We had to agree to keep you locked up till they come in tomorrow for a final settlement. Don't worry about that. We'll get you checked out by a medic, let you sleep in the hospital tonight. If you're okay, we'll get you in early tomorrow to the MP station. It looks like you got a nice egg on your head. They'll check for concussion. For now, just rest, we'll talk more later." I didn't argue; my head was pounding.

The medic thought I was okay, no sign of concussion. He didn't want me being interrogated tonight. Said I needed rest. That they'd monitor me overnight; make sure I stayed without symptoms. Mullen argued but the medic shut him down. "It's not up for debate, Colonel. Frazier needs rest. There's plenty time later to get the details. Good night, Colonel." So I was left alone, spent about 5 seconds before I fell dead asleep. When I dreamed about being surrounded by villagers, I knew it wasn't a nightmare anymore. But now I knew I survived.

Clep picked me up next morning, didn't have great news. "Colonel Mullen and I met with the Provost Marshal, General Smyth, and filled him in. He wasn't too happy. By the way, Percy's alive but you smashed him up pretty bad. Broke 3 ribs, a neck disc and both his collarbones. He'll be in the hospital a few weeks. Then he'll stand trial. But General Smyth thinks we're a bunch of shell-shocked cowboys from Chu Lai. He wants to get you out of here. Mullen did his best to paint you the hero but the general wasn't too receptive. He seems to think you over-reacted." He shook his head. "I'm not sure why."

My head still hurt but I gathered myself. "He's probably right, should have waited till Percy raped the girl and killed Callahan and me. Could have blamed it all on the VC and made it cleaner for him." I looked at Clep incredulously, "You have to be kidding me!" Clep was calm.

"I'm going to fill in General Smyth about the treason case, that you've been instrumental in the investigation. And that Percy is the key suspect in the treason case. I'll also mention Percy's history of violence. Not to worry, you'll be out of here soon. Till then, you're suspended from duty pending the investigation. Try not to get in trouble, huh, hotshot?"

I visited Sgt Stroh later that morning, asked about Callahan. "He's headed to the States. They set his broken wheel and'll let him recover at home. Prob'ly be home in a few days, lucky bastard. Can get an 'early out' if he wants ta. Come ta think of it, you can too. Might have ta stay at Ft Dix er somethin'. But they don't want ta pay ya 6 more months just ta direct traffic in New Jersey. Know what I mean?"

I was about to grouse about getting shit on by General Smyth when Stroh added, "By the way, ya did great out there stoppin' Price. Proud of ya. One helluva MP and I'm gonna tell the General that myself. Served under him before, know em good. Should be pinin' a medal on ya, not dickin' ya around." Stroh had a nice way about him; I decided to shut up, wait it out. I had a lot of good people who'd tell my story. I put my hand up to get his attention.

"Sgt Stroh, it's me that's honored to serve with you. I got drafted; you do this for a living. And thanks for watching my back."

I got a lift up to CID Headquarters. Wanted to let Fleming know what happened with Callahan and Percy. I also would go crazy with nothing to do, so I hoped I could help out. Fleming listened to my story, started to smile. "I'm not falling for one of your tricks, Frazier. It's December, April Fools isn't for 5 months." It took awhile but he finally believed me. "Jesus," was all he could say. He agreed to let me kill time, so I got all the suspect companies and employees lists, spent the afternoon seeing if anything popped out. Nothing did. I rubbed my tired eyes, went back to the MP camp. I waited for dinner; spent a quiet night with my sore head. I was having a hard time getting the names on the list out of my head. But the more I thought, the more my head hurt.

Clep walked into my hootch early next morning with a huge smile on his face. "What are you smiling about Lt? Did Fleming finally admit he's a secret agent for the VC?"

He kept grinning. "Pack your gear, Frazier. I'm taking you to the DEROS center myself. Colonel Mullen not only got you cleared, he got General Smyth to move up your departure. Unless you flunk the drug test, you'll be out of here in a couple days. Then you fly to Ft Lewis and wait for transportation home. You can get an early out and be a civilian by Ground Hog's day. That's what I'm smiling about!"

And that's how fast things changed. We road up to CID, I said a quick goodbye to Fleming. He frowned as he said, "Lucky prick." Shockingly, he gave me a hug. And then he pushed me away as if irritated, "Get outta here." That was as nice a going away as I'd ever get from my surly friend. I'd really miss that sour puss. I never got to thank Colonel Mullen.

Clep told me, "He really went to bat for you, Frazier. He convinced the General to put you in for a medal." And then he smiled, "But I doubt you'll stay in long enough to receive it. You're a cinch for an early out." Clep promised to thank Mullen for me. I owed him big. When I brought up the investigation, Clep shook his head. "Mullen's hellbent to nail Percy. The more we thought about it, the more likely Percy was the key. Maybe Burton was the brains but Percy killed him off so he wouldn't get caught. Maybe we'll never know but we'll do our best to fry that bastard."

I entered the DEROS station, was told where to stow my duffle bag. "Stay nearby; you'll get called for a drug test whenever the piss station clears out." I asked a guy lying beside me how long he'd been here.

"I got here a couple days ago. I'm still waiting to pass the piss test. First one didn't go so good. I had some weed in my system. Lucky I didn't do no blow, or I'd a been sent to detox." I nodded sympathetically, like I understood. I shook my head: Just what I needed, a screw-up sleeping next to me. I ambled over to the door. Some soldiers were milling outside, so I went out.

I learned they had a "gift center" nearby, so I explored. The center was full of clothes, cameras, watches, and miscellaneous gifts that departing soldiers forgot, couldn't pay for or had to leave behind when they went to detox. Most of the stuff was brand new and dirt cheap, so I got a Seiko watch and Nikon camera for $35! Savoring my treasures, I headed back to my bunk. My doped-out bunkmate was asleep, I hid my purchases.

The drug test was more of an adventure than planned. Literally seconds after taking a humongous pee, we got called to report for testing. Marching like cattle through a narrow room with urinals on both sides, we were told to "fill up the cup." To make matters cozier, they had MP's standing behind you to make sure you didn't fill up someone else's cup "by accident." Soldiers who were worried about failing paid big bucks for surrogate pissers. Only in Nam, I thought. Make money for taking a piss.

I grabbed my cup, chuckled, thinking about Fleming standing here one day soon, being irate that someone was looking over his shoulder. "What so funny," my MP escort asked?

I turned around, "You won't believe this my friend, but I pissed like a race horse right before they called us in. And now, for the first time in my life, when taking a piss is meaningful, the well's dry." And then the MP started to laugh; pretty soon the whole place was giving me tips on how to pee under pressure. After a gallon of water and milking the pump relentlessly, I squirted out the required dose. Naturally, I peed like a firehose all that night.

At dawn, a sarjent flipped on the lights, belted out a list of names, one of them mine. "You lucky sum bitches is headin' on a jet plane, don't know when you'll be back again." With no apology to Peter Paul and Mary, he herded us out, checked our paperwork carefully and got in the transport bus with us. We drove to Da Nang airfield; I spotted the huge TWA jet. I remembered my rocket attack arrival in Nam, scanned the horizon for action. It was dead still as we took off.

Nobody talked much for an hour or so. I kept thinking this wasn't real, that they'd suddenly veer the jet back to Da Nang. When I noticed the real stewardesses, it dawned on me it was really over. We could have anything to eat or drink, so I guzzled a couple Rolling Rocks, munched on a decent roast beef sandwich. It would be a long flight to Ft Lewis, just outside Seattle. I spent the time thinking about the crazy mess I'd just left. Leaving without solving the case tormented me. A few things bothered me, so I kept replaying the facts. I dozed some but mostly thought, hoping for a breakthrough. I thought about Callahan and Lenore as I fell asleep.

When I awoke, I saw in the TWA magazine map that Seattle was near Portland. Maybe I could see McCarthy. It would help if I could talk over the loose ends. Was it a coincidence that Percy happened to be in the village while we were nearby on patrol? Did Percy make the anonymous call to report the murder? At first I wondered if Stroh was involved but quickly dismissed that notion. I remembered the concern and caution when Stroh was on the radio as we navigated the dangerous village. No way could he fake that. Percy must have seen the day schedule, knew we'd be close; sucked us into a trap. I had consistently underestimated Percy's smarts. Mastermind?

I got settled in Ft Lewis, learned it would take a couple days to process our re-entry. We were issued new uniforms, shown our way around the base. Most of us were tan, easy to spot from the other soldiers. Whenever a pale soldier noticed us, we got a crisp salute. "Welcome, home soldier!" was echoed throughout the tour of base. Had to admit, I did feel proud. When I got my new clothes, it became obvious I'd dropped a lot of weight. Never noticed that in Nam; had other things on my mind.

I dug into my wallet, found Mac's telephone number. After chow, I called. Mary answered, was quiet when I said who I was. Then she asked, "Are you still in Vietnam?" I laughed, told her my good news. "Mike's going to be so happy. He talks about you every day. He's worried that something might happen to you; he's going to be so relieved. And guess what? He's at Ft Lewis right now. He'll be there a few more days finishing his rehab. You know how Mike is. He wanted them to pay for everything. He said it was the least they could do." She gave me the details; I went to find my buddy.

I spotted that red mop as I entered the rehab center. His skinny frame had already filled-out, he looked good. As he did squats with a light barbell, I snuck over, got behind him. When he dropped the bar to the ground, I asked, "Is that all your Irish candy-ass can manage? Even that pathetic bastard Fleming lifts more than that." Mac froze. He turned slowly, took a second to absorb I was really there, lunged at me, hugged me like a lost brother. He kept holding my arms, continued shaking me while he babbled,

"Holy shit. Holy shit. It's really you." We both had tears in our eyes; we had survived.

We went to the USO, caught up. He'd start Med school next month when he got his early out. Mary was teaching school, little Mike was staying with grandma. "Now that you're back, all is well with the world." He had been worried 'I'd do something stupid with Percy'. I exhaled, told him to sit back and hold his seat. Mac's eyes bugged when I told the gruesome story of my last days. When I said what was nagging me about the investigation, he nodded but offered no new insights. Finally, he said, "Let it go, time to move on with your life."

I looked at my buddy, "That's good advice. Wonder why I'm not smart enough to take it?"

Mac laughed, realized I wouldn't let it drop, so he listened to each new detail, theories on what they meant. We went back and forth on what made sense, what didn't. He agreed that Percy being in that village wasn't an accident. "He had to know you'd be the ones to respond. He was waiting for you." Mac sat back, drained his beer. "If you think about it, Percy just picked us off one at a time. First Jones; then got Ben so he didn't have to split the money. When we started snooping around, he got me, and then he went after you and Callahan. No loose ends. It all hangs together."

We closed down the club, agreed to meet early for breakfast. Our mistake had been taking Percy too lightly. He was as devious as he was psychopathic. I would get in touch with Nut, tell him they needed to focus on Percy, to dig deeper. There had to be a paper trail to him. I had to wait at Ft Dix to get an early release, so I'd use my time searching Percy's past. I knew Nut had the juice to get me hooked up with CID stateside. I didn't want Percy to get away with murder. I could almost picture him laughing at us. I fell into a fitfull sleep.

As I came back from shaving that morning, I heard my named yelled out. "Get your gear packed, Frazier. You're moving out. Meet me here at 0800." Mac joined me for the early breakfast, stayed as I waited for the plane. I knew we would stay in touch but I wondered when I'd see him next. Not like Philly and Portland were close by. It would be work to stay close friends. What would I have done in Vietnam without him?

We joked about what the future held for us. "Maybe I'll be a private investigator. Always thought about coaching but getting paid to snoop in others business is kind of cool. Want to partner up, Mac?" I heard that chuckling laugh, realized it would be awhile before I heard it again.

"Next time you see me, Dylan, I'll be doctoring babies and out playing golf on Wednesdays. I'll leave the Joe Friday stuff to you. But if you want my opinion, you're a natural spook. I mean that in a good way." We hugged. Had to admit I was choked up, had a tough time catching my breath as I walked off.

I boarded another TWA flight, looked out the window as Seattle faded away. I'd be met by MP's in Philly, get escorted to Ft Dix, wait for outprocessing from the Army. As I sagged back, my head hit the comfortable cushion; I fully relaxed for the first time in almost a year. I smiled at the thought of Mac taking care of crying babies and playing golf to soothe his nerves.

That thought jolted me. My eyes got big. Playing golf, huh? Just like that, one of those dangling loose ends clicked. And then it hit me like a smack in the face! Something had bothered me about our airtight solutions. I went to my dufflebag, dug out the notes I got from Fleming before I left for DEROS. As I scanned the names on the suspect companies, the subtle irony hit me. Could it be an accident? I didn't think so. Masters Protection, huh?

The MP's drove me to CID headquarters at Ft Dix. I was very agitated; they were probably worried I was shell-shocked. But finally they heard what I was saying, took me to meet the Provost Marshall, Colonel Lynam. The facts were so clear to me; I rattled the horrific story of treason and my need to track down Green Beret Captain John O'Hanlon, somewhere in Nam. Colonel Lynam shook his head sadly. "Sickening story. Give me some time, I'll see what I can do."

Less than an hour later, I was telling Nut my theory. He let me babble, hardly asked a question. "Too coincidental, Nut, has to be him. He played us the whole time. Shifted the blame elsewhere, eliminated the only witnesses, planned to sit back, wait for the storm to pass. Pretty sure I'm right. His only mistake was his love of golf. If he hadn't gotten too cute with the names, no one would have noticed. Not sure why I did anyway. Bad luck for him that I got to drive those guys around right before I left. Put the names in my head. Chase him down, Nut. Bastard needs to pay."

I did chicken-shit jobs at Ft Dix as Nut unraveled the tangled string. Within a week, he had Colonel Mullen under arrest. The fictitious employees of Masters Protection, "Jack Hogan" and "Samuel Arnold" were traced to him and Ben Burton. So far the CEO of Masters Protection was not implicated. I told Nut I didn't buy that. "I knew you wouldn't, Dylan, just wanted to run it by you. So far, you've been right on. If the CEO's involved, we'll catch him. Don't worry." He told me that Mullen caved under interrogation, admitted the weapons scheme but not to killing Ben. Did it really matter? His treason charge would get him life in prison.

The only troubling news was Percy was apparently not involved. Mullen said, "Percy was mentally disturbed and not part of this. He couldn't be trusted." I let that sink in, unsure. I asked Nut if he thought Mullen was afraid Percy would come after him when he got out. Maybe go after his family if he got sent to a mental institution and escaped?" Nut smiled.

"You really should be a detective when you get out." I disregarded the jab, still had more on my mind.

"Do you think Mullen sent Percy after Callahan and me?" Nut shook his head.

"He said no, but he can't be believed. He doesn't want another attempted murder charge to deal with. My guess is yes. It wouldn't take much to push Percy's buttons. He hated you guys, wanted revenge."

I was still convinced that Percy and Mullen were connected. Nut still some doubts that he needed to resolve. "So far Percy says he doesn't know what we're talking about. He says you and Callahan killed the papa-sahn and attacked him. Two against one, he just defended himself." Before I could explode, Nut added, "We got Lenore as an eye witness and Lt Clep gave compelling testimony; Percy's in deep shit. He definitely gets court martialled and does jail time. He's a decorated hero, might plead temporary insanity but he's not too credible. Push him hard in court and he'll go crazy.It might not be life but he'll be away a long time."

It took another couple weeks to get my early out. Colonel Lynam tried to convince me I had a future in Military Intelligence. He would get me in OCS and assigned to Ft Dix. I politely declined, avoided smart quips of my "devilish nature." I just wanted this over, was ready to start my life. I walked from his office, stood alone outside the barracks as I watched dad's car drive up.

Mom and Laura jumped out, sprinted at me. Laura almost knocked me over when she jumped into my arms and hugged me. Mom grabbed us both and we cried with joy. My mom kept saying, "God answered my prayers." Laura sobbed, "This is the best day of my life." Dad joined the circle as we tried to overcome our emotions. As I stood holding the most important people in my life, random thoughts poured through my tired mind. Would anything be tough after Nam? Would Sgt Wilson and Frances reconnect? Would Callahan find a way to get

Lenore to the States? Would Laura marry me, or was that a war-induced delusion? Did I have a gift for criminal investigation; was that my path? What would happen to Percy? Would he get a light sentence and come after me? I finally closed my eyes and rested.

CPSIA information can be obtained at www.ICGtesting.com
Printed in the USA
BVOW04s2202170215

388194BV00002B/27/P

9 780988 786219